MYSTIC QUEST

MYSTIC QUEST

BOOK TWO OF

The Bronze Canticles

TRACY AND LAURA
HICKMAN

ASPECT®

WARNER BOOKS

NEW YORK   BOSTON

Aspect
Warner Books

Time Warner Book Group
1271 Avenue of the Americas, New York, NY 10020
Visit our Web site at www.twbookmark.com.

The Aspect name and logo are registered trademarks of Warner Books.

Printed in the United States of America

First Printing: April 2005
10 9 8 7 6 5 4 3 2 1

Library of Congress Cataloging-in-Publication Data

Hickman, Tracy.
    Mystic quest / Tracy and Laura Hickman.
        p. cm. — (The Bronze Canticles trilogy ; bk. 2)
      Summary: "The second book in the dragon-laden Bronze Canticles trilogy"—
    Provided by the publisher.
      ISBN 0-446-53106-5
    1. Dragons—Fiction. I. Hickman, Laura. II. Title.
    PS3558.I2297M97 2005
    813'.54—dc22   2004027776

To our brothers and sisters

Gerry & Jana, Kim & Kerry, and Kari & Garrin
Edward & Marilyn, Warren & Delayn, Madeline & Sam,
and Sidne & Len

TABLE OF CONTENTS

Thrice upon a time
there was a world that was three worlds
One place that was three places
One history that was told
in three sagas all at the same time.

Thrice upon a time . . .
the gods foresaw a time
when three worlds would become one . . .
When the children of their creation
would face the Binding of the Worlds.

Thrice upon a time . . .
Three worlds fought to survive.
Their children would be armed
with the cunning of their minds
their fierce will to endure
and the power of newfound magic.

Thrice upon a time . . .
came the Binding of the Worlds.
Not even the gods knew
. . . which world would reign . . .
. . . which world would submit . . .
. . . and which world would die.

Song of the Worlds
Bronze Canticles, Tome I, Folio 1, Leaf 6

The
Calling

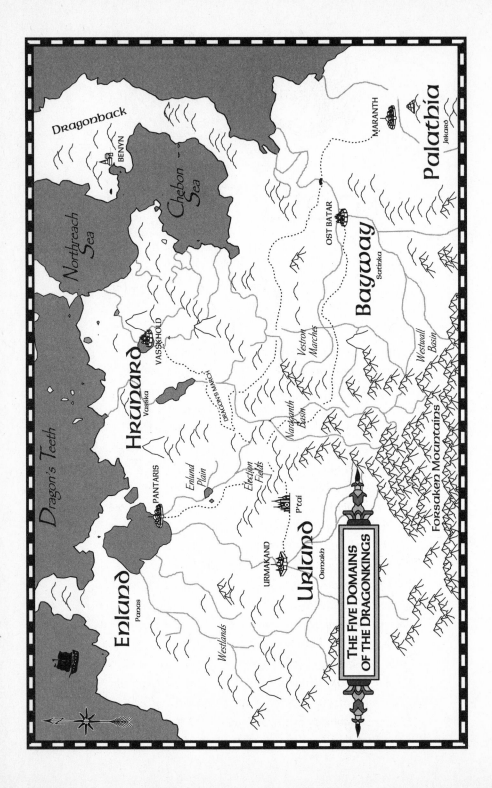

Fool's Errand

Near the close of the 492nd year of the Dragonkings, the revolt of the mystics on the Election Fields shattered the pact that for over four hundred years had limited the conflict between the dragons to a grotesque organized amusement. Satinka—Dragonqueen of Ost Batar—believed she had been betrayed in the Battle of the Election Fields and drove her remaining troops with blind rage to annihilate her retreating enemy. The broken lines of Vasska's warriors fled northeast, scrambling down the Dragon's March Road with Satinka's warriors at their heels. It was not until they reached the River Serphan that Vasska's insane Elect turned to make their final stand.

There, at Dragon's March Bridge, the battle raged for eight days before reinforcements from Vasskhold and its surrounding provinces bolstered the sagging and tired lines at the riverbank. Satinka's own reinforcing column was met as they moved north across the Vestron Marches by a second force under Vasska's banner that was marching westward from the coastal cities. They met at Waystead Gap, denying Satinka her reinforcements at the river but exacting a heavy price from Vasska's forces in blood.

Panas, Dragonking of Enlund, convinced the Grand Duke in Pantaris that these events were a sign from heaven and that his own troops must march down the Enlund Plain against Satinka's western flank. Her forces split, Satinka pulled back, but the Enlund troops smelled victory. The Grand Duke sent a second army south across the Plain of Umath in an effort to cut off Satinka's western retreat. But the Enlund royalty had not counted on the Thanes of Urlund, who under direction and support of their own dragon — Ormakh — rode their battle torusks against both Satinka's western retreat and the Emperor's troops from the north. It was then that the dragon Jekard saw his chance and drove his own warriors deep into the soft flanks of Satinka's lands.

The Five Domains had played at war for four hundred years — now their toys had broken and the struggle had become, for each of them, viscerally vital. To the common peasant, little had changed; the war before and the war now were one and the same. Sons and daughters went to battle. Sons and daughters died. That their numbers were no longer limited to the Elect was something of which no one spoke aloud. Yet in the halls of power the sad acceptance of ritual human sacrifice in the name of the common good had been replaced by something more desperate. The order of the world itself was now uncertain, and for the powerful atop their suddenly teetering thrones, the stakes could have gotten no higher.

By the 519th year of the Dragonkings, the escalation of the War of Scales ground into its twenty-sixth year with no end imagined. The memory of dragons has ever been long and the price of Satinka's insult on the Election Fields continued to be paid in human blood. It gushed from the wound of a dragon's pride that would not be healed. Open warfare between the Five Domains had settled into a dreary cycle of battle without conquest, sacrifice without purpose, and loss without victory. Battle lines swept back and forth across the same scarred patches of land that stank from death. War itself became the consuming preoccupation for the Dragonkings who perpetuated it, the Pir who struggled to end it, and the mystics who fought for their own survival because of it.

So it was that as all eyes cast their fearful glances toward one another, the doom of the world crept unnoticed even by the mystics, who alone were prepared to see it.

Yet all that would change in a single, fateful year.

BRONZE CANTICLES, TOME III, FOLIO 2, LEAF 23

"You!" a voice rings out from the darkness.

I peer through my conjured mask, an ornate facade of white and red painted leather in which I may hide. I squint into the void, trying to shield my eyes from the glare of the lights.

"Yes, you on the stage! Are you ready?"

"I don't know," I answer. "What am I to do?"

"Amateurs! All they send me are amateurs!" The voice bellows. "Just get off the stage and watch."

I can already hear an enormous thick curtain rising behind me. I glance awkwardly about, then jump gingerly over the unsteady flames of the footlights, landing on a giant plain that stretches to the twilight horizon.

The curtain vanishes into the sky, revealing a sparse setting. Painted wooden mountains hang from cords at the back of the stage, waving uncertainly in a breeze that drifts across the plain. There are several statues of metal warriors swinging at one side, while on the other side a false sea hangs just above the stage. All three of these pieces are suspended from an ornate bronze globe overhead, the sphere itself also suspended from the darkness. Each piece drifts slowly in the wind, sometimes circling forward on the stage while the other two circle back under the orb.

Then the players enter from either side of the stage. The footlights are inexplicably working against me, shining off the edges of the eyeholes in my mask. I cannot see the players clearly. My mask is supposed to hide me from them—not the other way around.

One of them is a woman with paper wings mounted to her back who dances beneath the false waves suspended over her head. I cannot see her face but she reminds me of my own mystic twin, the winged woman through whom the power of my Deep Magic is made real. She looks awkward as she dances across the stage, her faux wings bouncing unnaturally.

Nearby, a short, demonic little creature attempts a dance of his own beneath the metal statue suspended over him. As he dances, he is trying to carry something in his hands—letters and figures of some strange and unreadable script. He tries to be careful in his movements but the letters fall from his awkward hands, shattering against the hard floor and vanishing at once.

At the back of the stage, however, beneath the shadow of the wooden mountains, stand two tall figures—twins by the look of them, though their faces are hidden behind masks that are in every respect identical to my own. Each holds a sword in his hand. Both of them step forward.

"What do you think of it thus far?" says a voice in my ear.

I turn and find myself staring into the eyes behind another mask. Gasping, I step back.

This creature, too, wears a mask that is identical to my own. Its body, however, is hunched over, leaning on a walking stick clutched firmly in its left hand. A long gash rends its coat from the left shoulder down to the middle of the back, exposing a long, white scar. It gazes back at me with burning red eyes—vertical slits of darkness that are wholly inhuman.

"Who are you?" I ask.

"If you don't pay attention, you'll never get it right," the hunched figure snaps, ignoring my question.

I turn back to the stage, the wind whispering around the edges of my mask. The winged woman lies dead on the stage, her head severed from her body. Her blood seeps across the stage, a growing stain moving inexorably toward me. I shudder, trying to step out of its way as it drips off the stage, but it follows me as I move.

The players on the stage begin applauding, their sparse clapping echoing hollowly throughout the vast hall. I stare up at the masks of the twins—both still rapt in their ovation—knowing that one of them had destroyed this winged woman.

"Not bad for a rehearsal," the stooped figure calls out, his voice trying to carry over the sudden gust of wind. He grabs me by my

arm and pushes me up onto the stage. Off balance, I clamber upward, my hands sliding on the winged woman's blood. I stand on
the stage, aghast.

The stooped figure is suddenly beside me. It reaches down with
its right arm and picks up the sword from the stage. The breeze
that once drifted through the room has become a gale, howling
around the stage, blowing the scenery overhead to spin and twist
from its cables. "Enough rehearsal," he screams over the sudden
din. "Let the play begin!"

The body of the winged woman picks itself up off the ground,
her hand snatching her head from where it lay and deftly replacing it on her shoulders as she walks off the stage. The demon creature, too, has walked off, pulling a new set of symbols out of a
barrel just behind the proscenium of the stage.

I look back toward the twins — but only one figure stands at the
back of the stage. I look down at myself and see that we now wear
identical costumes.

"I won't do it!" I yell at the stooped man over the roaring of
the wind. "I won't play this part . . ."

"Everyone's part is his own," he insists.

The hunched figure puts the bloodied sword in my red-
stained hands.

BOOK OF CAELITH
BRONZE CANTICLES, TOME IX, FOLIO 1, LEAF 52

The winds were unusually cold for late afternoon, even in the early
spring. Caelith Arvad awoke with a shiver from his reveries and
pulled his hood down closer around his face, his cheeks chilled to a
bright, rosy blush. He shivered once more but knew deep within
himself that it had little to do with the cold of the approaching night.

He stood in the center of the broad avenue that had been the
main thoroughfare of the town known as P'tai—the Jewel of the East.
The wind played with a broken door somewhere, for the squeal of its
hinge and occasional banging of its remaining planks sounded an un-
easy tempo through the town. The wind lent its own mournful low

wail to the scene as it wound its way across the jagged edges of broken walls and the vacant blackness of shattered windows. The skittering dry leaves and ashes hissed for silence, but the wind paid no attention and continued to blow through the desolation.

The wind brought one consolation, Caelith thought as he sighed: it rolled down from the northern Enlund Plain, spilling over the Bounteous Hills before it cascaded down into the town. It filled his nostrils with the pungent smell of burnt timbers, blistered paint, and charred stores. It was unpleasant enough but he was grateful for it nonetheless, for the smell, he knew well from experience, could have been much worse.

It certainly *would* have been much worse had the wind come from the west.

A sharp, distant voice echoed among the fallen walls: "Prince Arvad!"

Caelith looked up in annoyance at the figure running toward him, weaving through the rubble of the fallen walls.

"Prince Arvad!" It was Lovich. He was new to the clan, only rescued from the Election in Waystead four months before. He was a talented mystic who showed promise in a number of areas—if he lived long enough to develop them. He had an enthusiasm and a blind loyal fervor that argued against betting in favor of his survival. Lovich breathlessly skidded to a halt just in front of Caelith. "Prince Arvad, I bring news!"

"Don't call me 'Prince,'" Caelith snapped. "A prince is the son of a king, and last time I checked, my father had not acquired a crown."

"But, sire, everyone calls you the Prince—"

"We are a clan—not a kingdom," Caelith said with a hint of force in his exasperated voice. He was inclined to like Lovich—probably a bad idea considering how easily one's friends die in the course of their work. Better to keep a distance. "Look, I know people back at the clanhold sometimes refer to me as the Prince, but that really isn't a good idea out here, right?"

"Yes, sire," Lovich gulped.

Caelith shook his head. Lovich was not that much younger than Caelith in years, but they were ages apart in experience. "You had something to tell to me, Lovich?"

"Yes, sire," the younger mystic replied. "Master Kenth says he's bringing everyone in."

"Let me guess," Caelith said, absently glancing around. "There's nothing left."

"Well, not much anyway." Lovich shrugged. "It looks like Satinka's army came down out of the Thanes' Rift east of here four days ago. They just marched down the road through the night before they got to the town. Master Kenth thinks old Thane Baerthag must have known they were coming, though, 'cause the townsfolk were already heading west with most of the Thane's army when Satinka arrived. He left part of the army behind to hold the town but apparently the Dragonbitch herself showed up two days ago and, well"—Lovich gestured around him—"they didn't hold on much longer after that."

Caelith nodded. Baerthag would have fared better if he had not been a thane in Urlund. All of Hramra, from the Forsaken Mountains to the south to the northern coasts of the Dragonback and from the western Desolation to the Gulf of Palathina on the east had been divided, since the fall of the Rhamasian Empire over four hundred years before, into the Five Domains. Each was ruled by a Dragonking—or, in two cases, Dragonqueens—under entirely different systems of governance depending upon the whim of the dragon who ruled that part of the land. Though each of those lands was touched by the Pentach of the Pir Drakonis and their religion to one degree or another, the actual system of rule varied from domain to domain. Thus, while Vasska ruled Hrunard and much of the Dragonback under a theocracy heavily centered in the Pir Drakonis, Ormakh preferred to rule Urlund through a less centralized collection of local thanes, each with its own militia and arms. Caelith was certain that Ormakh's intention was to keep each of the thanes sufficiently weak so that no one of them could challenge his rule as Dragonking. It may have been caution on the dragon's part, but it often left the individual thanes to fend for themselves, as the other thanes were reluctant to get involved in their neighbor's troubles.

Caelith started slowly down the broken remains of the avenue, Lovich falling into step next to him. "How far did Baerthag get?"

"Ten miles—maybe fifteen," Lovich said evenly. "It was pretty bad; Baerthag left the refugees behind and tried to make a run for it with what remained of his army. EvaLynn—you know, that Windtalker visiting from Clan Thais—she flew out and saw it. I can go and get her if you want to hear it from her, but she's pretty shook up about it."

"No." Caelith stopped and looked at Lovich as he rubbed his hands up and down the heavily patched sleeves of his tattered robe. "What's done is done. Baerthag brought it down on himself. He tried to push into Enlund through Satinka's lands and thought he could do it without the Dragonqueen noticing." Caelith took a long look at the smoldering fallen buildings around him. "Satinka, however, notices everything—and always balances her books."

"Have you seen one?" Lovich asked quietly.

"Seen one what?"

"A—a dragon?" Lovich breathed.

Caelith saw the look on the boy's face and started walking again. "By the gods!"

"No, really, sire!" Lovich stumbled back into step behind his commander. "I was just wondering . . ."

"You were a member of the Pir most of your life, Lovich," Caelith said, chuckling darkly. "Didn't Vasska, the Dragonking of the Pir—the center of your worship—ever deign to make an appearance for you?"

"Well, no," Lovich stammered, stumbling over some paving stones that had broken loose on the ground. "I mean, what with the war going on and all, I figured—"

"Lovich," Caelith said sharply, his anger boiling over. "The war is *always* going on! It's been fought back and forth across the plains of Enlund and the Urlund Expanse and the Vestron Marches and a dozen other lands you've never heard of since before you and I were even born! It's bled the clans, it's bled the Pir, it's wrung every one of the Five Kingdoms dry of blood, and the dragons go on! I promise you, Lovich, that you'll see your fill of dragons. The first time will be awe-inspiring and you'll feel a thrill at the power those magnificent beasts represent. You may even feel the need to fall down and worship such undeniable authority. But the next time—if you are fortunate enough to live to *have* a next time—you'll remember the people standing next to you who screamed as they burned under the dragon's flames. You'll remember the thousands of lives that die just to satisfy the hunger of their shredding gullet. You'll remember that the dragons prefer to cripple their prey rather than kill them outright because they like their meals *alive* when they digest them."

Lovich stopped, the color draining out of his face even in the salmon light of the fading day.

Caelith stopped and paused for a moment, thinking before he spoke again. "You will see far too many dragons, Lovich. I take it that Satinka's troops did a thorough job of ransacking the town?"

"Yes, sire, I'm afraid so," Lovich responded quickly. "There really isn't anything we can salvage for the clan."

"Well, that was expected." Caelith nodded. "I know it wasn't possible, but I wish they had held the town . . ."

"Sire?"

Caelith chuckled. "Well, I'm certainly no friend of Baerthag—or any of the Thanes of Urlund for that matter—but the outlying villages have been unusually helpful to our clan over the last few months. With the Thane and his army gone, the outer villages will flee west toward Urmakand. The remaining Thanes will be outraged and demand revenge—they may even work out an alliance with those lunatics in Enlund; that would heat up your war even too fast for you, Lovich. The Thanes will come back in force to take the land back for their *own* Dragonking, Ormakh. In any event, we'll find no friends here. We'll have to find somewhere else to get supplies."

"Somewhere else?" Lovich blinked. "Where else?"

"I don't know," Caelith said, running his gloved hand down his tired face. He then turned and looked around once more at the ruins. "P'tai."

"Sire?"

"The name of the town, Lovich," Caelith said sadly. "It was called P'tai."

The sky burned brilliant with the setting sun, red streaking the wispy clouds overhead.

"I guess we got here too late," Lovich said sadly.

"Late?" Caelith replied with surprise. "I should hope not! We couldn't have stopped this, Lovich; not with a hundred times our number." They had reached the edge of the town. The avenue be-came a wide, trampled road winding its way over gently undulating hills to the west. The fields to either side of the road were heavily trampled with the passing of the army just a few days before. Caelith gazed down the road to the west. "Find Kenth and have him gather up everyone else here as soon as possible. Have them collect as much wood as they can for a fire."

"Well," Lovich sputtered, confused, "if we couldn't have stopped this—and there's nothing to salvage—then, excuse me, sire, but why *are* we here?"

The distant hoarse braying of a torusk beast drifted down the road. Only then did they both hear the tones of an indistinct song echoing among the western hills, growing closer by the moment.

"We are here, it would seem, to be entertained," Caelith said as he smiled grimly in the fading light of day.

Teller of Tales

". . . So the merry work of blood and woe,
As onwardly we gladly go
To hear the ringing of our steel
And turn once more the warrior wheel!"

Warm baritone notes rolled out of Margrave's throat and carried across the scorched hills. He stood on the footboards at the front of the wagon, sure-footedly rolling with each jounce of the wagon beneath him, one hand pressing his fingers dramatically to his chest while the other was extended for its theatrical effect. His long black hair, carefully kept in a thick cascade of curls, framed his thin face and set off his bright blue eyes. The cuffs of his elegant, puff-sleeved shirt were frayed and its former white had settled into a complacent gray. His tight-fitted breeches, once obviously tailored with great care and expense, now sagged slightly from the effects of literally leaner times. Yet the single golden earring—symbol of his trade—was brightly polished and every gesture suggested a man who knew he was magnificent. Indeed, behind him in paint so faded and badly scarred as to be nearly illegible, the side of the creaking wagon proclaimed him

Margrave the Magnificent as it rolled slowly on wobbling wheels down the deserted road.

As no objection was heard from the shattered and scorched dead that littered the fields to either side of the road, Margrave determined to continue his song.

"The noble Thanes of Urlund called
For Ormakh, Dragonking of Night,
To come defend the city-walled—"

Margrave stopped in mid-verse, then glanced down past the emaciated torusk beast in front of him as it pulled him and the wagon eastward. Margrave sniffed the wind for a moment as he considered. "What do you think, Anji? 'City-walled' seems a bit forced, doesn't it?"

Anji, a short waif of a girl with mousy looks and a demeanor to match, walked along beside the front of the torusk beast, a huge stick in her hand. She herself seemed like a stick of a girl. Her large, dark eyes were unfocused somewhere on the road a few feet in front of her, almost hidden completely by a tangle of long brown hair.

Margrave continued without waiting for an answer.

"How about 'To come prevent a people mauled'?"

Anji did not look up from her blank stare at the road before her.

"You don't like that one? I thought it rather visual," Margrave said, warm in his own cleverness. "How about 'And make his enemies appalled'?"

Anji said nothing.

"No? How about 'To save the ass of Baerthag bald'?"

Anji continued to trudge the road.

"Oh honestly, there's no pleasing you," Margrave said, emphasizing his frustration by flinging both his hands passionately into the air. "We escape Urmakand with our very lives, witness one of the greatest battles yet fought in the War of Scales, slip through its devastation unscathed—and all you can do is criticize! We have an obligation—no, more than that, we have a *duty* to all humankind to chronicle such events." Margrave struck a noble pose at the front of the rickety wagon. "To sing for those who can no longer give voice to their deeds; to tell the tales of those whose tales should have been told but now cannot be told because they cannot tell them."

Anji sighed, tapping the torusk's tusk to urge it over the crest of the hill.

Color rose in Margrave's prominent cheeks. "Of course I know it needs work! Don't you think I know it's a terrible slogan? Honestly, Anji, sometimes I wonder if you're supporting me in my calling or not. Who else will tell the tales of the dead? It's our duty to stay alive so that those who don't will be remembered long after—"

Anji stopped, tapping the torusk on its good tusk. The torusk stopped suddenly, bringing the wagon to an unexpectedly abrupt halt. Margrave staggered slightly, fighting to keep his footing under him. He was momentarily upset that his grandeur had been compromised, but he forgot it all in an instant when he steadied himself and looked up.

Five cloaked men stood before Anji and the torusk, blocking the road. Beyond them, Margrave could see the road running down the hill and across three miles of fields to the smoldering remains of the town beyond.

Margrave barely hesitated before striking another pose.

"A delegation from the city!" Margrave said, opening his arms grandly. "I assure you it wasn't necessary, but the gesture is not lost on Margrave the Magnificent—Margrave the Loremaster of the Five Kingdoms! I humbly accept the generosity of the city of P'tai!"

Relieved of its burdens of the road, the wagon sagged against the broken wall on one side of what remained of the town square. It hid behind the canvas backdrop which Margrave had unfurled and hung between trembling lengths of supporting poles, a sagging cyclorama emblazoned with a fanciful map of the Five Kingdoms of Hrunard, illustrated with many small scenes that stretched from pole to pole. A fire sputtered in the center of the square, the late evening wind shredding its flames into shifting and uncertain light. Completing the circle around the fire stood a cadre of nearly thirty dark figures, each of them clad in worn and tattered robes, their faces cast in stark and shifting relief by the stuttering fire.

The young girl called Anji stood uncertainly next to the fluttering canvas, her large eyes blinking as her hands crossed in front of her. She shivered occasionally with the mounting cold, the fire offering no comfort in the chill wind. She shifted her slight weight from foot to foot as she silently waited.

Caelith stood on the far side of the fire with his arms folded tightly over his chest.

Next to him, Marash Kenth, a seasoned warrior from Vestron Marches, glared with his single good eye at the sight arrayed before them. He turned toward Caelith, his distaste obvious in his voice. "Master Arvad, have we force-marched three days into Urlund just for this shrill peacock?"

Caelith sighed. "That's what we are about to find out. My instructions were very specific. But before I bring this bizarre sideshow back with us, I want to be sure."

"'Tis a mad dream that brings us to ill ends," Kenth grumbled.

"Mad dreams I can understand," Caelith said with a chuckle. "Quiet, now. The show is starting."

The rising din of a drumhead rose slowly from behind the canvas, its tempo increasing. Just as it sounded a final hollow bang, the thin girl surreptitiously flicked her hand sideways, casting a handful of powder toward the ground. It erupted in a flash of smoke and light. Quite suddenly, Margrave stood before them, his hands upraised in anticipation, a grand smile on his face and the canvas behind him swaying precariously.

"Greetings, good friends!" Margrave intoned, his rich voice carrying over the heads of his grim audience. "Tonight you shall partake of the greatness of the ages! Fear not the power that I wield, for it shall harm none here! For I alone have tamed the power of the Soulless, the wandering carriers of the Emperors' Madness—that through those tempered demons you may experience yourselves the rise of your ancestors, the Thanes of Urlund, who from the most ancient of days were called forth by the Ormakh, dragon-god of Urlund!"

Margrave paused with dramatic effect, gesturing back toward the sweeping canvas behind him. That part of the backdrop representing Urlund suddenly seemed to lift as a ghostly apparition from the artwork. A visage of the past hung before the assembly. Caelith could only guess that he was seeing some apparition of the city-state of Urmakand sitting at the confluence of two rivers on the plains of the Urlund Expanse. Above it materialized the specter of a dragon—impossibly large—that spread its leathery wings from horizon to horizon. It looked down on the city beneath it, its glow illuminating the landscape.

Margrave turned with a smile toward his audience. The audience stared back at him with deepening grimaces, but Margrave barely missed a beat. The vision changed at a gesture, the dragon suddenly appearing threatening. The glow was gone, replaced by a deep shadow that blanketed the land below. "Yes, the *evil* god of Urlund, who, as you *conquerors* of the Eastern Empire well know, challenged the rightness of Satinka's domain and her benevolent rulership of the lands of Bayway!"

The dragon in the vision suddenly cowered and retreated as another spectral vision rushed forward from another part of the canvas. This time a different dragon, once more impossibly large, rose in the sky above a new landscape. The dragon swooped down from a towering peak high in the mountains, one which Caelith recognized as Mount Saethalan. As the company watched, it roared eastward over an illusory plain, the flames of its breath streaking down into a different city—walled with towering spires—whose stones exploded at their touch.

"I shall take you back down the centuries and you shall relive the liberation of Ost Batar from the Rhamasian lords who had held it captive in their madness since before time! You shall walk with me across the Vestron Marches as Satinka . . ."

Margrave caught sight of Kenth, who was livid at the mention of the conquest of his homeland. The scarred warrior bared teeth as he reached for the hilt of his sword.

"As Satinka brought her terrible destruction and iron domination down upon the once noble and free peoples of that land!" Margrave concluded. The enormous dragon suddenly diminished as the vision collapsed behind the Loremaster back into the canvas.

Caelith leaned over toward the still seething Kenth. "You have to admit, he's got an open mind."

"More like vacant, if you ask me," Kenth sniffed menacingly.

"Let us together peel back the years of war and find ourselves back in another time—a time of your ancestors; a time of their beginnings and ours," Margrave intoned with great solemnity, though beads of sweat were breaking out on the Loremaster's forehead. The images on the canvas behind him wavered, with different illusions struggling to be set free. "Just ask me! Test me! What story of your forebears will you have me weave for you tonight?"

"Tell us of Rhamas," Caelith called out.

Margrave turned sharply toward him, the Loremaster's face still a mask. "Do you want to hear a tale of the Mad Emperors and their just destruction before the power of the Dragonkings?"

Caelith stepped forward slowly, his hands still folded across his chest as he slowly shook his head.

"Ah! Then perhaps I could interest you in an older tale; something, perhaps, before the time of the Dragonkings themselves?" Margrave glanced around, a look of both fear and excitement crossing his features as he spoke. "You are a most interesting audience—most unusual in your tastes. There are such tales as you are seeking, but they are forbidden by the Dragonkings of all the Five Domains—dark tales of the Mad Emperors and a time that is no more."

"So you know these tales?" Caelith asked calmly.

Margrave smiled with a practiced coy modesty. "Margrave the Magnificent has seen more, heard more, and read more than any man breathing, sire, but such tales are lost in the mists of time. The scrolls of Maranth were rumored to have recorded such tales . . ."

"But they were buried beneath the city when the gray towers fell before Ormakh," Caelith finished, taking a few steps closer to the performer. "There were still other places where the stories were recorded, were there not—other legends of their existence?"

Margrave paused and blinked; a momentary hesitation that was not in his character. "Indeed, some say there were entire volumes carved into the sandstone walls of the caverns in Mount Evanoth where the scholars hid, sealing themselves within to protect their knowledge. Others tell tales of stray books, powerful in and of themselves so that they may reconstitute from their own ashes. Still others whisper about—"

"But what need does a Loremaster have for such magical books when he has been to Mount Evanoth himself?" Caelith smiled evenly as he stepped around the sputtering fire and stood facing the entertainer, his hands falling to his hips. "As the man who has seen more, heard more, and read more than any man breathing, surely you know the stories from that legendary place, don't you?"

"You flatter me too much, my lord."

"Perhaps." Caelith shrugged. "But you will tell us a true tale tonight—a tale from a cavern wall carved by the scholars of Rhamas about their empire's great cities and its power in the days before the Dragonkings."

Margrave leaned in toward Caelith, his voice dropping so as to be heard only between the two of them. "They are not very good stories, my lord. Might I suggest that they are not worthy of your good fellows' time?"

Caelith leaned in slightly toward the Loremaster, his voice matching in low conspiratorial tone. "You have eaten our provisions and now enjoy our protection. Might I suggest that we are not an audience to be denied?"

Margrave licked his lips, stepped back, drew in a deep breath and then began again, his voice once more booming over the small gathered crowd. "My friends, there was a time before time as the Dragonkings reckon such things. It was a time of men when all the lands of Hrunard—indeed, even the lands now lost to us—were governed for good or ill by the kings of the Rhamasian Empire. It was a sunlit time for men, for their ships sailed the waters of the fabled Gold Coast past the Pillars of Rhamas to legendary lands of myth and power."

The Loremaster gestured once more, this time toward the farthest lower corner of the canvas to his right. From a smallish rendition of a peak labeled Maranth roiled out an image of smoke and lightning. It seemed to Caelith as though they were looking into a thick haze or fog. Shapes and images emerged from its murky depths as though time itself was unwilling to give up its secret past. Graceful and ornate ships with two masts and great triangular sails sailed into view. The ships diminished in size until they were only the size of Caelith's thumbnail as they sailed between towering carved pillars of stone standing guard on either side of a busy passage. Then the mists folded and unfolded once more and Caelith saw rows of docks in the fog, beyond which stood ranks of buildings domed in gold and the dark mass of mountains beyond.

Margrave glanced again at Caelith.

Caelith smiled menacingly in encouragement.

The Loremaster turned once more toward the illusion. The smoke of the vision momentarily cleared as he spoke, revealing the flagging canvas. Margrave gestured across the broad expanse of the map as he spoke. "It is impossible for us today to comprehend it, for the rule of Rhamas lay over all the lands we know now as the Five Kingdoms and lands unimaginably far beyond. Rhamas was the center of thought and strength throughout the known world. The wealth of distant kingdoms flowed through her veins from the south along the magical Dwarven Road through the Mountains of Rhamas, bringing life, strength, and enlightenment to our ancestors. The great cities are, alas, no more. Each of them fell—Mithanlas the Prize of Hrunard, Agrothas the Beautiful, Rheshalthia the Citadel of Wisdom—each in their turn fell and only their bones remain. But the greatest of them all was Calsandria, the Throne of the Gods." Margrave's voice gained strength, his story surer as his hand swept downward before the canvas. Once more, the illusory mists tumbled outward from the canvas, this time from the center of its base until it filled Caelith's vision. "South . . . south beyond the snowcapped sentinels of Mount Aerthra and Hrudan, beyond the Tombs of Mnemia, down the long-lost Dwarven Road and hidden in the heart of the Forsaken Mountains, there still may lie Calsandria, the heart of man's hopes—the very home of the ancient gods!"

The mists thinned and Caelith saw what appeared to be a street running between rows of ornate buildings. Their carvings were delicate and intricate in their design as they wound their way up thin, graceful columns. It appeared as though the entertainer himself was standing on the cobblestones of the street itself.

Margrave turned, his face lit by the fire before him. "Calsandria! Think of it, friends! Picture yourselves there! Its broad streets beneath your feet are paved in granite stones fitted with such precision that no blade of grass could make purchase between them! Its buildings towered above you in alabaster carved with the most intricate of detail, each building a legend unto itself. The shores of Behrun Lake—an inland sea in its own right trafficking in the commerce of goods from beyond the horizons of the empire—laps gently at the docks nearby."

Caelith could hear the sound of the gentle waves coming from the fantasy before him. As he watched, the mists parted further. A great cliff face rose up beyond the glorious buildings, a long cascade falling beautifully down its face. At the top, with peaks reaching skyward, rose a magnificent temple of matchless beauty, the gold domes atop its tower glistening in sunlight.

"Above it all, you can see in the distance the Citadel of the Rhamas—the very Pillar of the Sky—cresting the top of Calsandria Falls, the glorious center of the Mad Emperors' Empire and the very thrones of the ancient gods of the Rhamasian people!"

Caelith smiled to himself. Margrave obviously felt he was doing well, feeling the warming interest of his audience at last. Caelith had heard enough but was somehow loath to interrupt just yet.

"The Rhamasian gods! What great power that they granted in those days unto men before the Mad Emperors brought them all to ruin!" Margrave paced in a circle on the illusory street, his arms outstretched as if imploring his audience. Caelith noticed, however, that the girl Anji tossed Margrave a small packet as he passed her near the canvas backdrop. Caelith shook his head and smiled.

"Here took place the tale of Ekteia and Hrea—the chief gods of Rhamas and how their ancient quarrel granted to man—!" Margrave thundered, his long curls quivering along with his voice. "—the power of MAGIC!"

Margrave flung his hands into the air. A ball of flame burst over him with a sudden popping sound, crackling with flecks of brilliant sparks inside a plume of white smoke.

The audience was stone silent.

Margrave held his pose for a moment and then turned to Caelith, frustration boiling over. The spectral street collapsed behind him back into the dim and quaking canvas. "What's wrong with you people? That flourish *always* gets applause!"

Caelith casually raised his hand over his head. A fleck of light suddenly burst into a sphere of brilliant blue no larger than an apple, tongues of shining flame curling continuously in on themselves within. One by one, each of the other cloaked figures raised their hands, producing identical spheres of light. The bright spheres floating above the surrounding mystics plunged their facial features into the dark shadows of their hoods.

"The Soulless!" Margrave's eyes went wide, his voice suddenly gruff.

Kenth turned to Caelith. "Are you sure about him?"

"Yes, he is the one. Get everyone organized and detail as many as you think necessary to get this wagon hitched back up to that poor torusk. We'll leave as soon as possible."

"Yes, Master Arvad," Kenth replied, then nodded toward Anji. "What about the girl?"

Caelith looked on the waif. Just then, she lifted her face, her wide, dark eyes shining back at him; bottomless pools of hope.

Caelith shivered suddenly and looked away.

"We had better bring her, too. She wouldn't last long out here without help," Caelith replied, then turned to the now trembling Margrave. "Loremaster, you seem to have fallen into bad company. However, as one who has tamed the powers of the Soulless, I've no doubt that you will feel right at home in the company of us wandering carriers of the Emperors' Madness. More than that, I can promise you that you'll be well treated where we are going."

"And where, may I ask, is that?" Margrave replied.

"Why, to my father's house." Caelith smiled. "He asked especially after you . . . and no one lightly refuses the request of Galen Arvad."

Galen's Ritual

The winged woman gazes at me with a sad silence.

We have often met here. The names of these places are unknown and perhaps unknowable, but she is always here, gazing at me in her hushed peace and pain. For more than twenty years we have come together in such places as exist only in this unconscious place, through fire and ice, good and ill. We have together striven to understand this power of the Deep Magic that binds us inseparably together and makes us dependent upon each other for the power it represents. Now, on this hilltop covered with bright flowers, I gaze on her with wonder, gratitude, and a sense of loss.

She destroyed my life even as she gave my life meaning — and I do not even know if she is real, this winged woman.

We stand on a hillside in my reveries and feel the wind blowing against us. She looks as she has always looked to me in this dream land; I stand somewhat ashamed as I hide behind the mask I have conjured for myself. I hate that I should have to hide from her. The petals of the flowers covering the hillside around us are tiny flames, burning brightly in the breeze. The winged woman opens her arms as though to release me. I feel her lightness within my body, my feet rising from the ground.

23

The wind carries me onward and blows against my mask, a masquerade that all mystics must now wear. It feels like soft tooled leather on my face, its surfaces painted white and black with the curled spikes from its forehead shading to flame orange and red. The shape and form of the mask must change each time I enter the dream, but this form is one of my favorites. I can hear the breeze whistling about the sides and flowing around its contours. Only lately in my dreams, I feel this wind grow with each passing day. I know that I must follow it and find meaning in its course.

The winged woman raises her hand in a gesture of farewell. I spread my hands out, surrendering myself to the wind's blustering flow. It blows me backward through the days and years, drifting on the breeze as a feather through the darkness and light. Each evening down the long years and in many different forms I have made this journey; it takes effort to undo time. But my masked self is weary and wishes now only to drift with the blowing of the wind, to give myself over to its whim and follow it where it may take me.

The years fall from my body until I float across the gentle slopes on the shores of Mirren Bay. I would that the wind had not driven me here, for it is a place of exquisite loss, I float through the chill of morning toward a humble little house on the northern edges of Benyn, drifting more slowly now, the breeze on which I ride taunting me as the cottage nears. The sounds of the Pir trumpets, too, are carried on the currents as I near an ill-fitting glass set in a windowpane. I turn away from the glass, for I cannot look upon the hopeful faces that would look back at me, so young and innocent of the tragedy to come.

The cottage has become a tree and I a leaf clinging to it, fighting against the wind. Yet it is as if I have dried and my season is finished. I cannot hold on to what is past and am torn from its shelter. Another leaf in brilliant orange is caught by the wind, too, and follows me swirling into the sky.

I twist on a new eddy in a sudden gust. The beautiful woman with elegant wings floats with me in the wind. She is ever there for me and never changing. Her presence comforts me for a time as the winds drive me away from my home.

And now there is another that is blown on this wind behind me. I can see her, too, tumbling in the gusts, the orange leaf that has taken human form. Berkita—my Berkita! We tumble down the path of years across the waters of the Hadran Strait and swirling across the plains and mountains of Hrunard. I try to reach out to her, to touch her, but the winds toss us about, conspiring to keep us apart. We swirl about the towers of Vasska's Temple, never touching in our dance of the winds.

I whirl away from the tower down different paths, skittering across the plains of Hrunard. Ten thousand—twenty thousand dead and more are pulled up by string from the blood-soaked ground of Election Fields, their tortured bodies once more whole. They dance like marionettes and take up arms. All around me the battle is joined and the slaughter rages. Again they die and the Dragonkings feast upon the dead. I try to stop, to help the dying, but the winds carry me insistently onward, south over the hills and into the forests beyond.

Then the winds drive me into chaos. I tumble in the currents, driven through the trunks of the trees, through hard winters of hunger and pain, through endless journeys, births, deaths, unions, and partings. Each place I touch urges me onward with no surcease.

At last the wind slows and deposits the winged woman and me back on the hilltop with the vibrantly flaming blossoms and into the now, if such a thing can be said to exist here. Two creatures, new to me, now rest before us, one a monstrous little demon that looks bewildered at our surroundings and the other a rust and white colored bird that sits on his shoulders. The little demon is new to the realm of dreams and I wish I could offer him some comfort. It happens often these days that someone new finds within themselves their link to this land of power and shadows. Their arrival always comes as a shock to them, and those of us who have walked the landscape of this shared dream do what we can to comfort them.

At least, most of us do. I think about my mask and hate it even as I know it must be strictly worn by all of our clan. Many years now have gone by since any of us could walk the dream as ourselves. Generally, I abhor disguises in all their forms, which makes my life doubly unfortunate.

This little demon before me is green and sports a scrawny beard. As I watch, ghosts wearing ancient armor stride up to him and drag him away from me. Poor little fellow; he probably has no idea that his life has just changed forever and that he has started down his own road without end and from which there is no turning back. I wonder once more if these visions of such creatures truly exist in some other place or if they are other metaphors for me to ponder.

The bird, however, remains behind. It flits through the air and lands on my shoulder. Its feathers are a brilliant white everywhere except for a ragged shock of black which runs down the cord of its right wing. It is odd to see a bird with coloring only on one side. With quick, jerking movements, it examines me with curiosity, staring at me with blinking, bright red eyes. I have not seen its like in the dream before, but the dream is full of the curious, wondrous, and all too often dangerous. Perhaps it wonders at who I am here behind my mask.

A gentle cry rends the air behind me, causing the clouds above to pause and fills me with bone-crushing despair. I turn to see my winged companion fall to the ground clutching at her chest. Her tears well up and I am moved beyond grief. I look about and quickly begin to gather up the flowers of the hilltop, their petals like flames burning cold against my hand. As she lifts her face toward me, I offer her the luminous bouquet. She accepts it with a glad smile. The flowers erupt into a pillar of flame, blinding me and forcing me back with its sudden heat. It vanishes as quickly as it came—the winged woman vanishing with it.

I sigh and turn to face northward, the great range of the Forsaken Mountains at my back. The winged woman is but a dream—bought too dearly at the cost of another who is all too real. I gaze across the tops of the Rhesai Forest trees. In my mind's eye, I look beyond the forest, beyond the foothills, and beyond all the intervening lands of Hrunard, I still look and know that she is there.

Each night I look to the north and remember my lost Berkita.

THE BOOK OF GALEN
BRONZE CANTICLES, TOME IV, FOLIO 6, LEAVES 32–36

"Father."

At the sound of his name, Galen Arvad withdrew from the realm of dreams to find himself on a ridge, gazing to the north over the crests of the God's Rim hills. Each evening for over twenty years, he had stood on an endless succession of hilltops in the waning light of uncounted afternoon suns. Some of those places had names, most of them did not, but in each of them, no matter where the clan had encamped, Galen closed each day by putting the setting sun on his left and looking northward beyond the horizon. In such times and places, he entered the Dream for his own purposes. It was the single touchstone of his day, that rare moment which he claimed entirely as his own.

Galen sat down slowly on a large stone at the crest of the hill, the pain in his effort finding voice in a prolonged groan. Twenty-six years, he thought, have exacted a terrible price on him. It was a long time to wander without a home. The long brown hair of his youth was now streaked with iron gray and his forehead seemed to have gotten much higher of late. His face had lost some of its fullness over too many hard winters with too few provisions and the lines had increased considerably in his weathered skin. He hoped idly that he did not look too different than he did when he was younger, and knew in the same moment that he did.

"Caelith! Welcome back, son."

"I am sorry to disturb you, father," the voice spoke quietly behind him. "I wouldn't have done so if . . ."

"That is quite all right, Caelith," Galen answered warmly. "I was finished."

"Oh, of course."

Galen laughed, turning slightly toward his son. "I don't suppose you know what I was doing, do you?"

"No, father," Caelith answered. "But everyone knows you come out each day wherever we are encamped—and that you are most strictly not to be disturbed."

Galen raised his peppered eyebrows with amusement. "They do, do they? And just what do *they* think I'm doing out here?"

Caelith stepped forward to stand next to his father. There was a lot of Galen in his visage, the same soft eyes and the slight purse to his lips. He had his mother's build, however, slighter and taller than his father. His mother attributed his sandy hair color to his maternal grandmother and his volatile temperament to some forgotten ancestor no one would claim. Caelith had been forged on the anvil of war and the fires of persecution. Both had beaten childhood out of him and tempered his metal in the cold waters of survival and necessity. The boy had never known a time without war or a time of rest. The demands of their times had aged him far too quickly. For all that, Galen decided, his son had tempered into a fine young man, though perhaps too soon. Looking at him now, Galen knew he was a grandson of which both Maddoc and Rhea would have been proud. He only hoped, wherever their spirits rested, that he had raised the boy to their honor and credit.

"Well, some believe that you gaze into realms of magic that you alone can see, searching for a new and more powerful Deep Magic," Caelith said, his own gaze looking northward past the horizon. "Others say that you look both into the past and the future, seeking the destiny of our clan and an end to our pain."

"And what do you believe, Caelith?" Galen asked.

Caelith thought for a moment before he spoke; then his lips curled into a half-smile toward his father. "I think you're just tired of everyone jabbering at you all the time and want to enjoy two quiet moments in a row."

Galen tossed back his head and laughed.

"I'm right, aren't I?" Caelith smirked.

"Ah, Caelith, you're a good son!" Galen said, slapping his thighs. "Do us both a favor, however, and don't tell that to anyone. I suspect it was your mother who put about such nonsense in the first place. She always understood the importance of such things more than I. Better that they believe such comforting twaddle. The gods alone know how much they need comforting."

"Speaking of twaddle," Caelith said, clearing his throat, "we returned with the requested entertainment."

Galen raised an eyebrow. "You found him, then?"

Caelith nodded. "As mother foretold; yes, in P'tai—or what was left of it. Satinka's armies had overrun it, as you predicted, and it now lies in ashes. Her armies had moved westward onto the Urlund Expanse, but I suspect only so far as to run Thane Baerthag to ground. We don't know for certain—our instructions were to return undetected."

"Baerthag was an idiot," Galen rumbled, shaking his head, "moving his troops into the Vestron Marches. What did he think, that Satinka wouldn't notice them near her own lair? The Thanes of Urlund will be on their heels now but Satinka won't press her advantage. She'll be satisfied once she's made a meal of Baerthag and pull back. She's too occupied by Hrunard and Palathia to deal with Urlund just yet. The bad news in this is that the thane may finally unite with Panas against Satinka. That could drive Urlund to ally with Enlund—which is something I'd rather not contemplate."

"There *are* those who prefer open war to slowly being bled to death," Caelith said quietly.

Galen looked at his son in surprise. "You side with Uruh Nikau on this?"

"No, father," Caelith returned quickly. "I would never disagree with you publicly . . . but I do see her point; we cannot stay on our backs forever."

"Perhaps," Galen said, drawing the word out. "Still, survival has its merits—and we have more immediate concerns. Baerthag's outland farms were supporting us. Now, with P'tai lost, those farms will be abandoned. We'll have to find another source of food."

"The third and fifth parties will be returning," Caelith responded. "Perhaps they have found some closer villages that can assist us. The townsfolk here in the Naraganth have had two different armies march through their towns in the last few weeks. They are always a bit skittish after deadly combat in their beet fields but it could work to our advantage."

"Let's hope the rangers' news is good then," Galen agreed. "We've just gotten through a tough winter here—I'd hate to ask these people to pick up and move again, even if the weather is clearing. So, tell me: what do you think of this fellow you've brought back to us?"

Caelith considered his response before speaking. "He's a peacock-plated buffoon who spends more effort on his hair than on any real work. Still, his control of the Deep Magic may be remarkably subtle and he appears to know a mind-numbing amount of history, geography . . ."

"And the ancient gods?" Galen asked casually.

"'The gods,' father?" Caelith raised his eyebrows in surprise. "Met any gods lately?"

"Well, certainly not the Dragonkings, if that's who you mean," Galen sniffed in reply. "You've seen just how mortal they are and there is no bottom to their selfishness, I can tell you that. I certainly have trouble believing in any god that was out only for himself—or a man who was, for that matter."

"So you're saying there are no gods?" Caelith persisted.

Galen looked up at his son in surprise. "You're serious, aren't you?"

Caelith stuck his chin out uncomfortably, looking away with some embarrassment. "Well—yes, I suppose I am."

"Well, that's a change!" Galen chuckled in surprise. "Where did this come from, may I ask?"

"It's started again in the camps—these stories about the 'old gods,' Calsandria, the Promised Valley—it could become a problem. You remember last time?"

"The Sedrich Expedition?" Galen snorted.

"He claimed to have seen it—all in the dream," Caelith said, stooping down to pull at the blades of grass about his feet. "Almost forty people followed him across the Vestron Marches and down the Old Imperial Road—right under Satinka's lair. If they found their gods, it was in the Pir's so-called Surn'gara after Satinka discarded their bones for trespassing on her lands. It could happen again—and perhaps worse—if this talk of the ancient gods gets out of hand again, and I'm hearing it more and more among the clanfolk . . ."

"And from your mother, no doubt," Galen coaxed.

"Well—yes, always from mother"—Caelith nodded, still looking away—"every time I return home. So—could there have been other gods before the Dragonkings?"

"I wouldn't know about that, son," Galen answered. "The Dragonkings are the only gods anyone has known for over four hundred years."

"Of course," Caelith agreed, "but mother says the Rhamasians worshipped other deities before the Dragonkings came. It's just—it's hard to know what to think."

"Your mother is unusually educated, son," Galen said softly. "She is well read and has visionary talents as well. We have spoken about this subject often, she and I. And it may surprise you to hear that this fool you have brought among us may serve us greatly in regards to this question."

"Indeed? So, have you made up your mind, father?"

Galen pressed his hands against his knees, stretching in his thoughts. "The gods of the Mad Emperors? I don't know. Your mother had read a number of ancient texts—collections that somehow managed to escape the fires of the Pir Inquisitas—that talk about the Lost City of the Gods, the Pillar of the Sky, and the heart of the Rhamas Empire from which all magic sprang as a gift from the gods."

"Then she shall find Margrave intriguing." Caelith chuckled darkly. "He talks about Calsandria as though he's been there, but it's all a child's tale to me."

"So you don't believe in these ancient gods, then?"

Caelith shrugged. "I believe in a sharp edge to my steel and the Deep Magic, father—that and finding tomorrow's meal and shelter. I believe what I've seen—and I've seen nothing of the gods or their city."

"Well, perhaps there are still a few things left that you *haven't* seen." Galen sighed. "But whether there is such a place—or the gods to go with it—Caelith, I honestly don't know—and that is something *else* you shouldn't let get around the camp either!"

"Yes, father, I'll be careful about that." Caelith stood easily and turned. "Still, that's not why I came out here to disturb your little ritual."

"If it's about protection of the glade tonight—"

"No, I'm already taking care of that, and yes, I'll make sure it is clear again right after I leave you . . . but that's not it either."

"I see." Galen sighed. "You've already seen your mother, haven't you?"

Caelith nodded with a wry grin. "She asked that I remind you to come home right away and have something to eat. She says she doesn't want your stomach growling in the middle of the Clan Council and having everyone think she isn't taking good enough care of you."

Galen nodded wistfully. "My dear Dhalia—that your mother wants me home, I have no doubt; but her reasons have little to do with feeding me. She is worried about tonight and is hiding behind the mask of my supper."

Caelith looked at Galen with a slight squint, not quite comprehending.

"You know why we wear the masks in the dream, son?" Galen said carefully. "We wear masks in life for the same reasons. Go to her, tell her I'll be back directly but I have a few things to take care of first. Will you be staying with us?"

"My company are now settled and I've dismissed some to stay with their own families," Caelith answered. "I suppose I can spend a few days away from them to eat your food and enjoy resting in your tent."

"Then I look forward to hearing all about your journey after the council," Galen said to his son with warm pride.

Caelith nodded and turned to go.

"Oh—and Caelith?"

"Yes, father?"

"Tell your mother . . ." Galen paused for a moment, unsure how much to say. "Tell your mother that I love her and that she has nothing to worry about."

Caelith nodded uncertainly and then walked quickly back down the hill. Galen watched his son until the youth disappeared among the shadows of the forest beyond.

"We have nothing to worry about," Galen repeated, rubbing his right thumb nervously against his left palm as he turned to face the horizon once more.

The wind was blowing from the north, and his wife feared what it would bring. He feared it himself.

The Clans

The Brotherhood of Galen became the foundation of the
Council of Six . . . six houses or, as they were then called, clans.
While pursuing the seedling mystical arts, each spent most of their
time and energies on survival alone. Hounded and despised by
both the lay members and priests of the Five Domains, jeered as
the Soulless wherever they went, universally blamed for the great
war between the Dragonkings that had raged for decades, the
mystics were outcasts of society, shunned and persecuted. They
were made up of farmers who could only long for land, craftsmen
dreaming of a trade, and women who yearned for a home for their
children. They became nomads by fiat, thieves by necessity, and
were hated all the more for it. They were the only hope of a world
winding down to its end — and the world would give them no rest.

Bronze Canticles, Tome III, Folio 2, Leaf 24

Caelith slipped quietly through the trees less out of design than
out of habit. There was no shortage of predators that hunted the mystics of Clan Arvad wherever they stopped. Some were beasts who
hunted the Reshalthei and Mathedran Forests for their own survival:
wild torusks that lay in wait before charging their prey, or small,

lightning-fast Kampocs—dragonhawks, as they were occasionally called—that could dart and weave through the thickets with incredible speed. Some were more cunning and deadlier still: human hunters who roamed the places beyond the walls of civilization hoping to claim the bounty offered on each mystic head by the Pir. Worse was the war itself that dragged the Elect to their deaths openly or killed them indiscriminately along with everyone else in its warrior path.

Caelith frowned as he stepped carefully from stone to stone over a small stream winding its way northward through the trees. All these were small matters compared to the worst threat of all. What they feared most endangered them no matter how light their tread nor how silent their breath.

Above all, the mystics feared one another.

According to the Pir, the clans of the Elect were composed of the insane—and they were not far wrong. The power of the Deep Magic, as they had come to call it, drove many of those who were susceptible quite mad. Indeed, those who were not outright insane were often ruined either by their inability to cope mentally or through bodily injury they may have suffered at the hands of the uncontrolled magic itself.

Supporting such a proportionally large community of mental or physical cripples was nearly impossible because little basic social structure existed beyond the broad ties of the clan. They were a society of broken dreams and shattered families—sons separated from fathers; daughters who no longer remembered their mothers; and parents whose children were lost to them.

Worse yet, those who had managed to somehow hold on to the dragon's tail of Deep Magic and retain some modicum of sanity and mastery at the same time were all too easily swayed by the power itself. Simple ambitions became dangerous obsessions when fueled by the explosive and dangerous power of the Deep Magic.

And the magic itself was unpredictable. The metaphors in the dream were cryptic; a language whose meaning was largely still unknown. It remained unclear to the mystics whether they controlled the magic—or the magic controlled them.

Thus, there was no greater danger to the mystics than their own kind.

Caelith stopped, alert and unmoving. An unnatural quiet had descended on the woods. He had learned to listen to the voice of the forest, and silence, he knew, meant danger. In his stillness, Caelith reached in his mind toward the place of dreams, drawing up its power within him. He only had a vague notion of what form the power would take but he would rather prepare than not. It was a fundamental fact of a mystic's life: be wary or be dead.

He sensed the movement behind him. He could not see his enemy but knew that one was there. One part of his trained mind fell into the dream, searching for a connection—for some image or idea that would empower him. Some few icons in the dream were known to him and he could count on them. The power surged toward him in the dream, taking shape in his mind as he drew it from the other world.

Caelith spun around, raising both his hands as they twisted and whirled through the air, forming the patterns from his mind. He only vaguely saw the shadowy figure rushing toward him as the long vines laying across the forest floor leaped upward in his defense. They wove themselves into a mesh as they flew, arresting the figure in its charge, throwing him backward against a tree with a resounding *thunk* that reverberated up the trunk and shook the leaves of the branches.

"Oh, no!" Caelith muttered. "Not now!"

The power continued to surge through him unbidden and turning wild. He had hoped only to bind this unknown stalker but soon even branches from the tree joined the vines in curling around the unknown person.

At last, Caelith was able to lower his hands. The vines were so effective that the figure was bound to the tree from the heel of his boot to the top of his head. Only the vaguest outline of the attacker could be seen through the foliage.

"Who are you?" Caelith demanded, still shaking from the magic. "What do you want?"

"Mmmffph murmuphth," was all the reply the encased figure could manage.

"Don't move," Caelith said harshly, raising his left hand and gesturing carefully.

Nothing happened.

Caelith sighed. *So much for control,* he thought as he pulled his sword from its sheath and started sawing at the vines. He quickly cut away some of the vines around the intruder's face.

"Well, if you can't take a little *joke,*" snipped a familiar voice, "I don't know why I even bother to visit!"

Caelith stopped in surprise, his face brightening as a rare, genuine smile broke on his face. "Lucian?"

"And who else would be bound to a tree in the forest?"

Caelith chuckled as he shook his head. "Lucian! I can't believe that you're here!"

"I might not be for long," Lucian grunted, "if you don't get these frightful vines off me."

Caelith gleefully sawed the edge of his blade across several more vines. "Diplomats and courtiers always think they can sneak up on the warriors; that's why we always hold our best magic just for you."

"No death too good for us, eh?"

"Hey, just relax and enjoy the embrace." Caelith grinned, stepping back and considering the predicament into which he had placed his friend. The lower vines were still tightening. He would need to work quickly before the upper vines got the same idea.

"Still having a little problem with control, are we?"

"Aren't we all," Caelith observed as he worked. "Nothing ever happens quite the same way twice. Whatever are you doing here?"

"Came with mother," Lucian answered in tones that seemed almost bored. "The Circle of Six is convening under most mysterious circumstances, you know; completely out of season and entirely irregular. Mother was quite put out."

"I see you managed to make the trip," Caelith replied flatly as he worked to free his friend's waist.

"Careful with that! Well, I thought I was making *remarkable* progress until I was bound to this tree," Lucian sniffed. "I had hopes that such an event might occur, mind you, but it always involved a comely young sorceress from Clan Arvad who wished to enslave me with her winning—or should I say 'vining'—ways."

Caelith groaned as he pulled the last of the vines away from Lucian's feet. "Then I'm sure you'll want to meet Magretha."

"Oh, indeed?" Lucian purred, the upward slant of both his brows rising precipitously. "And why is that?"

"Last month she presented her theories about the use of physical sensuality as a means of power and communication in the mystic arts," Caelith said pleasantly. "I understand it was an unusual presentation."

"That sounds like a course of study I should like to pursue most vigorously! Did it work?"

"No—but it was certainly worth watching," Caelith said smoothly as he pulled the last of the vines clear of his old companion's feet. "So why sneak up on me? You should know better than that by now."

"I wasn't *sneaking*," Lucian objected in hurtful tones. "I was looking for you, if you must know. *Sneaking* just made the whole thing more interesting. The truth is, I was sent to have a look at this glade of yours before the meeting."

"So you are in charge of your mother's safety this trip?" Caelith nodded. "Fair enough, but you've nothing to worry about. I'm on my way to check the glade myself."

"Of course." Lucian smiled like a cat. "Which is why my mother sent *me* to check on *you*. Lead the way!"

Caelith waved his friend on. "Go on, then—just upstream."

"Ah, well, if we must." Lucian sighed. "But upstream is definitely not my style."

Caelith followed his old friend as they walked against the slow and meandering course of the stream. Lucian was taller than Caelith by nearly half a head and somewhat broader. He had a pinched face like a triangle that came down to a jutting chin, and his small mouth held a perpetual smirk while his eyes always looked either sleepy or bored. He kept his hair cropped short, a bristle of blond as careless as his manner.

"It's good to see you again," Caelith said as they hiked.

"Yes, it is good to see me again," Lucian agreed at once, picking his way along the stream. "I cannot imagine how you have borne being separated from me. I know that I should be very upset at being separated from myself. How long has it been, Cae? Three years?"

"Two years," Caelith replied.

"Really?"

"It was the council on secession, remember?"

"Yes, I remember now," Lucian said and smiled in that peculiar way that Caelith recognized, with his right lip curling upward. "Uruh Nikau wanted to go to war against the Pir with or without the consent of the Circle. Your father talked her out of it."

"Actually, it was my mother," Caelith confided.

"No!" Lucian stopped in his tracks.

"Yes," Caelith nodded. "No one knows what mother said to Nikau or what she might have offered in exchange, but it worked."

Lucian raised his brows again as he looked at his friend. "I may have to be impressed with the Arvad family after all!"

Caelith smiled as he passed his old friend. "Well, I suppose everything has a first time."

"Still," Lucian sniffed, "it might have been just as well if we *had* gone to war."

They both stepped from the tree line where the stream opened onto a meadow full of activity. The white smoke of multiple campfires joined above them into a single light haze. A hodgepodge of shelters lined both sides of the stream in its course through the tall grasses. There were a number of large lean-tos mixed with tents in various states of disrepair. Children ran among the dwellings, their course determined largely by whim and a search for whatever grasses of the meadow remained untrammeled. Their mothers watched closely and scolded them quickly, if unenthusiastically, when they started to stray too far. The distant sound of a forge hammer rang over the encampment and already the hunters were returning from the forests.

"How many workers in your clan?" Lucian asked idly.

"Not nearly enough," Caelith replied, "Less than half our total number. We care for the drones★ as best we can."

"What about the dangerous ones?"

"The mad?" Caelith shook his head sadly, then looked up. "Well, we're all a little mad, aren't we? Maybe it's just a matter of degree— or time."

★Early mystic clan term for those members incapable of contributing to the general welfare.

"We've heard rumors," Lucian said casually, "that Uruh's been allowing the drones of her clan to be left behind."

Caelith looked away as he spoke. "Uruh's clan had a hard winter—but I haven't heard anything about her abandoning her own drones."

"I'd believe anything since the Edicts," Lucian said, squinting slightly.

"The Edicts?" Caelith asked

"Caelith!" An extremely large woman called from a lean-to whose interior roof she was attempting to repair. Her greasy black hair hung flat against her head down to her shoulders. Her neck was as wide as her head and carried at least two additional chins.

"Magretha," Caelith responded as he and Lucian walked past. "I hope you're keeping dry!"

"I am, Caelith, thank you . . . have you had a chance to ask your father about another audience?" Magretha shouted, wiping her broad, dirty hands against her even filthier dress.

"I have," Caelith answered, never slowing his stride. "He's just a little busy now . . . he promises you another audience before the clan masters as soon as he has the time."

Magretha called after him. "I've got some new insights into belly dancing and the dreamworld that I'm sure he will want to hear about!"

"I'm sure he will!" Caelith smiled as he responded, not looking back.

"*That* is Magretha?" Lucian whispered to Caelith.

"Yes, that is Magretha."

"The one who demonstrated the sensual—"

"Yes." Caelith nodded through an almost innocent grin, before he stopped, gesturing behind them. "Would you like to meet her now? Maybe I could arrange a special demonstration for you?"

"No," Lucian shook his head.

"Really, I'm sure she wouldn't mind. We could do it right now if you—"

"*No,* thank you." Lucian pressed earnestly as he grabbed his friend by the shoulder and pulled him forward once more. "Normally I wouldn't mind, but right now you were about to show me the Council Glade."

The old friends fell into step next to each other as they walked through the camp. It was an unusual feeling for the warrior; as a rule he had comrades in arms but no real friends. It seemed to Caelith as if no time at all had passed and it was not until then that he realized just how much he had missed companionship.

Caelith broke the silence hanging between them. "You were telling me something about some decree or law or . . ."

"The Edicts?" Lucian offered.

"Yes . . . what is that about?"

"Ah, yes." Lucian sighed. "The Grand Duke of Pantaris has decreed in the name of Panas—our most revered Dragonking, may he rot in his own bile—that the power of the mystics is actually some sort of plague. The Edict states that all who are in contact with them must die to 'purge the pure blood of Enlund' and that it is better to burn the grain and the weeds together in this season that the grain may grow healthy in the next."

"Strange thought, that," Caelith said, a chill running down his spine.

"Stranger truth," Lucian agreed, turning to his friend. "Entire villages have been razed, so we have heard. But come, you are entirely too serious around here."

"What do you mean?"

"The masks." Lucian tilted his chin toward the dwellings on either side of their path.

Each of the temporary shelters had one thing in common: on a front pole of each dwelling, no matter how humble or small, hung a mask. Most were of tooled leather intricately painted or stained with bright colors while others were carefully carved out of the most beautiful of woods. They were half-masks all, covering only the eyes and forehead, many of them crafted with long, waving points as if from a crown at their tops. Some had broken glass while others had what few gems were left to their owners embedded in their surfaces. Many were just plain or painted simply in an unsteady hand. Yet no matter what their circumstance, each of these temporary shelters was guarded at its entrance by a mask.

"It's their sign of agreement to the Law of Veils and, therefore, their support for the Circle of Six," Caelith explained. "No one walks the world of dreams without a mask."

"It's such a foolish rule." Lucian yawned. "I mean, it's because of this law that we have to travel practically the length of Hrunard just to be here. In the old days the Six would have just met in the dream no matter where they were and be done with it."

"Only in the most desperate circumstance; it's too dangerous otherwise," Caelith said, shaking his head. "Not everyone who connects with the dream supports the Council."

"And so we wear masks." Lucian rolled his eyes. "First we hide from the world and then we hide from each other. Really, Cae, how is anyone going to learn anything?"

"Father believes that until we can find a way to know who we can trust in the dream, it's better just to not trust anyone," Caelith said as he turned to wave at some children running around their parents' sagging tent. They continued making their way across the meadow as he spoke. "He says we should prefer to be anonymous rather than be betrayed. It has greatly inhibited progress in understanding the dream but the Council agrees with Father."

"Well, I think it's nonsense," Lucian rejoined. "Bad enough to have to conjure up some ridiculous pretense when you enter the dream, but to have to hang one on your tent? I wouldn't be surprised if the Council were actually making these masks at night and selling them on the side. It's all just a fad."

Caelith smiled broadly at the comical thought of the august heads of each clan slipping away in the night to tool leather goods. "I don't think so. The other night I was in the dream and found myself carried to a distant place I'd not seen before. There was what seemed to be a great amphitheater—an open stage like the ones you described having in Enlund."

" 'Had'—old fellow; 'had.' "

"Oh, of course."

"They were wonderful," Lucian said. "Some of the plays presented there were—"

"Are you listening to me?"

"Sorry, do go on—and on, and on—"

Caelith gave a sharp, frustrated grunt. It was hard to hold Lucian's attention, especially where serious matters were involved. "I was in this amphitheater in the dream, surrounded by a great crowd watching the players on the stage. I stood before the stage—in my mask, of course—and all the players stood before me in masks as well. One was a beautiful woman with wings like a butterfly—"

"Oh, I've heard of her before," Lucian interrupted. "Isn't she the one your father first met in the dream? You know, I even met a—"

"Will you just listen?" Caelith rumbled. He was beginning to remember things about his friend that he had conveniently forgotten. "The winged woman was wearing a mask, as were two brothers, both standing in shadows, as well as a short, dark man—a dwarf with a white scar running down his back. All were gesturing in their performance as though in a dance, but while I realize their movements had meaning, I could not understand any of it."

"So you watched a play you couldn't understand," Lucian said. "That's not uncommon, old boy; nobody who goes to plays really understands them. For a patron to attend a play and actually understand it would be highly insulting to the playwright."

Caelith gritted his teeth for a moment before he went on. "You're the one not understanding, Luc. I was watching these players moving on the stage when suddenly the winged woman fell dead at the feet of the shadowed brothers. The dwarf danced about her body while the audience laughed, cheering and applauding insanely. The blood of the winged woman ran down off the stage and crept toward me. I tried to move back through the crowd but the blood kept following me. I looked up at the brothers, their masks still in deep shadows, and knew that one of them had killed the woman, though I could not tell which one."

"When you have a vision," Lucian responded, "you certainly have a strange one."

"Yes, but I knew that if I had not been behind my own mask, I would have been on that stage and the blade would have been meant for me. It isn't just the other mystics of the clans that threaten us there, you know. There are others in whom the power is still awakening. Some of them, we believe, are being used by the Pir to spy on us. Father himself once knew an Inquisitas who had the gift."

"High Priest Tragget," Lucian finished for him.

"How did you know that?" Caelith asked, surprised.

"Oh, it's not much of a secret, Caelith . . . you can't keep a good juicy story down, can you?" Lucian replied with a shrug. "I heard they were once close."

"Father thought so." Caelith frowned, uncomfortable with the subject. "I don't know . . . look, do you want to see the glade or not?"

"Hey, sorry!" Lucian put his hands up. "Lead on into this most dangerous glade and we shall take on all foes!"

Caelith pushed past his friend and moved quickly down a winding path into a narrow hollow. The pond that had once graced this place had long since evolved into a grassy glade cupped in the hollow of the surrounding hills. Hardwood trees rimmed the glade, their new leaves casting dappled light on the soft grass.

"It is beautiful," Lucian concurred, "though not so much as I would travel a month just to see it."

"The most beautiful thing about it is that it is deserted," Caelith said as he stepped back toward the path. "Or at least *will* be once we leave."

"I thought you came to check on something?"

"I did—to make sure the glade was empty. It is—now let's go."

"Soon," Lucian said, holding back. "First, tell me what all this is about."

Caelith turned slowly, his jaw set. "Lucian, you know better."

"All the Circle of Six rushed here so quickly," Lucian stated casually, stepping to one side. "No explanation; just summoned by the great Galen Arvad? And they come—oh, yes, we all have come—but might we be permitted to think for ourselves?"

"Even if I knew, Lucian, I couldn't tell you." Caelith's voice was low and menacing. "Now let's just go before—"

"Wait!" Lucian's chin rose slightly. "Someone's coming!"

"By the gods!" Caelith swore. "Quick! Over there!"

"By *what* gods?"

"Just move!"

The two leaped as silently as the brush would allow into the undergrowth surrounding the glade. They held perfectly still for several long, careful breaths before a figure appeared coming down the same trail they had taken to reach the glade.

It was Galen. His features were more troubled than usual and his gait was slow and heavy. His fists clenched and unclenched as he walked and he looked altogether like a man facing his own death. Galen moved slowly into the glade, then just seemed to wait.

Caelith drew in a long, relaxing breath and moved to stand up but Lucian's arm restrained him.

The last sliver of the sun dipped down below the horizon. In that instant, a slim figure emerged from the dark shadows at the tree line. The robes were unmistakable in their design, black with a great hood trimmed in purple.

They were the robes of the Pir Inquisitas.

Panic seized Caelith. The Pir had hunted the mystics for two decades, relentless in their slaughter and persecution of any who demonstrated the power of the Deep Magic. Their vow was the extermination of the Mad Emperors on behalf of their dragon-gods. Now, one of their number walked slowly into the glade before Caelith's father, who stood alone to confront his enemy. Caelith wanted to run to his father's side, elements of the Deep Magic tumbling in his mind, but the shock of this unexpected visage held him still next to his old friend.

It was then that the Pir Inquisitas reached up and pulled back the great hood of her robe.

Caelith then heard his father utter a single name in a voice broken and somehow infinitely old.

"Berkita."

The Price

Caelith stared, his eyes widening in fear and wonder. He could feel Lucian turn a questioning gaze on him, but Caelith did not move.

"Who is that?" Lucian whispered.

"Quiet," Caelith hissed.

The woman's once raven hair was now streaked with gray, pulled severely back and knotted after the fashion of the Pir priestesses. Her face looked gaunt as though the years of her life had worn away its flesh and left little to soften the lines of her angular, pale face. Her wide mouth held a determined line though her brow was furrowed with obvious effort. She looked far older than Caelith would have supposed. Yet it was her eyes that called his attention; violet eyes that were still bright windows into a weary soul.

"You . . . you haven't changed," Galen spoke haltingly.

The woman drew in a deep breath, then looked away nervously. "Of course I've changed. We both have."

A breeze drifted through the trees; the sound of young leaves quaking drifted through the gulf of years between them.

"Berkita." Galen said her name with a deeper sadness than

Caelith would have imagined. "There is so much to say—so many questions . . ."

"Please don't," Berkita said, holding up her hand dismissively. "Twenty-six years; that's too many questions. The truth is, Galen, that I don't even want the answers anymore."

Galen nodded, then turned, gesturing. "It is nice to hear you say my name again. I've missed that."

Caelith froze at the sight of his father's hand pointing directly at him. He waited to be rousted from his hiding spot only to relax when he realized his father was indicating a large stone nearby on which Berkita might comfortably sit. The woman nodded and took the boulder.

"I was very sorry to hear about your father," he said with a forced casualness. "I realize it was a long time ago but I wanted you to know that."

"You heard about father's death?" Berkita asked.

"Well, yes." Galen's smile was rueful. "Word does occasionally come my way and yours was the only family I ever really knew outside the Pir. His death was before its time."

"He had to take over the forge after you left," Berkita said, her tones level and dispassionate. "You and Cephas were both gone and I couldn't go back. I never could decide if we broke his heart or the work did."

"You didn't go back? Why not?"

"Well, there were reasons," Berkita said wistfully as she leaned forward, pressing both her hands down against the stone. "The Pir Inquisitas put my case before the Pir Nobis. The priestesses there took me in for a time and cared for me. I had been told by High Priest Tragget that you and I would be together soon—at first he said we were going to meet you, then he said he thought you would come for me. I waited each evening, looking down from the towers of Vasska's Temple and wondering when I might see you walking up the Processional. I wept a river of tears, Galen, but one day the river dried up and I found that it had carried away all my hope for you."

"I wanted to come, Berkita," Galen spoke quietly. "There hasn't been a day in all those years that I haven't thought of you. I would have walked up that avenue for you, Berkita, if I could." He reached tentatively for her hand.

"But you didn't," Berkita said evenly, withdrawing just enough to stay beyond his reach.

Lucian nudged Caelith again but all Caelith did was shake his head. He felt ashamed of being here, of watching his father's dark past laid bare before him, and yet he could not turn away.

"No, I did not come," Galen said with a sigh, folding his arms across his chest. "I am sure there were a thousand reasons why—and they all taste like ashes now."

"And you married again," Berkita stated flatly.

"You and I were no longer married, Berkita," Galen said, clearing his throat. "The Pir saw to that."

"Yes, I know." Berkita would not be put off. "But you did marry again."

"It isn't what we had," Galen stammered awkwardly. "Dhalia was the daughter of two friends of mine I met after the Election. She is a gifted master of the arts and I married her to prevent a war among the mystics. It was for her protection and the protection of the clans."

"How characteristically noble of you," Berkita sniffed. "And you love her now, I suppose."

"Yes, I love her and have tremendous respect for her—but as I said, it isn't what we had."

"Nothing ever is."

"What of you?" Galen asked quickly. "Did you . . . ?"

"Find someone else?" Berkita smiled and shook her head. "No, Galen. I suppose there were some who tried to catch my eye but I never really saw them. I don't know. Maybe it was easier just not to let them into my life."

Silence fell awkwardly between them.

"I think back on that forge in Benyn," Galen said at last, his voice wistful. "I imagine that I can still feel the warmth of the tools in my hands and smell the air from the bellows. I close my eyes and I can still see our little cottage on the hillside and I see you standing in its crooked door frame smiling at my homecoming at the end of each day. I would give anything to go back to that life."

"We can't go back, Galen. None of us can."

"It was a good life, wasn't it?"

"Yes—it was."

Now it was Galen who looked away. "I am so sorry, Kita—so sorry for everything."

The priestess turned her gaze on Galen. "Look at me, Galen."

After a long, painful breath, Galen looked into the woman's face.

"I'm sorry, too," she said, her voice tightly controlled despite the tears spilling from her deep violet eyes. "More sorry than you will ever know. I loved you, too, Galen, but none of that matters anymore. The fates were seen in the dragonsmoke, and their ends were sealed by Vasska's decree. I accepted that long ago. I put away those precious and beautiful dreams. Everything I had ever hoped for in life is gone, and it isn't coming back no matter how hard I want it to. It is better to bury dead things, Galen. Better to let them rest."

"So this is why they sent you?" Galen forced the words through his lips. "Because you were the one who could hurt me? Isn't it enough that the Pir hunt us for sport, drive us like animals across the land and starve our children? Now they have to send you to destroy my past as well?"

"No," Berkita answered evenly, wiping the tears from her cheeks. "They sent me because I convinced them to do so. I told them I was the only one you would see—the only one to whom you might listen."

Galen stood suddenly, shaking his head in disbelief. Warily he rubbed his chin with his left hand as he considered. After several heartbeats, he turned back to where Berkita sat. "Apparently you were right. You are here and I am listening."

Berkita took a careful breath. "This war, Galen—for all these years—has come no closer to ending."

"It was a pretend war, Berkita—an amusement for the Dragon-kings paid for with the blood of mystics."

"Yes, but a necessary one. It kept the Dragonkings' bloodlust limited and contained. For centuries the Pir struggled to find a way to stop the killing, but the Dragonkings so hated all those who showed even the slightest talent for this so-called Rhamasian magic that they could only be appeased one way. The Election was a regrettable expedience—"

"Regrettable expedience!"

"But compared to open war and genocide? It was a choice, Galen; a terrible choice but one that had to be made. Then you and your clan brought it all down on the Election Fields. All the Dragonkings squabble over the injury they perceived was done on that day so long ago. The Pir have tried to put an end to it but the insult remains."

"Satinka." Galen nodded. "She would never let it go."

"Nor would any of the other dragons," Berkita continued. "But the Pir may finally have found a way to satisfy Satinka's insult; more than that—to end this war and perhaps even the Election forever."

"And just who pays for this little miracle?" Galen asked curtly. "I suspect the bill is about to land in my hands."

Berkita shook her head. "You always were so stubborn. Just hear me out, Galen. The Pir Inquisitas knows about the different clans' efforts to find the ruins of the Rhamasian Empire; most particularly, the city of Calsandria."

Lucian poked Caelith once more. The search for Calsandria has been the most heated subject the Circle of Six had debated in years. Lucian's Clan Myyrdin in particular researched it extensively and had pushed for a search for the lost city.

"Go on," Galen said simply.

"The Pir have found it."

"The Pir have found Calsandria?"

"Yes," Berkita answered with a nod, standing to face Galen directly. "The Pir have collected scrolls and writings from all across Hrunard. Many of them are heretical from before the fall of the Mad Emperors. Tragget himself authorized the research and now believe they know the location of this mystic homeland you've been looking for."

Galen shook his head slowly. "Four hundred years ago, the Pir and their Dragonkings brought down the Rhamasian Empire and the power of the Mad Emperors. Now you want me to believe that they want to send the very people suffering from the Emperors' Madness—the Elect they've been murdering for four centuries—*back* to land from where this mystic power supposedly once came?"

"The Dragonkings have decreed in their benevolence—"

"Don't talk to me of the benevolence of the Dragonkings," Galen growled. "They made crushing anyone who shows any sign of mystic ability into a religious duty. By the gods, they turned our deaths into a *holiday!*"

"You don't understand the trouble you've caused them, Galen," Berkita snapped. "Things aren't that simple. The Pir Drakonis are in a terrible position. Their Dragon-Talkers and priests are found in each of the Five Domains, but the dragons themselves are at war one with another. All of them blame you and your mystics but are violently at odds over how to deal with your threat. Jekard in Palathia wants to try to flush out the clans by making them outcasts and making her own people do the work for her. Panas, however, makes war on Jekard because he thinks that approach is weak; and he uses the Edict to commit genocide on the Pir and the mystics alike. Ormakh wants the thanes to take care of it for him; Vasska continues the Election and uses his army to battle the thanes; and Satinka appears to be using the mystics themselves against one another. The blood keeps flowing and the wound never heals."

"*Our* blood, Berkita," Galen barked. "Mystic blood."

"No, Galen—at the cost of the blood of the Elect *and* the blood of the Pir," Berkita replied. "We have all been dragged into this but the Pentach thinks that you might be able to solve that problem for all of us. You caused the escalation of the war, Galen. Your use of this so-called mystic power plunged the Dragonkings into unchecked slaughter and all the lands of Hrunard with it. The Pentach wants more than just an end to open warfare—it wants to end the war itself. The raids of the mystic clans in all the domains are only a constant reminder that *you* brought this down on the citizens of the Pir and perpetuates a conflict—"

"Raids, may I point out, that the Pir made necessary—"

"Raids the Dragonkings made necessary, Galen! Don't you see, if the clans moved to lands out of the thoughts of the Dragonkings—particularly of Satinka—then the Pir have some hope of bringing the fighting to an end. Each of the Dragonkings accuses the other of secretly supporting you. If the clans are gone—vanished from Hrunard—then we can bring peace to a land that has known none for over four centuries."

Berkita folded her hands before her. "The Pentach proposes to show you where this Calsandria is located. It is far to the south, well beyond the borders of Hrunard or any of the realms of the Dragon-kings. They believe the land about the ruins is fertile and workable for settlement. You conduct the clans to this place and the Pentach will grant you safe passage. All the Pentach asks is that you leave their lands and never return."

Galen considered for a moment. "What of those born later with the gift?"

"The Election will continue—"

"Never."

"Let me finish. The Election will continue, but we will arrange to deliver them quietly to you and your clans." Berkita looked up. "It's a chance for peace, Galen—a chance for your people to have a home."

Galen looked into the tree-shrouded sky overhead. The pale blue was darkening in the evening into a more salmon hue. "So after twenty-six years, this is what you have come to tell me?"

Berkita sighed and blinked uncomfortably. "No, Galen, it is not."

"But you just said—"

"I have told you what the Pentach has asked me to bring to your clan leaders," she replied, stepping away from him. "The message is what allowed me to come, but not what I came to say to you."

Galen cleared his throat uncomfortably once more. "I'm sorry, Berkita. Mystics breathe suspicion. For us, trust is too often followed by betrayal; betrayal comes an instant before death."

"You weren't always this way," Berkita replied, relaxing a little. "There was a time when you would believe anything I said."

"You're right," Galen agreed. "Please, what did you come to say to me?"

"The day of your Election—our last day together—do you re-member it?"

"Each day I relive it," Galen answered.

"I was so insistent that you be there on the square."

"For the blessing—yes, I remember it."

"Then you were screaming and the crowd took you from me. I

was panicked, Galen, and I tried to run from the square looking for Cephas to help me get you back."

"Yes," Galen said quietly. "Cephas told me."

"I didn't get out of the square quickly enough, Galen," Berkita said, clasping her hands behind her back and looking down at the ground at their feet. "The coins of blessing rained down around me as I ran weeping from the square."

"The coins of blessing?" Galen blinked, not understanding.

"Galen," Berkita sighed as she looked into his aging face. "We had a son."

Lucian and Caelith held quietly still until they were certain they were alone, Galen and Berkita having moved away separately from the glade.

It was long moments before Lucian spoke.

"A brother?" the Enlund mage said with interest, "and an older one at that, eh? Say, doesn't that make *him* the heir to leadership of your clan instead of you? You may need to take a look at a new trade, old boy!"

Caelith barely heard him. All he could think of was his dream of the two shadowed brothers and the dead winged woman at their feet.

The Pyre
of Victory

Once upon another time, in a distant land of myth, Xian, leader of the Kyree in exile, lay dead upon the Altar of Peace. His polished armor shone under the rays of light streaming down through the clear panels at the top of the dome that towered above the floor of the magnificent hall. His rugged features, lined with age, faced that glorious space above him, his eyes closed in uncharacteristic tranquillity. His hands lay across his chest, resting on the hilt of his sword, its tip pointing toward his booted feet. His magnificent wings had been arranged with care so that they folded around his body as if in a comforting embrace. He was the picture of a life well lived now passing into long deserved rest.

Seven halls radiated from the Altar of Peace. The lords and ladies, kings and queens of each of the five original faery houses, stood in their respective expanses at precisely the appropriate distance, the quintessence of profoundly studied silence. Row upon row of mourners filled each of the halls, each successive row situated in strict ascending order of station behind their betters. Each held a candle whose flame burned brightly in the dim recesses. Each row was ordered, as was the faery way, precisely by rank of caste. The lowest castes, representatives of the Third Estate gatherers and laborers, sat at the back. The Second Estate artisans, craftsmen, and the trades were further forward. Before them all sat the First Estate, each also holding their candle and, appropriately, it was a far more elegant candle than those of the castes below them. Queen Tatyana of House Qestardis stood with the entourage of her house caste. Lord Phaeon of House Argentei, his golden hair shining under the light from the dome, stood opposite her and looked displeased that his candle was less ornate than Tatyana's. He was surrounded by his personal honor guard, who also appeared displeased, but for them it was likely at the prospect of holding a candle rather than a sword. The Lady Milindral of House Mnemnoris, King Sithalian of Shivash, and even Queen Emaraud of far-off Vargonis; each had made their arduous and often dangerous way to attend the service and all held their own candle in homage to Xian.

From the sixth hall came a young Kyree man with raven hair and black wings. His own polished armor flashed in the columns of light as he stepped with reverence toward the altar.

Dwynwyn, Queen of the Dead, looked on from her own, seventh and final hallway. Her ranks were, no doubt, discomforting to all present, for they were ranks of the dead who wailed behind her in a gentle keening. She listened to the soft chorus of music welling through the hall, its mournful tones soaring through the space in honor of her onetime enemy. She gazed carefully on each face surrounding the altar. Each was a study in loss and compassion.

Masks, every one of them, Dwynwyn thought. Bad enough to have to deal with such lies in her visions these days, but to see such lies among the waking world was intolerable. It might have been a lovely funeral. It was a shame the entire proceedings here had less to do with honoring the life of her old nemesis than it did with taking advantage of a political opportunity.

The keening chorus of Dwynwyn's dead silenced as the young Kyree mounted the steps to the great altar. He had a generally dark countenance and a small scar at the corner of his upper lip always gave him the appearance of a smirk. Still, he carried himself with an air of confidence despite the burdens he had been left to bear. He had objected to this charade more than any of them but, in the end, Dwynwyn had convinced him it was their only hope.

For now her hope extended only to the urgent desire that the young prince not say anything that would upset anyone.

The young winged man lifted his head to address the assembled royalty and their considerable number of servants present. "I am Djukan, son of Xian and Master of the Dunlar Kyree."

Djukan paused. Dwynwyn held her breath.

"On behalf of my people, I thank you all for your . . . honoring my father in his passing."

Dwynwyn closed her eyes, slowly letting out her breath.

"Many of you have traveled from far lands to honor my father, one of the greatest lords over the sky," Djukan continued. "His deeds were those of epic song; for the Gods of Isthalos chose for him a time of woe and wonder. He sought the glory of the Greater Kyree Empire in its wholehearted service, but necessity drove him to a destiny across the courses of the seas and into lands of exile. His oath was to serve his emperor, and he fulfilled it by serving his people instead. He brought us to a land of strangers in search of a place where we could live, breathe, and find hope again.

"It is traditional among the Kyree to recount the great battles of our warrior dead . . ."

Dwynwyn blinked furiously. *Please, Djukan,* she thought. *Not now! Say only what we agreed on!*

"This we have done in private, for they are our tales alone. His burden, too, is ours to take up alone, and we shall do so for the greater glory of the Kyree, and to honor the life-struggle of my father. I thank you again, for myself and my people, for your honoring him this day."

Dwynwyn closed her eyes in relief. Djukan would behave. She held her breath, knowing that what was coming next was the first step down a long and uncertain road.

"Now," Djukan said, "we shall proceed with the cremation."

Dwynwyn's eyes flashed open. A wave of anxious murmuring rose from the assembly. Several voices, perhaps more practiced in being heard, cut like clarions through the noise.

"A what?" Lord Phaeon bellowed. "You mean right here? Now?"

A low murmur rose in the halls.

"We must," Djukan answered gruffly, motioning several of his lieutenants forward. Each carried large bundles of bound sticks. "We must have his bones for his Joining with the Ancestors. It's the final part of the ceremony. What do you think all the candles are for?"

"Barbaric!" Queen Emaraud intoned with her deepest disdain. "This is the Hall of Peace and I shall not stand silent against such desecration!"

The murmur grew louder, punctuated by several shouts of disgust.

Lady Milindral sputtered. "We're supposed to be putting this creature to rest, not roasting him."

"It is our way," Djukan said loudly over the crowd, clearly losing patience with the delay. The lieutenants were piling the sticks around the alabaster altar as he spoke.

"Burn him if you will," King Sithalian chirped in his high tenor voice, "it matters little to me, but have the courtesy to take him out in the woods where you don't have to force us to participate."

Suddenly, Lord Phaeon surged forward, his guards flanking him on either side. Their wings carried them quickly across the short intervening space as, with swords suddenly drawn, they surrounded the altar. Phaeon pulled Djukan forcefully away, the young Kyree flipping forward and rolling across the polished floor.

Phaeon drew his own sword. "This is territory of the faery and I will not allow some backward Famadorian ritual to despoil it!"

Djukan, using the momentum from Phaeon's throw, rolled to his feet in a single deft motion, his own sword in his hand. "You dare spit on our traditions? You'll pay for that insult in blood!"

"Good"—Phaeon smiled with bared teeth—"then at least if there is to be barbarity, let there be some sport in it!"

Dwynwyn closed her eyes—the wingless man was somehow there in her mind—gathering in the burning petals . . .

The rising noise of the crowd suddenly hushed. The flames of each of the candles lifted from their wicks and drifted over the heads of the astonished crowd. Increasing in speed, the tiny flames flew over the heads of Phaeon and Djukan, whose eyes were locked on each other as they prepared to strike, became aware of the fire gathering into a spinning whirlpool blaze over the altar. Phaeon's guards became aware, too, from the heat on the backs of their necks. They turned and then stepped slowly back from the altar.

In an instant, the whirling inferno collapsed downward, engulfing the altar and Xian on it. It burned with a hot, consuming fury, driving Phaeon back as well, though the faery lord still kept his distance from Djukan. With a white brilliance, the fire raged about the body, igniting the sticks and consuming them as well.

Then in a flash, the flames vanished as quickly as they had come. Only a small pile of blackened ashes remained. The smoke from the conflagration hung in a thin, horrible pall over the seven halls.

Dwynwyn strode forward, climbing the few steps up to the altar, and stood defiantly over Xian's burned remains. "Put your swords away," she commanded. "It is done."

"What right have you to interfere?" Lord Phaeon demanded, his wings fluttering angrily.

"I am the Queen of the Dead," she answered quickly. "This is my home and I have a right to govern my domain as I see fit. These are the traditions of the Kyree and I will have them honored in my house."

"I have not yet had satisfaction for that bird's insult," Phaeon yelled, pointing his sword at Djukan.

Djukan raised his own sword, ready to take up where they had left off.

"I have given you your satisfaction, Lord Phaeon, and it will be sufficient for you," Dwynwyn replied. "Or perhaps, Lord Phaeon, you feel these proceedings are unworthy of the attention of your house?"

Lord Phaeon blinked but held otherwise perfectly still.

"Each of the other Houses of the Fae has come to pay honor to this fallen warrior of the Kyree," Dwynwyn said easily, her voice echoing down the seven halls. "Would you—alone—refuse to do so?"

Lord Phaeon held his place for a moment, then slowly knelt down before the altar, lowering his sword. "No, Dwynwyn, I would not." He bowed his head as he knelt. "House Argentei has come far, indeed, to honor this great warrior."

Each of the rulers from the other houses, seeing Lord Phaeon kneel, quickly did likewise, murmuring their own phrases of honor and condolence. As their leaders knelt, each rank of caste behind them knelt as well. A wave of rumbling washed down each hall as row after row fell to their knees.

Dwynwyn sighed. It was all so predictably embarrassing. She turned to Xian's son, still standing astonished with his sword in hand. "Lord Djukan, here are the bones of your father. What must we do next to honor him in your traditions?"

"Oh, yes," Djukan replied suddenly, "we shall depart. The spirits of our fathers will not be at peace until their bones join those of their ancestors in Mount Isthalos. I, and a few of our number, shall endeavor to take them back to our homeland and put them to rest."

"But your empire was destroyed," Dwynwyn said, tilting her head to one side. "You cannot go back."

Djukan nodded and continued. "It has been many years. Perhaps things have changed. Perhaps all the Kyree may be able to return to our ancestral home. If we return, then we shall know."

Phaeon looked up from where he knelt. "The Kyree—might leave?"

"It would depend on the success of our quest." Djukan nodded sagely. "But—yes, it is possible. To return to our homeland has always been our greatest wish."

"Then, perhaps, from these ashes may come new life for your people," Dwynwyn intoned. She hoped their words did not sound as rehearsed to their audience as they sounded to her. "The House of Sharajentei—the Kingdom of the Dead—pledges itself to support you in this noble quest. I shall send five of our most talented Seekers to accompany your party and whatever provisions you should require."

"On behalf of the Kyree," Djukan said with a deep bow, "we would be most glad to accept your offer."

"Wait!" King Sithalian fluttered up from where he knelt. "The House of Shivash also supports this noble effort and offers twenty of its strongest laborers to help you bear the supplies for such a journey."

"Craftsmen!" Lady Milindral called out. "House Mnemnoris shall show its honor for Xian's quest with fifty of its expert craftsmen and the supplies *and* the laborers to support them as well!"

"Now just a moment!" Djukan said, hastily putting his sword back in its scabbard.

"What good are tradesmen in a dangerous world!" Lord Phaeon was recovering quickly from his previous embarrassment. "The Kyree understand that above all else. Warriors! House Argentei supplies one hundred warriors to the quest!"

Djukan shook his head, holding his palms up in front of him, gesturing for them to stop. "It's not what we—"

"One hundred?" Queen Emaraud sniffed. "House Vargonis offers two hundred!"

"Five hundred!" Lord Phaeon shot back.

"Five thousand!" shouted King Sithalian.

"No!" Djukan quieted them. "It's an expedition! If I show up on the borders of my homeland with five thousand warriors, we are no longer a quest—we're an invasion! All I want to do is honor my father in the way he would wish to be honored—and perhaps to find a way home for my people."

"Then we shall honor your father as well." Dwynwyn nodded. *It all hangs on this,* she thought. "May I make a suggestion?"

The lords and ladies of all the Fae turned toward her.

"Let each house send one—and *only* one—representative in support of this quest," she said sagely. "Let them be the best and the brightest from our houses. Let them represent us in honoring our fallen neighbor and friend."

The lords and ladies, queens and kings of the First Estate all nodded their consent. None would be represented more than another and the great balance between the houses would stand.

Dwynwyn glanced over at Queen Tatyana of House Qestardis. Of all the masters of the Fae houses, she alone had not uttered a single word.

It had been ugly and disorderly—two things that faeries detest—and nearly upset entirely by Lord Phaeon, but in the end, Dwynwyn knew, it had turned out exactly as she had planned.

Queen of
the Dead

Dwynwyn, Queen of the Dead, drifted out of the Hall of Peace and between the delicate, dark spires of the city of Sharajentis. She flew freely above its ever growing buildings, fortifications, and spires. Granite gray towers rose with great angular faces from the bedrock far below the ancient floor of the Margoth Woods. Sheer walls of stone with stark, razor-sharp angles radiated outward from the inner ward of the city, forming a cascading series of battlements, towering retrenchments, and ramparts that glowered down slick, polished vertical scarp above the enormous dry moat. Long strands of spiderwebs, woven at the behest of the necrodryads, hung from each of the spires, draping the city in a lacework shroud; a protection from assault by creatures of flight. A perpetual fog permeated the entire wood now, hiding the city from the eyes of the living yet allowing most of its citizens to see clearly the approach of any enemy.

It was the city of the dead—her domain—and its very existence threatened every one of the other Five Kingdoms of the Fae. For years beyond memory, the five original Fae kingdoms had struggled for domination, each over the others. A new, sixth kingdom threatened everyone—especially a kingdom with powers the other five could only envy.

The large stone garden surrounding the Hall of Peace fell quickly behind her. To her right she could vaguely discern the shadowy form of the Lyceum, itself a fortress of the living inside the Kingdom of the Dead. Dwynwyn could almost hear the recitations of the Oraclynloi—the Vision Pilgrims in training—drifting out from those long halls. Seekers from each of the Five Kingdoms journeyed at considerable risk to present themselves just to be considered for training in Dwynwyn's Lyceum. Some came at the bidding of their jealous masters; others out of nearly fanatical obsession to attain the Sharaj—the "Power" as they had come to call it. The limits of the Lyceum to instruct new Oraclyn initiates were exceeded almost at its inception. Many were turned away at the gates of Sharajentis, only to return again in the hope of learning the truth that Dwynwyn had discovered and the power of the visions they all shared.

What a strange fate has brought us all to this terrible destiny, Dwynwyn thought with a frown.

The Shadow Guard—formerly dead warrior faeries of the Third Caste—sailed about her in ever protective circles, their milk-white and pupil-less eyes darting here and there in their eternal watchfulness. Deython, Commander of the Dead, had insisted upon it, especially with his constant absence from the city. The truth of it was, Dwynwyn told herself, that when one commands the dead, there really is very little to fear from death itself.

The living, on the other hand, could cause you all kinds of trouble.

The labyrinthine streets and alleys below her seethed with movement. The restless dead never ceased their building, shaping, and expansion of the city both inward and outward. They built because they were driven to activity; to stop, as she quickly became aware some twenty-six years before, was to suffer the torment of their condition. It was the nature of that torment that had become the greatest question of her own existence. It was to answer that question that drove her now.

Dwynwyn pushed her wings a little faster, soaring easily in her weaving path between the great spiderwebs surrounding her palace.

The great tower rose high above the surrounding fortress, shining black obsidian from the fires at the heart of Sine'shai coaxed upward into a hideous shape. Its windows were darker pools reminiscent of eye sockets in skulls. The pillars surrounding the tower were shaped like great long bones, its arches formed into ribs. Its summit was crested with seven long curved towers in the shape of claws. It was repulsive to everything for which the faery stood, and after twenty-six years Dwynwyn still shuddered to approach it. Everything about the city's architecture said "go away." Her own palace seemed to scream revulsion to the very soul of the Fae.

It was, of course, all the work of the dead. The dead faery had little use for the living and found their presence troubling at best. But they looked to Dwynwyn as their queen and honored the living Sharajin—as Dwynwyn's Seekers were called—whom they served. So they built for her this city and made it a fortress which no one would want even if they should be able to take it by some means.

"My fortress," Dwynwyn sighed. "My prison."

Dwynwyn banked around a particularly thick cluster of webbing and settled on a large balcony nearly a third of the way up the black tower. Her black and purple robes blended into the obsidian so as to make her almost invisible. She sighed and stepped forward. The blackness parted before her as she stepped into the darkness. Her guards remained outside, hovering about the entrance, the sound of their wings suddenly silenced as the obsidian closed once more behind her. The sound of her own footfalls sounded loudly in her ears as Dwynwyn stepped down the smooth, black corridor.

Now fully in the darkness, she hastily pulled open the fasteners of the black robe of her office. It was heavy and loathsome to her now. She nevertheless caught it before it fell to the floor and, feeling her way in the short corridor, hung it carefully on a stone hook protruding from the wall just for this purpose. Dwynwyn shivered slightly in the cold, her light shift insufficient against the chill of dead stone. She closed her eyes, for she knew what was coming next, the most terrible thing that she was forced to endure.

She took a blind step and then another. She caught her breath as she heard the sigh of a second portal open before her. She saw the brightness rise abruptly behind her closed eyelids. Dwynwyn pressed her lips together and opened her eyes.

Tears blurred her vision. Dwynwyn choked on a single, unbidden sob that racked her. Her step faltered and she was forced, as many times before, to grip the railing in order to steady herself as tears rolled down her cheeks hot and unchecked.

The oval space was nearly two hundred feet in length and fully a hundred feet across. Painfully white alabaster columns soared upward higher and higher, their delicate latticework exquisite in its expression of peace and harmony. It arched upward into a dome where sunshine fell in gentle rays from between what appeared to be soft clouds drifting through an achingly blue sky. Twin waterfalls in the northeast and northwest quarters of the curved walls cascaded over crystal-laced stones, their soothing tumble quietly murmuring through the hall. The pools at the base of the falls then ran into two streams that ran around an oval dais before joining in a central pond. The floor of the hall was covered in a garden of unsurpassed beauty. The carefully molded shrubs and grasses were all shaded by the dappled light of impossibly graceful trees whose white bark ran upward into delicate silver-edged leaves that flashed in the gentle breeze. A small flock of birds fluttered through the air, their song a melody of contentment and rest.

It was the Garden of Dwynwyn and she wept each time she entered it. It was a pure, white heart in the center of death and darkness, her refuge and her strength. It was the symbol of life, beauty, peace, and joy. It represented everything that her kingdom denied and all that she had sacrificed for the sake of the dead.

Existing among the dead could be endured, she knew—one grew numb with them, unfeeling and cold. It was coming back to life and its warmth that hurt—for only then did she fully appreciate what she had lost.

"Dwynwyn? What might I do for you?"

"Cavan." Dwynwyn sniffed behind her sudden smile. "You always ask me that each time I return."

"It needs the asking each time you return," Cavan replied. The aging sprite had been Dwynwyn's nearly constant companion for as long as she cared to remember. Now he hovered with some effort in the air, holding the collar of her royal receiving coat for her as he had each evening upon her return. He helped her into the white-and-silver-lined garment as he spoke. "Out you go into that horror you call your kingdom each day and then expect to fall back into this island of sanity without missing a step. Honestly, you fall apart every time you return. Then it's my job to put you back together into some semblance of your former self." ·

"Well, at least you know you'll always have a job." Dwynwyn smiled. She collected herself and breathed deeply of the sweet air in her garden. It settled her further. Cavan was right; perhaps if the transition from the darkness to the light were more gradual she might not feel its pain so acutely, she thought. She could talk with Deython about it if she chanced to see him again soon. Perhaps he could explain it better to her subjects than she had.

"Your Majesty," came a voice from a single faery standing in the garden below. "I beg your forgiveness for intruding on you."

She is always so formal, Dwynwyn smiled to herself as she closed her eyes and took in another deep breath. *I wish she would relax a little.* "Yes, Shaeonyn, of course. What is it?"

"Your Majesty, the appointed time is at hand. I submit my humble personage to confer with your august self."

"Your 'august self'?" Cavan snipped, wrinkling his nose. "Just what kind of manners do they teach those Seekers down in Mnemnoris?"

"Be kind, Cavan." Dwynwyn chuckled. "Shaeonyn *is* my apprentice."

"And has been for too long, if you ask me," Cavan replied. "Those Mnemnorian Fae—they speak more and say less than any other faeries I know!"

"And there certainly are none more skilled at the Sharaj than Shaeonyn," Dwynwyn said.

"With the exception of yourself," Cavan added quickly.

"You should certainly hope that is the case," Dwynwyn chided, "or she could rival us both. I am fine now, Cavan. Would you do me the favor of securing the hall as you leave? I have urgent business to attend with my apprentice."

Cavan hesitated for a moment. "I live to serve—as does all my house, Dwynwyn—but are you certain you—"

"Yes, Cavan," Dwynwyn interrupted him in her haste. "Please leave us. I wish to be undisturbed."

Cavan nodded, though disapproval showed in his eyes. "As you wish," he called as he quickly fluttered away through a side portal.

Dwynwyn waited until she was certain the portal had closed behind her sprite friend. The Sharaj, they called it—the Power—for lack of any other word that might do. The advent of this New Truth into the world had shaken the very foundations of the Fae. That Seekers should call truths into existence from their Orsyl—their visions—was a terrible and frightening thing, yet it was manifestly true and could not be denied. The Fae had given it a name largely out of fear; they hoped that by giving the thing the form of a word it would somehow be diminished. It would take more than semantics of the Fae language to contain the Sharaj.

Shrugging her shoulders as though the weight of her royal coat somehow did not sit well, Dwynwyn fluttered her wings and sailed over the railing toward the floor of her garden.

"Has she come?" Dwynwyn asked as she approached her apprentice.

"Queen Tatyana of Qestardis awaits your pleasure, Your Majesty. I have taken the liberty of securing your garden personally and delight in telling you that your words will remain private. Will there be anything else before I withdraw?"

"Yes." Dwynwyn nodded as she softly alighted on the dais next to her apprentice. "There are two things I want. First, stay and hear what we say to each other. It concerns you, and I would rather you understand more fully the truth of what we are trying to accomplish."

"Yes, Your Majesty," Shaeonyn murmured, her large eyes cast downward as she spoke. "And the other?"

"Please call me Dwynwyn."

Shaeonyn hesitated, her silence speaking volumes.

"Well, perhaps we'll just deal with one thing at a time," Dwynwyn said, relieving her shy apprentice of the awkward moment. "Please conduct Her Majesty Tatyana to the garden at once."

Dwynwyn watched Shaeonyn as she floated toward the western portal of the garden. She was lithe and beautiful, even among the Fae, with a long, delicate neck, smooth copper skin, and full lips. Her eyes were large dark pools that bent down slightly at the corners, giving a perpetual sadness to her countenance. Her hair was a flaxen color—a peculiarity that marked her as one of the southern Fae from the House of Mnemnoris.

She was the first, Dwynwyn reflected, to join her in her exile. Shaeonyn had arrived one day as uncalled for and largely unwanted as the storm that had preceded her, in the encampment near this same spot over twenty years before. Dwynwyn still remembered looking out from under the rain-soaked awning at the wet and shivering faery Seeker who had left her homeland, her lady, and her caste because of a vision she had had of a faery Seeker calling her to a place she had never known.

Dwynwyn had asked that shivering girl what she wanted.

"To see the vision clearly," she replied haltingly, "to heed the call of the Sharaj and to master it."

In all those years since and through all they had shared together—both in the vision's mystery and in life's struggle—Dwynwyn had never been able to get beyond the reverential deference that Shaeonyn always showed to her. That Shaeonyn was driven by her visions was clear to Dwynwyn, but just what those visions were remained a mystery beyond the stone wall of her strict and proper bearing. Dwynwyn wondered if beyond that cold formality lay something too delicate to touch without bruising her apprentice.

She was skilled beyond even Dwynwyn's abilities. Yet, for all that, the strength of her powers had been disappointing. She had an elegant command of the subtlety of the Sharaj but always seemed to tire easily, and the power of her creations from the vision were never as strong as Dwynwyn would have liked. The Queen of the Dead still hoped for some new truth that could explain the problem, for she saw her successor in Shaeonyn.

Now, Dwynwyn knew, the visions of the Sharaj that had carried this seemingly fragile Seeker to the Queen of the Dead were now about to carry her away. A wind was moving through Dwynwyn's visions, too, and she knew them to be carrying her apprentice eastward on a desperate task. Its success was far from sure, for her vision did not carry that far.

Its failure, however, would certainly doom all the Fae as surely as it had doomed the Kyree.

Fae Diplomacy

Queen Tatyana, the Faery Mistress of Qestardis, floated into the room on her magnificent, undulating wings. She still wore the dark funereal cloak about a dark traveling dress. Her face was drawn, her lips pressed tightly together, as she approached the dais.

Shaeonyn, following a respectful distance behind, bowed as Tatyana stopped. "Your Majesty, I beg to present Queen Tatyana of Qestardis."

Dwynwyn herself started to bow, but a quick, reproving glance from Tatyana checked her.

"You are looking well, Dwynwyn," Tatyana said casually. "We were concerned for you."

"Your Majesty . . ."

"Please"—Tatyana smiled ruefully—"you must call me Tatyana. We are equals now, you and I."

"Only because you have made it so—madam," Dwynwyn responded, sighing, suddenly appreciating intimately why her own apprentice had trouble with informality.

"Because I made it so?" Tatyana asked, her right eyebrow rising into a high arch. "We are both of us carried inexorably toward our

fates. Your army of the dead defeated Phaeon and his army on my behalf. I owe my reign and the peace of my kingdom to you. Giving
you your own kingdom, here in the Oaken Forest, was a just reward."

"My kingdom was not so much a reward," Dwynwyn said, gesturing for the Queen to drift beside her as Dwynwyn floated over
one of the immaculately kept flowering beds surrounding the dais, "as
an elegant solution for your problem. You welcomed our help but we
ourselves were not welcome in your land."

Tatyana drifted comfortably beside Dwynwyn, her eyes flashing
brightly. "You were always a very gifted Seeker, Dwynwyn. New
truths rarely elude you. No, the returning dead were and are an
abomination. I personally cannot see how you abide them and my
subjects are horrified by them. They would not be welcomed in
Qestardis by my subjects, nor would you find any better reception in
any of the other four kingdoms."

"The dead," Dwynwyn responded, "do not much care for the
company of the living, either."

"Then the solution was to our mutual betterment. By rewarding
you with lands of your own, I have legitimately and truthfully claimed
that you act independent of my authority. By granting you lands in the
Oaken Forest, I arranged that your new kingdom sits poised to defend
my own and keep the expanding Kyree settlements to the east in
check. The masters and mistresses of the other houses have all seen the
wisdom in this, which is why they sanctioned your kingdom."

"Yes, they have," Dwynwyn agreed, ill at ease, her wings fluttering nervously. "Each of the houses needs Sharajentei to exist; but each
hates and despises my kingdom at the same time."

"True, we do," Tatyana smiled, "but not nearly as much as we hate and
despise one another. Each kingdom—mine included—sees Sharajentei as
tipping the long and delicate balance that has existed between the Fae
houses for eons. As long as each house believes it has a chance of influ-
encing you on their behalf, they will continue to support your house."

"Including you," Dwynwyn said as she nodded her head.

"Yes, including myself," Tatyana agreed. "Though sitting here in
the midst of the horror you call your kingdom, one might be
tempted to question the sanity of such support. My entourage has not

slept since entering your borders two days ago and, I suspect, will refuse to do so until they are safely beyond your borders tonight."

"And what of you, Tatyana," Dwynwyn asked, leaning forward slightly in the air. "How have you slept?"

Tatyana merely smiled tightly, changing the subject. "Is our truth to be told before other ears, Dwynwyn?"

The Queen of the Dead turned slightly. Shaeonyn floated behind them at a respectful distance but certainly was listening. "I cannot leave Sharajentei. Shaeonyn must be my eyes and hands in this matter; she must know what I know that she may act as I may act."

Tatyana nodded her consent. "So, you have arranged everything to your liking, Dwynwyn?"

"I believe I have served us both in my arrangements, unless I have misunderstood your own intentions in this matter," Dwynwyn rejoined.

"Indeed, you have served us both," Tatyana said as she drifted slightly ahead, bending forward to examine a carpet of fragrant gillyflowers beneath her, her brows furrowing slightly. "All of this because of a string of pearls—those black pearls you gave to my daughter."

"They saved her, Your Highness," Dwynwyn said evenly, "and ultimately they saved your kingdom as well."

"I know the story too well, Dwynwyn." Tatyana's eyes narrowed under her brow in disapproval, threatening to wilt the flowers under their gaze. "Thirty-six pearls became thirty-six Lords of the Dead because of this 'new truth' you discovered. The thirty-six Dead Lords then called out thirty-six hundred of the dead from the sea and marched through my kingdom against Lord Phaeon's armies."

"There was little choice left to either of us by then." Dwynwyn could hear the defensive tone in her own voice. "You had announced your intention to resist Lord Phaeon and his armies were already marching on Qestardis. My job was to find a new truth that might stop him and his armies."

"You did not stop his armies; you destroyed them!"

Dwynwyn had no greater respect for anyone than Queen Tatyana, but the implications of her words were hurtful. "Would you have preferred Lord Phaeon's troops flying the banner of his house over Qestardis?" she demanded.

"I am not ungrateful for the victory," Tatyana snapped, "but the loss of life was terrible that day. Had Lord Phaeon known what his armies were facing he might have withdrawn."

"Had anyone told Lord Phaeon that he would be facing an army of the dead he would never have believed them," Dwynwyn said carefully, trying to keep her own temper in check. "The critical always speak from the security of hindsight. No one regrets the death of so many faery more than I, Your Majesty."

"Even so, the truth is that you more than doubled your own army that day."

"I did what was necessary to save your daughter . . . and your kingdom."

Tatyana suddenly lapsed into a smile that was gracious if less than heartfelt, her arms unfolding in a gesture that seemed to take in all of their surroundings. "And have I not been grateful?"

"You rewarded me with banishment from my homeland, to rule a kingdom of the dead who never rest." Dwynwyn spoke quietly as she floated closer to her guest, their faces uncomfortably close. "A kingdom that continues to grow despite my every effort. More dead flood the city each day and nothing I have tried has stemmed that inexorable tide. Look around you, Your Majesty; since that day I first made camp here, the dead have laid stone on stone to build a home for their fellow dead. At first there was order and reason to it and I did the best I could to direct it. The center of the city, this tower, the Hall of Peace; all these I did my best to control but more came all the time. Then the Seekers started coming and we built the Lyceum for them but still it wasn't enough. They just kept building! Soon the structures took on the peculiar perspectives of the dead, this horror and abomination over which I rule, and still the city grows! Indeed, Your Majesty, I dare not stop them, for unless they are kept occupied every moment of the day and night, the dead stop to reflect on their condition and break into the most terrible wailing sound you can imagine and begin some destructive rampage of their own. So my kingdom grows night and day, insane in its constant construction of crypts for the dead, defenses for the dead, and monuments to the dead. This is my life now, and such is the harvest of your gratitude, Your Majesty!"

"Dwynwyn, please," Tatyana said, raising her hands in front of her as she drifted backward to open the distance between them. "You speak truth—to your credit and my shame, yet what else could we do, you and I? These are our fates, set on their course at the foundations of the world."

"I do not know, Your Majesty," Dwynwyn said, shaking her head as she turned away. "Perhaps our fates are not as set as we believe."

Tatyana frowned deeply. "Take care, Dwynwyn, when you speak against the fates."

Dwynwyn sighed, still looking away from her guest as she spoke. "I have seen so many of the truths we once held as inviolable called into question by the very nature of the Seekers here, Your Majesty. The truth of the Orsyl and its Sharaj cannot be denied. Look around us, Your Majesty; this is the evidence of a power that may be greater than the fates themselves."

"Then it must be stopped, Dwynwyn," Tatyana rejoined. "A power so great could destroy us."

"A power this great *did* destroy the Kyree," Dwynwyn said, turning to face her old friend and ruler. "That is the point. For many years, Xian told me about the strength and success of his empire and how quickly the fall came. All they knew were rumors of an unusual faery that had been brought before the Kyree emperor. There were apparently many different accounts of what happened there—no two of them the same and all of them contradictory lies. But all of them mention this faery with abilities that were obviously those of a Seeker who showed signs of what we would now call Orsyl."

"So, you believe the Kyree were destroyed by a Sharajin Seeker because of a few lies?" Tatyana asked skeptically.

"No, Your Majesty," Dwynwyn answered. "I believe it because my apprentice saw it in the vision. She spoke to the Seeker herself."

"She spoke to the Seeker who destroyed the Kyree?" Tatyana's eyebrows arched upward in astonishment.

"So she has told me," Dwynwyn nodded as she glanced at Shaeonyn hovering quietly nearby, "although the contact was fleeting between them. I myself have never met this person in the vision, but Shaeonyn says this Seeker appeared as one who was dead, his largely transparent form congealing from the mists that tumbled in an eastward-blowing wind. She is certain that it is the figure of a male faery and has seen it several times. She recognizes it by—"

"By the bright white tear through its left wing," Tatyana finished.

Dwynwyn gaped in astonishment.

"Spies in your court?" Tatyana responded with amusement. "No, my dear old friend, though it would not have been for a lack of trying on my part. No, the wind in the vision—this Orsyl, as you call it—does not blow in Sharajentei alone. A Seeker—newly discovered in my own court—confided this same vision to me. My new Seeker not only confirms what you have told me but also something you have left unsaid: that this mysterious and misty faery who doomed the Kyree knew the answer to freeing your dead."

It was Dwynwyn's turn to remain silent.

Tatyana smiled. "So long as we understand each other. The Kyree want this expedition because they still long for their homeland and the glory that, no doubt, no longer exists. Typically shortsighted of Famadorians but it works to our advantage. If you had mounted an expedition in secret, then each of the other houses would have been obliged to hinder you in secret. By forcing the expedition to be made public, you have managed to limit the involvement of each of the houses to a single representative, satisfied their honor, and trusted that you and I would instruct our representatives to work in concert with one another. That, of course, would be *our* advantage."

"Court intrigues are a new game to me, Your Majesty," Dwynwyn said, bowing slightly.

"Ah, new perhaps, but I suspect you play it quite well," Tatyana said, drifting next to Dwynwyn and taking her arm in the crook of her own. "However, sometimes the fates deal us more fortune than we might like for our measure."

"And what is it that you want out of this expedition, Your Majesty?" Dwynwyn asked casually.

"Two things," Tatyana answered. "The knowledge that this terrible power remains safely out of the hands of the other houses."

"And the other?"

"That it remains safely in our own hands, of course!"

Dwynwyn laughed as they drifted together across the stream to the far side of the garden. "I have missed you, Your Majesty. So you have a new Seeker in court? I am surprised you have not sent them here for training. Seekers from all the houses show up here unbidden day and night trying to enter the Lyceum for training. I certainly would have heard about a Sharajin-loi from the House of Qestardis!"

"Well"—Tatyana's smile dimmed somewhat—"as I said, sometimes the fates deal us more fortune than we might like for our measure. This Seeker only recently demonstrated the talent for the Sharaj but she is promising—and she is the one I have appointed to represent Qestardis on your expedition, though with no small reluctance. I think it is time that you meet her. She is waiting. Will you call her in?"

"By all means," Dwynwyn said, a look of puzzlement crossing her face; then she called loudly to the side portal. "Shaeonyn?"

"Yes, Your Majesty?" the apprentice answered at once.

"There is an Oraclyn-loi waiting in the hall," Dwynwyn spoke firmly. "Please present her."

"As you will, Your Majesty," Shaeonyn replied even as she left the garden.

"You are appointing an Oraclyn novice as your representative on the expedition?" Dwynwyn whispered, leaning over toward Tatyana.

"She is uniquely qualified and will most definitely tip the balance of the expedition in our favor," Tatyana said, though Dwynwyn noted the Queen no longer was smiling.

The lithe figure of a faery woman flew slowly into the hall, her brightly patterned wings undulating with stately grace. Her large eyes were as unmistakable as the soft lines and the full lips of her beautiful face. She had changed little since the Queen of the Dead had seen her. Yet there was no mistaking the unique and terrible thirty-six black pearls around her elegant neck.

"No!" Dwynwyn breathed.

"It was fated," Tatyana sighed.

Shaeonyn drifted just behind the Oraclyn-loi as she spoke. "Presenting Aislynn, Princess of Qestardis and Seeker to the court of Tatyana."

The Novice

D o I really have to wear this?"

Aislynn looked critically at herself in the three oval mirrors arrayed about her in the shallow alcove of the dressing chamber. The panels of her robe had been fitted in a modestly flattering way but the severe black was unbroken by any other color. The pants and hose under the robe would take a bit of getting used to and the high, pointed collar seemed a bit fussy to her, as did the tightly fitted sleeves that gathered just below the elbow and came to a point at the back of each hand. The hem was several inches above the floor, which to her seemed ungainly. The cut in the back made an easy exposure of her wings, which, she flattered herself, were elegant in and of themselves, but otherwise the entire outfit made her look rather dull.

"It is the garment of the Oraclyn-loi." Shaeonyn's voice was several degrees colder than the chill chamber itself. "By this garment we are known throughout the lands of the Fae. It is the recognized symbol of our being set apart from the castes, of the depth of our commitment to the Dwynwyn Seekers and the power of the vision that it represents."

"But it isn't much as a statement in fashion," Aislynn observed as she frowned at herself.

"It is not meant to be a statement in fashion." Shaeonyn breathed out her words in ice. "It is a statement in power."

"Hmmm." Aislynn shrugged. "Well, I suppose it shall have to do for now. Maybe with a few changes it could become rather fetching. Some silver inlay, perhaps, or bright trim—"

"It is what it is because it functions," Shaeonyn spoke firmly. "It shall remain what it is until a form is found that functions better. That is all that need concern you, Aislynn. You would be better served worrying about learning your craft than about how you look to others. Now, if you are quite finished being critical of the way we all dress, would you accompany me to your quarters in the Lyceum?"

"Of course," Aislynn answered imperiously. "You are permitted to lead the way."

"You do not 'permit' anything!" Shaeonyn's lip curled in disdain as she spoke. "Dwynwyn has offered you to me as an apprentice candidate; as my Oraclyn-loi. I have not yet accepted you. If I am to be your mentor, we must be clear: when I speak, you listen; when I lead, you . . . ?"

"Think about it?" Aislynn replied hesitantly.

Shaeonyn swallowed her own reply before turning toward the portal. The dark strands of the door contracted at her approach, pulling themselves aside. Beyond the portal was a deep and chilling darkness. Shaeonyn passed into it without a glance behind.

Aislynn hesitated in the door, shivering at the sight of the ghastly space beyond. The enclosed forecourt of Dwynwyn's tower plunged down nearly forty feet from the ledge on which they stood to the cobblestone floor below. There, the dead flowed into the forecourt through three sets of iron doors, each portal forged with horrible figures in wide-mouthed torment. The dead then took flight on their green-flecked wings, following the black shafts of polished stone that rose up from below in columns melded into the surrounding walls, ribbed as though formed from the spines of some great beast. They moaned as they drifted upward past where Aislynn hovered with unsure fluttering of her wings. The dead continued past Aislynn upward another thirty feet, at which point the sickening columns bent into a sweeping curve over a high wall and into a dark and foreboding place deeper into the keep beyond.

The portal slammed shut behind Aislynn, nearly catching the back of her new robe. She yelped involuntarily and was instantly reprimanded by a look from Shaeonyn.

"Please respect this place," the Seeker said quietly. "These are the newly arrived. They are lost and confused. They cannot find rest until they have been given tasks to keep their minds and their bodies occupied. Come with me. We'll watch the ceremony of their induction as your first step into—"

"No," Aislynn said with a shudder.

"No?" Shaeonyn raised a cool eyebrow.

"Please, could you just show me to my accommodations," Aislynn said nervously. "I don't—I don't feel well."

Shaeonyn lowered her eyebrow slowly into a look of disdain. "This way," she said simply, turning her back on the Princess.

They drifted downward through the vast darkness of the forecourt. At their approach, the constant procession of the dead parted before them. Their images were each uniquely terrifying. They retained the form they had in life and, depending upon how long ago they had died, some retained much of their former material selves. Those longer dead, however, made up for their physical losses by reconstituting their form from whatever materials were at hand. Thus the dead that marched about them were sometimes composed in some measure of brackish seawater, gathered moss, or wet clay. Several were horrifically molded from writhing worms and insects that had gathered to form the corporeal figures. Some were clad in the remnants of clothing representing every caste known to faerykind and of every age. Others wore nothing at all and some less than nothing, as their physical forms had not fully gathered themselves anew. Regardless of their station in life, they were alike in death, and they moved through the hall with agonized purpose.

Shaeonyn was pushing quickly forward on her wings through the right portal of the forecourt and Aislynn was having a little difficulty keeping up with her proposed mentor. The Princess folded her arms tightly in front of her and, setting her jaw with determination, flew through the same portal, brushing past the dead and into the outdoor plaza beyond.

The sight shook Aislynn anew: the Plaza of the Dead. This large open space ran completely around the massive black tower behind her. The damp cobblestones paved every patch of ground in the plaza, each joint so tight that Aislynn was sure no plant would ever take root between them. The open flat space of the plaza ran nearly one hundred feet to the surrounding wall—seven enormous walls that ran between seven watchtowers around Dwynwyn's central tower. From each of these towers, incredible flying buttresses arched overhead to the huge central tower, all of which supported a complex latticework of spun webbing. Beyond the wall itself, she could make out the dark shapes of the town's buildings just beyond.

Aislynn had little time to wonder at the sight, for Shaeonyn was moving quickly across the plaza toward a great gate in the wall on the far side of the plaza. At least there seemed to be enough room overhead so that she could fly to the gate. The top of the gate itself, however, was low. Shaeonyn passed through the gate just before Aislynn.

"What is this place?" Aislynn stuttered as she caught up with the Seeker.

"This is Mourning Lane," Shaeonyn said. "We'll take a turn down Weeping Way and make our way down the back passages to Lost Way. It's not badly crowded at this time of night and we should be able to get to the Lyceum fairly quickly—what's wrong now?"

The avenue ran as a twisted river down among a jumble of buildings all constructed in varying shades of gray stone. Side streets writhed in their own path from where they intersected at the base of the Queen's Tower, their course vanishing around sharp corners of architectural canyons within less than a hundred feet of where she stood. The buildings which lined these chaotic passageways loomed overhead in a cacophony of styles, all sharply angled and without grace. Spindly towers thrust up into the sky from which a mesh of massive spiderwebs sagged under their own weight and obscured the roiling gray sky above. All around her, the dead continued in their procession, moving around Shaeonyn and Aislynn as a river flowing past rocks in a stream. Shaeonyn alighted on the slick stones of the street and began to press forward through the crowd down the crooked street to their left.

Aislynn was finding it difficult to breathe as she landed behind the Seeker. "Please, couldn't we just fly over them?"

"Who?"

"The dead—please."

Shaeonyn continued to make her way down the street but turned slightly as she shook her head. "You do not know the way through the webs as yet and they are intentionally treacherous. The Arachnis serve the Queen of the Dead but are as hungry for living blood as they are zealous in our defense. They have a tendency to eat first and ask who their victim was later. Better we should make our way on foot through the streets."

Aislynn felt light-headed, a headache building at her temples, but she followed Shaeonyn, the soles of her delicate slippers soiling on the slick stones. The dead choked the street before them, slowing their progress despite their efforts to get out of the way. Aislynn followed closely, still clutching her hands to her chest as she walked.

Aislynn looked up. Shaeonyn was pushing through the throng ahead of them and Aislynn was having difficulty keeping up. The space between them was filling with animated corpses in various states of decay.

"Shaeonyn!" Aislynn called out. "Wait!"

A strong, cold hand took hold of her shoulder, turning her about in the crowd. Aislynn found herself looking into the face of a beautiful faery woman with dark skin and bluish lips.

"Please, help me!"

"What?" Aislynn responded. The woman was holding her firmly now by both shoulders. "What is the matter?"

"My child!" the woman said, anguish contorting her face. "I've lost my child! They've taken him! Help me, please."

"Taken him? Taken him where?"

"This way!" the woman said, pointing down a dark, narrow chasm between the tortured buildings. "Please, if we hurry we may save him!"

The woman turned, dashing desperately down the black-shadowed passage, calling back over her shoulder, "Hurry! Please help me! Help my child!"

Aislynn ran after her. The shadows in the alley seemed colder than she had ever felt before. She ran as quickly as she could, but the woman in front of her kept disappearing around the various contortions of the narrow passage. Several times, the alley broke into different paths, an increasingly complex maze confronting the Princess, but each time she saw a fleeting glimpse of the woman and was able to follow.

The alley abruptly opened into a deserted cobblestone square looked down upon by black windows in the surrounding tall buildings. The faery mother knelt in the center of the square, its gray cobblestones stained dark where she knelt. Aislynn hurried toward her. "What is wrong? How can I—"

The woman turned. Aislynn saw a terrible smile on her face.

"Hello, my child!"

Aislynn stopped, her pulse suddenly pounding in her ears. Glancing around, she saw them—the dead—pouring out from the black doorways, sharp tools in their hands. They filled the alleyways. The webs overhead were thick and impassable.

"Don't worry, my child," the woman said with a grin. "They've gotten quite good at this. They barely leave a mark anymore. Look at how well I turned out."

The woman split open her bodice, revealing a ragged hole cut between her breasts.

Aislynn took a staggering step back, confusion engulfing her thoughts. "You—you lied to me!"

"You'll be free, child," the woman said, taking another step toward Aislynn. "You'll be free with us!"

Aislynn reached up, grasping at the necklace around her throat.

The blue woman snarled.

Aislynn cast the pearls down to the stones. In a moment, they transformed, uncurling into the massive, powerful form of the Lords of the Dead. Towering faery men formed of foam and sea, they surrounded the Princess at once, their shining blades menacing the throng.

The dead were not intimidated. The crowd screamed at the

guardians, circling them as they waited to pounce, adding to their numbers in order to overwhelm the guards. The Lords of the Dead drew in closer to Aislynn, preparing to make a stand.

"Enough!"

The dead quelled and parted before Shaeonyn as she entered the square from the alleyway.

"This Oraclyn-loi is under my protection—and that of Queen Dwynwyn," said the Sharajin as she walked quickly toward Aislynn and her surrounding magical guardians. "You will allow her to pass in peace or face the displeasure of the Queen. Now, *back!*"

The dead shuffled away, the square clearing slowly.

"You too, Philida," Shaeonyn said to the bluish faery woman. "I'm surprised at you trying such a thing with anyone wearing the robes of the Sharajin—and in the middle of the day."

"Sorry, Shaeonyn," Philida replied with a smile and a shrug as she skulked off to one of the surrounding structures.

Aislynn peered out between her encircling guardians. The square appeared to be clear once more. "Is it safe?"

"Yes, Oracyln," Shaeonyn said, sighing. "It is safe."

Aislynn took in a deep breath. "Deython?"

The tallest of the guardians turned, staring at her with his blank eyes.

"My—my thanks," she said.

At once, Deython nodded and in that moment the entire group of guardians curled once more into the form of black pearls, strung together on the ground at her feet. Aislynn reached down hesitantly for them, then secured them around her neck once more.

Shaeonyn glared at Aislynn. "When I lead?"

"I follow," Aislynn responded at once. "It's just—"

Shaeonyn stopped and turned impatiently toward the princess. "Just what, Aislynn?"

"Please," Aislynn could not stop shaking. "Please take me away from the dead."

Aislynn sat in a chair next to the lattice-crossed window at the far side of her room, staring out into the courtyard beyond. The beautiful garden below was surrounded completely by the Lyceum itself, its windows looking inward on this place of loveliness and peace rather than on the terrible ugliness of the city beyond. Just knowing there was such a place at hand had calmed Aislynn's panic.

"It's just that it never seems to get any easier for me," she said in a quivering voice. She did not want to meet Shaeonyn's eyes. "The dead, I mean. I speak to them and listen to them and watch them but there is always some part of me that wants to scream and run away. You would think that I above all the faery would feel differently. The dead saved my life and my mother's kingdom. I even knew many of the dead that came to our rescue those years ago, my own guard among them."

"I remember that part of the history, too." Shaeonyn nodded. The Seeker sat forward on her own chair. "You knew him as Deython when he lived. Now he's Lord of the Dead?"

"Yes." Aislynn smiled slightly at the thought. "He was—well, he was a good man and a loyal subject of the Second Caste. He had such a wonderful warm smile. Even when he was so formal around me on our walks, there was something soft about the way he—" Aislynn shivered suddenly, her hand rising involuntarily to her throat. Her hand hovered there for a moment. "You would think that after all I have been through that the dead would not bother me. But they do. They just do." She quickly pulled her hand down and folded her arms once more in front of her. "It is hard for me to bear touching them."

Aislynn saw the Seeker's eyes drop to stare at the thirty-six black pearls that lay—as they had for many years—as a dark circle around her neck. Her words were a statement of wonder when they came rather than an accusation. "The Lords of the Dead touch you always."

Aislynn kept her silence.

"I have, of course, heard the story of their coming into the world from the power of the vision—as have all the Sharajin—although I had never thought that I should see them myself. The story is that they are kept below the Queen's Tower, in a special crypt reserved for them alone. Yet are they here before me?"

"Yes, they are the Lords of the Dead," Aislynn said, sighing. "And they touch me always. I never said that I like it."

"May I ask you something?" Shaeonyn spoke quietly.

"Of course," Aislynn replied quietly.

"Dwynwyn asked me to be your mentor." The golden-haired Seeker spoke softly. "More than that, she asked that I be your guardian as well—though if the Lords of the Dead are accompanying you, I can hardly see how I am needed in that regard. Still, the journey you have undertaken is more arduous than you might imagine. So I ask: why are you doing this?"

Aislynn turned from the window to face Shaeonyn, tears still staining her face. "Because I cannot deny that I have seen the vision. The magic has awakened within me. I did not ask for it to come, nevertheless it is within me. More than that, it has called me to some purpose I do not yet understand. The wind is blowing in the vision and I must follow it."

"The wind is blowing, Oraclyn Aislynn." Shaeonyn nodded with satisfaction. "And we shall follow it together, you and I. I accept you as my Oraclyn-loi and my novice; even as Dwynwyn accepted me."

"Will you help me find my purpose?" Aislynn asked hopefully.

"You are my apprentice, Oraclyn Aislynn," she said, taking the hand of the Princess with an easy smile. "We are both called to follow this wind and we'll find its source together."

"Yes, Mistress Shaeonyn," Aislynn said, smiling in gratitude. "Besides, with you and I—and the Lords of the Dead—together, what could possibly go wrong?"

Common Myth

Everything had gone wrong.

Galen sat stiffly on his chair at the southern edge of the glade, his knuckles white and his grip threatening to splinter the wood of the armrest. He cast his eyes once more around the circle that had been carefully arranged around the grassy hollow and tried to discern in the faces about him just what had changed them so radically in the last two decades to bring them to this loud and vicious impasse. His mind wandered from the argument for a time as he tried to assess the people who would settle it.

All of his guests had come with their own entourage. This was to be expected; indeed, no mystic would dare travel any of the roads in the Five Domains without escort. So here they were, hovering about the chairs of their clan leaders as though even here in the Circle of Six they were a fortress under siege.

To his left in the circle sat Thais Mistal now of Enlund—a girl he had known from that life before the Deep Magic had changed everything. Back in Benyn, when they had shared that town in common and little else, she had been a young girl he had barely noticed. But now they were both among the Elect and somehow the magic had chosen her as well to be one of the Thirty-six. She had followed him into battle on the Election Fields and she had followed him south across the hills and into a destiny that she could scarcely imagine. Now she was the head of Clan Mistal, a woman of elegant features whose eyes turned slightly down at the corners, implying a deep sorrow in her soul. Her cloak was feathered in vibrant purple and blue, hiding her frailty. Her once golden hair was now nearly white from the strains of her duties. Behind her waited several of her personal guard and her son, Lucian. Galen remembered that the young man had once been a companion to Caelith. Standing there, he somehow seemed amused by the argument raging before them.

Farther to the left beyond Thais sat Cyrus Myyrdin of the Dragonback, though Galen understood that the man had originally come from Southport in Hrunard. Galen had joined with Cyrus when he entered the Dragonback many years ago in search of Dhalia. They fought side by side then but had since grown apart. Still, Galen liked the older leader of Clan Myyrdin and had insisted that he remain among the Six over the objections of several other clan leaders and those of Cyrus's own son, Evath, who wished to take his place. Cyrus was somewhat deaf in his left ear, which led to his disconcerting habit of turning his head away from Galen whenever he could not hear the speakers in the Circle properly. He was a powerfully built man, shorter than Galen but with broad shoulders and a grip like iron, although many now said his blade was sharper than his mind these days. His head was rimmed with a wreath of carefully trimmed gray hair, though the top of his head was so smoothly bald that Galen jokingly wondered if the man actually polished it. He was obviously having no trouble hearing what was going on in front of him now as he glared with bright and angry eyes from deep beneath the heavy brows of his broad forehead. Evath, ever present with his father, hovered nearby scowling just as deeply.

To Galen's immediate right sat Uruh Nikau, the Palathian with the flawless dark skin. She sat with her arms folded over her chest, her head cocked to one side as she studied the spectacle before them.

Galen was no different, and he certainly felt under siege himself. Caelith stood next to him clenching and unclenching his fist.

The object of their common concern was Brenna Caedon of Hrunard. She stood in the center of the glade, the whiteness of her fur-lined robe contrasting with the near-purple of her face, which was framed by her carefully woven cascade of long soot-black hair. Before her, equally outraged, stood Haggun Harn, now of Urlund, though, like Thais, Galen had also known him from Benyn. His tall, older frame shook with rage beneath his own shabby robes, his slicked-back white hair quivering. Brenna and Haggun had been going on for some time and neither of them showed any signs of slowing.

"Your argument is worse than stupid, it's unconscionably danger-ous!" Brenna railed, her voice, Galen feared, carrying well beyond the glade. "All the Pir understand is force! We've tried to placate them for centuries and all it has *ever* gotten us is more death!"

"But you heard Galen," Haggun shouted, his left hand jutting out toward the master of Clan Arvad sharply. "If we accept this offer, we put an end to all that!"

"What offer?" Brenna spat back. "To pack up our clans and travel to some mythical land to the south on the word of the very people—the *very people* who have spent the last four hundred years trying to destroy us man and child? Half of us would die from the journey alone!" Brenna glared directly at Galen. "That's not an offer; that's suicide."

"And what would you have us do, Brenna?" Uruh said, her deep voice rolling evenly like a cool breeze across grass. "At least with his proposal, we have the hope to fight for a homeland that is our own."

"Fight, surely! Yes!" Brenna said, stepping forward, her fist clenched, "but for something *real!* Fight for our own land here and take back that which was taken from us. The power of the Deep Magic should no longer be held like some caged beast. It should be released over the land, to strike down our enemies and win back the land for our sake and the sake of our children."

"And when you have released this beast across the land, how will its hunger be satisfied?" Thais snapped. "Two decades of toil and struggle and we still know so little of this power to which we are nei-ther master nor slave. If we become the plague upon the landscape, how then do we justify ourselves as being any better than those who hunt us now? You would argue for open war—"

"Better open war than to sell our future on the word of this Pir bitch," Cyrus growled as he squirmed in his chair. "The Pir are mighty in battle, to be sure, but they give nothing with the right hand that they don't take twice with the left. The application of a wee bit of keen-edged steel would gain us more in negotiations with that lot than all the words in the world."

"But, just think for a moment, what if it's *real*," Haggun spoke with emphasis. "What if the Pir are as weary of the war as we are? Think of the lives we would save and not just our own, eh? Think of us in a land that is our own and not just any land, but Calsandria, the very center of the ancient—"

"The center of smoke," Brenna countered. "The center of misplaced dreams. You're hanging our very survival on a phantom, Haggun—you and Galen both—on a place where the grasses are softer and the fruit falls from the trees into your basket. It's only children's stories. It doesn't exist, Haggun—it just doesn't—"

"It does exist," Galen said, standing slowly.

"You've deluded yourself, Galen Arvad, if you think—"

"Mistress Caedon, your words have blown across the council quite effectively," Galen said with a voice that commanded attention. "I think we all know its direction. Now you shall have to endure a little breeze of my own."

Brenna abruptly sat down in her chair, the palms of her hands pressing down on the armrests and her elbows bent outward. She was quiet for the time being but it was obvious she was far from finished. The boy standing next to the chair laid a hand on Brenna's shoulder, which seemed to calm the woman a bit.

Galen turned around toward Caelith. The young man nodded curtly in response and ducked quickly back into the woods behind him.

"Calsandria," Galen began, shaking his head as he turned back to the Circle. "The Throne of the Gods; the Pillar of the Sky—it's all a myth, a story to distract children, a 'phantom,' I think you said, Brenna. I believe you're right. The Mad Emperors are gone and with them the glory that was Rhamas. Maybe they had the powers of the Deep Magic, as some have supposed, and lost it. Maybe they had another power that we know nothing of. Maybe it is just as well that they are gone into the mists and now no more than a half-remembered tale."

Galen could hear the rustle of leaves behind him.

"Or, perhaps, it is more real than we know."

Caelith burst from the brush at the edge of the glade. A brightly clothed man with long, curled hair was firmly in Caelith's grasp, his hands bound tightly before him. Caelith shoved the man forward, pushing him off balance and causing him to tumble into the center of the glade.

"May I present Margrave the Magnificent, Loremaster."

Margrave rolled painfully up to kneel in the grass of the glade and then looked around. "By the gods!" he murmured with wonder, then broke out into a radiant smile. "The Mad Masters of the Soulless! How wonderful!"

"Margrave," Galen said, stepping forward.

The Loremaster struck a noble pose, the picture of the bound martyr, speaking to some audience seen only by him. "Brought in chains before the Dark Council . . ."

Galen blinked. "What chains?"

Margrave looked up and winked. "Don't worry, sire, I'll fix it all up later. This is going to make a *great* epic song! Just work with me and everything will be fine."

Galen sighed. "Margrave, tell us the truth of Calsandria."

Margrave closed one eye, cocked his head, and considered for a moment. "There may not be that much to tell of the truth, sire. But if you will permit me a small indulgence, there is a great deal I could tell you that *isn't*."

Galen shook his head.

Margrave shrugged.

"Just answer my questions directly. Does Calsandria exist?" Galen asked quietly.

Margrave looked up. "Of course, sire!"

Galen could feel Thais lean forward in her chair. Uruh had not moved but her eyes were on the Loremaster, considering him. Cyrus squinted attentively.

"How do you know?" Galen said with studied ease.

"Well, sire, I've seen records of it." Margrave smiled, then cocked his head to one side as he considered the matter. "The Pir have confiscated most of the ancient writings, of course, but not all of them. They still exist in places here and there across the land. I've seen fragments of trade records on the Dragon's Teeth Isles, lists of goods shipped from Calsandria long before the time of the Dragonkings. Oh, and there were pillars in Vasskhold, before the Pir obliterated them, that spoke of the southern trade routes—the ancient Dwarven Road—and mentioned the name of Calsandria as—now how did they put it—oh, yes, as 'the end of all roads.' The stones of Mount Evanoth had extensive records from the period that talk about the fall of Calsandria but say little of the city itself and nothing at all of its location." Margrave turned his head to look upon his audience with his most winning smile. "Even so, be assured, my lords and ladies, Calsandria did indeed exist."

"Are we now taking council on what is truth from an—an *actor*?" Brenna sputtered in derision.

"Madam!" Margrave responded, his dignity apparently wounded. "I am a Loremaster! We are entertainers and historians with very strict guild laws and ethics! We know more than anyone that one has to know the truth in order to tell a convincing lie. I assure you that nothing is more important to a Loremaster than the ability to know where the truth ends and the lie begins."

"That's all well and good for you, Loremaster," Uruh chuckled to herself, "but that leaves us with a liar who assures us he is telling the truth."

Galen stepped forward to stand next to the Loremaster. "Lady Dhalia attests to his voracity. She saw him in her vision and knew that he carried the truth of this. He only confirms her long study of this matter. Her word will be sufficient for this Council."

Galen glared. None of the Council would challenge Dhalia's ability or her word.

"And so what if it does exist still?" called a high voice across the glade.

Galen looked up, surprised that the words were coming from the figure still standing with one hand on Brenna's shoulder. Only now did

Galen realize that it wasn't a young man at all, but a tall woman with cropped hair dressed in a traveling tunic. "Every child among the clans was raised on stories of Calsandria and the great lost Empire of Rhamas. They helped us sleep at night in our innocence but now we have grown and are facing the waking world. The Rhamasians could not save themselves; how does finding them save us now?"

Uruh shifted in her chair. "Mistress Eryn, you forget yourself. Your voice is not to be heard within the Circle."

Ah, Galen realized. Eryn Caedon—Brenna's daughter. Galen smiled. From what he had heard of her, the dragons themselves could not prevent the girl from expressing her opinion, and the more contrary, the better. "Even so, her point is a good one and I shall answer it. You are right, Mistress Eryn, the stories of Calsandria have been instilled in the hearts of all of us. We have long wondered if its avenues really were golden or its walls crusted with jewels or whether the Throne of the Gods really existed. But more than anything, we have wondered if they were our forefathers—if they held the Deep Magic in their time. Is this power we know so little about the same power that made them great? What did they know about it that we do not? Most important of all—if they with all their power were doomed to fail, what might we learn from them that we could avoid their same fate?"

"You ask a great many questions, Galen," Cyrus muttered. "Questions that cannot be answered."

"No, Cyrus, they must be answered," Galen intoned. "The Edicts of Enlund are only now going into force; humanity slaughtered because the dragons themselves are mad for our destruction. If Urlund joins them, then where are we safe? Where can we hide? More than just hide; where can we live? The Pir are offering us all a way out—for their survival and ours. We must act and we must act *now*; we must gather the clans and prepare them to leave—"

"It's too hasty," Brenna interrupted. "We must wait—"

"We cannot wait!" Haggun shouted.

"Hold!" Galen said, his voice booming over the rising objections. "There is a more acceptable way!"

They all turned toward him. He took a deep breath before continuing, his voice more even as he spoke. "We can quietly gather our clans to ourselves. While we do, we shall send a company of scouts ahead. If they do not find Calsandria, then we shall be in no more danger than we are now. But should they succeed and discover this fabled land, then—and *only* then—shall we follow and leave the Five Domains forever."

Thais chuckled briefly. "Indeed, Galen, should this company actually discover Calsandria, I doubt any of us could prevent the clans from taking up a pilgrimage. But who could we all agree on to determine the truth of this illusive Calsandria?"

"I will go," Eryn said. "I want to see this child's fable for myself."

"My son Caelith shall lead an expedition," Galen said, ignoring the young woman with a voice that defied dissent. "His raiders have but recently returned and they are available for such a quest."

Thais shook her head. "Galen, we all owe you much, but I think we would trust you a little better if you learned to include us in your grand plans."

Galen smiled in return. "I should think Caelith would also appreciate the company and protection of his friend, Lucian of Clan Mistal . . ."

The young woman's voice was more adamant this time. "I said that I will—"

"Mistress Eryn should hold her tongue until she can learn when to use it! Nevertheless, I suspect that Clan Caedon will insist that their favored daughter join as a witness to the expedition, is that so?" Galen cast a questioning glance toward Brenna, who nodded with a polite smile. "As I thought. They shall take Loremaster Margrave here with them as well. His knowledge of Rhamasian lore should—"

"Truly?" Margrave beamed. He stood at once in his excitement, somehow instantly releasing himself from the ropes that bound him and tossing the cords to an astonished Galen before bowing deeply to the Circle. "I present myself gratefully before this majestic assembly and put all my understanding at your disposal in this noble quest! And my promise to you all is that I shall unfailingly immortalize every terrifying moment, torturous maiming, and tragic death in song and poem upon my return."

Galen interrupted the speech by gathering Margrave's costume in his large, powerful hands and pulling him backward abruptly. The Loremaster staggered into Caelith, who grabbed him quickly with his powerful left hand while slipping the tip of his dagger under the Loremaster's chin with his right. Margrave smiled once more but held his tongue.

Galen continued. "As I was saying, his knowledge of Rhamasian lore should help us determine if the true Calsandria has been found or not."

"And who, do you propose, to lead this group into the Forsaken Mountains?" Haggun asked. "The noble Caelith's abilities are formidable but have the Pir told him the way?"

"Inquisitas Berkita has provided us a guide—a Pir monk who knows the location," Galen answered haltingly.

"Why do they not just tell us where to find it?" Uruh asked cautiously.

"It is a condition of their telling us. They want to verify their discovery as much as we do."

Cyrus sniffed. "And just who is this monk we are supposed to trust with leading our sons and daughters into lands from which no one has ever returned?"

"Jorgan Arvad." Galen tried not to whisper. "He is—I have another son."

Ghosts of the Past

Caelith looked up and set his jaw, reluctant to take another step yet knowing that he must. Down the long years he had charged into battle or run grimly down foreign and menacing trails whose ends were dark and unknowable. Fear had been his companion on many of those occasions, but never before had he hesitated as he did now at the base of the hill leading to his mother's tent.

The path before him wound its way back and forth under the star-filled sky, climbing higher and higher up the gently sloping hillside under the soft glow of fading twilight until it crested at the warmly lit opening in the large canvas tent that was the only real home he had ever known. There, as she had for uncounted nights over the long troubled years, Dhalia stood her vigil. She gazed into the night and murmured her thoughts to the Deep Magic and her prayers to whatever unnamed gods would hear her. This was Dahlia's ritual, as strictly maintained as Galen's own, every evening for as long as Caelith could remember. This image of his mother silhouetted against the flickering light of the evening fire haunted him through the blurred seasons of their exile, down every muddy, dusty, and forgotten road he walked. It shivered next to him in the rain outside every unnamed village where he and his fellow raiders searched desperately for anyone who would trade with them for food. It watched him in the cooling abandon after battle when the world stopped and a sense of lonely frailty filled his heart to call him back from despair. No matter where their wanderings took that huge and battered tent, regardless of its being pitched in mountain glade or desert hilltop, here Dhalia stood each evening and her image called him home.

Tonight was different. His footfalls were heavy, and Caelith grew more grim with every step.

At last he reached the hilltop, a clearing rimmed by the towering hardwoods of the Rhesai Forest. Somewhere nearby in the cover of those trees, the Order of Galen stood watch; thirty-six warriors of the clan chosen to protect Galen and his family. They were ever present and never seen. The clanfolk spoke of their ability to be invisible as being both figurative and literal; that they had mastered not only the arts of silent combat and stealth but used the Deep Magic to disappear from the senses of man and beast. Caelith thought much of their reputation to be mere storyteller's smoke, but he had to admit that it was easier for him to leave knowing they watched over his parents.

Would that they could protect us from the truth, Caelith thought solemnly.

She stood there as he had always remembered her, though her silhouette in the open flap of the large tent had grown smaller over the years. Yet her back was straight as she stood, her arms folded in front of her, looking out with eyes that saw both onto the world beyond the horizon and into the infinity within.

Caelith forced a tight smile, though he was fairly certain that his eyes belied it, and stepped quickly toward her. "Mother."

"Ah, Caelith," she said, returning from the far place of her thoughts. "It's over so soon?"

She made no move toward him; welcoming arms had never been the way of his family, though Caelith thought his father would have preferred it differently. It was perhaps a sign of their times; his mother had feared to love her boy openly in the early years of his life when so many of the clan's young had not survived. Self-preservation had over time translated into a physical boundary between mother and son—or so Caelith tried to tell himself.

"The Council is adjourned and there is much to discuss—much to tell." Caelith hesitated for a moment. "Father should be here soon."

"I've no doubt that there is much to tell—and I'm just as sure that you'll enjoy telling it."

Caelith looked thoughtfully at her face. The red hair of her youth had faded nearly to gray. Her face was careworn and lined but her eyes were still bright, though now rimmed with red. Seeing her cheeks stained with tears, he hated what he had to do—what he had come to say. "Mother?"

"She has come, hasn't she?" Dhalia said with a wistful smile as she lowered her head, averting her eyes. "All these years—and now she has come."

Caelith cocked his head slightly, trying to catch her eyes. "Yes, mother, she has come, but—but there is more."

Dhalia nodded as she turned and looked down the hillside. "Yes, of course; much more indeed."

Caelith turned to follow her gaze. It took a few moments for his eyes to adjust to the starlight, but there, down at the base of the long slope of the hill, stood the unmistakable form of his father. There were two other cloaked figures with him: a slightly shorter, younger man with a heavy traveler's pack and a woman.

"Is she beautiful?"

Caelith blinked; there was not much time left. "Mother, you know that father . . ."

"Loves me?" Dhalia hugged herself and smiled reflectively. "Of course I do, Caelith. Your father is above all things a man of honor and honesty. He has told me that he loves me and I believe him. It's just that—well, he loved *her* first. I don't know if you can understand that, son; love is a living thing and when it dies it must be mourned. Your father never had that opportunity; they were separated by the fate of the gods rather than their choice. The specter of that past has haunted us ever since—and I must admit that I feared that ghost more than the living woman who embodied it."

"You needn't worry about the past, mother," Caelith said, look-ing back into her face once more. "It's done and gone."

"No, Caelith, and you remember what I tell you," Dhalia said quietly, her eyes locked uncomfortably with Caelith's own. "The past is still with us—in the here and now. We are what our past has made us and we live now with who we were. If the Deep Magic has taught us anything, it is that our choices haunt us down the long years, for good or ill; and it is the unexpected consequences of those choices that can be the most dangerous."

Caelith steeled himself; he could not put it off longer. "They had a son."

Dhalia took in a long, slow breath.

"Father didn't know," Caelith continued, carefully watching his mother. "She must have been expecting when he was caught up in the Election."

"So you have a brother to trouble you as well," she said gruffly, her brow furrowed in thought.

"A half-brother." Caelith nodded, uncertain as to what his mother was trying to tell him. It was her eyes, as always, that gave him his best insight into her thoughts. They had steadied with re-solve and strength.

"But a brother, nevertheless," Dhalia replied quickly. Her focus again seemed to be on a far place and time only she could see. "And an elder brother at that. He comes to us, but not to dwell in his fa-ther's home. He has other purposes in mind."

Below them, the figures were moving. The cloaked woman reached up for the face of the second man, pulling his head toward her. He bent forward slightly, lowering his pack to the ground. She kissed his forehead, holding him there for a long, tender moment be-fore releasing him. Then she quickly turned away, moving purpose-fully into the forest's edge below.

Both Galen and the second figure watched her go for a moment, but the woman never hesitated and never looked back. Galen then reached down to pick up the pack, but the young man deftly snatched it up and shouldered it himself. Galen turned slowly and began mak-ing his way up the hill toward the tent, the younger man in tow.

Caelith watched his father, thinking he looked more tired than usual. It was as though a great and old burden had either been removed or renewed. Caelith did not know which it might be, but his father seemed to have aged in the last few hours.

Behind him followed the stranger advancing from the obscurity of darkness into the warm, flickering glow of the tent. The harder Caelith studied this man the more impossible he found accepting him as his own brother. This man looked so different from his own family. Since hearing of his existence, Caelith half expected the fellow to be a copy of himself; a few minor differences, perhaps, but nevertheless recognizable. But this stranger had a soft chin and a rounder, more oval face than either he or his father. His nose was larger and hooked slightly in a way that reminded Caelith of a bird of prey. His build was larger, stockier than Caelith or Galen for that matter. More remarkable still was his nearly complete lack of hair; his scalp, cheeks, and chin were all scraped completely bare, making his large ears stick out.

In his right hand, however, he carried a dragonstaff. Caelith could feel the Eye of the Dragon shift across him, its cold shiver running down his bones. Though the early mystics had learned quickly how to ward off the more frightening aspects of the dreaded device, its presence nevertheless was an uncomfortable and dangerous warning to any magic-bearers under its gaze; it clearly proclaimed Jorgan to be one of the Inquisitas priests of the Pir Drakonis and an enemy of the clans.

Galen halted in front of his wife, his eyes averted, though he spoke to Caelith and Dhalia while gesturing at the newcomer.

"This is—Jorgan."

Dhalia gazed for a moment on the young man before she curtsied, bowing her head slightly before him. "You are welcome in our home, Jorgan. I've prepared a meal for—"

Jorgan abruptly chuckled, his baritone rolling out his words in smooth, liquid tones. "Thank you, ma'am, for your efforts but I have not come to enjoy your hospitality."

Caelith examined Jorgan more closely, dragging his gaze away from the dragonstaff. The Inquisitas wore an olive green hooded cape, dark trousers, high-top boots, and a dark tan shirt under a striking padded doublet. Though his general costume was drab, the doublet was a deep maroon elegantly and intricately embroidered with silver threads.

"That is an unusual garment," Caelith said, nodding toward the doublet.

"It is a symbol of my order in the Inquisitas; a special gift from my mother," Jorgan replied through a careful smile with a hint of condescension. His startling violet eyes locked on Galen as he spoke. "She would have preferred a rose-color cloth but none could be found."

Galen coughed uncomfortably.

"Ah." Caelith's response hung in the air between them all, failing to fill the deepening silence.

"I should have thought he would look at least a little like you, father," Caelith said, crossing his arms over his chest.

Jorgan's eyes, creased with his enigmatic smile, shifted back easily toward the young mystic.

"No," Galen spoke slowly, "but I think he favors his maternal grandfather, Ansal Kadish. He is the very image of—"

"Please," Jorgan said, clearing his throat. "I am sure it is awkward and difficult for all of you. It hasn't been that long since I myself learned that I not only had a father still living, but that he is the most—well . . ." His words trailed off as he shrugged, smiling once again.

"The most what?" Caelith's tone rose.

Jorgan drew in a long, considered breath as his gaze locked on Caelith. His words were disjointed from the lightness of his pleasant face. "Why, the most hated and reviled apostate in all the Five Domains."

Caelith narrowed his eyes and closed his hand unconsciously around the hilt of his blade.

"Well, yes." Galen chuckled sadly. "I believe that fairly describes my current status with the Pir Drakonis. But there is more to me— more to all of us—than being the object of your hatred."

"Hatred?" Jorgan spat. "The word comes so easily to you, but it's in your own hearts you need to find it. It was not my hatred that turned a small conflict into unbridled warfare that has butchered the faithful Pir for more than a quarter-century!"

"The mystics were being butchered long before that." Galen's tone was heavy. "Table meat for the Dragonkings was all any of us ever meant to them. All we wanted was to end the slaughter."

"It is late," Dhalia interjected. "Let us leave this outside for one night and—"

"Oh, so all you wanted was to end the slaughter—by forming a mob of heretics to bring down the divine order of the world?" Jorgan sneered with contempt. He turned to face Dhalia. "I thank you out of common courtesy for your offers, madam, but I cannot reside among you or the community of your faithless, godless clansmen. I shall make camp and return in the morning for such councils as are required. Then I shall do as my faith and duty direct me: lead you and your sorry, misguided clans to your precious Calsandria—may Vasska save you when the truth at last is known!"

Jorgan picked up his pack and, flashing another grin, bowed before stepping back into the darkness. He strode confidently down the path under the starlight toward the base of the hill, his dragonstaff glowing with cold blue light.

Caelith looked at his father.

The old clan leader blinked up at the stars overhead and then spoke gruffly. "The order will be disturbed by his presence unless I find a secure place for the boy to camp."

"You had better go and see to it, then."

Galen glanced at his wife uncertainly.

"It's all right, Galen," she replied. "I'll be right here waiting for you."

Galen smiled tightly and then turned, making his way down the hill behind his first son.

"He comes to us, but not to dwell in his father's tent," Dhalia murmured.

"Are you a prophetess, mother?"

Dhalia chuckled darkly. "No. I only wish that I were! Like all of us, I walk the dream of the Deep Magic, searching to apply that talent with which we are either blessed or cursed. I, too, feel the wind that blows through our dreams—don't look so shocked—but the vision that gives it all meaning and context remains the elusive province of the ancients. But, son, I believe there was a time when such mortals walked the earth and knew the will of the gods."

"He says he can lead us to Calsandria," Caelith said with more assurance than he felt.

"Calsandria?" Dhalia smiled. "So the Pir think they have found it. That should interest your father a great deal, I should think. This isn't the first time he has sent someone to look for it."

Caelith turned to his mother in irritation. "Not the first time? When? Why wasn't I told of this?"

"Because he thought it a fool's errand at the time," Dhalia said, turning to face her son. "He wanted so much to believe that Calsandria existed—as I suppose all the mystic clans want to believe, but he wanted to be sure of it first. He sent his closest friend, the one who could travel the Forsaken Mountains and whose word he could trust on his return."

"Cephas?"

Dhalia nodded. "Cephas Hadras—that blind old dwarf who used to carry you on his back when you were a boy. He was your father's best friend even before his Election and no more honest, capable, or trustworthy creature ever walked the face of Aerbon."

"Good old Cephas." Caelith nodded. "I'd wondered where he'd gone off to. I take it that Cephas didn't find Calsandria then."

"We don't know," Dhalia said, concern clouding her face. "He left over a year ago and we still haven't heard from him."

Thux

By the twenty-sixth year of the reign of King Mimic, the forces of the Grand Subjugation Army had extended the boundaries of the Dong Mahaj Mimic Kingdom to consolidate and conquer the opposing kingdoms, clans, and empires from the Cynderlond Wastes to the southern boundaries of Kranc.

However, it was not until the GSA set siege to the heart of the Jilik Dynasty that Mimic accomplished the greatest prize of all in the capture of Thux, the Grand Wizard of Jilik.

AN ORAL HISTORY OF MIMIC
TOME XVII, FOLIO 2, LEAF 12

"Just a minute!"

Thux, Grand Wizard to the Goblin Emperor of the Jilik Dynasty, was almost finished.

That, at least, is what he had absently told his wife each time over the last hour that she had stopped in her panicked rush to plead with him. Phylish's tone had grown increasingly urgent and demanding and, he supposed in the back of his mind, rightly so. His experiment was taking longer than he had originally thought, but then, he realized sorrowfully, it always did.

Standing a head taller than the goblin wizard, the wooden frame was lashed together with reeds from the nearby swamp, which he had cultivated there for just this sort of thing. Inside the frame were several gears, their axle rods bolted through a wooden shingle, though he was still having trouble getting them to line up properly. These gears led to a set of plates surrounding a strand of cable that ran from the top to the bottom of the frame. It was a complicated device designed entirely by Thux, and if it worked he was sure it would revolutionize the entire wizard industry throughout Jilik.

Which may not have been saying a great deal, since Thux *was* the entire wizard industry in Jilik. Thux reached up, removed his flat blue ceremonial hat of office and slapped it against his filthy pants several times to shake off some of the rubble that had fallen on it. Flopping it back on his head, he scratched his short beard and gazed critically back into the workings of his device.

Then another massive booming sound literally shook the stones of the large vaulted chamber. Phylish shrieked, diving under a heavy nearby table, scattering the rumpled mass of clothing she had been carrying. Broken chips of stone fell from the cracking mortar of the stones overhead, trailing long cascades of fine dirt sifting through the air. One of the stone chips fell irritatingly into the mechanism itself. Thux growled to himself in disgust and leaned forward to blow the newly fallen dust and small rock slivers out of the device.

Phylish was hastily gathering up the garments from where she still knelt beneath the heavy workbench. "Thux! We've got to get out now! They've come! They'll be here any moment!"

"I know, dear," Thux answered absently as he reached in to adjust another gear mounting. "Just one more minute and—"

"Just one more minute and we'll both be dead!" Phylish shrieked. Thux could tell that she was doing her best to control her considerable temper. "The Emperor and the entire Grand Army of the Dynasty will be lost for sure!"

"I don't think so, dear," Thux said casually as he worked. "The Emperor left with the Grand Army of the Dynasty this morning on a scouting expedition to the south."

"But the titans are coming from the north!"

"Which is why I think the Emperor and his army will keep their casualties to a minimum." Thux shrugged.

Phylish glared at him from under the table. "We'll be murdered in our beds if we don't get out now, I just know it!"

Thux looked over at his wife through the haze caused by the cloud of dust in the large secret laboratory. He always called it his "secret laboratory." Really to anyone who would listen, including a few goblins from Kranc who had wandered in by accident while looking for the lavatory. Thux was not sure what a lavatory was, but it could not possibly be grander than this room. Thick pillars rose into arches that supported the stone ceiling overhead. Numerous heavy tables lay between the pillars, each crowded with cogs, wheels, cables, rocker arms, and sundry other mechanical objects in various states of disrepair, dismantling, and dysfunction. Each represented a separate course of investigation for Thux and he felt a momentary pang at the loss they would represent when he did, indeed, finally leave with his wife. Their large traveling trunk lay on the last table in the row, its lid open wide and its contents seemingly desirous of escaping its confines. Phylish, now crawling out from under the table, had been trying to stuff objects into the case for the last hour with little success. Thux would have gladly helped her but could not interrupt his work, especially now that he was so close to a breakthrough.

"Phylish, they aren't going to murder us in our beds," Thux said matter-of-factly. "Our home was the northern edge of town. They have no doubt already burned both the house and its bed to the ground. Why don't you just finish packing, dear, and I'll be right with you. It will take only another minute—"

Another muffled detonation rattled the hall, followed almost at once by an even louder explosion. Phylish yelped, crawling backward with remarkable speed under the table and covering her head against the falling debris.

Thux eyed the device critically. "Just another minute and I think it will be ready for a test."

Suddenly, an immense stone shook loose from the ceiling, whistling slightly as it fell. The granite block crashed directly down through a table opposite where Phylish huddled. Covered in billow-

ing dust, the goblin woman bolted from her hiding place, still clinging to the wadded-up clothing. Because the ground below them was
still reeling and bucking from the impacts, her steps were uneven.
Smoke from the fires outside was beginning to flow into the room.

"Hmm," Thux observed. "They appear to be getting closer."

Phylish threw her bundle into the trunk. The lid would not close
despite her frantic efforts. "Thux, honestly! What is so important
about that thing?"

"Ah, I'm glad you asked, dear," Thux said brightly. He rather suspected that his wife asked him about his work primarily to make sure
he was actually listening to her, but the goblin wizard did not mind.
He always fancied that he impressed her with his brilliance and he
loved to talk about his work. "I call it the Thux Variable Grabber. Tell
me, what happens if you are hanging from a cliff by a rope and you
let go?"

The ground shook violently again. "Thux! Please, there really
isn't time for—"

"No, I promise I'll be brief and you'll really think this is interesting," Thux assured her even though he was pretty certain that she would
not find it interesting at all. "What happens if you let go of the rope?"

"You plummet to your stupid and well-deserved death," she answered with obviously overtaxed patience.

"Exactly," Thux responded brightly once more. He felt he was
really connecting with his wife. "But what happens if you just hang
on to the rope?"

"You dangle there stupidly until you die?" Phylish's tone suggested it was less of a question than a suggestion.

"Of course! But what happens if you let go of the rope *just a little?*"

Phylish's eyes narrowed. She answered him through clenched
teeth. "You get to the end of your rope?"

"Yes, but *slowly*," Thux replied, clapping and then rubbing his
hands together with glee. "And *that* is what my new invention does.
It lets go of this cable just enough so that whatever is attached to it
goes down slowly. I tell you, the Thux Variable Grabber is a major
technological leap forward which will—"

The western wall of the chamber suddenly bulged inward with

the sound of cracking stone and collapsed downward into the room with a deafening roar. Smoke and dust billowed across the chamber through the opening. Phylish ran as quickly as she could to get away from the collapsing wall, her large feet staying just ahead of the tumbling boulders. She reached for Thux's hand as the dust cloud enveloped them both.

Thux choked on the billowing cloud, hacking the dryness out of his throat even as he turned. Phylish's hand was still tightly in his grasp. He began feeling his way toward the other end of the laboratory. He knew their only hope for escape now lay past his Variable Grabber. Some part of him wondered for a moment if the Variable Grabber would have worked and he suddenly felt very sorry that he might never know.

The goblin wizard could hear his wife struggling behind him. "Come . . . quickly, my dear," he wheezed between agonizing coughs. "I think . . . you were right. It's time—it's time to leave."

A sudden wind blew through the opening in the collapsed wall. The dust and smoke swirled under its breath and cleared. Thux turned, drawing his wife nearer to him as they saw sunlight streaming in through the ragged hole, its rays forming shifting columns in the debris-filled air. Then, just as suddenly, the sunlight was cut off.

An enormous face, fully thirty feet tall, was peering through the opening. Its skin was made of pocked and rusted iron and it gazed down at them from enormous eyes, blank with no pupils. Its nose was short and upturned and its mouth small with thin lips. Part of its head was missing on its right side from the forehead back, exposing a chaotic jumble of pipes, some of which were cracked and hissing with leaking steam.

Thux took a step backward, pulling his terrified wife carefully with him.

The gigantic face turned toward their movement.

Thux stopped. *Titans!*

A scream of metal being forced to twist into new and unnatural positions filled what remained of the broken chamber. The face contorted, and Thux realized with a start that it was *smiling at him.*

"Thux," Phylish whimpered. "I think it wants you."

"I think you're right, dear," Thux stammered.

"I think we really need to leave now." Phylish gulped.

"Yes, I think that would be a good idea."

They both turned at once, running past the Variable Grabber toward the stairs as quickly as their feet could carry them. The doorway lay at the end of the supporting pillars of the hall and led into the deeper reaches of the Jilik Palace. The interior corridors on this level were complex and narrow, Thux reasoned as he ran, and might offer them an opportunity to escape.

Phylish screamed, her large deep-set eyes widening with fear and disbelief.

The ceiling in front of them crumbled, its debris falling in front of the doorway. A colossal metallic hand and arm were plunging down through the stonework, four of its original five fingers curving with the terrible sound of scraping metal, reaching into the room for them.

Thux yelled a wordless cry of anguish as he skidded to a stop. He still held tightly to Phylish's hand, pulling her around him as he stopped. There were several exits from the secret laboratory in order to accommodate the numerous visitors and occasional tours that the Emperor liked to conduct. One of them had to lead to safety; one of them had to offer him a way out of his own folly.

The gigantic hand rushed across the floor toward them, its arm carving a gash through the ceiling overhead. Hot sparks flew from the rusting metal as it scraped against the stone flooring.

Wildly, Thux thought of the Variable Grabber. Perhaps if he could use the device on one of the outside cables that supported the palace, he and his beloved could slide to safety. It would be a daring and romantic rescue the likes of which had never been seen in all the history of the goblins. It would endear him to his wife forever and make him the stuff of legend and myth for generations to come. He would be the hero of Jilik, the greatest wizard that had ever lived.

He tripped, stumbled, and fell. His head landed, wizard's hat and all, in the supporting framework of the Variable Grabber.

Yes, he thought. *I'll be a hero after all. I'll just lower the mechanism slowly, take it out of the framework, and escape!*

Gazing upward at the Variable Grabber suspended above him, he activated the device.

It did not work as expected.

I was suddenly on a hilltop blinking at the clouds racing over-head. They were blood-red in a strange twilight. I sat up carefully, wondering what fates had brought me to so strange a place. My immediate concern was for my wife, who had been with me but moments before but who now had vanished from me or I from her. Large gears, cogs, pistons, and other assorted pieces of machinery lay half buried in the rich and loamy ground of the hill, partially obscured by the soft grasses that waved about me.

"Phylish!" I called. "Phylish! Where are you? Where am I?"

I heard a sound behind me growing louder by the moment. I quickly stood up, fearing that perhaps the shouts were coming from my wife, and I turned my face into the wind.

It was a small goblin the likes of which I had never seen before with large, leathery wings. He seemed to be having some difficulty navigat-ing in the wind that was blowing about us. His arms were flailing as he whirled tail over head. This odd goblin flipped over suddenly and smashed into the ground. He was still rolling along among the blades of grass when the wind caught his partially open wings once more and lifted him backward just above the ground and directly toward me. I put my hands out to protect myself but the impact still tossed me off my feet. More by instinct than any design, I wrapped my arms around this strange being, folding his wings under my arms. He fell on top of me as I pitched over back-first onto the hilltop.

"About time you came!" the winged goblin replied. "I've been looking for you for the longest time."

I struggled to push him off me with little success, for his flop-ping wings made it difficult. "What are you talking about? Who are you?"

"Me? How can you ask such a question?" The strange little creature sounded as though his feelings were hurt. He rolled off me, his wings rattling awkwardly in the breeze. "Don't tell me you've forgotten your old friend Lunki?"

"Well . . . of course not!" I responded with all the confidence I didn't feel. His features were obviously those of a goblin, and there was something familiar about him, though I couldn't place it at the time. He had a streak of brilliant white running through the otherwise rust-colored shock of hair at the top of his head. Certainly I would have remembered someone with so distinguished a feature! I truly had no idea who this creature was, but did not want to appear unsociable. He obviously thought that he knew me and his name seemed vaguely familiar. "Well, well! So, my old friend Lunki, eh? Has it — has it been a long time?"

"Far too long!" Lunki grinned, his sharp teeth glistening. He reached toward me. "But that's not important now that you're here. Wonderful! It is simply wonderful!"

"Lunki, perhaps you can help me," I said, pretty certain he couldn't help me at all. "I seem to have misplaced my wife and — hey, where are we going?"

Lunki had taken my hand and was dragging me across the top of the hill. "No time to waste," he said, his wings flailing in the wind. "You've got to meet the right people — make the right connections — and then you'll really learn something; you'll learn a <u>secret</u>, Thux. There's nothing more powerful than a secret!"

He pointed over to a pond of water among the hills and then dragged me in its direction. As we got closer, I saw that there was a glass tube sticking out of the water on one side. One long plane of metal ran down its length twisted into spirals around a central shaft. At the exposed end, the shaft was connected to a large crank and handle. It was a fascinating arrangement, one that I had not seen before.

"Beginnings and endings," Lunki said with a broad grin. "What will happen, Thux? Why don't you see what will happen?"

I nodded and stepped up to the crank. I turned it one way and watched the spirals of metal turn inside the glass cylinder. Nothing happened, so I tried turning it the other way.

To my astonishment, the water was being drawn up the tube by the spirals of metal. The more I turned, the higher it rose until it began spilling out the top of the glass. I was elated, turning the handle faster and faster until suddenly I realized that no more water was coming out and the pond itself was empty.

Lunki danced gleefully and flitted uncertainly over the now dry bed of the pond. There he found a pair of leathery wings like his own. He bounced through the air back to me, and when he handed them to me, I suddenly found that they were sprouting from my back like his.

Then the wind caught Lunki's wings, dragging us both into the air. We tumbled high over the grassy fields, bouncing across two other hilltops before sprawling onto the grassy crest of a third.

A tall creature approached us from the base of the hill. His face was covered by a mask in the form of a highly unusual goblin, and his build was extraordinarily tall and emaciated for any of the goblin-kind I knew.

"Lunki," I asked, "who—or what—is this?"

The figure only held up his hand and covered its mouth. Whatever it was, it appeared to be in no hurry to speak to me. Instead it pointed away from the hill toward a distant mountain.

"He is one of the ancient titans," Lunki whispered loudly in my ears. "He is showing us the way! He will lead us to our destiny!"

It was then that I noticed the wind had grown into a terrible gale. It blew about me with great force but in silence. As I watched, the cogs and gears embedded in the hillside rose up, carried by the silent wind. They floated away from the hilltop, borne by this strange breeze in the direction that this masked titan-creature pointed.

I thought of my own leathery wings. They stretched awkwardly from my back, and I understood the difficulty that Lunki was having with them. The rushing wind picked both Lunki and me up to wheel among the flying cogs, gears, and pulleys in the sky. I couldn't help but smile as I floated on my own upon this river of air over forests and foothills until I came at last to soar among the craggy peaks of impossibly tall mountains. Lunki, the old friend that I still could not remember, tumbled alongside me, his laughter bright over the roar of the wind.

A valley appeared between those mountains below us, and at

the sight of it, I was filled with dread. I tried to move away, to fly in some other direction, but the currents of the air were stronger than I and my wings were new and unfamiliar to me. The various device parts that floated with me were spinning down toward that valley and both Lunki and I with them, our speed faster and faster until the floor of the valley seemed to rush up at me.

I closed my eyes. I could hear nothing but terrible wind and Lunki's hysterical laughter . . .

CONVERSATIONS WITH THUX THE FIRST
BOOK I, PAGES 53–59

Thux jolted awake, sitting upright with a start. "Where are we? What is this place?"

"Quiet, dearest," Phylish said, rubbing a large bump on her husband's head, one that threatened by the moment to grow even larger. "We're still in the secret laboratory—well, what's left of the secret laboratory."

"What happened?" Thux said, blinking.

"You released your device and it landed on your head."

"It didn't work?"

Phylish shook her head.

"Well," Thux said, blinking furiously as he tried to focus, "at least I'm back."

"Back?" Phylish said. "Back from where?"

"I'm not entirely sure," he replied. "But I think I may have seen Ag'nar."

"God of the wandering goblins?" Phylish's eyebrows beetled. "Oh, you poor dear, it must have hit you harder than I thought!"

"*Silence!*" boomed a voice through the shattered laboratory. "KNEEL BEFORE YOUR CONQUEROR!"

Phylish and Thux turned as one toward the voice.

It came from the gigantic face of the titan, still peering through the broken wall.

"Do you think it's talking to us?" Phylish asked, her voice a full octave higher than normal.

"I believe it is," Thux replied in awe.

"KNEEL BEFORE YOUR CONQUEROR OR DIE!" came the thunderous voice from the motionless blank face.

"What should we do, Thux?" Phylish asked.

The wizard shrugged. "Kneel?"

Phylish nodded. "That seems appropriate."

They both carefully knelt facing the rusting face of the titan, Thux carefully removing his official wizard's hat and holding it in both hands in front of him.

Something green dropped from the nose of the titan, then stood. It stepped confidently toward them, waving a short stick in its hand as it approached.

Thux's jaw dropped. He knew he would hear words about it later from his wife, assuming they lived that long, but he could not help himself. The young goblin woman that stood before them had long, perfectly pointed ears set off with fiery red eyes sunken back under a heavy brow of mottled green skin. Her round, firm potbelly was touched by long, thin sagging breasts all held loosely under a linked-armor vest tinted green. She was the most exquisitely beautiful goblin Thux had ever seen.

"Who are you?" he managed to say.

"Are you Thux? The so-called Wizard of Jilik?" the woman said, her croaking deep voice the embodiment of goblin seduction.

"Uh-huh."

"Consider yourselves both the just spoils of war," the woman replied coldly. "You are now my prisoners."

"And by whom do we enjoy the pleasure of being captured?" Phylish asked with barely contained annoyance.

The stunningly beautiful goblin stuck out her potbelly, the daylight shining into the room from behind the face of the titan illuminating her as she struck a suitably dramatic pose. "I am Lithbet, Warrior Princess of Dong Mahaj Mimic, King of the Goblins."

King of
the Goblins

His hands and feet hobbled in loosely wrapped chains, Thux was accompanied into the magnificent court of Dong Mahaj Mimic by two squat goblin guards.

Thux almost forgot to rattle his chains as he stepped into the enormous hall, slack-jawed in abject, unabashed awe. Immediately in front of him was a troop of dancing gremlins who apparently were hired for the victorious procession. Each little creature wore torn, clinging clothing that showed off their large feet and potbellies to their best advantage. They were supposed to be the conquered goblins of Jilik, but the actual conquered goblins had apparently drunk too much at the "Welcome Prisoners" party the night before and were in no condition to be presented before the Dong. The gremlins were hired at the last minute, thereby narrowly averting disaster for the conquest parade.

Behind Thux were foot soldiers from the GSA carrying treasures looted from Jilik for additional presentation to Dong Mimic. The wizard would have thought that the best goods from Jilik had disappeared long ago, vanishing among the army ranks, but the occasional glances he stole over his shoulder told him there had still been some first-rate items remaining—most of which he recognized as looted from his own secret laboratory. Such discipline and restraint in a goblin army was unheard of so far as Thux knew.

Leading them into the hall was the Warrior Princess herself, Lithbet. She strode into the hall confidently, declared the conquering of the Jilik Dynasty to her father, and then motioned for the parade to begin.

Thux barely took notice of the gremlin beauties swaying and slapping each other to the music of the drums, lutes, and horns of the goblin band at one side of the hall. The Grand Palace of Dong Mahaj Mimic was the most magnificent structure in the known world—at least according to the guide who was ushering small groups of goblins in and out through the towering rusted doors—and Thux was inclined to believe that it was true. Mimic had completely renovated the hall to its former glory back in the time of the titans—again, something he had overheard the dull-voiced guide say as he had entered the hall. The ancient arches of steel beams and the original corrugated curving metal plates had all been removed. Now the walls were formed by the torsos and heads of titans, some of them missing only a jaw or an eye, whose faces were bowed forward and whose arms were raised to form their own towering arch nearly fifty feet overhead. Between these arms was laid a latticework of stained glass carefully designed to present the scenes of Dong Mimic's history.

Thux trudged forward, his chains rattling loudly as he stared up at the glass overhead. There, on the left, was Dong Mimic, leader of the engineers, striding over the plains of Cynderlond in search of the first True Device with Ebu Gynik at his side. Then on the right was the depiction of Mimic marching triumphantly into the city of the Dong, armored in the ancient armor of the titans and holding in his hands the True Device as female goblins gathered around him in droves but are fended off righteously by Ebu Gynik. Then, in a large middle panel spanning the full forty-foot width of the hall from titan armpit to titan armpit, was a depiction of Mimic, once more in titan armor leading an army against Dong Mahaj Megong, light breaking through the clouds as Mimic triumphs over Megong with the stunning Ebu Gynik at his side.

The beauty of it almost made Thux cry.

To either side of the hall, untold riches were piled up with a decadent casualness. Gears and even entire gearboxes whose value might easily support the average goblin family of thirty-seven for years lay half buried beneath pulleys, wheels, belts, shafts, and, Thux could scarcely believe it, *pistons.* Thux glanced again at his hands and feet. *They are even bringing me in bound in* chains, he thought, and could barely grasp the reality of such wealth.

In front of him, the dancers were finally gyrating to a halt. Then the band climaxed on a triumphant blaring note, and the courtiers all applauded, whistled, and hooted their appreciation. The Mimic Gremlin Dance Troupe always gave a great conquered people's performance; they were especially appreciated for the way they knew when to give up on an encore and get offstage. They split to either side and scampered to the back of the hall, their feet flapping against the polished stone floor in anxious anticipation of being paid . . .

And thus Thux found himself suddenly standing before the Great Thrones of the Goblin King. Three large gears of decreasing size formed a stepped dais leading up to the twin thrones. To either side, tall swamp reeds grew out of great pools of stagnant water. The jawless head of a titan arched over it all, suspended from the ceiling by cables.

There, before Thux, sat King Mimic himself—Dong Mahaj Mimic. The squat little goblin had grown impressively fat over the years, his breadth seemingly in competition with his height and possibly winning. He sported a huge and luxurious spike of orange hair fully three feet in length, legendary in itself since, as all goblins knew, it was a hairpiece crafted from the less than enthusiastic donations of his dead enemies. It was also rumored that he had a great many hairpieces just like it. He wore an ermine robe that flowed down from his throne and over the gears to the floor directly before Thux. It was hopelessly long as a cape, but, no doubt, could easily double as a carpet for the short king as needed. Thux considered this the ultimate in both economy and practicality.

Next to him sat the glory of the court, Queen Gynik—Ebu

Gynik to her subjects. Time had only enhanced her incredible beauty. Her round belly hung down over her lap in no fewer than three folds, the sight of which had driven several courtiers into mad fits of lust. Though her long ears now drooped more than they once might, it was a sign of maturity that only endeared her the more to her subjects. Her yellow eyes were still bright and keen; her mind still as sharp as her teeth.

Yet it was the gorgeous Lithbet, standing between her father and mother, that eclipsed them both. "Dong Mahaj Mimic—Ebu Gynik—I present the spoils of our conquest: the Wizard of Jilik known to us as Thux."

Thux was so stunned at his introduction that he dropped the chains off his hands. They slid to the floor, clanking noisily against the polished stones.

"Your Majesty! I am so sorry!" Thux blurted, bending over quickly and picking up the pile of chains. He hurriedly tried to bind his hands with them once more, but the chains seemed to have tangled. Thux was abashed. "I trust, Your Glory, that they were not damaged by the stones."

"Hah!" Mimic bellowed a laugh that rang down the length of the hall. "A polite wizard, eh? I don't think we've ever met a wizard before, have we, my prized darling?"

Gynik barely bothered to glance up from sharpening her fingernails. "No, my king."

"Capital! Absolutely capital," Mimic snorted, then pushed his considerable bulk forward in his throne. "You may keep your chains if you like."

Gynik did look up at that, however. "May I remind you, my sweety-poopsey, that he *is* your captive? I think you are too generous to your conquered slaves."

"Oh, I think we can afford to keep this particular captive in chains, my beloved honey-woobie!" Mimic gurgled. "He isn't just any prisoner, you know. No, indeed—not just any prisoner at all." His eyes narrowed slightly, however, making Thux a little uncomfortable. "I understand your wife was captured as well—Phylish, isn't it? Did she not see fit to attend this morning?"

"Not at all, Your Majesty," Thux stammered. The truth was that Phylish had laid claim to a major headache this morning. It was understood between Thux and his wife that such headaches covered a very broad number of conditions usually involving some egregious offense Thux had perpetrated and of which he was usually completely unaware. "She was much fatigued by the arduous trip from Ploktick last night and the prospect of meeting your glorious self caused her to swoon and faint."

"Quite understandable and proper," Mimic pronounced as he slid off his throne, his bulk shifting under his link-metal tunic as he plopped down onto the train of his royal robe. He gestured behind Thux toward the treasures held in the hands of the foot soldiers. "I see that my daughter has brought back treasures from your fabled laboratory. Tell me about them, Thux!"

"Sire?"

"I was a magnificent engineer before I was the King of the Goblins," Mimic sniffed in irritation. "As one old engineer to another—show me your best stuff!"

"Ah, of course, Your Majesty." Thux bowed deeply once more, struggling to hang on to his chains. He straightened up and turned around, casting his eye across the devices held by the goblins behind him. "Well, uh, let me see—oh, here is a nice one over here!" Thux stepped quickly between a pair of soldiers until he stood in front of one who had pushed the tall wooden frame into the audience hall. "This is what I've been working on lately. I call it the Thux Variable Grabber. You see, when you pull this lever down, it causes the plates to expand just enough so that—well, now that I think about it, perhaps we should look at this one over here. That one I'm still working on."

Thux skittered sideways between the soldiers, desperately searching for something else. "Ah, here is something! I think you'll find this interesting."

"A steel rod and a triangle of wood?" Mimic asked questioningly.

"Well, yes, it is a steel rod and a triangle of wood, Your Majesty—very good! But it is the application of the steel rod and the wooden triangle that makes the difference. You see, I've discovered—excuse me, Your Majesty." Thux considered for a moment, then took the chains on his hands and quickly wound them around his neck for safekeeping. Then he took the steel rod and the wood from the soldier and walked toward the throne dais, placing the block in front of the huge gear on which Mimic was standing. He inserted the flat end of the steel rod under the protruding lip of the gear just below where Mimic stood and rested the rod over the block of wood. As he spoke, Thux moved down toward the far end of the rod—now hanging several feet above the floor. "This is simple, Your Majesty, but really quite amazing. I discovered that by moving the block of wood closer to the subject, you can move heavier and heavier things with the rod. I call it the Thux Variable Rod Lifter."

Mimic's eyes narrowed. "Thux, it would take ten of my best guards to lift this . . ."

"Just a moment . . . sire"—Thux huffed as he pushed down on the end of the bar—"I just need to move out a little farther . . ."

The great gear at the base of the goblin throne suddenly rose upward several inches. Mimic staggered slightly but, Thux was relieved, managed to keep his balance. It would have been disastrous if he had toppled the throne altogether. He dropped off the end of the rod, allowing the gear to fall back to the floor with a loud clank.

"Sorry, Your Majesty," Thux stammered again as he retrieved the rod and block from before the throne and tried to return it. The goblin soldier who had brought them in now seemed reluctant to touch them, so Thux laid them on the floor.

"You impress us greatly, Thux," Mimic intoned.

Gynik yawned.

"But there is one test I must give you," the Goblin King continued. "There is a device I discovered. He turned to a goblin groveling near the throne. "Bring in the pipe!"

The goblin scampered quickly behind the throne.

"The—the pipe, sire?" Thux asked quietly.

"Just a little test," Mimic replied with a shrug.

The groveling goblin returned. In his hands was a length of brass tubing, half a hand wide and nearly three feet long. Thux took it from the quivering attendant and examined it. It had a crank and handle attached to one end of a rod running down the center of its length. Thux peered down the opening holes at either end of the tube.

He saw spiraling planes of metal.

"Your Majesty." Thux was dumbfounded. "Where did you find this?"

"The same place you found it." Mimic smiled broadly, showing his sharp teeth. "Show me."

Thux took in a deep breath. It seemed impossible to him, yet here he was holding a device identical to the one he had dreamed about a few days before. He glanced around, noticed once more the pond next to the throne and stepped over to it, thrusting the bottom of the tube into the dank water.

He turned the crank.

Green-flecked water spilled out of the top of the tube and onto the polished floor.

"Well, well," Mimic rumbled through his smile. "The Wizard of Jilik indeed. You are officially appointed to the post of Best Friend to the King."

Gynik, Thux noticed, was no longer paying attention to her nails. She, instead, was leaning toward her warrior-daughter, who had bent down to hear her mother's softly spoken words. Gynik continued to speak to Lithbet, but her eyes never left Thux as Mimic stepped down from the dais and threw his arm around Thux's shoulders.

"We have much to talk about, you and I," Mimic hissed. "Not the least of which is why the wind in our dreams blows us both toward the south."

Technomancer

Thux flapped wearily through the door in the heel of his luxurious dwelling, dropped onto the down-stuffed tarpaulin cushions that elegantly covered the couches in the large room he had come to think of as the Great Fallen Arch, and let out a long, exhausted sigh.

"Thux?" screeched the familiar voice from around the curve of the little toe. "Is that you? Are you home?"

"Yes my dear," Thux replied, staring up. He still wore his ceremonial flat blue cap, for he was too tired to get up and put it on its special hook in the heel.

The wizard gazed absently about. Phylish and Thux had been living here for three weeks, installed at the express order of Dong Mahaj Mimic, and already it was hard to think of anywhere else as being home. The idea made Thux a little wistful, for neither he nor his wife had ever before enjoyed such opulence and the thought that they had gotten so quickly used to it made him a little uncomfortable, especially since he was the Dong's prisoner. Aside from the royal complex itself, his was the most elegant dwelling in all the known goblin lands. On the outside, it resembled a gigantic metallic foot, huge even by titan standards, raggedly cut off just above the ankle, with a cone of fitted metal set on top to keep out the elements. Inside, it was entirely hollow, its space having been converted into one of the most talked-about dwellings in all the goblin lands. It was simply—and somewhat reverently—called "The Foot," and whoever dwelt there was the envy—and social target—of every goblin, gremlin, gnome, and imp in the conquered lands of Mimic and, no doubt, far beyond as well.

The curves of the interior of the Foot were fitted with multiple levels of metallic flooring, dividing up the enormous space into smaller areas linked by ladders and stairs. The interiors of the toes then became—from the big toe down to the little toe—the bedroom, storage, kitchen, guest room (which had never held a single guest in all its history as a dwelling), and, completely unheard of among goblins, an interior bath behind the curve of the small toe.

Thux glanced mournfully at one of the platforms just around the curve of the Fallen Arch, down where an indentation in the ball of the foot was planked over. It lay just outside the entrance to the bedroom in a hollow that was the best hidden from the prying eyes of the main entrance. It was also the one space in their new habitat where Phylish would allow him to study the various and increasing number of contraptions and, more recently, various books he was dragging home from work each day. Now the large table that originally dominated the space had completely vanished from view under the accumulated flotsam of his investigations: gear casings, governors, pulleys, one entire drive assembly taken from the finger of a titan, and, most annoying of all, the screw pump that Mimic had shown him the first day they had met—the mechanism he had unquestionably seen in his own dreams. Yet here it was as real as the pain in his head and he could no more understand its existence than anything else the mad mechanics of Mimic had eagerly shown him.

"There's another 'Welcome Prisoners' party tonight," Phylish called as she stepped from the little toe, spitting on her hands and then slicking her hair with them until it stood nearly vertical on her head. Thux reflected that Phylish could be quite attractive when she made an effort. "Do you want to go?"

"It's just the Free Fascists again," Thux groaned, shaking his head.

"Oh." Phylish slumped with disappointment. "Haven't they been conquered twice already?"

"That's twice since we were conquered," Thux agreed as he closed his eyes and flopped back onto the couch. "The Free Fascists fight for a while, the titans walk all over them, smash their buildings, carry them here in chains, and then within a few days they stage an elaborate escape. The GSA almost always discovers their complicated plans before they are acted on, but Mimic has standing orders to let them escape no matter how foolish their plans. He then sends the GSA up there every week or two to wage war on them and capture them all over again."

"Isn't that a waste of time?" Phylish considered as she sat on the end of the couch.

Thux rubbed the tips of his pointed ears absently. It seemed to help his headache. "I asked Mimic the same thing; he says it's good for testing the new weapons and keeping the titans fit for more serious conquest. Besides, Mimic says that the Free Fascists seem to enjoy being crushed and then rising up against repression. It's apparently part of their cultural identity." Thux sat up slowly, looking around and wondering how he could possibly tell his dear wife what he knew he had to tell her. "Dearest, would it be all right if we stayed home tonight. I'm not feeling much like a party . . . even if it is a bad one."

"Well, I suppose," Phylish sniffed, "but . . . what's the matter, Thuxy? There's something you're not telling me . . ."

"It's . . . oh, my dear Phylish," Thux moaned, shaking his large green head and dropping it down to hide behind his large hands. "I've wondered all day how I was going to tell you. I just don't know if I can!"

Phylish's large eyes filled with watery concern. "What is it, Thuxy? We've been through war and capture and it's always worked out before. Whatever it is, we'll see it through together. What is it?"

Thux gathered his courage. There was no going back now, but as he gathered up the threads of his thoughts, he was having trouble deciding where to begin that would make sense.

"Phylish, you've watched me working for years now, haven't you?"

"Why, you know I have," Phylish answered with a sigh, clasping her hands together to remain calm.

Thux appreciated his wife's willingness to wait for him to work through to his point, no matter how long or needlessly complicated he made it. "Well, you have to understand that the basis for everything I've done as a wizard was built on simple ideas, one on top of the other. Rocks fall down and not up; square objects don't roll as well as round ones; a thrown rock will continue to fly until someone's head gets in the way; all those are simple ideas. I call it Thux's Invariable Law."

"I know that one," Phylish interrupted, furrowing her mottled brow as she tried to remember, her hair lock quivering with the effort. "It goes, uh, oh yes: 'stuff we do makes other stuff happen and . . .'"

"Yes!" Thux encouraged. "And . . ."

"Oh!" Phylish brightened. "'And when other stuff happens, someone did something to *make* it happen!'"

Thux was so proud of her that he almost forgot the dire point of what they were talking about. "Right! Very good, my dearest!"

"Well, it wasn't too hard to remember." Phylish smiled, her sharp teeth gleaming behind her thin lips. "It's the only thing you ever invented that didn't have 'variable' in the name."

"Yes, well, be that as it may," Thux harrumphed, "it is the basic rule of everything I've created; everything that ever worked or almost worked. If something moves, something connected to it moved it. If something floats, then something connected to it is holding it up. Rods push rockers. Shafts turn gears. Different parts in machines *touch*. It's always the same; there's always a connection. All my work and my entire career as a wizard are built on this."

"Well"—Phylish nodded enthusiastically as she gestured at the Foot around them—"it seems to have worked quite well!"

"But that's my point," Thux shouted in exasperation. "It doesn't work at all! Just after we got here, King Mimic took me down to the Very Secret Laboratory."

"You've been to the Very Secret Laboratory?" Phylish said with astonishment. "Why, I've heard of that place! It's where Mimic keeps all his magical powers that resurrect the titans. Everyone in the city says it's the most secret place Mimic has!"

"It most certainly is," Thux agreed gravely.

"Can you show it to me?" Phylish asked, her eyebrows rising.

"Certainly, we can both take the tour later if you like . . . but that's not important right now," Thux said, trying desperately to get to the point, to shed himself of his burden. "The point is that I've been working at the Very Secret Laboratory ever since that day. I've tried to study their methods, learn what they have learned, and merge their understanding with my own. The thing is, the more I study it, the less I understand."

"The less you understand . . . what?

"Technomancy!" Thux cried. "That's what they call it. It has something to do with a mystical power in the books of the titans. Somehow the books are connected to the machines of the titans, but the harder I look, the more elusive that connection is to me. The Technomancers hold on to these books. Some of them dance with them. Some of them sing to them. Some of them mutter strange words over them or run their fingers over them in circles. None of it makes any sense, but when they do these strange things clockworks start to tick, water flows through pipes, and before you know it titans are raising their arms or their legs and walking as though the centuries since they fell never passed."

"These books must be very powerful," Phylish said in awe.

"Yes, but *why?*" Thux got up suddenly, jumping down from the couch platform to land among the devices and books on his study platform. He gestured with frustration around him. "There has got to be some connection—but I can't find it. Are the books holders of some kind of unseen connection? Are they just something like pipes that convey this invisible connection? Or does this Technomancy have nothing to do with the books at all? I've been burning ideas night and day trying to understand it, and all the while in the back of my mind was growing the frightening thought that maybe I was wrong—maybe Thux's Invariable Law *was* variable after all."

Phylish was suddenly unnerved. "But you—you said yourself there had to be a connection—that Thux's Invariable Law was—"

"Invariable; yes, I know." Thux looked up at his wife and then looked away shyly. "Well, I still think so, too . . . which is why I tried an experiment today. There was this titan whose upper arm was mostly missing. The Technomancers were having trouble getting it to rise properly, which didn't surprise me since most of the mechanism was missing. They danced and howled and waved their books and it did move but not nearly well enough. Anyway, I happened to be watching all of this and noticed that there were two pulleys mounted to the exposed shaft of the arm. They were lined up but only the upper one was turning. I had used something like this in my Thux Variable Grabber mechanism. I realized that with the pulleys aligned like that, all you needed was a big rope or leather strap to connect them. Then the top pulley could turn the lower pulley."

"What did you do?" Phylish asked quietly.

"I asked the Technomancers to stop." Thux sighed. "I picked up a length of rope and climbed up on the scaffold next to the arm; it wasn't a difficult reach. I looped the rope around the pulleys, climbed back down, and asked the Technomancers to try it again for me."

Thux sighed again and kicked at a clockwork armature near his feet.

"What happened?"

"The top pulley made the bottom pulley turn, too." Thux nodded, his eyes averted.

"So, the Thux Invariable Law *is* invariable!" Phylish beamed.

"Yes . . . but . . ."

"But?"

"But because of me the arm worked *perfectly* after that!" Thux growled, tears welling up in his eyes. "I had fixed the arm by making that connection."

"Well, of course," Phylish said, now confused. "You said that connections make—"

"You don't understand," Thux said, shaking his head angrily. "I connected the pulleys, but the pulleys weren't connected to anything else. The connection should have made no difference."

"Oh," Phylish murmured. "I'm so sorry, Thuxy."

"It's worse," Thux continued.

"Worse?"

"The Technomancers were so impressed with my genius in getting the arm to work that they reported me to their superiors."

"No!"

Thux nodded. "Word even got as far as Mimic himself."

"Oh, Thux," Phylish sniffed, tears welling in her eyes. "Did they . . . oh, please tell me they didn't make you a—a *manager.*"

"Worse."

Phylish bit her fist in fear.

"They made me *Boss* Technomancer—Wizard of the Titans," Thux rumbled.

Phylish fled sobbing into their bedroom.

Thux did not know how to console her. Phylish was unusual among goblins; she had no ambition beyond having a small family of twenty or so children and living her years quietly with Thux. Most goblins considered her retiring personality flawed, but it was part of why Thux, himself unique among goblins, loved her so much. Now, through no real fault of his own, he had brought them to live in the exalted Foot *and* attained the high position of Boss Technomancer. He could think of no other way he could have made either himself or his wife a bigger or more inviting target.

Thux slowly climbed the gleaming steel ladder and tossed himself back onto the couch, closing his eyes. The whole thing was really getting to him lately. His dreams were becoming more vivid and disturbing. They always involved a tall creature in a mask showing him wheels and gears spinning in the air for no reason at all. There was also an ugly, tall female with wings that kept throwing bones at him, and always that Lunki creature beckoning him to the south.

There just had to be some connection.

Lithbet

ithbet, Warrior Princess of the Dong, burst forcefully into her
mother's chambers without permission or preamble. It was her
way. The concept of asking anyone permission simply never occurred to her. So the doors slammed open with a resounding clang, rebounding with such force that they very nearly closed behind the young
goblin maiden as she stomped into the room. Her back was hunched and
her arms swung wildly with purpose and haste. Jaw jutting determinedly
forward, she smacked her large feet loudly against the fitted stones of
what were generally known as the Queen's Apartments.

The Foot may have been a popular focus for the envy of the majority of goblins, but it paled entirely against the rooms in the palace
occupied by Ebu Gynik, Most High Queen of the Goblins. The audience chamber was a round room thirty feet across covered by a low
dome of arching metal girders. A dazzling array of intricate pipes
threaded a mesmerizing pattern overhead, just above long, milky rods
of glass that ran in lines from the center of the dome out to its edges.
There were metal doorways that interrupted the curved wall of the
room at three of the compass points, while three large frames—two
of which held actual glass in their panes—shined dim, golden light

into the room. Beyond the glass lay the Very Secret Laboratory whose floor was far below, putting the heads of the titans being reconstituted in there by the Technomancers on a near eye level with Gynik's rooms. More tantalizing still, each section of the curved wall between these points was covered with shattered glass plates and intricate objects protruding from the metal walls.

Nothing was too good for Gynik, as she so often reminded her husband. The finest of rooms, the most elegant decor, the rarest and most delectable of foods; all of these were the just due of Gynik, and she accepted them with all the grace and charm that a goblin who knows she is deserving can muster. In the middle of this sumptuousness, a huge, ancient desk curved into a nearly complete circle. Gynik sat in a chair that actually still swiveled, leaning forward with her hands reaching in dreamlike distraction for the panels on the desk. Through the windows, yellow light from the setting sun cast long shadows across the smashed dials that no longer measured anything, as Gynik flipped impotent rusted switches and twirled useless knobs.

"Mother!" screeched Lithbet. Her voice was used to commanding armies with great effect. It rarely worked on her mother.

"Ah, Lithbet!" Gynik smiled, baring her teeth, her yellow eyes flashing in the failing light of day. "How good of you to come and visit me."

"This is no visit, as you well know," Lithbet snapped. "You summoned me here!"

"Of course I did," Gynik purred. "And how else was I going to see my own daughter who is too busy to visit her ailing old mother."

"I'm in the middle of preparing the Grand Subjugation Army for our next glorious campaign," Lithbet rumbled. "Of course I am too busy to visit you."

"Exactly my point." Gynik smiled disarmingly, as she turned her back on her child and contemplated with relish the complex patterns of controls inlaid into the desk. "Magnificent, aren't they? All these delightful switches, buttons, and dials, and all of them are paying homage to me."

Gynik reached forward with her long right hand and flipped a random switch in the shadows. "You know, Lithbet, hundreds of years ago a titan—of high rank to be sure—sat right here where I sit today. She looked out on all these wonderful devices around her—much the same way I do today—and knew everything there was to know. She could see what everyone did, even their very thoughts, and if she didn't like what she saw . . ."

Gynik reached forward and flipped another switch closed.

"She just got rid of the problem—simple as that."

"And I take it there is a problem you would like someone to get rid of for you?" Lithbet asked, crossing her arms in front of her. "What is it, mother—who do you want me to kill this time?"

"Kill?" Gynik replied with surprise. "I should never!"

"All right, then." Lithbet sighed. She hated playing these guessing games with her mother. "Who do you want me to blackmail or rough up, or have their legs broken or their teeth pulled or their hair cut while being forced to serve in the Grand Subjugation Army?"

"Oh, you are a tease." Gynik smiled easily. "No, I've called you here to discuss your upcoming wedding."

The Warrior Princess gaped at her mother for three heartbeats before she even breathed. "I'm sorry—what did you say?"

"Now what would be wrong with a mother discussing her daughter's wedding," Gynik said, standing up from the chair, her smile filled with sharp teeth, "especially such an important wedding as that of the goblin princess."

"I can think of a number of things that might be wrong with that," Lithbet snorted with derision, "the first being that I'm not getting married."

"Oh, but of course you are," Gynik replied with light charm. "Every goblin maiden—well, perhaps, *most* goblin maidens at any rate—look forward to finding that special someone in their life—or several some-ones—whom they can use to really make them powerful."

"Mother, if you hadn't noticed—I am in command of the army," Lithbet said.

"And a lovely little army it is." Gynik nodded, taking Lithbet by the arm and guiding her toward the windowpanes at the side of the room. "Very powerful, indeed—but for how long, my child? Your father is getting older and won't be much longer for this world, I should think. When he is gone, who then will be King of the Goblins? Who will inherit the lands you have conquered in your father's name? And, more importantly, when *someone else* becomes king, what use will they have for a warrior princess whose father is dead?"

Lithbet thought for a moment as she looked out through the broken window. The ranks of titans before them glowed in the deepening sunset. The Warrior Maiden then eyed her mother suspiciously. "So, I thought I should come and tell you that I am going to be married, eh?"

"Most sensible of you." Gynik nodded.

"Perhaps you might remind me," Lithbet said, a sudden twitch developing in her right cheek, "just who it is that I am going to marry?"

"Well, my dearest dear, it cannot be just any goblin who falls out of a tree," Gynik said thoughtfully. "Your father created the power of the Technomancers, and it is that power that has kept him in his position all these years. I think what you really need in your husband is someone who understands this power as well as, or perhaps better than, your father does. Someone who can take over and continue the grand tradition of conquest your father started. There are a number of talented Technomancers your father has collected over the years but none of them seemed right. Until today, this is."

"A worthwhile Technomancer?" Lithbet said skeptically.

"Oh, this one is *very* worthwhile and *very* powerful." Gynik nodded. "Just today he dumbfounded all the Technomancers in the Very Secret Laboratory with his incredible skill. All of them are jealous and looking for some way to get rid of him, but so far none have dared make a move! Your father promoted him to boss just an hour ago."

"Sounds promising," Lithbet agreed. "Who is the unfortunate idiot?"

"Thux." Gynik nodded firmly.

"Thux? The Wizard of Jilik?" Lithbet stamped her considerable foot. "Are you out of your mind, mother? I just captured him last month. He's impossible to talk to, only interested in those devices of his, has no understanding of combat or tactics or strategy or *anything* that is interesting at all! And he's *old!* We'd have nothing in common."

"Exactly." Gynik nodded. "It's perfect. Since you won't have anything in common, you won't have to worry about talking to each other at all. He won't bother you in the least and all you have to do is keep him under control."

"And just how do I do that?"

"Oh, it's easy, darling—I'll teach you," Gynik said, patting her daughter on the arm.

Lithbet withdrew from her mother and stepped back to the window. She missed riding inside the titans, seeing the land roll under their gigantic strides and taking them into battle. Things were always so much simpler out there than they were at home. You win or you lose and you always know the difference. Still, she was a warrior and a princess, and she was equally savvy on both battlefields. Her father was getting older and would one day weaken. Should he fail altogether before there was a clear successor, then the titans—those great toys—would no longer belong to her.

"Thux would be acceptable," she said at last. "Although I suspect that his wife would have some objection to our marriage—the goblins of Jilik were peculiar in that way."

"Nothing, however, that I am sure could not be handled in due time," Gynik said. "All we need to do is make sure that Thux stays near court. You can work on him when you return from your next conquest and, in the meanwhile, I'll see what I can do about his poor, unfortunate soon-to-be-late wife. Whatever it is, I'm sure it will be tragic but ultimately work out for the best."

"Well, then it seems we do have a wedding to plan," Lithbet agreed with a smile. "I'd like a dress of pure burlap with an armored train."

"Anything for my prized darling." Gynik beamed.

"We should hold it the week after I return," Lithbet said, her mind working quickly through the logistics of the ceremony. "That would give us another week to cement the marriage and then two weeks after that for me to prepare for the next campaign. In total, it wouldn't cost me more than a month and I'd be right back at work."

"Sound thinking," Gynik agreed cautiously, "but a marriage does require more than just an occasional visit to really work. You have to be able to communicate: your demands, your instructions, your wishes—not to mention the whole technique of him thinking everything in his head is his own idea. Those things take time, Lithbet, or the marriage won't succeed—at least not long enough for you to stay in power."

"Yes, mother." Lithbet nodded impatiently. "You'd know better than I would."

"Indeed I would," Gynik replied, sitting back down in her chair, idly twisting knobs to no effect. "Thank you for coming—and congratulations on your impending wedding."

"You are most welcome, mother." Lithbet bowed so deeply that her shock of hair touched the floor. She turned and was nearly to the exit when she stopped. "Mother, how long do you think father has before he will become gravely ill?"

"He is already showing signs, my dearest, though none but myself seem to see them," Gynik said with sad tones carefully injected into her voice. "Of course, I would trust that our conversation would be kept in the strictest confidence. I wouldn't want your father to hear about this and upset himself."

"Of course, mother," Lithbet said with slight exasperation, "but how *long* does he have before this grave illness takes him?"

Gynik shrugged and turned back to absently flipping dead switches as she spoke. "Oh, I should say he could survive no longer than the third week after your wedding—whenever that may be."

By His Majesty's Pleasure

The dream started as it always did; with me sitting at the crest of a hill, staring at the blood-red clouds overhead as they race toward the south. Phylish was not there, and I had come to expect her absence. The soft grasses all around me waved in the breeze. The pieces of machinery poking above the level of the grass were like landmarks to me, identifying this place as what I had come to think of as *my* hilltop in that strange dreamworld.

"Hello, Thux! I was so hoping to find you here!"

I turned in surprise, my soul having difficulty believing what my eyes were seeing. "Your Majesty?"

Mimic bowed, the tips of his ears drooping slightly toward the ground. His royal robes of ermine were missing and, instead, his squat bulk wore the orange vest of an engineer and a traveling sack slung over his shoulder. "I am glad to see you here. The Technomancers often frequent this place but they really don't have much of a mind for engineering, just between the two of us." Mimic straightened his old body painfully and swung his arm about him in a wide arc, his palm up and open. "Do you know what this place is?"

"No, Your Majesty, I do not."

"This—this is the realm of books," Mimic said, a broad grin breaking out on his pinched face. "This is the place where the books live. All the power of Technomancy comes from books, but all the power of the <u>books</u> comes from here!"

"But, Your Majesty," I stammered, "this place is only a dream."

"That is the great secret!" Mimic shouted with glee. "You've got it!"

"Got—what, Your Majesty?" I replied, not entirely sure of what King Mimic was talking about.

Mimic leaned closer to me, his voice a conspiratorial whisper. "The books are the keepers of the dreams! I think they hold all the dreams of the titans inside them, locked up between the sheets. Sometimes I think that's where the titans went, Thux—right here inside these books—and that's why they have the power to bring the old machines back to life again."

It was difficult to bring my thinking around to a new concept. "You mean—there's a <u>connection</u> between these books and this—this . . ."

Mimic beamed. "That's why you're the boss! I knew there was something about you that I liked. You're not like other goblins, Thux—you're 'the Wizard of Jilik.'"

"That was largely a ceremonial title, Your Majesty."

"What does it matter now, Thux." Mimic spoke with an exuberance that belied his advancing age. "You're the Boss Technomancer and that means you are the most powerful man in the kingdom next to me."

I hung my head, feeling rather awkward in the moment. "I didn't mean to be, Your Majesty."

"Well, don't feel badly, Thux. After all it wasn't your fault—I was the one who appointed you to the position." Mimic smiled again knowingly. "More than that, I made sure you set up your household in the Foot. I daresay there isn't a single one of my subjects that has not heard about you by now and, no doubt, each of them has spent considerable time figuring out just how they can knock you over and take your place. Yes, Thux, there probably was not a single thing more that I could do to make you the most desirable, powerful, and dangerous target in all of my expanding domain."

"But why?" I stared open mouthed at the King, the wind at our backs blowing through the meager strands of his hair. "Haven't I been a good captive? What have I ever done to you?"

"Oh, it isn't what you've done _to_ me, son!" Mimic said, hoisting his flabby green arm and landing it heavily on my shoulder. "It's what you're _going_ to do for me. <u>That's</u> what it is all about!"

Mimic turned me around so that we both were looking to the south, the red clouds streaming over the rolling mounds before us. In the gloaming, I saw the distant mountain peaks and oceans, caverns and rivers, and strange towering buildings.

"There," Mimic said, pointing with his fat, free hand, "that is what you must do for me—for us both. I am old, Thux, old and vulnerable. The power of the books can do only so much for me now. But I feel the wind, as do you. There, to the south, lies the answer to our questions: the answer to this connection that you keep talking about, and the answers that I have looked for all my life. I cannot make the journey but you can make it for us both."

"You want me to take a trip—in my dreams?"

"Bah! Listen with your ears and hold my words in your head for once!" Mimic bellowed. "We dream when we sleep, but the books are still there when we awaken. What is that law of yours you keep babbling about?"

"The Thux Invariable Law?"

"Yes, what does it say?"

"Stuff we do makes other stuff happen—"

"Exactly!" Mimic jumped up and down as best he could, his more than ample middle rebounding around his girth. "Well, stuff we do <u>here</u> makes other stuff happen <u>there</u> when we are awake."

"So there _is_ a connection!" I declared with relief.

"Yes," Mimic nodded, "and the answer to that connection is there beyond the horizon. That's why you're leaving—right now."

"Leaving?" Once again I felt lost in the reasoning of the King, and I'm not so surprised that some have taken to calling him Mimic the Mad.

"Oh, you have to leave — and the sooner the better for you, I should think," Mimic said as he plopped himself down in the grass. "None of us will be out of danger until you have gone."

"Go? You mean leave the city?"

"Absolutely. There isn't a moment to waste." Mimic nodded, pulling a gear out of the ground. He examined it as he spoke. "My wife has already taken notice of you. You're the most obvious candidate for a son-in-law to come along in years — and that's why it is in your best interest to leave at once."

"Whatever you say, sire," I answered in astonishment. Court politics were not a game that I knew how to play. "It may take some explaining to Phylish, but both of us can leave within —"

"No, Thux." Mimic looked up, shaking his wide head, his ears flapping in the wind that constantly drifted around us. "For both your sakes, you have to leave her behind."

"No, sire!" I blinked, not believing what I was hearing.

"You must," Mimic said with sudden earnest. "My wife is set on this union. Your wife would be a minor inconvenience easily disposed of if you remain. On the other hand, should you leave at once, your wife would become a <u>hostage</u> — someone whom my wife could use to lure you back from this mission on which I am sending you. Take Phylish with you, and you will be hunted; leave her behind and you will return with more power than even my wife can cope with to keep you, your Phylish, and, needless to mention, your King Mimic safe from harm."

"I understand." I sighed, full of sadness. "But what do I say to Phylish?"

"Unless you can guarantee that the Queen won't find a way to stop you, better to say nothing and just leave." Mimic shrugged. "I'll tell your Phylish of your secret mission tomorrow and that you'll return soon."

"I see. And where am I to go?"

"Your answer will be found in the Courts of Og, in the South Crags," Mimic said as he pointed beyond the strange landscape toward which all the clouds were flowing. "I have a titan — very fast — waiting for you east of the city. Istoe — an imp in my service — will join you there. He is the greatest explorer of our time, Thux, and will be an invaluable guide to you. Just present the glass ball to the Technomancer . . ."

"What glass ball?"

"The one in your pocket — no, not now, after you wake! Pay attention. Give it to him and the titan will take you south until you reach Og. Present yourself there as High Ambassador with Secret Agency of Dong Mahaj Mimic, King of the Goblins. Once you are there, you will know where to look for our answers."

"How do you know this?" I asked, more than a little skeptical.

"Because a mutual friend has told me so." Mimic laughed and then turned again to face the south. I followed his gaze and was astonished at what I see.

There, on the next hilltop, danced the small, winged goblin with the long white scar. He called to me to join him, to fly with him to the south.

Lunki.

CONVERSATIONS WITH THUX THE FIRST
BOOK I, PAGES 67–71

Thux awoke.

He sat up in the dim light of the burning oil pots set around the interior of the Foot. Phylish had lit them and then gone to bed, trusting that her husband would follow her there as soon as he roused himself from his nap. Thux turned on the couch, looking toward the toe. She would no doubt be there now, a fact confirmed almost at once by the rumble of her snores rolling from their bedchamber.

Thux sat up and dropped his head into his hands. These dreams, he thought, were getting more vivid every day. He remembered every detail and every word of the conversation he had with—with what? Was that really the King commanding him to go on a secret mission to spy on a kingdom to the south, of which, so far as he knew, no one had ever heard? It was impossible—insane, really—that he should think the King of the Goblins should issue him commands while he took a nap on his own couch. *Why not just call me into the throne room,* Thux thought, *smack me on the head and tell me what he wants?* Of course, if the King had really wanted to keep the thing secret, what better way than to come to him in his dreams when no one else was around to hear them?

A great shiver rolled up and down Thux. *What am I thinking? Am I as mad as the king?*

Thux stood up and stretched. Well, he certainly was not going to make a fool of himself. Ambassador with Secret Agency, indeed! The very idea was preposterous now that he thought about it. It must have been the pressure of the last few days, this unwanted promotion and all his frustration with the whole concept of Technomancy. Maybe he could find a way to quit the position or, better still, get fired from . . .

Thux froze.

He had absentmindedly thrust his hands into the front pockets of his engineer's vest. His fingers were closing around a small, chill, and smoothly spherical object as his dread was mounting. His right hand lifted it up unbidden in front of his face.

The flickering light from the oil pots played through and off the object.

It was a glass ball.

Thux stared at it, breathing heavily, his mind racing to come up with an explanation for how it got there, who might have put it there, and what it all meant.

All he could think of was Mimic in his dream.

Connections.

It does not really mean anything in and of itself, Thux told himself, slipping the glass ball back into his vest pocket. It was still just a dream. Perhaps he had forgotten about picking up the glass ball earlier in the day and had remembered it only while he was asleep.

Or, he thought while exhaling a shuddering breath, there was a titan waiting for him east of the city.

Thux set his jaw. No, he refused to believe it, but he knew that he would not be able to sleep until it had been proven false—and there was only one way to do that.

The Boss Technomancer made his way back to the heel and grabbed his heavy cloak, tossing it over his shoulders as protection from the night air. He discovered his hat was still on his head and cursed himself for forgetting to hang it up earlier as well.

Thux opened the door of the Foot and stepped outside. He was fully confident that he would be back before dawn to regale his wife with his foolish journey into the night.

In this, he was absolutely wrong.

Partings

The long banners of the Kyree Orders rustled in the morning winds, forming brilliant silky waves over the courtyard of Kien Werren. These forty great pennants had each been carefully worked with an intricate design symbolizing the virtues of the founding Articles of the Kyree; the code of laws by which their entire society had been governed for nearly a thousand years. Above this vibrant, shifting canopy of color, the tower of Kien Werren—an ancient keep of the faeries that was the original southeasternmost outpost of House Qestardis—rose into the brightening sky, its delicate features cast into sharp relief in the slanting light of dawn.

Below, lining the sides of the great courtyard itself, stood the Kyree in carefully ordered ranks. Each stood tall, their posture achingly straight and their great feathered wings tightly folded against their backs, the tips of their long primary feathers crossed with precision behind them. Their arms were each held crossed in front of them, the right arm resting crisply atop the left, the fingers of both hands held knife-flat and as rigid as iron. The stoic looks on their faces belied the energy that seemed to charge the air like lightning.

Atop the walls surrounding the courtyard, a series of long trumpets were separated by ornately painted drums. The finely crafted instruments were ordered by lengths and breadths, from small to massive. The drums beat a constant rhythm like the slow beating of wings while the horns sounded precisely in their turn, weaving chords and patterns of sound that rebounded against the walls of the courtyard with their power and majesty.

Aislynn's wing motions fell into step with the cadence of the march without her thinking about it. There was something about the pageantry, the barbaric music pulsing through her flesh that called to her. Raised as the Princess of Qestardis, she had been at court all her life and had participated in every kind of ceremonial event known to the Five Kingdoms. Yet never had she been as profoundly moved as she was this morning.

Aislynn was among the faery delegation entering the courtyard right behind Djukan and his two lieutenants. Djukan was arrayed in his father's polished black battle armor. His father's helmet—symbol of the honors accorded his family in life—rested firmly beneath Djukan's tightly squared arm. His lieutenants wore their own armor, polished leather that glinted in the morning light. All three flew at a stately pace into the courtyard, their wings catching great scoops of air as though controlled by a single mind. They, like Aislynn, beat their wings to the tempo of the drums and the fanfares overhead. Behind the faeries were two ranks of ten Kyree, each holding a golden rope that supported the ornate black, polished chest, inscribed with gold symbols of the Kyree. Herein lay the ashes of Xian, the late, almost religiously revered leader of the Kyree. Though Aislynn could not see them, she was equally sure from the rumble of feathers behind her that the honor guard bringing the ashes into the courtyard was beating the air in meticulous synchronization with their masters at the head of the procession.

Behind them all was a single, aged Kyree. He did not fly, but purposefully walked behind the procession, one hand on the polished chest, his feet bound in sandals as he trudged the ground, his wings hung outward, and both tips pointing toward the ground.

"Such a wonderful beginning," Aislynn gushed, barely able to contain herself. "I can't think of anything more thrilling."

Shaeonyn held her silence for a time before she spoke. "It will be a long and arduous journey, my Oraclyn-loi, on a road known only by the Kyree through lands we know to be infested with our enemies. What is more, not all our enemies may come from beyond the circle of our traveling companions. It would be to your credit to remember that truth."

Aislynn glanced past Shaeonyn down the single line of faery delegates nervously awaiting their prescribed moment to enter the courtyard as part of the procession. Beyond Shaeonyn to Aislynn's right, the four delegates from the remaining kingdoms struggled to maintain the exacting line dictated to them by Djukan. Of course, Sharajentei—the Kingdom of the Dead—was technically a sixth kingdom, but thus far the original five had not managed a consensus on approving that particularly thorny change in the language of the Fae. Indeed, if the current delegation was any indication, that would be a long time in coming.

Next to Shaeonyn floated Obadon, a tall, broad-faced faery from the court of Lord Phaeon. His head was completely bald—a startlingly unique trait for a faery—and his eyes were a disturbingly intense shade of blue so pale as to seem almost radiant. Though still slighter than the Kyree, Obadon had obviously been an accomplished warrior in the service of House Argentei. Even at a casual glance, it was obvious that so far as Obadon and Shaeonyn were concerned, no known measure of distance would be too great between them.

Next to, and constantly being crowded by, Obadon drifted a female faery of the Second Estate from House Vargonis, a distant kingdom that rested on the southern shores of Mistral Bay on the far side of Mnemnoris. Aislynn knew little about this woman beyond her name—Valthesh—and the fact that she was originally of the Fourth Caste and therefore an artisan. Her appearance, however, was intriguing; she wore her long dark hair in a loose cascade down her shoulders and back, her bangs partially obscuring her eyes. While combed with great care, her hair was nevertheless left unbraided and natural, completely contrary to the elaborate and controlled styles almost universally found among faeries at all levels of caste. Her dark wings, despite the overwhelming pulse of the drums and the horns overhead, continued to beat at their own pace, almost in defiance. A slight smile played at the edge of her lips as her sleepy green eyes moved easily from side to side, surveying the ranks of Kyree around her.

Then there was Gosrivar, an aging scholar from House Shivash. His long white hair ran back from the crown of his head, ending in delicate strands at the base of his fading wings. His chin was soft under the curve of his nose, giving him something of the appearance of a wrinkled bird. Aislynn had enjoyed pleasant conversations with him on the occasions that she had visited Shivash on diplomatic business for her mother's court. But she could not think of why King Sithalian would send such a piece of stiff old leather as his delegate.

Finally, there was the faery delegate of House Mnemnoris, the besieged kingdom whose borders unhappily faced, in one way or another, all of the other Fae kingdoms. His name was Ularis and his skin was far darker than Aislynn's own dusky tones, almost the color of night itself. His hair, however, was closely cropped and light gold like Shaeonyn's, while his large eyes were a chestnut color that Aislynn had not seen before. He wore a beautiful tunic of linked silver rings so small that it was hard for her to make out one from the other even at this close range. Beyond his name and what she had observed, however, Aislynn knew nothing of this young dark faery.

Aislynn decided Shaeonyn was right.

At the head of the procession, Djukan and his lieutenants had flown in stately dignity to the top of the stairs. As if by some unspoken command, they then wheeled as one, folded their wings, and dropped the distance of a single hand-width down onto the top step of the keep. In that instant, the tempo horns and drums above them resounded with a thunderous chorus. The honor guard slowly pulled the golden ropes, raising the platform holding the polished chest until it was among them. Then the honor guard took hold of the long handles on either side of the platform, slowly settled to the ground, and folded their wings as they lifted the bier onto their shoulders.

The thunderous chord suddenly ended, dropping a silence over the assembly more profound than the music.

Aislynn waited breathlessly.

The only movement came from the banners overhead; the only sound from their cloth snapping on the wind.

Slowly, Aislynn became aware of a figure making its way around the right side of the formation. It was the old Kyree who had followed at the rear. He was limping slightly as he moved. His mane of hair was an iron gray that still showed signs of the brown that had once dominated its coloring. He came to stand at the base of the stairs, just in front of the faeries, and then slowly, painfully, lowered himself to kneel, bowing deeply.

Djukan's voice cut through the silence. "Dekacian Sargo, you served our Lord Xian with unreserved honor. Will you now serve his memory in this, the hour of his final struggle?"

The old man tottered gamely to his feet. "I serve Lord Xian to the end of all honor and glory, My Lord."

"Then, Dekacian Sargo," Djukan said, his voice quivering with emotion, "you are appointed Guide of our Fathers. May the aeries of our ancestors smile down the paths of Mount Isthalos and guide you in the ways of honor in your endeavor."

Aislynn caught her breath. Djukan had briefed them all the evening before concerning this part of the ceremony. They were about to take their first step down an irrevocable path.

The old Kyree bowed once more, then slowly stood erect, clasping his hands together near his throat. His voice wavered with age but nevertheless was strong. He turned slowly as he spoke, his words a ceremony called out to all the assembly. "I, Dekacian Sargo, am Guide of our Fathers to Lord Xian of Dunlar! Fear you the honored paths of the dead!"

Djukan stepped forward, descending several steps before raising his fist into the air and calling out, "I beg the honor of following the path!"

"And I," rang out both of his lieutenants nearly simultaneously as their fists, too, were thrust upward.

"And I," Aislynn called out as loudly as she could, her own right arm thrusting her fist into the air. Shaeonyn, too, called out in turn, followed by each of their fellow faery.

"And I," shouted the twenty Kyree behind them, raising their free hands curled into fists.

"To the honor of this house!" shouted Sargo. "To the honor of our fathers! To the blessing of the warrior Xian!" With that, he threw back his weathered head and let out a roaring shout with all the breath in him.

At once, every Kyree present threw back their heads, adding their voices to Sargo's. The shouting grew to a deafening roar as Sargo stepped to where he had followed the black chest into the area—only now he was facing the great doors of the courtyard. The honor guard simply turned around where they stood, changing the hand that gripped the poles on either side of the bier.

Aislynn turned as well. Clever, she thought, that the last of their number should suddenly be first when the procession reversed itself. She wondered if there was truth or significance in that fact.

There was little time for her to contemplate it, however, as the great gates were opening. The procession, now led by old Sargo, took flight and, with resolute beating of their wings, flew at a stately and grand pace through the main gate to the still deafening cheers of the assembled Kyree.

As they cleared the north-facing main gate, the procession turned slightly toward the northeast. Aislynn had a feeling that she had just passed the portals of the life that she knew. Ahead of her lay a dangerous territory whose landscape was unfamiliar to her. Just beyond the horizon of the gentle grasslands of the Shezron Plain lay a land inhabited by Famadorians, the feared enemy of all the Fae, and a vague notion of a sea to cross and a lost civilization to be rediscovered.

One thing above all troubled her, though, as she looked toward that horizon; she had an image in her mind's eye of the figure of a handsome faery with a bright white scar on its wing, beckoning her toward that horizon.

And the wind was pushing at her back.

The Hralan Glade

The glade was the southern outpost of Clan Arvad—indeed, of any of the clans. Nestled in the hardwoods of the Rhesai Forest, the glade sloped downward until it met the banks of the Serphan River. From here the river ran northward twenty miles around a gentle bend and under Fate Bridge before it joined as a tributary to the larger Naraganth. Those were dangerous paths, for the Fate Bridge was the gateway to the Election Fields and its stones had been trod by more armies down the centuries than any other bridge in all of Hrunard. The armies of the Elect from the lands of both the dragons Satinka and Jekard marched proudly to their doom across this bridge, and never in over four hundred years did they return. Though the days of the Election Fields were past, the war that it caused ground on. The rules of war had changed but its purposes remained the same, and thus Fate Bridge was still in use carrying men to their deaths.

Such dark paths were well to the northeast of Hralan Glade, a name taken from an ancient map fragment passed down to the inhabitants of the local small villages—also well to the north—and whose origins had long since been forgotten. It was a place of peace and beauty, blessedly situated out of the way of warring human and dragonkind and therefore remained untouched.

Caelith considered it all for a moment, rooted where he stood on a small knoll rising amid the gentle slope of the glade, his arms folded across his chest. Was this grassy expanse named for some ancient conqueror or just some forgotten local hero? From the sound of it, the name was fairly obviously Rhamasian, but was it a place, or a person, or a feeling, or just meaningless syllables that someone thought pretty? It was idle speculation, he realized, something to keep his mind occupied rather than dwell on the things that were of real concern.

"Master Caelith," came the gruff, familiar voice behind him. "The company is assembled per your instructions."

Caelith nodded without glancing at his lieutenant. "So the mists have gathered, have they, Master Kenth?"

The aged warrior chortled. The company was given the title "Mists of Arvad" by the clan elders in recognition for their service several years before. What had once been a source of embarrassment had since become a label of pride. "Aye, gathered and awaiting your word."

"Would that the rest of our party was as prepared." Caelith frowned, his gaze still fixed across the glade. Several hundred feet away, Margrave was making a fuss in a voice that was entirely too loud about having to leave their wagon behind. Throughout his histrionics, several warriors from his company were trying to load their supply saddles across the back of the braying torusk. The young servant girl did her best to comfort the beast while Eryn Caedon stood nearby studiously ignoring everyone around her despite the horrendous din.

"Which do you think is louder," Kenth sniffed. "The torusk or that plumed fool?"

Caelith cleared his throat and scowled. "What difference does it make; either one could give our position away to any deaf man within ten miles. Honestly, Kenth, I'd prefer a straight-up fight with Vasska himself to baby-sitting this lot on holiday." Caelith suddenly called out down the slope. "Lucian! Why the delay?"

The tall mystic extracted himself from among the supply saddles and jogged quickly up the slope toward them, stopping several feet away and holding his hands up.

"Master Kenth," Lucian asked with a flash of humor in the corner of his eyes. "My good fellow, do you think it safe for me to approach your fearsome leader? The last time I surprised him in his reveries—"

"You became intimately acquainted with a tree, I believe," Caelith finished without a smile.

"Ah, but you do not look nearly as formidable as you did on that day," the tall man said, dropping his hands and casually approaching. "And it is a beautiful day to begin such an adventure as merry fellows. I detest beautiful days."

"You detest them?" Caelith asked, knowing even as he did that he did not want to hear the answer.

"Indeed I do, sire." Lucian nodded in mocking solemnity. "For a beautiful day is never so wondrous as it is in memory—and impossible to enjoy properly at the time. Moreover, I believe bad rehearsals—as our friend Margrave may be inclined to say too loudly and too often—make for good performances. We seem to be starting out, as it were, in the hole."

"Hmm," Caelith grunted in reply, folding his arms critically. "Well, I told you I don't know anything about formal theater, but if you are looking for a bad rehearsal, I think you're looking at one now."

Lucian turned to look back down the slope. Margrave was now in full voice, gesturing wildly about him, barely missing hitting the warriors as they lifted the heavy bags onto the moaning torusk.

"How long has he been doing that?" Kenth asked.

"About half an hour, I should think," Caelith responded. "But I've been watching him; the entire time he has been complaining, he's also been unhitching the torusk from the wagon and packing his traveling pack from his own provisions."

"So, he's getting ready to leave the wagon," Kenth considered with scorn, "but insists on protesting it."

"You know," Caelith said, "I keep thinking that he'll run out of words—but so far they just keep falling out of him."

Lucian drew his head back and laughed heartily. "Very good, old boy!"

"Well," Kenth muttered. "If you'll be excusing me, will there be anything else, Master?"

Caelith glanced over at the craggy, weathered face that seemed somehow uncomfortable with the conversation. "Of course, Master Kenth; check everyone's gear—I'll let you know as soon as we're ready to move."

"At your word, Master." Kenth bowed and slipped back toward the warriors milling behind them.

"I must say," Lucian chimed in brightly, "you have assembled a cheerful outing. Kenth there is bursting with good humor, we have ample entertainment in Margrave's bellowing, and what about the women—handpicked by you, I take it!"

Caelith groaned.

"Oh, come now—can't be as bad as all that!"

"How much worse could it be? That girl with Margrave—what is her name?"

"Anji?" Lucian offered.

"Yes, that's it—why can't I ever remember that? Anyway, just look at her," Caelith said, pointing to where the young woman was standing next to their emaciated and very sad-looking torusk beast, now heavily loaded with their supplies. She was hugging the creature's broken tusk in an apparent attempt to comfort it. "How will she survive?"

"So why bring her?"

"We shouldn't bring her—but Margrave insisted; truth is, he demanded that we bring her," Caelith said brusquely. "Father and I both tried to dissuade him, but here she is nevertheless. In any event, we needed a torusk driver and she apparently has some ability in that if nothing else."

"Two fools for the price of one, eh?" Kenth sniffed.

"Three if you count me for bringing them both," Caelith concluded. "Then there's Mistress Caedon."

"How romantic of you to invite her along." Lucian beamed.

"It was *not* my idea either," Caelith snapped, then took in a considered breath. "Brenna Caedon went to my mother and complained that much as she likes me personally, it would be better for the rest of the clans to have Eryn along as an 'impartial pair of eyes' to corroborate any actual discovery of this 'so-called' Calsandria."

"What does that make me?" Lucian asked in surprise.

"Partial, apparently." Caelith shrugged. "In any event, she talked to mother—mother talked to father, and that was pretty much the end of it. I argued against it but I really didn't have a choice."

"I thought you liked her," Lucian asked with affected nonchalance.

Caelith held perfectly still but could feel the corner of his eye twitch just the same. "She's a fine mystic and a dependable warrior."

"Just a comrade in arms, eh? Well, that's not how I heard it," Lucian purred. "The story that came to me is that the two of you were spending a lot of time together whenever Clan Caedon was visiting. There were even rumors of a few extra and not all that necessary journeys you made yourself to Clan Caedon."

"Distance exaggerates the story in the telling," Caelith said with perhaps a little too much force. "We did see each other but that's apparently all done with now. Besides, I think we have bigger problems that require our attention."

"I assume," Lucian said easily, "you mean our guide."

"I mean our guide," Caelith said.

Jorgan sat in an area of the glade removed from the rest of them. He was motionless with his pack and walking stick next to him, waiting apparently for Margrave to finish his tirade.

"Has he said anything about the road ahead?"

Caelith shook his head. "Only that our path lies up the Serphan River toward a place called Spirit Valley. Eventually we'll be entering the Forsaken Mountains wherein—huzzah—lays our supposedly fair Calsandria. Beyond that he refuses to say."

Caelith looked over at his elder brother—the thought of even having an elder brother jarring him—and wondered how he would ever understand this man. Both he and his father had spoken with the disdainful and arrogant Jorgan over the last week's preparations, trying to get some understanding of where they were going, but the Pir Inquisitas remained calmly aloof and refused to divulge anything of import.

"So, tell me about your big brother," Lucian prodded. "What's he like?"

"I have no idea," Caelith said abruptly. "He always sleeps away from the clan encampment, refusing my mother's repeated invitations to stay with us. He prepares his own meals from his own stores and eats alone. He has been forthcoming when it comes to provisions and supplies for this journey. But there is always an air of contempt about him—contempt and something else that I just don't understand yet."

"Well, maybe that will come in time; after all, you've only had an older brother for about ten days now." Lucian slapped his companion on the back and drew in a deep breath. "You and I are setting forth into the dangerous unknown with your ex-girlfriend, who is both armed and skilled; a storyteller whose voice will call down every deadly creature within ten leagues if we don't find a way to shut him up; his waif of a servant girl, who wisely never says anything; and—lest we forget—your dear long-lost brother, who I strongly suspect might just as soon kill us all as sneeze."

Caelith and Lucian both cast a sideways, skeptical glance at each other.

"Well," said Caelith sourly, "as long as we know where we all stand. We'll need my twenty-seven warriors just to protect us from ourselves."

"Indeed," concurred Lucian. "A good start."

Caelith shook his head with a grim smile, then called back loudly over his shoulder. "Kenth!"

"Aye, Master!" came the reply at once.

"Get everyone on their feet," Caelith snarled as he strode across the field toward where the torusk stood, whining. "Bring the company down and form up in front of the torusk. Let's get this over with."

Eryn was apparently done with listening to the complaints from Margrave and had her hand on the hilt of her sword. Anji could barely be seen cowering behind the enormous bulk of the torusk.

Eryn, Caelith thought. *What gods brought you into this?* He had pushed her out of his mind, buried her memory under a barrow of more urgent tasks and dire circumstances. Yet now she was here again, still beautiful, stubborn, and strong. She was the only thing he ever ran away from in his life and his shame still gnawed at him. He knew strength; it was a thing of battle and survival; it would get him past his doubts about Eryn, too.

"The morning shadows are shortening," Caelith said loudly

enough to cut through Margrave's jabbering. "It is time we were off. Lovich, is that beast loaded yet?"

"Y-yes, Master Caelith," the young warrior responded, pulling quickly on the last strap as he spoke.

Margrave quickly raised his hand and moved toward the company commander as he spoke. "If I might just say a few words, Master Caelith—"

"Not now," Caelith interrupted. "Eryn, did you check the harness on the torusk?"

Eryn shrugged her shoulders, reseating the straps on her traveling pack. "Anji checked it—"

"I didn't ask if Anji had checked it," Caelith said with force.

"Yes," Eryn replied, glowering at Caelith. "I checked the harness and everything is ready."

"Thank you. I guess all we need is the guide." Caelith looked around and was surprised to see Jorgan still sitting exactly where he was before.

"I guess we go to him?" Lucian asked.

"I guess we go to him," Caelith answered, thinking that if every day was going to be this difficult, it would take forever to fulfill their quest, if they ever did. "Master Kenth, get everyone moving; our first journey apparently is to find the guide."

Caelith led the company and the massive torusk across the slope of the glade. There, amid the grasses, Jorgan still sat motionless, his eyes moving only to follow the approach of the group.

"Are you ready, Jorgan?" Caelith asked with exaggerated patience as he stopped in front of the Inquisitas.

Jorgan faced his brother; the crooked smirk remained on his face. "I am always ready—are you?"

"Absolutely," Caelith said, ignoring the tone in Jorgan's remark. He turned around to address the group, assembled now by Kenth in a clear order of march. "Very well. Lovich, Beligrad, Tarin, Phelig, and Warthin—you'll take perimeter for now. Eryn—"

"Mistress Caedon will remain with the torusk while your warriors trail behind," Jorgan said, his voice carrying over Caelith's. "Three scouts will be sufficient in rotation—"

"Inquisitas," Caelith answered with strained patience, "these men answer to me."

"No," Jorgan snapped as he stood up, his slightly larger frame imposing itself over Caelith. "I am in charge here, and you will follow my instructions."

Caelith turned around, his own discipline barely able to prevent his arms from shaking with the rage that welled up inside him. "You are the *guide,* sir," Caelith responded without giving a thumb's-width of ground, "You may know the way, but *I* lead this expedition."

"Excuse me," Margrave chimed in again. "Before we go—"

"'Lead the expedition,' you say?" Jorgan sneered. "To where? It is by the grace of the Pir that you are even being shown the way at all— and it will be by *my* grace that we move!"

"*Your* grace be damned, sir," Caelith snarled back. He could feel the heat of his anger on the back of his neck—as well as the eyes of every member of his company watching this unexpected spectacle with earnest. "Your orders are to be our guide. You show us where to go; *not* tell us how to get there."

"Stop it, both of you!" Eryn stepped between the two brothers, planting her open palms on their chests in turn and pushing, with great effort, both of them back a step. "Not five minutes and you're butting heads? We don't need a pissing match—not now!"

"Then tell this Pir puppet to do his job and lay off doing mine!" Caelith raged.

Jorgan seethed. "You simpleminded bastard son of a whoring . . ."

"Excuse me!"

Everyone turned toward the shout.

Margrave, gaining attention at last, struck a pose atop the heavily laden torusk and spoke. "In the days of the Dragonkings, five heroes struck out with a company of valiant warriors on an epic quest. One was a balladeer of humble reflection who chronicled their adventures, their dooms, and triumphs of fate. Among them were two brothers: one a priest of the Dragonkings, pious and humble in his service; the other the son of the greatest mystic of their age, a powerful and noble sorcerer of the forbidden arts—enemies at heart but joined at the soul. With them came the mystical friend filled with a humble warrior's heart and the woman of mystery whose bow shot straight through the heart of their foes and whose eyes could steal their hearts as well."

Caelith, Jorgan, Eryn, and Lucian all stared at the bard in disbelief. Someone among the ranks of warriors unsuccessfully tried to stifle a laugh.

Margrave was in full dramatic voice as he concluded. "Together—this noble band set out on the greatest quest of their age: to recover the days of glory and the power of their ancestors! Together with one purpose and one heart, the Heroes of the Lost City set out on the greatest quest of theirs or any age!"

"Oh, why don't you shut up?" Eryn said in disgust. She turned and began stalking off to the south.

Jorgan snorted, then turned back to Caelith. "If the show is now concluded, do you think we might move on before the woman tries to get there before us?"

"Yes, I quite agree," Caelith said, his voice carefully controlled. "Lead on—please."

Jorgan turned and began walking toward the south, his dragonstaff swinging easily in his hand with each step.

"Master Kenth," Caelith called ruefully, "let us follow the priest."

With a loud protesting trumpet from the torusk, the assembled company finally began moving down to the riverbank, following it and the course of the Pir priest toward the south.

Lucian chuckled, alone in his slow and hollow applause for Margrave, "Well done, old boy!"

"Did you like it?" the bard asked eagerly. "Of course, it's just a rough idea right now."

"You left Anji out of it, though," Lucian observed.

"I'll put her in later," Margrave said with a wink.

Over the treetops, Caelith could occasionally catch a glimpse of the tall peaks rising to the south. They seemed farther away than ever to him, and yet he knew that their final destination was to the south far beyond.

He glanced once at Eryn.

It was going to be a very long road indeed.

The Quest

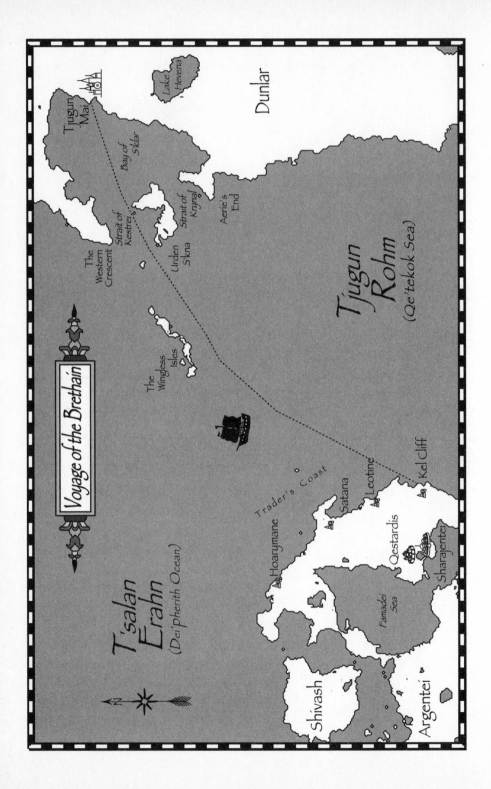

Off the Map

"It awaits you, Aislynn," says the voice behind me. "It awaits all of us."

I drift along the crest of a gentle ridge, carried by a breath of wind, and alight delicately at its crest. As many times as this has happened to me lately, it still seems strange and new to me—a sin against reason somehow. It is not real—cannot be real—and yet here it is in my thoughts and my experience. As I look down, I see what seems to be the great expanse of the entire world, though I know that it cannot be so—it is but a symbol in my mind of other things. Below me is a winding shore whose contours are strange to me. Smoke curls into the sky from tiny villages that lay along the coast.

My eyesight is extraordinary, for I can see beyond the coast to a shore that is strange: foothills with a gleaming city at its base whose towers move and whose walls change at a whim. Beyond the foothills is a great country of towering mountains that seem to touch the veil of night itself. There, between the peaks, is a burning darkness, its rays shooting out from the crags and drawing light and warmth from whatever it touches. There, from its center, emanates a chorus whose words are indistinct, muffled by the ocean and continents between us.

I turn slowly, without fear, toward the voice behind me. I know this voice, although I have never heard it before in waking life. And there he stands. The faery I have seen so often these last few weeks in this other place, his right wing ruined by the long white scar. His long dark hair blows luxuriously about his face from the eternal wind blowing between us. It is his eyes, piercing and filled with pain, that capture my attention. "Who are you?"

"It is not important," he replies with a smile of infinite sadness. "The drama is about to begin, and you must meet the other players."

The world before me flattens and changes so quickly and subtly that I wonder for a moment if it was ever real in the first place. The hill upon which I stand is now a wide floor of polished stone. The distant ocean is roiling fabric of translucent blue that shimmers at my feet, while the hills, cities, and mountains of my horizons have flattened into painted shapes, depictions of reality. The sun becomes a glowing globe above and behind me, the fiery darkness still emanating from between the wooden pinnacles of the painted mountains before me.

"Players?" I ask, uncertain of his meaning. "Is this a game?"

"It is, indeed, a game, but like no game you—or any of your kind—have ever played before," the scarred Fae says as he floats in a circle around me. He is costumed in a baffling array of garments; his tunic bears the color and markings of an artisan—the Second Estate, Fourth Caste—but his cloak is trimmed in the silver of the Musicians Caste—strictly First Estate. His shoes are those of a Gatherer of the Third Estate, yet his collar is carefully inlaid with the golden symbols of the First Caste royalty.

The Sharaj is all so new to me; the vision disturbing. Shaeonyn says that what I see here is a representation of something in the waking world, but that truth does not help me determine what these visions mean or how they are connected. I have no idea what this man bodes by his strange and irreverent appearance.

"Like no game played before?" I ask, struggling to understand.

"For you, it shall be a game and I shall show you the way of it; but we must be quick," he says, gesturing widely with his hand, "for all the world is waiting on us!"

I turn to follow the wave of his hand and am astonished.

The stone floor on which I stand is now a platform surrounded on three sides by a room of such enormity that my senses reel. The floor of this greater space slants upward and away from me, its great curve arching from one side of the stone platform to the other. Three more concourses of balconies are situated above the floor, each arranged with the same arch and slant as the one below it.

More than that, I can see that the entire floor and each of the concourses above it are filled with all kinds of creatures. Faeries from each caste are jumbled together next to the fell beasts of the Fourth Estate; Famadorians of every vile kind and description. Centaurs, satyrs, merfolk, Kyree, and others completely unknown to me; one-eyed giants, wingless men both short and tall, hulking hairless brutes, muscular, gray-haired animal-men with feline faces, and short green monsters with long pointed ears and white tufts of hair on their heads. The sight is appalling to me and grotesque in the extreme; an affront to the natural order.★

The globe of the sun is encased in a box in the ceiling, its light shifting to shine brilliantly on me alone. As it does so, the entire assembled crowd leaps to their feet, shouting, cheering, and clapping their hands together with a frightening enthusiasm.

"You see how you are adored by the world?" the scarred faery whispers to me through the tumultuous noise. "Give them what they want and they will always love you!"

"Is that the game?" I ask, still frightened by the overwhelming noise of the mob.

"It is part of it—but only a part," he says comfortingly. He then flits around me, floating between me and the crowd. "Ladies, Gentlemen, and Good Beings, the great show is about to begin! A comedy! A tragedy! A place of masks and illusions, deceptions and betrayals! The strings of the puppets are pulled, the curtain is drawn and—behold our players!"

★The faery were racial purists at the time and had been for several millennia. They held a firm belief in the divine superiority of their race and their manifest destiny to lord over all "lesser creatures." This was maintained through a rigidly strict and fanatically maintained caste system. As difficult as it may be to consider such thought in our own age, Aislynn's comments here must be taken in the context of her time.

I turn once more toward the flat depictions of mountains be-
hind us. From between them come several creatures onto the stone
floor; three wingless men—two tall and one short, a wingless
woman, three faeries, and two of the small, ugly green creatures
with the tufts of hair. To my astonishment, each of them is wear-
ing a covering over their face; an artful depiction of a face.

"And where is your mask, Aislynn?" the scarred faery asks.

I am suddenly deeply ashamed.

The dark-haired faery snickers, then pats my head as though I
were a little child. "That's all right, Aislynn. You won't need
one—and it probably wouldn't do you any good anyway."

FAERY TALES

BRONZE CANTICLES, TOME VIII, FOLIO 3, LEAF 10–13

Aislynn awoke with a start in the darkness.

A hand closed over her shoulder. "Steady, Princess, it's almost time."

Aislynn shook from the chill on her shoulders and drew her cloak in tighter around her. She must have fallen asleep as they waited at the edge of the woods for the night to deepen. It came as no surprise to her; the long days of travel had left her tired to her very bones.

She wondered idly to herself whether all such adventures start out gloriously and so quickly collapse into a kind of numbing boredom shattered by moments of abject terror. Their trip had started with the pomp and ceremony of the Kyree funeral. Once they had passed the first few grassy undulations of the Shezron Plain, they made their rendezvous with the three supply cloudships, held there by Kyree volunteers who had brought the supplies out and loaded them into the gondolas suspended from the floating globes. These were merchant cloudships, not nearly as elegant or sleek as the nightrunners that Aislynn was used to riding in during her travels on behalf of Queen Tatyana. Obadon questioned momentarily just who had supplied the cloudships for the expedition, seeing as they were clearly of Qestardian design, but Djukan assured him and the rest of the faeries that no favoritism was involved; the ships had been purchased by the Kyree for the expedition and therefore belonged exclusively to the winged warriors. Moreover, Djukan said with a hint of conceit, the cloudships would be propelled not by the usual slave castes of the faery but by beasts trained for the purpose. Djukan then called out a flight of Pegasi, great winged creatures with dark eyes and four strong legs. The Kyree proceeded to fit the monsters in specially crafted harnesses, much to the astonishment of the faeries, for the Pegasus is known to be untamable. The Kyree clearly had a knack for it, however, for the winged beasts took flight on command, six of them to a team, before each of the three cloudships. The astonished faeries fluttered to catch up, each struggling to take a place on one of the pitching cloudships before they were left behind. Smug Kyree took to the air themselves, laughing at the faery, who could not keep up.

The cloudships moved quickly over the ground; more quickly than their design accounted for, making them bump along, bobbing and jouncing with every whim of the air. Soon the grasslands of the Shezron rolled under Aislynn and her companions in a monotonous but constantly uncomfortable flow.

Their first day ended with them settling onto the open plains, the Kyree posting watches through the night. The second day saw a repetition of the plains beneath them, ending only when they descended to the banks of the River Karga. It was the last landmark she knew by name, the boundary between the Shezron Plain and the unknown and unknowable lands of the Famadorians.

The third day found them skimming just above the treetops of a great forest which carpeted the nameless, undulating low hills. Just as the sun was setting, the ships crested one last tree-covered rise, and Aislynn saw for the first time the vast Qe'tekok Sea. She wondered aloud if it were possible to see the other side. Djukan laughed at this; the Kyree knew it to be at least five times wider than any sea the Princess had ever seen before. She could not comprehend it and silently decided for herself that the idea must have come from stories told by Famadorian seamen—and were, therefore, lies.

As the day closed, Djukan directed the cloudships hidden in a clearing surrounded by a thicket of trees. The encampment set and the guards posted, Djukan announced that he and Sargo would be going into the port town to the north to secure a ship for our expedition. The distinguished Fae representatives, Djukan made clear, would remain in camp for their own protection, as the presence of so many faery in the town would most likely cause more trouble than was necessary. Even Obadon was eventually satisfied as to the wisdom in this.

Aislynn, however, had kept her silence and never agreed to anything. She had known Djukan for the entire span of his life, yet she still did not trust him despite having dealt with him both personally and formally on several occasions. Or perhaps it was because she had dealt with him before; he was even more mercurial than most Famadorians, judging by the few she knew. He held his own people above all others—a sentiment which Aislynn could easily understand—but he was rash to judgment and often stood in obstinate and unreasonable defiance of the truths the Fae represented.

Shaeonyn, noticing the young Oraclyn's silence, mentioned to Aislynn that the development bode ill. The Fae should be represented at any such critical meeting or who could say what arrangements might be made against them. Yet, the senior Sharajin frowned, who among them could move among a city of the Famadorians without fear for their lives?

Aislynn, fingering her dark pearls, knew it was up to her and felt perfectly justified in following the two Kyree into the night. Djukan was outraged when she caught up to them within an hour of their leaving, but Aislynn stood firm in her insistence on joining them on their expedition—and even Djukan could not argue with her reasons.

Now, Aislynn sat quietly hiding next to Djukan and Sargo at the edge of the unnamed woodland, gazing down wearily through the thickening night on the Famadorian port of Kel Cliff.

The town itself was an abomination. The buildings were entirely angular with no curves or architectural delicacy. They appeared to be made of butchered wood,* hacked, shaved, and stabbed with iron into shapes that reflected the Famadorians' bad taste. Its streets were also crooked and angular, with stones hammered into place as paving. It reminded Aislynn of an even more grotesque version of the City of the Dead.

---

*Faery architecture deals with shaping living wood through Surface Magic rather than the cutting, planking, and nailing methods used by most other races.

It had two redeeming features, however; it sat curled around a small harbor at the base of towering white cliffs. And there, above the horrible slanting and crooked rooftops, swung the gently undulating tops of several sets of masts.

"What do you think, Sargo?" Djukan asked in a whisper.

"Looks about right, sire," the old Kyree replied, peering down into the streets, which began nearly three hundred feet of open ground away from where they waited. "The lights in the town are dying down on the edges. Most of them are bedding down for the night. The seaport taverns, however, will be another matter entirely."

"As we intended." Djukan smiled, flexing his wings slightly to push out the stiffness. He turned back to Aislynn. "This is really no place for you."

"We've been over this, Djukan," Aislynn huffed. "You cannot enter the town in force, but you cannot guarantee you can leave without it. I am your best hope on both accounts." Aislynn fingered her black pearls in the moonlight.

Djukan cast a skeptical glance at Sargo.

The lieutenant shrugged. "Sire, she's right. The other faery may not know about the magical warriors in those pearls, but I've fought them in your father's time and it is only by the choice of the fates that I live to tell you about it."

"Fine! When I walk into this den of thieves, I'll take comfort in knowing I'm being watched over by a faery and her jewelry," Djukan mumbled, then turned to Aislynn. "Follow me closely, don't make any noise, and if you see or meet anyone—for Skreas's sake, just keep walking!" He turned back to the town, gave it another look, and then sprang out into the open field.

Sargo leaped after his young master, a long leather case slung across his back. Aislynn took in a deep breath and followed as well into the cool night breeze.

The moonlight was strong coming through the open clouds streaming over the ocean, illuminating the darkened streets of the town in shades of deep blue. In moments the open field gave way to narrow streets winding between ramshackle buildings, which Aislynn felt sure were leaning precipitously over her head. The blackened windows to either side held mysteries that she dared not consider, while the occasionally lit portal she studiously ignored, unwilling to witness what might be going on inside. She was convinced that in the heart of a city of monsters, everything happening must be of dark and dire consequence. It had not occurred to her that she might observe the normal commerce of life; that the centaurs' one-story homes with their wide doors and open interiors might reveal a stable of mares and their children huddling together for the night. Her mind could not imagine that the tall, multistoried buildings might display nothing more evil than satyrs eating their evening meal, or that the fauns and nymphs would be engaged in nothing more nefarious than unwinding from the toils of the day. So Aislynn, faery Princess of Qestardis, kept her eyes averted, concentrating on Djukan's quick feet ahead of her and holding on to the aged Sargo with a grip so tight the old warrior actually winced.

Strange, she thought, that she should cling so desperately to one Famadorian out of fear of others of his kind. Perhaps the evil one knew was of more comfort than the evil of the unknown.

The village smelled of wet hair and rot, but as they turned yet another corner, the smell changed. It was both fresher and riper all at once, a tangy bite in the air. The ground in front of her gave way from stones to weathered wooden planks. She hesitated to step on them, horrifying as they were, but the thought of losing sight of Djukan was more terrible than the violated wood. She plunged ahead, her fingers tightly gripping Sargo's arm.

Djukan's legs stopped before a building that rose in their path. Only then did Aislynn look up.

The structure was shoddy, even by Kel Cliff's low standards. The paint that had once adorned the construction was all but missing, scrubbed away as time and wind sought to etch their own mark. The carved wood sign swinging over the doorway depicted a monstrous serpent wound around a large tankard, which overflowed with some sort of foam. Beneath it, in Fae shortscript,* Aislynn was surprised to read "The Kraken's Flagon."

---

*Fae shortscript is a symbolic representation of concepts or names in phonetic format used to convey simple ideas and truths without extensive detail. Rarely considered complete, it is not used in polite conversation, as it is too low a form of language for anything but signage and map work, where brevity is more important than totality.

It occurred to Aislynn that she had been so focused on not seeing anything in the town around her that she had no real idea how she had gotten here or, worse yet, how she might get back out. Looking about her frantically, she realized that they had passed completely through the village itself and were now standing on the crude quays of Kel Cliff's harbor. Several tall-masted ships were at anchor in the curving bay behind her, the white cliffs to the north shining under the moonlight. The only way out would be through the town, and Aislynn was sadly sure that she would be immediately lost in its maze of streets and unable to find her way.

Djukan, standing before her, ruffled the feathers of his wings and carefully folded them flat against his back. After a deep breath, he pushed open the door in front of him, plunging into the fire-lit room within.

Aislynn followed at once, determined not to think before she acted lest she talk herself out of it.

Shouts, sounds, and smells assailed her. The common room of the inn had a low ceiling supported by massive sagging beams that threatened to come down on the heads of the varied and terrible patrons under it. Since it was rather late, the room was not crowded, but to Aislynn it felt filled beyond tolerance. To the right of the door, three satyrs warmed themselves before a great blazing fireplace, its light spilling over the room. As she watched, one of the satyrs tossed another piece of cut wood onto the fire, its heat making the space pleasantly comfortable for the satyrs, though increasingly uncomfortable for everyone else. Standing next to one of the tall tables, a pair of male centaurs glowered at the satyrs and took long, thoughtful draughts from their tall flagons, their tension seeming to increase by the moment. A long, high counter of dark wood ran almost three quarters of the length of the far wall and was tended by another centaur, larger than either of the others in the room, who was washing out tall ceramic mugs without seeming to notice, or care, about the noisy satyrs by the fire. A rickety staircase—a unique feature of Famadorian architecture*—led past the bar upward, presumably to more rooms

---

*The winged Fae do not have stairs, since they simply fly to the various levels of their buildings as need requires.

above. A wet, ripping sound came from one of the tables where a hulking creature covered in coarse brown fur with sharp horns sprouting from the forehead of his hideous flat face tore with relish into the cooked flesh of some beast that topped the dull, metallic platter that had been set before him.

Ailsynn's impact on the room was instantaneous. One of the satyrs, seeing her, sharply kicked the one next to him who was jabbering away to get his attention. The creatures in the room then turned almost as one toward the door, a profound silence descending over the scene as all the beastly eyes trained themselves on her.

Aislynn trembled, frozen under their gaze.

"Cor!" crooned one of the satyrs, his red eyes flashing by the light of the fire, his long tongue flicking over his sharp teeth, "lookin' as a faery queen gracing the pub, mates!"

"Ner so yer noticesess," a second satyr added, a wide grin splitting his face nearly from ear to ear. "She's a love come for me! Her price yer no making, Kakh!"

Aislynn could not make herself move or speak.

"Ner so either," said the first, rising from his chair, his cloven hooves rattling against the floorboards as he moved slowly closer to her, "she er love me fair free!"

TWANG! The satyr's face was suddenly obscured by a round iron cooking pan swung with vicious speed by the huge centaur who had come from behind the bar. The satyr limply dropped to the floor, unconscious.

"Pardon, lady," the centaur rumbled. "No trouble my pub, see?"

Aislynn looked into the lantern-jawed face of the huge centaur. Unsure of what he had said and what was happening, she was stuck shaking before him.

Djukan reached for her free arm, guiding both her and a rather amused Sargo toward the alcove booths at the left side of the bar. "Remember? I said to just keep walking! Never mind—just sit down and try to stay out of trouble!"

Aislynn slid onto the bench, looked across the table, and tried desperately to shrink into the corner of the booth.

The creature across from her that leaned back with a defiant airiness was a Famadorian man unlike any she had ever seen or heard of. He was barrel-chested and incredibly muscular, and he wore a long coat open to his narrow waist and a tight cloth that wrapped the top of his head and tied at the side. His face was vaguely reminiscent of the Kyree and might have been considered handsome, if it weren't for his black-tipped, flat cat's nose, feline eyes, and the layer of shorn gray fur that completely covered his face and body. When he smiled at her, she could see his sharp incisors.

"Well, if it isn't one of the high and mighty herself," he purred, "come to pay us a visit in our own humble dwellings."

"What are you?" Aislynn blurted out.

"Now, isn't that an interesting question, mates?" the creature said, winking at Djukan and Sargo, who had just sat down next to Aislynn. "I'm a new truth for ye, dearie! That's what you faery are all about, isn't it, new truths? Well, never mind the name then—I'm a Mantacorian; does that help?"

Aislynn shook her head.

"No," the beast said, casually leaning back again, "I suppose not."

Djukan turned to Aislynn. "This is Captain Bachas of the brigantine *Brethain*. Captain Bachas, this is Aislynn of Qestardis."

"Ah, a fine name from a fine nation," Bachas responded, smiling, his fangs glinting in the firelight, "though I've never before had the pleasure of meeting any of your fellow Fae."

Aislynn swallowed. Her hand was shaking beneath the table and she could not seem to make it stop. She could hope only that no one noticed.

"Are you ready?" Djukan asked quietly, as he leaned over the table.

"Always ready, mate," Bachas said, leaning as well. "Though the crew is a bit nervous about this entire affair. Not me, mind you—I trust you with my life—but the *crew* would like to know there is a little proof regarding our destination and our—understanding as it were. They would hate to think they were sailing into the watery gulf with naught on the other side but promises."

Djukan turned to Sargo and nodded. The older Kyree reached behind his back and freed an old leather case. Unscrewing the top, he reached inside and pulled out a large, rolled piece of treated papyrus.

"Just a moment, lads," Bachas said, holding up his long-fingered hand. He turned to face the bar. "Hhruhr! My friends here are parched! Ales for—what, do you say, gents?—ales for the three of us and, oh, something nice and sweet for the lady, eh?"

The centaur barely looked up as he nodded.

"There." Bachas smiled again. "That's more friendly like. Please, do go on."

Sargo glanced once more at Djukan, who nodded. Then he placed the scroll on the table, unrolling it carefully until it was only partially open.

"This is the Famadei Peninsula here," Sargo said, pointing along the arch of land. "Here is Kel Cliff—up here is Leotine, Satana, and Hoarymane."

Aislynn leaned forward, examining the map as well. She recognized the outlines of the coasts at once. It was Sine'shai, her own lands, they were talking about, but the names on the map were all wrong.

"Trader's Coast." Bachas shrugged. "I know it like my own smell."

"No doubt." Sargo smiled, and then unrolled the papyrus slightly more. "Here, however, is the Tjugun Rohm—the great sea of the east. Look here; these are the bearing markers, times, dates, headings."

Aislynn considered the names and the territories. *The Tjugun Rohm? They must mean the Qe'tekok Sea.* This map was obviously not drafted by the scholars of the great hall. This was a Kyree map whose borders extended far beyond the realms she knew; a map of lands the Fae had fled in the ancient times and whose memory was now lost to them.

"Aye," Bachas said more soberly, "with such markings a man might sail such seas and make the port of his choosing." He then leaned back, his large, long hands knitting comfortably behind his head. "But what ports would they be, mate? My crew would not be satisfied with visiting some backwater village with nothing to show for it but some fish, eh?"

Sargo carefully unrolled the map a little more.

Djukan cocked his head to one side. "Well, with one such map one might find the Wingless Isles."

The captain leaned forward slowly, his eye never leaving the map. "Now, *that* might be worth the crew's attention." Bachas casually reached forward to splay the scroll even further. "But surely there are other ports of call beyond which—"

Djukan's hand latched onto Bachas's wrist, arresting its movement above the parchment. Sargo quickly rolled the papyrus back up, slipping it quickly into its case.

Bachas snatched his arm back with a low growl.

"There are other ports indeed." Sargo nodded, his voice low and even. "Ports which are our destination. They contain the wealth of the lost Kyree Empire; more wealth than your ship could possibly hold. I know, for I sailed these same waters when the empire fell and I alone am left who knows the way."

Just then, the large centaur appeared at the table and conversation ceased. Aislynn dutifully accepted her tall flagon and surreptitiously sniffed at it. It smelled sweet and fruity, though there was something about it that reminded her of the cleaning preparations her hand-maids had used to wash her mirrors at home. Nevertheless, it had been ages since she had had anything to eat or drink and everyone else seemed to find it acceptable.

"Then, gentlemen, I believe you have convinced my crew of the rightness of your cause," Bachas said, after the centaur had made his way back across the floor. He took a deep draught of the dark liquid.

Djukan and Sargon hoisted up their own flagons, tipping them slightly toward Bachas before taking their own long swig.

Aislynn was too thirsty to question the offered Famadorian fare and took a long pull on her own drink. It had a slightly bitter taste, as though the fruit had been left out too long, but it felt warm on her throat. Still, it seemed harmless enough.

"We have provisions," Djukan said. "Provisions and people that are better boarded beyond the sight of prying eyes."

"Understandable," Bachas said, nodding, drinking deeply before he continued. "I entirely agree. Personally, I wouldn't want anyone knowing what we were about either—it always gets so messy when there's competition about, eh?"

Aislynn took another swallow, the liquid coursing down her throat. It was not all that bad once you got used to it. At least it no longer reminded her of cleaning preparations.

"What do you suggest?" Djukan was beginning to sound to Aislynn as though he were speaking from a great distance.

"There is a cove about three miles south of the harbor, popular with smugglers," Bachas said. "Or so I've heard. We could meet you there at high tide?"

That seemed like a good idea to Aislynn. The tide would be a good thing. She loved the tide. In fact, the tide was probably her most favorite thing in the world.

Aislynn finished her flagon before anyone else at the table found the middle of their glass. Bachas thought it only polite to order her another as she apparently liked it so much.

It was the last thing she remembered.

Djukan was tired; more exhausted than he could recall. He pushed aside the flap of his campaign tent, which had once been his father's, and rubbed his hands across his eyes. His wings shuddered suddenly, trying to shake off the weariness they carried.

Within, his lieutenant had already made preparations for his return. A lantern shone with a warm light in one corner while his Kyree field perch, a three-legged cot strung with a sleeping canvas, was set up and waiting for him. It looked inviting, beckoning him to settle into its comfort before the inevitable hangover arrived.

He turned toward the east, yawning wide as he did so. He knelt down unsteadily on one knee and bowed his head toward a land that he had never seen and the tombs of his ancestors he had only heard about. As he knelt he thought of his father and the fathers before him. It was difficult through the haze in his mind, however, and he decided his ancestors would be better served by remembrance in the morning, thundering head or no.

He rose carefully, if unsteadily, to his feet. He kicked off his boots and fluttered his weary wings to position himself over the center of his perch. His weight settled into the center of the welcoming canvas as Djukan folded his wings around him, his head coming to rest near one of the supporting poles.

He sighed and closed his eyes. It was that faery woman, he thought. Bad enough that she had forced herself on their rendezvous in Kel Cliff, but to have to carry her back, passed out and senseless, was intolerable. Sargo had been highly amused, but Djukan failed to see the humor. They had dumped her, snoring loudly, among the supplies in one of the cloudships. The night would be warm enough and better she should sleep her intemperance off among the rest of the baggage.

Djukan closed his eyes and sighed.

"Master Djukan!"

"Go away," the Kyree leader groused, keeping his eyes resolutely shut.

"Master Djukan, I must speak with you!"

"By Skreas," Djukan roared, uncurling his wings and angrily, if not entirely steadily, flapping himself out of his perch. "Enter and be damned for it!"

The tent flap pushed aside, revealing the face of a young Kyree warrior with field-brown wing feathers. He seemed reluctant to come farther.

"Thush," Djukan rumbled the name in his throat. "What in the name of the ancients could possibly justify disturbing me now?"

"Master," Thush spoke with surprising resolve considering his nervousness. "I am the lord of the dead watch tonight."

"Please tell me," Djukan replied, running his hand over his tired face, "that you haven't come to report."

"Master," Thush said and swallowed before continuing, "I was setting the watch per your orders. I know we just sent the sentries out to their posts, but I thought I should check on them tonight—you know, personally . . ."

"Very commendable." Djukan sighed, closing his itching eyes. "I'll give a good word to your captain when we—"

"No, sire," Thush interrupted. "I found something."

Djukan opened his eyes.

"Something I think you need to see, Master."

The stars were brilliant in the clear sky, not yet obscured by the moon in its rising. They shone down on the small clearing in the woods with a soft blue radiance that painted the grasses and surrounding woods in stark contrast, illuminating two winged creatures, their eyes cast downward where the gently waving tops of the grasses were marred by a depression.

A third figure lay among the grasses, still and unmoving, frosted eyes staring up without seeing the glory of the night sky.

"Who is it?" Sargo's whisper was gruff.

"One of the Fae ambassadors." Djukan knelt down among the tall blades of grass. His eyes were more than adequate, for the Kyree could see well in starlight, preferring to do their hunting and warring at night. "I don't recall—Ularis, I believe was his name."

"What killed him?" Sargo asked. "I don't see much blood."

Djukan stood back up, his sharp features softened as he looked quickly around. "Not what—but who; it wasn't animals, or they would have dragged off the body. Fae are supposed to be good eating, or so I've heard. There's only one wound to the body and it's precise. Someone wanted this faery dead and did a very tidy job of it, too."

Sargo's eyes narrowed. "It might be the work of one of the natives. The Fae are always going on about how these Famadorians are all out to get them."

"No, Sargo." Shaking his head, Djukan knelt down once more. "Look at the grasses here. It's all compacted but just in this one place. The Fae are proud and foolish but more than anyone else they know how to run from an enemy. Ularis would have just taken flight— look, his wings are undamaged. Then there's the wound itself." He pulled his own dagger, prodding at the wound, probing its direction and depth. "Slit him just under the rib cage and straight into the heart—with a blade that is thinner than my own. You'd have to be standing directly in front of him and probably need to be holding him with your free hand just to get the blade in far enough. The Fae never let anyone get close enough to them to inflict this kind of wound. Unless—"

"Unless—what?"

"Unless they knew the person." Djukan rose.

"So, Ularis knew the person who killed him?" Sargo chuckled. "It had to be one of the other faeries then."

"So it would seem."

"Well, whoever it is, this should be simple enough," Sargo responded. "We'll just ask each of them if they killed Ularis and they'll confess. Faeries can't lie."

"That's what they keep telling us," Djukan said flatly, "though I'm not yet convinced that's true."

"A faery that lies?" Sargo said slowly. "Well, in any event, this will certainly delay the mission. Once the faeries learn that this fellow is dead—"

"We aren't going to tell them."

"Sire?"

"Not yet, anyway," Djukan said, turning toward his aged friend. "Our quest is too important to let something like this stop us."

"But if we have an assassin with us?"

"Better we deal with him in a place where he cannot escape," Djukan said, turning his face to the east and into the breeze from the shore. "The Fae cannot fly far without exhaustion, my friend—and it is far, indeed, from shore to shore."

Tjugun Passage

Hang him high from the billowed sail
Toss him over the leeward rail
Tie his belt to a hitch and he will not flinch
'Cause a Dead Man does not pinch!

Aislynn came most reluctantly to her senses. Some deep voices far away were singing. Their guttural sounds penetrated an enormously painful fog that seemed to be somewhere inside her head. There was also unbearably bright light on the other side of her eyelids and she felt in no hurry to open them—or do much of anything else for that matter. Her head seemed to be lolling from side to side for some reason, her forehead rubbing against something cool and hard. She was surprised to be able to move her arms and managed somehow to reach up. Her hands closed around something angular and hard, so she pulled herself up slowly and cracked open her eyes.

The world was slanted so badly that she had to close her eyes for a moment before she could try coping with the world again. When she opened them again, things had not improved much. She was looking out through a window, she was certain, but beyond was the sea and its entire horizon was tilted at a strange angle.

"No," she murmured through a distinctly horrible taste she found in her mouth, "the horizon is fine; I'm tilted."

"Princess Aislynn," a voice said behind her. "How are you feeling now?"

Aislynn turned unsteadily. She discovered she was sitting—or, rather, lying limply—on a long bench situated just below a curving row of windows. The cabin was wide, although the ceiling was entirely too low even by Famadorian standards. Gosrivar, the aging Shivash faery, stood leaning back against a large, heavy table which occupied most of the room's center. Valthesh sat leaning back in one of the ugly carved chairs, her booted feet casually crossed upon the table's edge and her arms crossed impatiently in front of her. Obadon stood near a door situated in the center of the far wall. He did not seem to want to look at Aislynn. The Princess could not tell whether the Argentei warrior was listening for danger from outside the room or from within.

That accounted for the faeries except . . .

"Shaeonyn and Ularis?" Aislynn asked at once. "Where are they?"

"The Sharajin is—how do they say it—she is on deck," Gosrivar said a little too quickly. "But you have not yet answered my question: how do you feel now?"

Aislynn took a deep breath. "My head aches. It pounds in ways that I had not thought possible. This is one new truth I really would have preferred not to learn."

"Famadorian drink," Obadon grumbled. "I would have thought the First Estate of Qestardis would have known to avoid such common poisons."

"My desire was diplomatic," Aislynn asserted, managing to sit up on her own.

"Yet your result was nearly catastrophic," Valthesh said calmly. "The House of Qestardis has suffered some humiliation, I would think, in having its favored daughter brought back from Kel Cliff rendered completely senseless by an act of her own choice while in the very center of a Famadorian township—worse still for having to be hauled aboard a Famadorian ship with all the dignity of a sack of beets."

"I well note your—enthusiasm regarding my social standing," Aislynn said, reaching up to rub her temples with both hands.

"Not to mention that it may have contributed to other losses," Obadon griped.

"*May* have?" Valthesh asked with a droll inflection.

"Other losses?" Aislynn looked up, blinking her squinting eyes as she tried to concentrate. "What other losses?"

"Princess Aislynn," Gosrivar responded with a sigh, "the emissary of House Mnemnoris is missing."

"What do you mean, missing?" Aislynn replied, shaking her head to clear it and immediately regretting the action. "We're on a ship— how far could he have gone?"

"He means," Valthesh spoke just as the old Shivash faery drew a breath to answer, "that Ularis never came aboard. He has disappeared."

"The last time anyone saw him was last evening, before you chased after Djukan and entered that vile Famadorian town," Gosrivar continued, annoyed at being interrupted. "He spoke to Shaeonyn shortly after you left. He said he had an urgent message for you, then left down the same road you took. You didn't see him?"

"No," she answered, puzzled. "I don't remember seeing him."

"As I understand it," Valthesh said with a smirk, "you didn't remember seeing anything at all past a certain point."

"In any case"—Gosrivar's words cut emphatically into the conversation—"he never returned to our encampment. Obadon instituted a search for him but found nothing."

"He may have been taken on the road by Famadorians," Obadon mused darkly. "A lone faery would have been a tempting target for renegade centaurs and certainly easy prey for their meal."

Aislynn felt the color drain from her face at the thought.

"We do not know the truth of what happened to Ularis," Gosrivar said quickly. "In any case, we were forced to come to the anchorage and load our own provisions aboard this boat. We left signs for him to follow us, but as the tide was going out, we were forced to set sail without further delay."

"Set sail?" Aislynn suddenly realized. "You mean—we've already left the shore?" She turned at once toward the windows behind her, grasping hold of the open sill and thrusting her head out.

She could feel the stiff breeze crossing her face from her right. By the motion of the water below, she realized that she was at the back of the boat, the ship cutting a path through the waves beneath her. She raised her eyes toward the horizon, which still seemed somewhat tilted to her. It was a single, hazy, and unbroken line as far as she could see.

"We've left!" she yelped, her voice breaking slightly in her surprise.

"Why, yes, Princess," Gosrivar replied, "several hours ago, in fact—wait! Where are you going?"

Aislynn had reached her feet only to bang her head against the low ceiling. This amplified greatly the pain already throbbing behind her eyes, but she was determined and walked unsteadily toward the door at the front of the room.

"This is not wise," Obadon said flatly, his right arm blocking the door.

"You will let me pass." Aislynn said it as a matter of unquestionable fact.

"We have lost one of our number already on this expedition," Obadon said with equal force of fact. "I would not risk the life of another of the High Caste so quickly."

"And you let Shaeonyn leave before me?"

"That is different," Obadon said too quickly. "She is . . ."

The Argentei warrior lapsed into silence.

"She is what, Obadon?" Aislynn returned hotly. "A Sharajin witch? It is well known to us Argentei's opinion of Queen Dwynwyn and her Sharajin. You would do well to remember in the future, Obadon of Argentis, that the Sharajin came to that place of death not out of choice but through the compelling power within them—a power, sir, which they did not seek and which many of them would gladly deny if they but could."

Obadon stood straight as best he could in the cramped space, his eyes smoldering.

"In the future, you might remember Shaeonyn's life to be as precious and worthy as my own," Aislynn said with an easy force that years at court had taught her. Her stomach was beginning to roll as badly as the boat. "Now, I *will* be going out, as I am badly in need of fresh air. If you think it dangerous, then perhaps such a great warrior of the Argentei should accompany me. Otherwise, you should get out of the way before what is left of last night's dinner becomes part of your wardrobe."

Obadon's brows rose precipitously and he gracefully stood to the side, opening the door and holding it for her. Aislynn thought there was a smile played lightly across his lips as he did. "Who would stand in the way of the determined Qestardi royalty?"

Aislynn stepped into what appeared to be a very narrow hallway, grateful that there were railings mounted along the walls to help steady her in her passage. Once, she stopped completely and closed her eyes, trying desperately to stop the world that seemed to roll all around her. When she felt it safe, she opened her eyes once more and half walked, half pulled her way around the corner of the corridor and opened the bright-windowed door at its end.

The sight that greeted her took Aislynn aback, stopping her where she stood at the base of a ladder that rose just off her right hand. The main deck of the ship spread before her in all its busy glory. An amazing and complex system of heavy lines and tarred cables reached from the deck railings up to the masts, whose tips seemed poised to pierce the sky. The enormous complexity of the ship was nothing compared to its crew. Across the deck was a wide and terrifying assortment of monsters: Mantacorians clad only in trousers, the fur of their muscular upper bodies shining with sweat in the sun; a fair number of Arachniads, most of them aloft in the rigging but several others of their half-spider kind clattering across the deck on their hard-clawed legs; a pair of satyrs, who were jabbering at each other in their own inexplicable tongue, and, judging from their gestures, were about to come to blows.

"Well, well," came a familiar rough voice above and behind her. "I see that you've risen at last."

"Captain Bachas," Aislynn said weakly as she folded her wings carefully behind her. The Fae Princess turned carefully on the gently pitching deck and grasped hold of the ladder's railing tight enough that she thought her hand might break. It felt comforting, somehow, to be in as close contact with anything solid around her as possible. She slowly and deliberately climbed to the quarterdeck. "I have risen indeed, though I feel more as one who has come back from the dead and, in truth, am not sure as yet that I have fully returned to the land of the living." Aislynn reached the top of the ladder and quickly latched on to a thick, tarred cable from the mainmast. The cold, hardened tar coating felt greasy under her hand, but it steadied her in a world that seemed incapable of steadying itself.

Bachas stood easily before the helm, seeming to enjoy the pitch of the ship as it moved under him. Aislynn had never met a Mantacorian before Bachas. They were tremendously muscular creatures, roughly the shape of wingless faeries although larger in build and with legs whose knees bent after the manner of the satyrs. Their faces were rimmed by a mane of the same fur that apparently covered much of their bodies, framing their deep-set, piercing eyes and black, flat-tipped noses. They also had a disquieting way of baring their fangs when they smiled.

Two other Mantacorians stood on the quarterdeck as well, one near Bachas and the other holding the great wheel of the helm steady. Beyond them, Djukan stood against the far rail, the wind blowing through his hair and a look of blissful amusement on his face. Shaeonyn was aft, her hands and arms lying easily on the rail she was leaning against.

"Where are we, Captain Bachas?"

"We are at sea, madam," the Mantacorian said, his muscular arms folded across his barrel chest. There was amusement in his yellow eyes. "Indeed, some of us appear to be more at sea than others. My apologies for not tending to you personally, but your companions felt it best that you remain in your cabin until you were—how best to say it?—more fit for proper company."

"I might well agree," Aislynn said, closing her eyes once more for just a moment. "I am not certain that I care for my company right now either."

"And I am certain of it," Shaeonyn said disapprovingly. "Oraclyn-loi, your dress is indefensible; where are the robes of our order?"

Aislynn drew in a deep breath. "I have not yet had the opportunity to dress, Shaeonyn, and I have no servants to attend me."

Bachas bared his fangs as he smiled, shaking his head. "Faeries!"

"Nor shall you," Shaeonyn said stiffly. "An Oraclyn stands alone in the world, trusting in nothing but their gift of the Inner Truth and Sight."

"Yes, Shaeonyn."

"You have much to learn, Oraclyn-loi." Her mentor spoke disapprovingly.

"Yes, Shaeonyn," Aislynn repeated, turning to descend the ladder and return to the cabin. She momentarily lost her footing on the deck, however, catching herself by swinging from the hand that still gripped the backstay. Regaining her footing, Aislynn glanced up once more. Above her she saw the dizzying array of ropes leading up to the masts on either side of her. Some of the sails were billowed open while others remained gathered up. As she watched, the top of the mast swayed back and forth with the motion of the ship beneath her, scribing wild paths against the racing clouds overhead.

Aislynn's stomach lurched once more and she felt her limbs shaking. "Captain Bachas?"

"Aye, madam," the captain answered, amused.

"Are we making good time?"

Bachas lifted his head as though to smell the air. "We are on the reach with ample sail and a following sea."

"Is that good?"

Aislynn could see the sneering smile on the face of the helmsman. Bachas laughed loudly before he turned to face her. "It is good. We are, as you say, making very good time indeed."

"How long, then, before we get to—to where we are going?"

"That, of course, assumes that I have been told where we are going," Bachas said with a chilling smile, "but my best estimate says that it should take us only a month—two at the most."

"Two—*months*," Aislynn gasped. "Two months at sea—like this?" Suddenly, the Princess realized her stomach could no longer be either ignored or denied. She turned quickly, leaning far over the railing, and heaved what little remained in her.

Bachas seemed to take no notice as he glanced across the deck of the ship, surveying it as he thought, *Like this? Yes—if we are lucky.*

Aislynn shuddered and heaved once more.

"Welcome, Princess, to the *Brethain*."

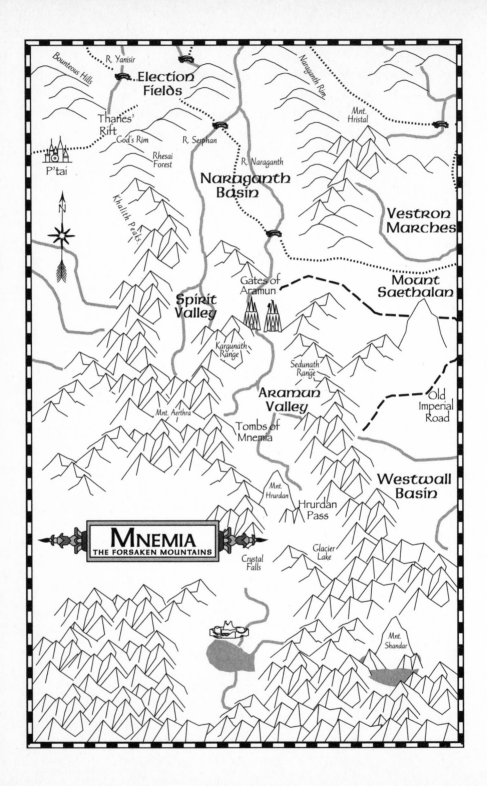

Gates of Aramun

The Forsaken Mountains, as they were known during the reign of the Dragonkings, formed a continent-spanning region, a maze of smaller ranges and intermittent valleys extending roughly from the Enlund Delta southeast to the shores of the Sea of Rhamas. It encompassed the Urlund Expanse at its northwestern end, but was largely known as a land that was truly to be forsaken; those few who ever returned reported a land barren and bereft of value. The lure of the ancient Rhamasian wealth called many opportunists to explore its secrets, but if any of them had penetrated to the interior of that lost empire they did not survive to take credit for the achievement.

THE COMMENTARIES OF IGNASTUS
BRONZE CANTICLES, TOME XXI, FOLIO 13, LEAF 12

"Master Caelith!"

The mystic commander's eyes sprang open, his mind desperately reeling in the threads of his dreams. He stood somewhat unsteadily from his bedroll, trying to get his bearings. "Yes, Master Kenth, what is it?"

"Begging your pardon, sire." Kenth was looking away uncomfortably. "It seems the Inquisitas has decided it's time to go. He stood up a moment ago, said his usual 'this way' and started off on his own."

"'This way,' eh?" Caelith repeated gruffly. "That's all the notice any of us have had every morning since we began this—this outing. 'This way,' the man says, and damn the rest of us. Have the outer sentries reported back as yet?"

"No, sire," Kenth answered. "They weren't due back until the sun broke over the camp."

"Well, they'll just have to catch up to us wherever we are." Caelith sighed. The chill ground was hard under his feet, but he welcomed the chance to move. The cold night and ground had stiffened his muscles and he relished warming them up again with a good stretch of his legs and a fair piece of ground moving under them.

Not that their current location was a bad one. The trees around their encampment were the softwoods of the higher altitudes situated as a lush carpet of forest in a gap between Mount Kargunath on the north, the rest of the Kargunath Range to the south. From the small clearing nearby, they could look down on the beautiful expanse of Spirit Valley to the west and the bright waters at the confluence of the Greater Serphan and Lesser Serphan Rivers below. Caelith normally would revel in the strong scent of pines and the beauty of an occasional stand of aspen, but he was leery of staying in one place too long.

He was certain that they were being followed.

"Master Kenth?"

"Aye, sire?"

"I want you to send ten scouts out from the company—five pairs of two," Caelith said, shouldering his pack. "Trail three pair; one to our rear and the two others on our left and right flanks following the line of march. Send the two remaining forward to the left and right. Have all of them keep us just in sight and together; I don't want anyone out there running into trouble alone."

"You expecting danger, sire?" Kenth asked.

"Let's just say I'd prefer to know about it before it's entering my house," Caelith responded. "We'll rotate the assignments at noon—and get the company up and moving before we lose sight of our guide altogether."

"Yes, sire," Kenth said, pressing the open palm of his right hand against his left shoulder in salute. He turned, nodding toward the tall mystic as he approached. "Sire Lucian, good dawning."

"Good dawning to you, Master Kenth," Lucian, his traveling pack already shouldered, said as he stepped up to Caelith, his voice discreetly lowering as he approached his friend. "Though what there is good in it I'm failing to see. Is that our guide stomping off on his own toward the brightening east?"

"It is," Caelith responded, glowering through the trees at the figure that was growing small by the moment.

"And did he give his cheerful and ever popular command?" Lucian asked.

"You mean 'this way'?" Caelith huffed. "He did indeed."

"Ah." Lucian nodded. "And here I was afraid he wouldn't tell us."

"Keep that to yourself," Caelith smiled more to himself than his companion. "It's better if he thinks he's in charge."

"So long as he only *thinks* it."

"Where is Eryn?"

Lucian nodded behind them. "Back with Anji and Margrave. They were having a little trouble getting the torusk back in harness this morning, but they are ready to move now—not that it matters to our fearless guide."

Caelith shouldered his own pack, letting out a low guttural rumble. "I don't know how much of a leader he thinks he can be without anyone following him. One of these days, he's likely to lead himself into oblivion. He'll look back and none of us humble old followers will be there to pull his fat out of the fire."

"Well, old boy, if he *does* wander off all alone," Lucian said with a smile, "I only hope I'm there to watch."

Caelith was about to say something but was stopped short when he considered the remark. He decided that silence was a better response, turned, and started to follow their Inquisitas guide. He could barely make out Jorgan walking through the woods ahead of them

So far as Caelith was concerned, the farther ahead the better.

They had traveled nearly seventy miles south from their point of origin, following the banks of the River Serphan, climbing slowly through the Rhesai Forest until the river spilled out through rougher terrain between the Khalith Peaks on the west and tower Mount Kargunath on the east. The way through that terrain had been more difficult; they had to pick their trails among the boulders and out-croppings on the western side of the angry white water until they passed the gap. There, in the Spirit Valley nestled between the Kargunath and Telgunath mountain ranges, the upper river was wider and far calmer. The company forded the river on their eighth day at a wide spot three miles below the confluence. They stopped to pro-vision with fresh water, but Jorgan had continued heedlessly on, and they were forced once more to continue their march, turning and climbing toward the eastern gap.

It was during their brief stop at the fording that Caelith noticed the movement in the trees. It was nothing more significant than a flushing of birds taking wing about three miles behind them. It was insignificant by itself, yet there were other signs that followed over the course of the next two days as they climbed eastward out of Spirit Valley, signs that added up to an unknown companion tracking them and their movements. At first he sent out individual scouts to discover their stalker but none had returned with any success.

It galled him, Caelith thought, glancing behind him with frustra-tion, that he could not find this pursuer. He hated the unknown. It was always the unseen blade that struck you, the missed dagger that found you in the back. You do everything you can—plan for every possible outcome—and it is always that one, unconsidered power that cuts your knees out from under you.

"You have told Eryn about our mysterious guest, haven't you, old boy?" Lucian asked casually.

"What?"

"You were thinking about our unsolicited companion in the woods," Lucian said as they walked along. "I mean, it only stands to reason that—"

"Yes, I have told her," Caelith snapped. "She's the best tracker we have. Besides, if I hadn't told her—"

"She would have figured it out for herself," Lucian finished, "and then you would never have heard the end of it. Of course, you'll never hear the end of it from *me,* but then I suspect you've grown accustomed to that by now."

Caelith often found himself out of step with Lucian's thoughts. "Never hear the end of what?"

"Why, never hear the end of how our most secret mission—known only to the members of the Six and, say, about thirty-five trusted traveling comrades, not to mention a guide who is otherwise our sworn enemy—seems also to be known by a party thus far completely unknown to us." Lucien's tone was more serious than either of them were used to. "I mean, it's all well and good we have our own little holiday traipsing about in the woods and mountains and all, but I cannot abide—nor trust—an uninvited guest."

Caelith nodded ahead of them. "What about him? He may very well know who is trailing us. I'm thinking we should ask him."

Lucian considered for a moment, then smiled. "Oh, the problems of command seem to weigh heavily upon him. Why should we burden him further with an actual threat—especially when he is so generous as to be at the very front of the expedition?"

Just then, Eryn padded up behind them. It was a conscious gesture of politeness on her part; Caelith knew that had she wanted to, her approach could have been absolutely silent.

"Your friend is still with us, Caelith," she said quietly as she joined them.

"I posted scouts," Caelith groused. "It shouldn't be this hard. Are they close?"

"Let's just say I would not advise looking in his direction right now," she said quickly. "He's moving higher up the saddle to the south."

" 'He'?" Caelith asked. "You think there's only one?"

"Yes—and he's getting ahead of us."

"Really?" Lucian asked with surprise. "Do you suppose he means to intercept us?"

Caelith shook his head. "If he had meant to catch us, he could have done so on his own by now."

"Your sentries and the wards would have killed him." Eryn was gnawing at her lip—an old habit that always signified to Caelith that she was frustrated or upset. "Of course, if he knew we set up Deep Magic wards to defend us at night . . ."

"Then he wouldn't approach that way," Caelith agreed.

"Well, whoever it is, they don't appear to move very quickly during the day," Lucian observed.

"And yet they are still getting ahead of us," Caelith said, shrugging.

"Which means they are also moving at night." Eryn nodded, pulling out her bow. "I could track him down if you'd like and we could all have a nice long chat with him."

"No, not yet," Caelith said slowly as he considered. "He's an unknown. If we're going to do something about him, I think we should act in numbers."

"It will need to be soon," Eryn said, replacing the bow across her back.

"I agree." Caelith nodded. "We'll give him one more day, and then if he hasn't shown himself by then, we'll act. Meanwhile, I'll get with Kenth tonight and see if we can come up with a plan. How are our other traveling companions faring?"

Eryn looked away for a moment and drew in a deep breath. "Did you know that Mount Kargunath was once the site of a quest by some guy named Adena-something-or-other whose beloved woman, Princess Forget-her-name, had thrown herself from the peak in a fit of depression over being married to an evil king whose name is unpronounceable. The story of his triumph and tragedy in climbing the mountain only to find his beloved woman's face now a part of the peak is—I assure you—a tale that takes hours in the telling and the ending of which you are going to force me to endure if you make me go back and tend those two helpless souls once more."

"What?" Lucian said, his eyebrows arched high. "The tale of Adenathanar and Ummathrace? That's a classic play; I've seen it several times."

"You sat through a play that was seven hours long," Eryn said in complete disbelief, "more than once?"

Lucian looked at her askance. "My dear, what are you talking about? It was two hours of the finest theater in all of Enlund!"

"Well, if you enjoyed it," Eryn retorted, "then perhaps *you* could go back and hear the long version from Margrave."

"Thank you for your offer," Lucian said as he bowed to her, "but I think I may prefer the shortened version."

"No doubt. Carry on then, good sirs; I wouldn't want to miss the big finish," Eryn said.

"I say," Lucian asked, looking over at her. "Dangerous a woman as you appear to be, are you sure our new friend is a man?"

"Of course," she replied with an edge to her voice as she stopped, letting the two men continue. "Who else would sneak off in the night without a trace?"

At that, Caelith's face flushed beet-red, but he kept his stride without missing a step.

By afternoon, the company of mystics had left the saddle between the peaks well behind. Now, spread out in a vista before them, the southern reaches of the Naraganth Basin sloped upward from the north. Down below, the Naraganth River curved inward as it ran to the north, winding its way into the basin, eventually, Caelith knew, to make its way across the distant plains of the Dragon's March. To the northeast, in the far distance, he could barely make out a hazy line, dust, on the horizon—the road from Ost Batar, the city at the heart of Satinka's lands in southern Bayway.

"What is that, sire?" a voice came from behind him, young and eager.

"That, Master Lovich," said Caelith quietly, "is an army on the move."

"An—army, sire?" Lovich responded in awe.

"Yes," Caelith answered with a sigh, folding his arms across his chest. "Probably sixty miles away from where we stand, six thousand—maybe ten thousand—swords are moving toward doom or victory. That's the billowing dust from the feet of warriors whose time has come or is about to end—the poor, noble souls. Don't worry, Lovich, they're too far away to even see us, let alone do anything about us."

"By the gods," breathed Master Kenth as he pointed to the southeast. "Have you ever seen the like?"

Caelith turned, his eyes following a broken, sweeping scar that cut down the center of the Naraganth Basin below. It was all that remained of the Old Imperial Road—its once fitted stones all but reclaimed by the grasslands, weeds, and the blowing dust. Its line led directly to the ruined glory known as the Gates of Aramun.

The entire company stood there for a moment, all halted by the spectacle except Jorgan, who heedlessly moved ahead of them a little way down the slope. The vista of the ancient towers, built by the hands of a centuries-dead empire, stunned them into silence. Even Lucian was at a loss for words. Eryn stood next to Caelith. She was as beautiful as he had ever seen her, her short reddish hair blowing away from her eyes in the gentle wind. He longed to share this moment with her but did not know how to bridge the years. Would there ever be a time in this journey when he could try to voice words that had been too long silent between them? He wondered how he had let things go so terribly wrong. He turned, washing his face with the wind and feeling alone again in the midst of so many.

"Have you ever seen the like before?" Kenth whispered as they stood in the meadow looking toward the south.

"No." Caelith turned back to look at the gates and consider them with reverence. Battlement walls extended from the slopes of the mountains through a series of delicate turrets. Most of these had fallen, but the two great towers standing watch over either side of the gate itself remained. The top of the eastern tower had collapsed but the dome atop the western tower was still intact. Sunlight through the broken clouds played across the valley, casting shadows and light across the entire scene. Caelith whispered almost to himself. "It is beautiful."

"To this day, no one is certain of their purpose," Margrave intoned, injecting a hint of mystery in his voice. "Yet what is known is tantalizing. There never was an actual gate per se, but the towers on either side of the river were worshipped by the ancients as the sentinels between which flowed all the wealth of Rhamas down to what they knew as the Northern Provinces. The towers represented two of the greatest gods of Rhamas—Hrea and Ekteia, the gods of justice and mischief . . ."

"Justice and mischief?" Eryn said. "Both in the same place? That makes no sense."

"But you see, it made perfect sense to the Rhamasians," Margrave said. "They believed in balance in all things and accepted the aspects of both these gods as symbols of the order of the world. Hrea was the more powerful of the two but was always kept in check by his own humility and sense of honor and law. Ekteia constantly challenged his rule but her powers were always too limited."

"Her?" Eryn asked ruefully.

"Well, no one is really sure whether either of them was male or female." Margrave shrugged. "The Rhamasian language itself uses pronouns that are gender-neutral and the descriptions that have been found talk of both of them as being man or woman. In either case, these ruins you see before you represented them as the watchers of the Northern Provinces and the patrons through whom flowed all the bounty of Rhamas. Barges loaded with goods of every kind from the Gold Coast of southern Rhamas and lands beyond would float down the Naraganth like the lifeblood of the empire itself. Then Rhamas, fell; Calsandria went silent and one day commerce along the Dwarven Road from the south simply halted. The lifeblood of the empire dried up, and with it, the empire died. Now those towers mark the boundaries of the Dragonkings' lands and the beginning of fallen Rhamas, where their silent gods stand watch over lands long lifeless. They stand as the guardians of the Valley of Aramun, where the Tombs of Mnemia were carved into the base of Mount Aerthra and paths that only the dead are allowed to walk."

Caelith looked askance at Margrave.

"Well—so they tell in the tales." Margrave grinned.

"Well, there's one thing I think it is safe to say: it is not dead down there," Eryn said, stepping up next to them and pointing. "There, at the base of the western tower."

Caelith looked closer, then his eyes widened. "Smoke!"

"A campfire by the looks of it." Eryn nodded. "It seems our friend has made camp."

"That has to be a good fifteen miles!" Caelith said with wonder. "How could he get such a distance over us?"

"Who are we talking about?" Margrave asked with a nervous smile.

"Oh, not to worry, old fellow," Lucian said easily, slapping Margrave on the back. "Just an acquaintance of ours—no one, I'm sure, whose name you would recognize."

Margrave nodded, though without assurance. Jorgan was walking back up the slope toward them. "There is a small glade down the slope to the south. It is about five miles but we should make it easily before nightfall. Good shelter and well hidden from the valley floor. We shall make camp there for the night."

"You know of a hidden glade five miles from here?" Caelith asked skeptically.

"You find everything hard to believe—that is your weakness, brother," Jorgan said in bored tones. "Has my information thus far been wrong?"

"No," Caelith said through tight lips. "Your information has been very good thus far."

"A little too good," Kenth muttered under his breath.

Jorgan turned to the craggy warrior. "Perhaps you would prefer to wander through these mountains under your own aimless guidance should you find the accuracy of my information in question. My instructions are quite specific and have no room for your petulant pride or your snide disdain. I know of only one path to our destination—a specific path walked and charted long before any of us—and any deviation from that path will be disastrous, is that clear?"

"Most clear, sire." Kenth bowed as slightly as he could.

The Inquisitas turned from them all and began walking once more down the mountain path.

"This way," he said, motioning them to follow, without looking back.

Eryn adjusted her pack and began to move forward, but Caelith reached out and took her arm, holding her back.

"Hey," she began to protest.

"We're camping five miles to the south," Caelith said quickly, his eyes still on the distant tower. "Jorgan's taking us to the towers. Our unknown guest is apparently already there, but I'm betting he knows where we are going to camp already."

"Let go of my arm," Eryn said.

Caelith released her but she did not move.

"What is your point?" she said.

"Our uninvited friend will be only ten miles away," he replied. "Just far enough for the two of us to do a little scouting on our own."

"Sire," Master Kenth interrupted, shaking his head, "we've got lads in the company for that kind of work."

"Normally I would agree, but this fellow has proven slippery more than once, and now he builds a fire that can be seen for miles."

Eryn nodded. "You think it's an invitation, is that it?"

"Yes, and I think we should be the ones accepting it."

"You're sure this isn't just some way of getting me off in the woods . . ."

"Hey, have I ever been that subtle?"

Eryn sniffed. "No—not once."

"Then what do you say?"

Eryn considered for a moment. "All right. If his camp smoke is still there by nightfall, we'll both go. But Jorgan isn't going to like it."

"Then why ask him?" Caelith grinned. "Master Kenth, a few words with you if you please as we catch up with our guide once more. I believe tonight I'm going to stretch my legs."

Caelith and Eryn slipped out of the grassy mountain bowl of their encampment shortly after nightfall, quickly making their way down the eastern slope of the Kargunath. It was a cloudless night, the quarter of the waxing moon obliterating all but the brightest stars in the sky. Its light was welcome, however, as it was sufficient for their vision and sped them on their way. The two then worked old paths of forest game southward among the foothills until they came to the banks of the Naraganth River. This would be their guide, for the Naraganth passed between the Gates of Aramun.

Caelith reveled in the night. Unburdened of their packs—not to mention the lumbering torusk or even his company of raiders—he and Eryn were free to traverse the land as quickly as they wished. It was exhilarating for him to dash across open country, the grasses whispering behind him as his legs brushed their blades in the night.

He was moving with purpose and speed and free from duties and responsibilities. His feet padding quickly across the ground, the fresh night air filling up his lungs and open land as far as he could see— Caelith felt more alive and joyful than he had in years.

There at his side was Eryn, matching him step for step, stride for stride along the grassy banks of the river. He could hear her breathing next to him, sense the determination in her movements. Why had he left her? Why had he broken her heart so callously? He knew that there had been reasons at the time, but their importance and urgency seemed to be fading with every stride they took. Not that it mattered now, he thought. He knew her too well to believe she would ever take him back. He ached just to slip his arm about her waist and kiss her as he had so many times before. Awkward words of apology and explanation rose unbidden to his lips. He swallowed and realized that in this still and dark canopy of night, silence was more healing than anything he might say or do.

Yet out here in the night, it seemed to Caelith for just a moment that it might be possible for the two of them to outrun anything— even their past.

The tower was older than anything Caelith had ever seen. There were other ruins of Rhamas scattered across Hrunard, but none could come close in their history to the ancient Gates of Aramun. There was a crude elegance to it, Caelith thought as he gazed on it under the scant moonlight; a demonstration of superiority and might. For who now had the skills or the power to build such a structure? It was nearly three hundred feet wide at its base and certainly rose more than a thousand feet in height at the topmost tier. The original alabaster had been stained by time, causing ancient figures in the carvings to appear to weep.

Still, he reminded himself, this was not the reason for their coming. A stand of scrub oak trees had laid claim to the area between the river and the base of the enormous tower. Both Eryn and Caelith could make out the light of a brilliant campfire still blazing away somewhere amid its rough bark and twisted trunks, its smoke still curling up past the tower as it had since earlier that day.

Caelith and Eryn exchanged looks at the edge of the stand of trees. Eryn quietly pulled her bow, nocking an arrow onto the bow-string. Caelith noted there was a deep blue glow around the edges of the arrow—Eryn had summoned mystic powers. Caelith readied his own staff, searching within himself for the touch of the Deep Magic, and was reassured when he felt it there, channeling into the staff through him. As prepared as he could be, Caelith stepped carefully between the gnarled trunks of the short trees.

It was difficult to move forward silently. Despite the dampness of the ground, the thick layer of old leaves threatened to crackle noisily at their every step. The thick trees impeded their ability to move eas-ily through while keeping track of each other in the darkness, as the leaves and limbs of the trees overhead obliterated the scant moon-light. Still, they were on the hunt and the adrenaline rushing through Caelith urged him on, the light of the fire becoming brighter before him with every cautious step.

Caelith paused at the edge of a small, stony clearing. He was cer-tain Eryn was somewhere to his right, though he could not see her now. In the midst of the clearing, a carefully laid ring of stones con-tained an enormous, blazing bonfire. The larger pieces of wood were arranged carefully in a tent-pole fashion, leaning against each other, the fire blazing upward about them. Nearby, a large pile of cut wood was stacked and next to it lay an open bedroll and a pack.

Caelith considered the scene for several minutes. Someone had made camp here, and whoever it was had gone to a lot of trouble to get ahead of them and then announce his presence in as conspicuous a way as possible. Moreover, it would be far better for the stranger to show himself first to Caelith, rather than the other way around. At least it was evident from the pack and bedroll that Eryn was right; there was probably only one individual involved rather than a group. There were mysteries and peculiarities here and Caelith feared the unknown, but his mind eased somewhat over the risks they were running; he felt confident that he and Eryn could handle any indi-vidual presented to them.

Time passed and Caelith was content to wait out the stranger. He was in no hurry to give up any advantage, single opponent or not.

Eventually, he heard a rustling coming through the brush on the other side of the clearing.

Tense, Caelith readied his staff as he once more drew on the Deep Magic in his mind.

A short figure emerged from the trees on the other side of the bonfire. Caelith was having difficulty seeing clearly around the towering flames, catching only glimpses of a stocky body clad in what appeared to be traveling clothing. He could hear the sound of heavy boots stomping the ground and the rumble of a deep voice. Then the squat figure stomped around the ring of the fire pit, shouldering a massive axe in one hand while dragging a long section of cut tree trunk with the other. His face was framed by a nimbus of wild hair that stuck straight away from his scalp and merged with an equally wiry and erratic beard. All of the hair was held in place by a broad piece of thick red cloth tied over his eyes.

Caelith laughed loudly and bounded into the clearing, startling Eryn, who, as it turned out, was crouching with her bow drawn not twenty feet away from him.

"Cephas!" Caelith called in genuine amusement. "I never thought I'd see the day when I could sneak up on you."

"Caelith Arvad," the old dwarf rumbled, a wide grin splitting his dirty face. "Nay ever could sneak up on this blind dwarf er is!"

Tombs of Mnemia

"Would you mind telling me what all this is about?" Eryn's words stabbed at the night air. "Who is this—this . . ."

"Dwarf, ma'am," Cephas said with an extravagant bow. "Cephas be common a dwarf as er is."

They all stood next to the blazing fire Cephas had prepared, its bright flames obliterating all but the brightest stars above them.

"He's an old friend of the family," Caelith said, shaking his head, "although *how* old is anyone's guess."

"You *know* this thing?" Eryn glowered.

"This lass excited as er is," Cephas chortled. "Be she chasing you all this way?"

The female mystic's face flushed noticeably even in the warm light of the fire. She took a threatening step forward, her fists raised. "Why, you filthy little . . ."

"Easy, Eryn," Caelith said, stepping smoothly between Eryn and the dwarf. "This is Cephas Hadras. I'm surprised you haven't met him before now; he and father have been practically inseparable since before the clans were even formed."

Eryn eyed the dwarf with sudden recognition. "You're Galen's dwarf—the one who fought at his side on the Election Fields?"

"Aye, that er Cephas be." Cephas smiled, exposing his widely spaced teeth. "Twer I what taught Galen his metalcraft back when he were but a sprout. Cephas and Galen were a friendship forged, yer might say!" The dwarf threw back his head and laughed heartily at his own joke.

"Fine!" Eryn huffed, turning to Caelith, "but what is he doing here?"

Caelith folded his arms across his chest, considering. "Looking for us, I suppose."

"Looking for us?" Eryn repeated. "A *blind* dwarf's been looking for us?"

"Nay," Cephas rumbled, shaking his wide, dark head, driving the ends of his frizzed hair to bounce back and forth. "Cephas not looking er Caelith; Cephas waiting till *found* er be."

"Now what is he talking about?" Eryn was exasperated.

Caelith turned toward the dwarf, whose eyes were always tightly bound under that ubiquitous thick red cloth. "I suppose what he means is that it would have been dangerous to approach us. I'd posted both sentries from the company and a rather serious set of mystical traps around our encampment each night. He's been gone so long that most of the members of my raiders wouldn't know him on sight; most that did are either dead or replaced. Coming to us might have provoked a nasty response—but by getting *ahead* of us and building this absurdly large fire . . ."

Cephas flashed his wide grin once more.

Caelith shook his head and smiled knowingly. "It was safer for him if we found him rather than the other way around."

"Caelith sharp as onyx." It was an old dwarven saying of approval. "Come, this old dwarf has to join yer quest er quick as Cephas heard. Long and far er I searched for yon Calsandria; belike me now to feel her stones under my hands, if real they be. How came Caelith by this path when old Cephas walked the wild south er these ten months with no result?"

"We have a guide," Eryn said flatly.

"Things have changed a great deal since you've been away," Caelith interrupted. "Calsandria may be the only hope for the survival of the clans."

"Surface-folk be talk of changes always." Cephas shrugged casually. "Dwarves know the mountain stone; rain, wind, or snow, the mountain remains er is. Surface-folk always worry for change. Dwarves know better; nothing new. Who be this guide er is?"

"A Pir Inquisitas," Caelith said with studied ease, watching for the dwarf's reaction.

"Caelith's guide be of Vasska's priests?" The dwarf's brow furrowed with thought.

"Yes." Caelith nodded. "He and the rest of our company should arrive tomorrow. My guess is sometime early in the afternoon if they keep their pace. Then the next morning we'll pass between these ancient towers and look in earnest for Calsandria. And there is one other thing—this Pir Inquisitas that is our guide . . ."

"Aye," the dwarf coaxed.

"He's apparently also my older brother by Berkita," Caelith said quietly.

The old dwarf sat down so suddenly that clouds of dust exploded from his clothing. "Break my bones!"

"So now do you think nothing new er is?" Caelith asked.

"Sit!" the dwarf commanded. "Tell the old dwarf your story from first to last!"

It was late in the day by the time the Inquisitas arrived at the Gates of Aramun with the rest of the expedition in tow. It had taken them that long to coax the torusk down out of the mountains and follow the wide plain southward to the towers. The sun was just touching the tops of the western mountains, their long shadows reaching across the valley floor toward the ancient ruins.

"An armed camp er is," Cephas said. "Arrive here er long, eh?"

Eryn nodded, though the gesture was lost on the dwarf. "And just when you predicted, Caelith."

All three awaited the approaching company from the north, but Caelith did so with a special satisfaction. Kenth must have done his duty at the beginning of the day, telling Jorgan where the missing Caelith and Eryn had gone, why and where they expected to meet up with them. Now, the dust from their feet shining in the afternoon light, his company and the lumbering torusk behind them were approaching. Everything had worked out better than he had planned it; he had discovered that their mysterious and potentially dangerous follower was a friend and ally; and had done so without losing any time on the journey.

Jorgan was in front of the company, as usual. That Caelith managed to get to the towers ahead of their guide also filled him with a smug satisfaction that he had to admit was worth reveling in. He called out to the company as they approached. "Welcome to the Gates of Aramun—what kept you?"

Jorgan looked up as he approached, his eyes locking momentarily with Caelith's. The look, however, was inscrutable, his face devoid of any reaction or emotion. The Inquisitas brushed past Caelith as though taking no further notice of him, the rhythmic swinging of his staff continuing without hesitation.

Caelith turned in anger, his smoldering gaze following his brother. He had expected—well, he was not sure *what* he expected— but some reaction.

"Who be that?" Cephas asked.

"Jorgan," Eryn said before Caelith could answer. "Notice any resemblance?"

Caelith's head snapped back to glare at Eryn, who returned his gaze.

"Sire!" called the familiar voice from the company.

Caelith turned, standing a little straighter. "Ah, Master Kenth! I see that you have managed to get my company back to me in one piece."

"Aye, sire, that I have." Kenth smiled wearily.

"Eryn," Caelith asked quickly. "Please take Cephas over to Lucian. It's been a few years but I'm sure Lucian will remember him."

"Fine," Eryn said without enthusiasm. "Just how do I do that?"

"Take my hand er lass," the old dwarf said. "Then this blind old dwarf won't get lost."

Eryn wrinkled her nose and reached down for the dwarf's outstretched palm. It was wide, dirty, and calloused, but she held it nonetheless.

"Thank ye, lass," Cephas said with a blissful smile.

Kenth watched the two of them walk through the milling warriors in the direction of the torusk. "I thought dwarves were *never* lost."

"They aren't," Caelith answered lightly. "But Eryn doesn't know that."

"Well, it seems you've at least made a dwarf happy today," Kenth said.

Caelith turned, grasping the shoulder of his lieutenant firmly with his right hand. "More than I can say for you, I'm sure; I hope the priest wasn't too hard on you."

Well, sire," Kenth began, sighing. "I've served long enough to know that bad news bodes ill for the messenger. That's a soldier's lot, isn't it, sire: to deal out punishment to his enemies and to endure it from his masters?"

Caelith chuckled darkly. "That it is. I'm sorry, Kenth; it couldn't have been pleasant."

"That's just it, sire," Kenth returned with a puzzled look on his face as he nodded toward where the Inquisitas was walking toward a platform of stones at the base of the near tower. "I told him, but all he did was raise his eyebrow and say, 'The poor fool doesn't even know how little he knows.' Then, calm as you please, he tells me we need to reunite the company with—begging your pardon, sire—with their 'blunderingly heroic captain.'"

"What?"

"I'm just repeating his words, sire." Kenth, old warrior that he was, still flinched. "I mean, I've seen men yell, hit, draw a weapon or cook off some deep magic in a rage at such news—but I've never seen anyone just *smile*. I mean; it ain't natural-like, sire."

Caelith looked back at Jorgan. The man was settling with his back against the stones at the tower's base, gazing out over the clearing where the smoke from the previous night's fire still curled skyward.

"Thank you, Master Kenth," Caelith said absently. "Have the company set up camp here for the night. We'll try to make an early start in the morning."

"Aye, sire," Kenth acknowledged, then turned, his voice booming. "All right! Break out your gear, we're making camp for the night."

All the while, Jorgan sat with his back against the wall, his legs crossed in front of him. Caelith watched him for a while before seeing to the evening meal.

Jorgan never spoke, nor did he move.

The sun was climbing higher into the sky, its rays streaming between the clouds that were gathering. The sun has risen over the towers since before time was counted yet never before on so curious a scene as this particular morning as it lengthened toward midday with agonizing slowness.

The company of warriors stood in their ranks, shifting occasionally from foot to foot. The torusk beast stood pawing occasionally at the ground, held in its place by a thin, silent female barely more than a child. The representatives of the clans of mystics shuffled back and forth in concern but did not speak. Even the bard was silent. Caelith stood with his arms crossed, fuming.

Across the clearing, Jorgan sat as he had since the previous afternoon, his staff laid over his crossed legs, his eyes closed as his head rested against the stone wall at his back.

Lucian stepped up to his old acquaintance, fully aware of the signs Caelith was giving of exploding at the slightest provocation. "Isn't he supposed to say 'this way'? I mean, every morning since we started he says 'this way' and then we all 'this way' with him; isn't that how it is supposed to work?"

"He was supposed to say it over an hour ago," Caelith responded through clenched teeth.

"We've got to do something," Eryn said.

"I could hold a sword to his throat," Caelith seethed. "That might get his attention."

"Why don't you just *talk* to him first," Eryn snapped.

"She has a point, old boy," Lucian interjected. "I mean, it would be hard to converse with him *after* you slit his throat."

"Fine!" Caelith huffed. "We'll talk to him!"

"We?" Eryn sniffed. "What do you mean, 'we'll' talk to him?"

"This was your idea," Caelith growled. "Kenth! Set the men at ease but keep them in order. I'll be right back. Now, as to the rest of you, let's go."

Caelith crossed the clearing with quick purposeful strides, the rest of his companions quickly trying to keep up. He leaped up onto the platform of ancient, fitted stones and stood towering over the Inquisitas, who sat with his eyes still serenely closed.

"It's time, Jorgan," Caelith said flatly. "Let's go."

The Inquisitas opened his eyes and fixed them momentarily on his brother—then closed them again.

Caelith could feel his companions looking at each other uncomfortably, unsure as to whether to involve themselves or not.

"Sit down," Jorgan said calmly.

"There's no time for . . ."

Eryn caught his eye. She was shaking her head in warning.

Caelith held his breath for a moment, then slowly sat down on the stone platform.

"You are worried about the discipline of your troops," Jorgan said, his eyes still closed. "They are seeing their commander—whose word must always be obeyed—defied by a Pir priest who does nothing more than sit still. You are wondering what would happen to your ordered world if they all just sat still. This from a man who cannot sit still himself; who is so obsessively controlling in other's lives because he is so uncontrolled in his own life. Ironic, is it not, brother?"

Hair stood up on the back of Caelith's neck. This was not what he wanted; not what he needed now. "I realize now that I should have consulted—"

"You deserted the rest of us to pursue your own selfish whim, but I don't know why I would have expected any more from you." Jorgan shook his head. "You're the bastard son of a man who walked out on his wife to pursue a debased and corrupt life. Come to think of it, considering the family history of abandonment, I don't know why I would have expected anything less."

"I did what was best for the safety of everyone in this company," Caelith rejoined.

"The brave hero makes us all safer by sneaking off into the night?" Jorgan sneered, opening his eyes for the first time, fixing their penetrating gaze on Caelith. "We're about to enter lands that no human has walked upon in four hundred years and lived to tell the tale. Where will you be then when lives are on the line? Not just yours—I could care less if you throw your own life away—but are you going to toss everyone else's life away, too?"

"There was a threat," Caelith snapped back, trying to wedge some response in among Jorgan's barrage of questions.

"A threat?" Jorgan tilted his head in disbelief. "A single blind old dwarf is a threat to the great mystics of Clan Arvad? This is what justified you and the girl vanishing into the night?"

Caelith drew in a deep breath, trying to keep his own anger under control. "I didn't think . . ."

"No, you most certainly *didn't* think." Jorgan smiled at his younger brother, pity in his eyes. "You just did what you wanted without any thought for the rest of us. Let's be honest with each other, shall we? You hate me; that fact is in everything you've said or done regarding me. The truth is, however, that you don't know me well enough to truly hate me. You don't understand my faith and my conviction because faith is not part of your life. But I'm trying to stop a *war* here—a war that has been killing good *people,* innocent *people*— even your own faithless, misguided clans—for as long as both of us have drawn breath. I'm tired of the smell of their blood on the wind. I don't need your approval or, thank Vasska, your friendship. But I *do* need you to do your duty to your own troops, if not to me. Just follow me to this fabled land, verify that we've found it to your precious council, and help me stop the senseless killing. Then you and all your faithless followers can vanish into the mountains for all I care."

Caelith held his breath and his tongue. He was finding it difficult to breathe.

Jorgan stood, smiling down on his brother. "I know what I believe and who I am. You believe in nothing and know less about yourself than anyone around you. So let's be clear: play soldier all you want with the lives of those men who blindly follow you, but know that between the two of us, I'm the only one who knows where we're going—so you *must* follow me."

Jorgan stepped confidently past his brother and stepped off the platform. He then turned away, stalking off toward the south as he called back to them, "This way."

"So we *are* leaving after all?" Margrave said in bewilderment.

Jorgan spun around. "Thanks to the dwarf and his enthusiastic signal fire there isn't a pair of eyes in three dozen miles that won't know we're here. We're going now. Besides, Caelith seems to make better time running away from things than toward them."

Caelith, losing his temper at last, leaped to his feet and lunged for his brother, but Lucian stepped in front of his friend, holding the mystic back. Jorgan simply turned and continued to the south.

Caelith's breath was ragged with the rage beating through his veins. As he calmed he could see Kenth, the lieutenant's eyes questioning what to do next. He suddenly realized how foolish he had been to be baited by the priest in front of his men. He steadied himself as best he could, speaking as evenly as he could. "Master Kenth, assemble the company and—follow after the priest."

"Aye, sire," Kenth responded at once. "Let's go, lads! You heard the captain!"

Caelith drew in a long, shuddering breath.

"Touchy these brothers as er is," Cephas observed.

"You've no idea," Margrave said with a sigh. "Well, come along, Anji, and stop dawdling! I know you would have liked to stay here and study these towers for another night but our master has called us on. By the gods, how I hate road engagements."

"Do either of you think that there *is* a pair of eyes within three dozen miles of here?" Lucian asked.

Eryn looked at the ground for a few moments before she faced her companions and spoke. "I've been thinking—maybe Jorgan was right."

"What?" Caelith snapped. "How can you possibly—"

"Stop, Caelith—think about it for a moment," she continued. "If someone in your raiding party did to you what we did to him last night, how would you have reacted?"

"How can you say that?" Caelith fumed. "This is entirely different!"

"How?" she asked quietly. "How is it different?"

"The man is a menace, you can see that!"

Eryn shook her head. "What I see is a man surrounded by people he thinks are his enemies—one of whom is a brother he did not know he had before he was thrust into working with him. I see a man who is carrying a lot of pain around with him."

"Pain?" Caelith said with disbelief. "*He's* carrying around pain?"

"Look, you both are, all right," Eryn said with exasperation, "but he's the one who can get us where we need to go. We've got to find some way to work with him or we'll never survive this." She turned and with quick, purposeful steps hurried after the Inquisitas.

"What are you doing?" Caelith called.

"Someone has to talk to him," she called back.

The Sedunath and Kargunath Mountains were further divided beyond the gates to rim the Aramun Plain. They followed upstream the circuitous course of the Naraganth River as it curved first eastward toward the Sedunath Mountains and then southwest in a nearly straight line for the towering, snowcapped peak of Mount Aerthra in the hazy distance.

The company had settled into a routine that, while not comfortable, was nonetheless predictable. Jorgan snapped orders from the front of the line while Eryn struggled to engage him in conversation. Caelith and Lucian would amuse themselves with the dwarf Cephas, who began describing his own attempts to penetrate the Forsaken Mountains. Occasionally, Caelith would deliberately lag behind to gain more space between himself and the priest until he realized this only put the dwarf in dangerous proximity to Margrave, an event that always precipitated an argument over local lore.

"Daft as er is!" Cephas bellowed. "The Tombs of Mnemia be restful er is! Dwarven built and strong stone nay like human work! See er self!"

Mount Aerthra loomed large, though it was still some thirty miles distant. Even at this range, however, the colossus of carved stone that marked the entrance to the ancient tomb was visible, its visage shimmering slightly with distance.

"The texts all say it is haunted," Margrave insisted casually as he walked next to the torusk. Normally the bard preferred to ride, but the torusk had developed a sore claw and the less pressure on it the better. "Haunted, they say, by the souls of the warriors who failed to hold secure the Gates of Aramun from the hordes of the Dragonkings advancing against them from the north. There, in the failing light, they retreated to the North Gate of Mnemia, hoping that the Dwarven Road would lead them to safety. Yet, when they arrived, they found the great doors of the North Gate sealed from within by the very lords who had commanded them into battle. When at last the pursuing armies of the Dragonkings hunted down the armies that had fled south before them, they found them dead before the Tombs of Mnemia, their hands reaching for the closed gates. Since that date, the North Gate doors remain sealed from within, held closed still by the spirits of the coward dead who fear lest they should ever be opened by mortal man and their sins revealed."

"Nonsense drivel," Cephas huffed, his human language always getting worse when he was upset. "Mnemia granite sides of the mountain er is. Dwarves of the Khagun their work be of those doors made! If closed from within the doors of the Dwarven Road, then closed they stay until time ends—haunted or not!"

"I say, Cephas," Lucian asked casually, "you keep going on about this Dwarven Road. I didn't know dwarves build roads."

"The dwarves of the Khagun built the greatest road ever known to any race—dwarven, human, or dragonkind," Margrave began, his face waxing rapturous. "The miraculous, magical gift of the Dwarf King Garl Thimlos to Emperor Rhamas–"

"Shut your trap!" Cephas yelped. "What can yon whelp know of dwarven lore? The history of the Undercities, the dwarves to tell best er is!"

"You'll probably get it wrong," Margrave sniffed.

"Cut my beard if I do! See er is, Master Caelith—and ye, too,

Master Lucian." Cephas spoke carefully, reminding Caelith strongly of the days when the dwarf would try to teach him on his stumpy knee. "Yon peacock right in some ways er is; King Garl Thimlos the Dwarven Road built er the Emperor of Rhamas yon many year ago—nigh more three hundred year afore the Dragonkings. 'Twere said amongst the dwarven Thimlos thought er keep the problems of the overworld out er the Undercities. See er is?"

"Yes, I think I see," Caelith replied with a chuckle, not at all sure. Often with Cephas it was better to let him continue and hope to catch up later on down the path, so to speak. "So this was a magical road?"

"Magic? Bah!" Cephas threw back his head and laughed. "Magic in the dwarves no er is—nay then; nay now! 'Twere build by the dwarves' craft. Eight hundred miles and more under the mountains of the Khagun the road ran but er a skill unknown in Cephas's day now. A man starting that road er the South Gate be walking out the North Gate one ten-day later fresh as er is, mark old Cephas's words!"

"Eight hundred miles—in ten days—and without magic?" Lucian shook his head. "It isn't possible."

"Possible er not." Cephas smiled. "Dwarven skill er is what done it!"

"Well, at least he got the distances and times right," Margrave groused. "Still, I think his version lacks color, drama, or any flair for the tale."

Caelith shrugged, adjusting the weight of his pack on his shoulders. "So, Cephas, did you use this amazing Dwarven Road on your own travels?"

"Nay, Master Caelith," Cephas replied with a heavy sigh. "The Dwarven Road closed er is and its gates er lost and hidden. For Calsandria I looked nigh on the ten-month. Down the eastern Urlund Wall tried I the Forsaken Mountains to enter. Wandered the maze of valleys to the south but no pass found I. Even skirted the Desolation er is. Nay passage er is."

Caelith pointed ahead of them. "Our friend Jorgan up there thinks there is."

"Right may be," the dwarf allowed grudgingly. "Cephas's path to the west er is; Jorgan's through the east and south. Which right er is, we see soon."

The river slowly turned in its course toward the southeast once more. Jorgan and Eryn had both stopped ahead of them, and they stood on the banks of a wide riverbed which once fed into the Naraganth. The dry wash continued to the southwest, winding its way toward the base of Mount Aerthra.

"This way," Jorgan said as they approached, pointing across the riverbed to the south.

Caelith took a moment to look toward the southwest, to catch a glimpse once more of the intricately carved mountainside in the distance.

"Farewell, Tombs of Mnemia," Caelith whispered, "I would have liked to have seen you."

For a moment, however, he thought he could see one of Margrave's phantom spirits—a giant, walking down the river toward the peak of Aerthra and the magnificent tombs at its base. It was a towering man encased in metal that shimmered against the sky and then vanished as quickly as a dream.

He then turned with his companions and, carefully picking his way over the dead bones of the lost river, began crossing the brown grasslands to the south.

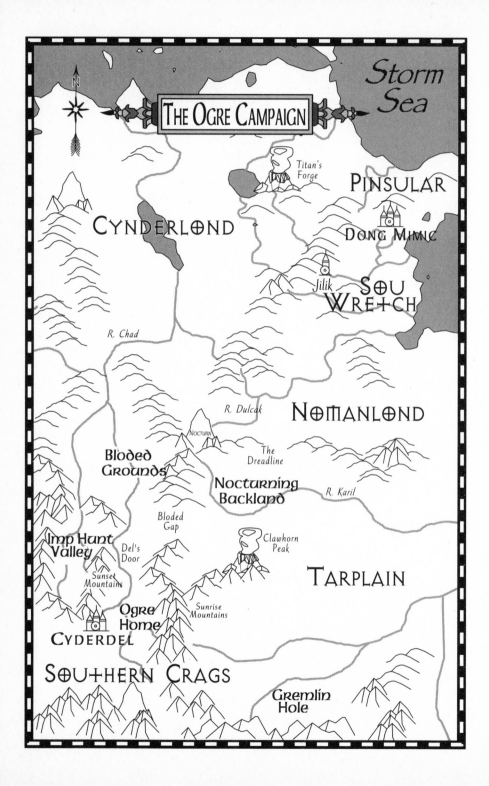

The Ogre Lords

W here are we again?" Thux yelled from his seat in the empty brainpan of the titan.

Istoe, the imp who had been driving the mechanical man for the last week, rolled his large eyes and yelled back in the general direction of what he had lovingly come to refer to as "his cargo." That Thux objected to being called "cargo" made Istoe all the more pleased with himself for thinking of it. "About ten steps farther than the last time you asked me!"

Istoe sat in a wicker seat suspended in the empty eye socket of the titan. It was not a very big one as titans go—Istoe had driven larger ones in his time—but it worked quite well and could be spared for "special duty." Istoe made more than abundantly clear on several occasions during their trip that this "special duty" was a stupid waste of his time.

Thux sat just above and behind the driver in a large open space at the top of the titan's head. This brainpan was his living space during the long trip. His hammock stretched from the inside of one ear of the titan to the other, providing him a place to sleep each night. There was even a couch back there to relax on and a table on which to eat the meals Istoe reluctantly hauled up from the titan's stomach each morning and evening. As head boss he could also, of course, explore the other areas inside the titan in all their intricacies to his heart's delight, and he did so on some evenings. Yet despite all these wonders, his favorite place remained his perch here at the top of the titan's head.

The goblin Technomancers in the capital had cut off the top of the head of this particular titan, raised the skull plate a foot or two, and then forged it into place with supports. Thus, from where Thux sat, he was afforded a magnificent view of the distance in all directions but was afforded shade and protection from rain. If the sun beating down on the displaced metal skullcap had a tendency to be uncomfortably warm, at least there was enough ventilation.

Thux gazed out the top of the titan's head and contemplated the horizon. He was having a little difficulty relating what he was looking at from his high perch atop the titan to the names and landmarks that constantly seemed to be shifting around him.

"When will we get there?" Thux asked, his voice sounding a little like a plea or maybe a prayer.

"About ten minutes sooner than the last time you asked," Istoe snapped back.

"Look, I wouldn't ask if I knew where we were," Thux said with irritation.

"Look, we are really, really, really close," Istoe said. "You see that mountain up ahead?"

"Which one—there are so many . . ."

"The big one—the one that's white on top!"

"Oh, yes, I see it."

"That's nothing, forget about that one. Now, look over there just to the left of that big one. See the *other* one with the white top?"

"Why, yes! I do!"

"Well, that's Mount Thurl on the west side of the Sunset Mountains. The Sunrise Mountains are behind us to the east, and this whole plateau is called Ogre Home. Just keep your eye on Mount Thurl."

"Mount Thurl; got it. Is that where we're going?"

"No."

"Oh."

"No, we're going toward it because the city is at the base of the mountains that are in front of that mountain," Istoe said as he pulled and pushed levers on either side of his chair. "It's a city of the ogres they call Cyderdel and now you know as much about it as I do. All we need to do is follow this river down the right-hand fork and we'll get there."

According to Mimic, Istoe was the most renowned explorer of the age—and Istoe himself would tell you so about as often as possible. Thux had not met an imp before, as they generally hailed from regions west beyond the Cynderlond, but he had heard plenty about them. Vanity was their most defining characteristic and they could as easily be recognized by their audacious costumes and jewelry as by their diminutive size. It was often said by the goblins that all imps weighed the same; the smaller the imp, the more heavily ornamented they were. The largest members of their species could reach as tall as three feet, but the vast majority made their way through life somewhere around two and a half feet in height. They were universally skinny and their quick minds matched the nimbleness of their hands. They were generally a mottled deep red in skin tone with large watery eyes and two small and entirely useless leathery wings protruding from their backs. Alarmed at first, Thux feared the imp might be the same creature he had met in his dreams, but the face was all wrong and the wings in the dream were long and luxurious compared to the stubby flaps sported by Istoe. Worse, however, was that all imps exude a terrible stench, which, for some reason, can only be smelled by goblins—much to Thux's discomfort. It made him long all the more to arrive at their destination.

Even Thux could tell that the base of the mountains was getting closer, so he was beginning to feel relieved. The journey, which had started over a week ago, had been a circuitous and, in some ways, harrowing one. After getting over the shock that the titan was, in fact, waiting for him, he realized that his beloved Phylish was truly in danger so long as he was near her. So he climbed aboard the great mechanism with Istoe at the helm and hoped for the best. He did wonder just where he was going, and the why of it still nagged at the back of his brain from what he could recall of his dream. There was something in the city—this Cyderdel—that Mimic needed and, apparently, Thux needed as well. So he and Istoe had left the capital heading east for a day or so before turning south to traverse the wastelands of the Sou Wretch. When they reached the Dulcak River, they followed it to the west, and for several days the titan wandered tirelessly across the dreary plains. They followed the meandering course of the river until Nocturne Peak could be seen in the distance—southwest of them by the path of the sun overhead. Istoe then turned the titan at right angles to the sun and headed south, passing what the helmsman called the Dreadline between a range of low hills before entering some place Istoe referred to as the Nocturning Backlands. They headed straight south, ignoring an entire village of gremlins that attacked the titan in force. Istoe generally paid no attention to the assault and kept the mechanism walking, casually stepping on one or two by way of discouragement. They continued for two days toward Clawhorn Peak, crossing the River Karil and then turning west once more through what Istoe said was something called the Bloded Gap. It was at about this point that Thux was beginning to think the journey would never end. Then they came upon the River Chad, following it upstream to the south until they passed through a narrowing of the mountains into the Ogre Home itself.

"Well, Boss High Ambassador with Secret Agency," Istoe said drolly. "Have you given any thought to how you're going to approach these savages?"

"No. How did you approach them when you came here before?"

"*I* didn't approach them," Istoe said with a rueful smile. "I stood my titan outside the gates and was pelted by rocks, some of them large enough to dent my titan."

"Well, what do you suggest?"

Istoe turned around in his chair to face the wizard. "My personal suggestion would be for us to camp out here for a few weeks, make up some fantastic story about where we had been, the incredible things we had seen, and the heroic deeds we had done—then return for a reward."

Thux blinked, not understanding. "I thought you were the greatest explorer of our age?"

"Now you know *how* I became the greatest explorer of our age."

"Well, we can't do that," Thux concluded, thinking of his poor Phylish's life hanging by a rather frayed thread. "I've got to be a spy and that's all there is to it."

"Glad to hear it," Istoe said, "since that makes my job a lot easier."

"What is your job?"

"My job is to spy on the spy!" Istoe said through toothy, wide grin. "You spy on the ogres; I spy on you; everyone does their job and we all get paid."

"So you're spying for Mimic?"

"Hey, court intrigue is a tough business. Even a king like Mimic can't be too careful."

"I suppose that makes sense—but who spies on you?

"So, since we apparently *are* going to approach the ogre city," Thux sighed, "do you have any other suggestions?"

"Well, I'm going to stop this monster about three miles from the city gates in a little ravine that's out of sight; then you and I will walk up to the city gates . . ."

"And then?" Thux prompted.

"Then let's hope you're good at dodging rocks."

Grand Emperor Uthank sat on the great marble throne in the great hall, his most glorious Empress Mook at his side.

To be completely accurate, they were not exactly thrones. They were actually large marble tables situated at the end of the hall. But since they appeared to be the right height for the ogres to sit on and were conveniently located in a very auspicious place, they had for many centuries been pressed into service as thrones.

The roof of the hall had collapsed and its remnants lay scattered across the floor where they had fallen. The eastern wall bulged slightly inward and, it was thought by many of the ogres who passed through the hall each day, would one day give way, possibly bringing down the entire structure with it. All agreed that it would be a sad day for the ogres when this happened, so everyone was especially careful when walking near that particular wall.

On either side of the hall, a large number of ogre men and maids stood swaying in anticipation. Most of the males of the species were twelve feet in height, with the women smaller by about a foot. All of them, regardless of gender, were massively strong and powerfully built, though their heads were elegantly small atop their great frames. Necks were a feature completely lost on ogrekind.

Emperor Uthank Oguk the Ninety-seventh wore the divine mantle of his office, a long velvet curtain that had been taken up by the first Uthank centuries before. Threadbare now, it was nevertheless revered by all the ogres of Og, and nowhere more so than here in the walled city-state of Cyderdel. Though his head was bare, at his right hand sat a massive helmet with but a single dent in it, the symbol of his office. Around his waist he wore the traditional ogre man's leather warrior's kilt.

Empress Mook Oguk-Gruk was no less impressive in her own long velvet curtain, which was draped around her shoulders. Her tresses began halfway back on her head, falling in long curling tendrils behind her. Her left hand gently rested on a black-granite globe, nearly encompassing its foot-wide diameter. Her dress was of the whitest cloth bartered from foreign lands. She was the only woman in white; all the other females were similarly clad but in various colors.

While Uthank and his wife watched, at the opposite end of the hall the great stained doors were carefully pushed open by two massive hands. An ogre wearing bronze armor that was demonstrably too small for his chest bent over nearly double in order to enter the hall through the main door. He stood slowly as he entered, the pattern on his kilt markedly different from that of the common ogres standing around the periphery of the hall.

"Emperor Oguk!" he called in his resounding bass.

"Guardian Oof! What news?"

"Two emissaries at gates. They want present themselves before you."

A low murmur passed among the assembled ogres in the hall.

Oguk's deep-set eyes narrowed as he thought. "Bring before us and we hear them!"

Oof bowed once more, and then gestured forward with his great open hand.

A tiny green figure walked hesitantly into the hall shaking so badly that the tips of his ears seemed ready to beat against his own tall tuft of white hair. Next to him, a shorter, slighter figure was dressed in an ornate vest glittering with metals that jingled as he walked. Both of their heads, to the ogre eye, were absurdly large.

"You goblin of the north," Oguk rumbled sagely. "And come with faithful servant imp."

Empress Mook raised a great, bushy eyebrow as another murmur, much louder this time, rolled through the crowd.

The shivering goblin, its hands clasped nervously to its chest, staggered forward at the insistent urging of Oof's powerful hand.

"What you name?" Emperor Oguk demanded.

The small figure blurted out, "Thux!"

The ogre emperor frowned. "What he say?"

"I think him call you bad name, Great Emperor!" Mook said with astonishment. "It sound like dirty word!"

"Your Greatness—Your Majesties—my name is Thux, the—uh—the Wizard of Jilik," the goblin stammered. "I am also the Ambassador with Secret Agency from Dong Mahaj Mimic from a land far to the north."

"And I am Istoe," the imp chimed in.

"You also a wizard, Istoe?"

"Well, sure!" the imp responded.

"Wizard Thux and Wizard Istoe, in name of the Og," the Emperor intoned, "we welcome you."

"We are also spies!" Istoe chimed in cheerfully.

"Spies?" Oguk repeated, his huge head leaning over them, drawing nearer as his eyes inspected them closer.

"Why did you tell him that?" Thux snapped at the imp.

"Well, we *are* spies, aren't we?" Istoe blinked in annoyance.

"Of course we are," Thux said angrily. "But we're not supposed to tell them that! They're supposed to figure it out for themselves; that's how spying works."

"Oh." Istoe nodded sagely. "I'll try to remember that next time."

"So you *spies?*" Oguk demanded.

"No, Your Greatness," Thux said quickly. "I mean—listen, yes, I was sent here to spy on you. As soon as I report back what I've learned, I think our king is going to send his army of giant titans down here to attack your city! But if you'll help me, I think—"

"Ambassador Wizards," Oguk said as he stood up, showing himself to be a full three times the height of the goblin quaking in front of him. "You have come as spy?"

"They made me do it, sire, but I assure you that if you'll just listen to me, work with me, I'll—"

"A spy for invading army?" Oguk intoned solemnly.

"Well, yes! That's why, if we can work out a deal—"

"Master Wizard-Spy." Oguk smiled. "That wonderful news!"

Thux blinked up at the ogre lord towering in front of him. "Excuse me—perhaps I didn't make myself clear—"

"All Og be glad giving," Oguk said, his face looking proudly over the assembled ogre crowd, "that in our lifetime we fulfill orders of ancients! This great news, Master Wizard-Spy! Your coming, indeed, welcome!"

"See, I told you." Istoe socked Thux happily in the arm. "These ogres aren't bad once you get to know them."

"We hope you will have pleasant time spying on Og," Empress Mook said graciously from her table-seat. "Ask us anything and we do all to make worthwhile."

"But you don't . . ." Thux's voice sputtered to a halt. "I just don't think you understand . . ."

Conspiracy
of Silence

G et out!" Djukan raged. "Get out before I throw you out!"

Obadon rose from the chair in the captain's cabin, his jaw set and fire flashing in his eyes. He turned his muscular back on the Kyree prince, who was seated on the opposite side of the table, and stalked to the door, his head bent forward to avoid the low ceiling. He forcefully pulled the door open and stepped out between the two Kyree warriors standing guard.

The door slammed loudly shut behind him.

"Not a word!" Djukan bellowed. "Not a single word!"

"That's three now," Sargo said. He sat at the end of the table, parchment splayed out before him, quill in hand, inkpot nearby. So far, the parchment contained the names of only the five faeries on board. "The last said less than the previous two put together."

"And the first two said nothing at all." Djukan rubbed the bridge of his nose.

Bachas leaned languidly against the corner of the room, his arms folded casually across his broad, powerful chest. "Aye, it's hard to make any headway when you're becalmed. There be a definite lack of wind in this room."

"Damn him!" Djukan slammed his fist forcefully against the heavy tabletop. "Damn him and all the faeries with him!"

"Well . . . maybe here be just a little squall," the Mantacorian captain purred.

Djukan's face soured at the remark. "I suppose you have a better idea?"

"Nay, Master Djukan, I have only my humble advice to give; the faeries are long known to my people. We've dealt with them and fought with them and sometimes done both at once. They're an odd lot, to be sure, and arrogant beyond all reason. For a lot who cannot lie they are damnably difficult to get to tell the truth."

Djukan set both his elbows on the table and pressed his throbbing forehead against his hands. It had all seemed too simple to him and should have been the shortest inquest ever conducted into a murder. He had a set of suspects, none of whom could tell a lie. All he needed to do was bring them into a room, confront each of them individually until he found the one who either confessed to the deed or, knowing faeries, just refused to answer.

Yet thus far he had called in Gosrivar, Valthesh, and Obadon, each in turn to sit before him and answer his questions. Each in turn had been shocked when confronted with the facts as he knew them and then each had gone silent. Gosrivar said that he did not kill Ularis but then went immediately silent afterward. Valthesh allowed that she had known Ularis but would say nothing beyond that. Obadon was the worst of the lot, sitting in the chair for a full two hours and refusing to answer even the most mundane questions put to him.

"There's nothing left for us to do but press on," Sargo said, leaning back in his chair, his wings drooping dejectedly to either side.

Djukan rubbed his hands across his tired face, trying to press some enthusiasm into his features. "Who is next?"

"Shaeonyn, I believe," Sargo replied, referring to his short list.

"Dwynwyn's apprentice?"

"Yes, sire."

"Well, this should be entertaining," Djukan said as he yawned, stretching his arms over his head and shivering his wings to relieve the strain. "Very well, show her in."

The guard opened the door and stepped out into the corridor.

"Do you think she'll confess?" Bachas smiled.

Djukan chuckled darkly. "I had no idea you Mantacorians could be so droll."

Shaeonyn stepped through the doorway, her bright golden hair in perfect coiffure as it framed the elegant dark features of her face. "Lord Djukan, how may this humble Sharajin be of service to you?"

"Mistress Shaeonyn." Djukan's words were perfunctory. "I regret to inform you that Ularis, a faery ambassador of this mission, was found murdered shortly before our ship sailed. The purpose of our inquiry is to ask—"

"If I may ask," Shaeonyn interrupted. "How was the deed done?"

Djukan's eyebrows arched upward. "A single thrust of a blade to the heart. It entered just beneath the front of the ribs and—"

"Was this a very thin blade?"

Djukan kept his eyes on the faery standing before him, though he could hear the sound of Sargo's quill scratching furiously next to him. "Yes, Shaeonyn. May I ask how you would know—"

The Sharajin nodded solemnly. "You have been bringing each of the faeries on our expedition into this room throughout the day. I suspect you have questions you would like to ask me; questions you have been asking the other Fae before me. May I also suggest that you have had little fortune in getting any answers from any of them on this or any other subject? Am I correct in such assumptions?"

Djukan leaned back. "Any assistance you can be in this matter—"

"May I sit?"

Djukan gestured to the chair on the opposite side of the table. Shaeonyn sat, arranging her robes around her, then clasping her hands in her lap.

"The knife was most likely a krisheen—an assassin's weapon not uncommon among the Fae," Shaeonyn said, concern furrowing her brow. "And you suspect one of the faeries accompanying us on this mission to be such an assassin?"

Djukan leaned forward. "I have a few questions—"

"I should be delighted to answer any of your questions that I can."

"Are you an assassin?"

"No, I am not."

"Did you cause the death of Ularis?"

"No, I did not."

Djukan glanced at Bachas. The Mantacorian nodded approvingly.

"Do you know who might have—"

"Forgive me, Lord Djukan," Shaeonyn spoke through a slight smile. "I must ask: are these the questions you put to the other Fae?"

"Essentially, yes."

"And what kind of responses did you get to your questions?"

Djukan blinked, and then leaned back as he considered for a moment his answer.

"Silence, of course," Shaeonyn answered for him, nodding gravely. "I have seen this before, Lord Djukan. It is a difficult thing, even among the Fae, to discover the truth. The faery cannot lie but there are ways to hide the truth; even ways to answer your questions in such a way that the truth remains hidden. The easiest and most sinister way is to enter into a conspiracy of silence."

"A conspiracy of silence?" Sargo looked up from his writing. "What does that mean?"

"I heard tales of this up in Leotine," Bachas interjected. "Seems some Qestardis faery was running from one of these assassin blokes. The way he told it, if a group of faeries all got together and gave the assassin just a part of what he needed for the job, then no one of them could have been responsible for the fellow's death. You could ask each of them all day if they killed the bug and they'd tell you flat out no."

"Because no one of them was responsible for the deed," Shaeonyn finished. "I believe what you have encountered is a Fae conspiracy of silence—the agreement between two or more individuals to kill another Fae. If this is the case, then the assassin remains among us and threatens each of us as well as this mission, whose importance demands that it must not fail. Moreover, the conspirators are also likely among us as well."

"We've questioned three of the faeries thus far and each of them has gone silent," Djukan mused. "So they're all in on this."

"No, that is not true," Shaeonyn said.

"But you just said—"

"Silence in a Fae does not necessarily mean they are complicit in murder." Shaeonyn gazed thoughtfully out the windows and over the sea beyond. "They may have other secrets which they are merely protecting and suspect that your questions may delve into subjects they do not wish revealed. It would be difficult to discover the truth without considerable effort and time. Unfortunately, your assassin may strike again before you discover the truth. No, we must assume any of the Fae who are silent are hiding something from us and are complicit until we know otherwise."

"What do you mean, 'us'?" Djukan eyed the Sharajin with suspicion.

"The Kyree, the crew of the Brethain, and myself," Shaeonyn answered. "Our goals are not the same, but they are in support of each other. I wish to know what the fall of your nation has to do with the living dead; you want to know if your nation can be reclaimed, and Captain Bachas—well, perhaps it is best to characterize his interest as a matter of commerce."

Bachas spoke up. "This is a fine cargo I've brought aboard. What do you suggest we do?"

"I would leave that to your decision," Shaeonyn replied calmly. "Whatever you decide must be done soon, before this person or persons can strike again."

"We still have one interview after this," Sargo said to Djukan. "Perhaps we should hear what Aislynn has to say."

"Of course," Shaeonyn added. "But may I suggest to you that if Aislynn, too, holds her silence your problem would be all the more acute."

"Aislynn?" Djukan scoffed. "I've known her nearly my entire life. She's no assassin."

"As you wish," Shaeonyn demurred. "But might I suggest that it is an axiom of the faeries that the best assassin lives closest to the heart. If she holds her silence, you must consider her."

"If she *is* part of this," Sargo said thoughtfully, "then we really do have a problem."

"Those pearls again?" Djukan asked.

"Sire, if she is part of this," Sargo replied, "there aren't enough Kyree on twenty ships that could stop her."

"That makes no sense." Djukan shook his head. "If that were the case, she could take us all right now."

"No, not until she achieved her objective," Shaeonyn said. "She would wait until then—which makes it all the more imperative that we strike against this conspiracy before it is allowed to strike us."

"Even if that were true," Sargo said, "those pearls that guard her are more than a match for the rest of us."

"I can deal with those pearls," Shaeonyn offered, "if you will give me the aid I ask for in doing so. Once that threat is neutralized, you should easily be able to deal with the rest of the conspiracy."

"Only if Aislynn has anything to hide," Djukan said flatly.

"Only should Aislynn hold her silence, of course."

Djukan stood up to look out the windows at the aft end of the compartment. The waves receded, a jumble of foam tumbling behind the ship. Their convolutions were ever changing and unpredictable; their complexity was wonderful to look at. Yet through them the ship cut the straight line of its course. He wished his own course were so obvious to him.

"Why do you not hold silence, Shaeonyn?" Djukan asked at last.

"Because I need your help, Djukan of the Kyree. I shall stay here as long as required and answer whatever questions you put to me until you are satisfied."

"Why?"

"Because regardless of who this assassin is, I suspect that their next target will be both you and me."

Night was falling when Aislynn saw Shaeonyn step out of the aft cabin and up toward her on the mid-deck. The horizon had settled into a gentle pink haze in the distance behind them.

"Mistress Shaeonyn," Aislynn said, rushing up to her as best her newly acquired sea legs would allow. "What is going on?"

Shaeonyn was about to speak when a Kyree guard called out from the cabin door. "Mistress Aislynn, come!"

Aislynn took a step aft but Shaeonyn caught her arm, holding her just long enough to speak.

"Whatever you do," she whispered into Aislynn's ear, "*hold your silence!*"

Trove

N ow *this* is what I call spying!" Istoe grinned as he lay back on a divan, sunning himself in the light that streamed down from the window behind him. "Rumble your tummy and they feed you. Lack anything; they bring it. Your feet feel a bit tired and they push a soft couch under you. I tell you, Thux, I wasn't all that interested in this spy business of yours, but it really seems to be paying off!"

Thux sat opposite the imp—indeed, as far away as possible—on a worn stone chair. The goblin leaned forward cradling his head in both hands looking dejectedly at the floor. "But we haven't spied at all! We've been here for three days and haven't found out *anything!*"

"Of course not!" Istoe snorted as he cleaned out his ear with a long, sharp fingernail, flicking the wax in Thux's general direction. "Look, these ogres are a single step above rocks on the brain scale. If we find out everything there is to know about them on the first day we're here, no one back at good old home is going to believe us— especially not good King Mimic. You really need to learn a thing or two about adventuring."

Thux raised his head and looked around their quarters. Emperor

Oguk had given them a spacious suite of rooms whose windows looked out on the main gate of the city. They had their own sleeping rooms, which were adjoined by a common sitting room and dining area. Down a flight of stairs, the door opened onto the wide street that curved just inside the outer wall of the city.

More than just the comfort of the rooms and the eclectic furnishings provided by the ogres, it was the constant attention lavished on them and their every need that promised to make their stay as spies on the city one that would be the envy of any goblin in all of Mimic's kingdom. Istoe at this moment was lying back and, when not cleaning his ears, enjoying chewing on an enormous bowl of grapes without much discernment between the fruit and the vine.

"I just want to get this over with," Thux moaned.

"Now there you go again, no vision," Istoe groused, spitting out the juicy remains of a half-masticated grape as he spoke. Imps may have been fastidious in their dress, but their manners were abhorrent even to goblins. "You can't have an adventure finished right off! The trick to being a great hero is to pick your adventures carefully so that you can get the most result for the least amount of work—but just as important is to make everyone *think* that your adventure was harrowing, dangerous, and perilously difficult. I'll admit that this mission of ours had me worried at first—it looked like I'd actually have to do some work—but now that we're in and have the help of the ogre emperor—well, we can take a few days to get around to the work. If we return too soon, the whole thing just won't look believable."

Thux stood up nervously. "Look, I'm going to do some spying this afternoon. I've already made the appointment with the Emperor Oguk."

Istoe made a face and a rude noise at the same time.

"Look," Thux said with impatience, "it may be all right for you to lie around and do nothing, but I've got to get my spying finished so that I can get back to my wife and some real work."

"Fine," the imp said, sitting up reluctantly. "What is this thing you're supposed to spy?"

"I don't know."

"You—don't know what you're supposed to spy?"

"Mimic said I'd find it in the Courts of Og." Thux shrugged. "But here we are in the Courts of Og and I haven't seen anything yet that might remotely interest Mimic. But I do have these dreams . . ."

Istoe rolled his eyes back in disgust.

"I have these dreams about this big stage with strange things on it and creatures on it," Thux continued with a bit more force in his voice. "I think it may have something to do with why we're here; some new device, perhaps, or a weapon of some kind. I don't know— I just hope I know it when I find it."

"You're looking for something—but you don't know what it is?" Istoe said, shaking his head slowly.

"Yes, I guess that's about right," Thux agreed.

"This could take longer than I thought." Istoe lay back on the couch. "Let me know when you find it."

"Aren't you coming to help?" Thux asked.

"I never volunteer for anything," Istoe said, once more chewing on a string of grapes. "You go ahead; I'll find some way of taking the credit later."

"What you think of our city?" Oguk said as he walked down the broken paving stones of the wide street.

The ogre's footfalls shook the ground slightly, making Thux— who was scampering to keep up beside him—more nervous than ever. "Your Imperial Master," the goblin croaked, "from what I have seen, your city is a wonder the likes of which I've never dreamed— well, that's not entirely true; I mean, I *did* dream of a city once not long ago but—"

The ogre reached down, gathering the back of Thux's robe in his massive hand. Thux squawked but it was too late; the ogre was already lifting him into the air. In a single motion, he placed the squirming goblin wizard on his shoulder. "There! Now you shall see our city much better," Oguk rumbled as he started climbing a wide staircase up onto the city wall.

Thux had seen the wall, of course, from the outside when he approached the city. It looked to him like a great smooth vertical cliff with massive towers evenly spaced around the great curve of its outer face. It was a tremendous structure, running outward from the vertical granite face of the mountain in a great arc whose radius must have been at least two miles in measure. There were but three breaks in the stained but otherwise seamless fortification; one heavily grated passage which allowed the River Chad to continue its course out of the city, and, flanking the waterway, two massive gates whose bronze was shaded with a deep patina. But his ability to get a bigger picture of the weathered interior of the metropolis was limited to the narrow streets made narrower by the towering crowds of ogres who were trying to pass one another in their busy lives. Since being brought into the city, his most overwhelming impression had been of walking at the bottom of a narrow canyon—rather claustrophobic and stifling.

Now, however, as Oguk climbed the stairs to the battlements, the true vista of the city spread itself before the Wizard of Jilik.

"Well, Master Spy," Oguk said with great pride, "what do you think of our city now?"

Thux was struck speechless. It was incredible. It was miraculous. It was so—familiar!

"The titans, in days long past, had love for curved lines," Oguk mused as he surveyed the city below them. "I, too, have love for curved lines."

Thux could understand where the ogre got his affinity; the outer wall of the city encompassed two more interior walls whose curving faces sectioned the city into smaller rings set against the face of the granite cliff. It was, however, the innermost ring that immediately caught the goblin's eye, a collection of buildings that seemed untouched by time. Thin, graceful towers still reached skyward above several domes shrouded in a veneer of green. He thought he could even make out the outlines of some sort of large, overgrown garden.

"What is that place?" Thux asked, pointing anxiously and forgetting for a moment the dizzying height to which the ogre had brought him.

"That is Trove," Oguk intoned solemnly. "That is purpose of our existence."

"The purpose of your existence?" Thux repeated. "Why? What is it?"

"In the Days of Strife, we Og served Titan-Whitat with honor and dedication," Oguk said, a wistful expression crossing his wide, flat face as he spoke. "One day, many ages ago, Titan-Whitat left us for Last Battle Against Enemy; against Titan-Blakat. They leave us here in outer city and, as they marched off, they stop and give Two Laws of Og."

"Incredible," Thux thought, more bewildered than ever. "So what were these two laws?"

"First, defend Og until Whitat return!" Oguk said with reverence.

"And?"

"Second, don't touch anything!"

Thux waited for a moment before speaking. "That's it? Nothing more?"

"What more we need than Two Laws of Og?" Oguk smiled with rapture. "Since that day uncounted years ago, the Og have kept trust. We wait for Titan-Blakat to attack us so we might defend city as in our law, and we touch nothing within the Trove, awaiting day when Titan-Whitat return."

The ogre turned to face Thux, who was still clinging desperately to his shoulder. "Now, Wizard of Jilik, you come as spy for Titan-Blakat. You come to fulfill the prophecy of ancients. How we help you?"

Thux considered for a moment, his eyes slowly drawn to the center of the city. "I should very much like to spy *in there.*"

Oguk considered this for a moment. "No ogre entered Trove since loss of the Titan-Whitat," he said slowly. "But you small and must spy as your destiny and calling. You allowed to spy in the Trove."

"Thank you, Your Imperial Immenseness," Thux said with a smile.

Oguk's eyes narrowed on the goblin. "Just don't touch anything!"

The gates to the Trove rose above, streaked by years of rain coursing down the polished silver. They had been closed nearly four centuries before by the hands of titans, sealing within the valued symbols of lives now centuries lost. Thux stood before the closed portal in awe, reverence filling him as he looked at them and pondered the reality and deep sadness that lay just beyond the gates. Did the titans know on that last day that they were shutting the doors forever, and did they mourn what was to be lost? From what Oguk had said he thought it was unlikely; they seemed to think they would be back shortly. They left in innocence of the doom that awaited them. It was up to Thux, a little goblin whose ancestors no doubt were slaves of the titans then, to look on their wonders and ponder their loss.

The ogre guards at either side of the gate unlatched its locking mechanism—a manner of its design in itself a tempting vision to the eyes of the Boss Technomancer—and, wrapping their massive hands around the ornate handles, pulled carefully. At first, the doors made no motion at all, their hinges weathered by time and the elements. At length, however, the great gates yielded to the ogres' strength, shrieking as though they were the waking dead. Thux could see the pain crossing the guards' wide faces, for in all their years of service—indeed, in all the years of their ancestors' service down the generations—they had never touched these gates. Not even the assurances of their Emperor Oguk, who had gotten dispensation directly from the ogre shamans who kept and interpreted the Two Laws, could fully assuage their anxiety. As soon as the gates had split sufficiently for Thux to pass between them, the little goblin held up his hand, allowing the relieved guards to stop.

Thux took in a deep breath, then let it out slowly. "Don't touch anything," he whispered to himself before stepping through the gap between the gates into a time four centuries before his own.

He walked across a plaza just inside the portal. A wide fountain sat in the center, surrounded by what might have once been a carefully tended park, but which had long since become overgrown. Three trees, gnarled and ancient, still grew here, their roots lifting up the paving stones, crushing part of the once smooth roadway. Indeed, the paving had buckled in many places from plants that had, over the centuries, finally asserted their authority. As to the fountain itself, its central figure, a delicate carving depicting four horned griffins, stared with dull eyes toward the sky. Beneath them, a shallow pool of black, still water—remains of collected rainwater, no doubt—mirrored in its surface the rising lines of the architecture surrounding the square.

The ruins were amazingly intact. Each structure was a surprise in its design, a unique expression of a time before the memory of any goblin. Pillars were carved into fanciful expressions of plants, heavily ornamented with depictions of many creatures, including goblins, which marched in colonnades around central towers. These towers, in turn, took many other complementary shapes: the unopened bud of a rose or two enormous hands pressed together or vertical elongated eggs. Other buildings rose in sweeping waves of stone curling slightly at their peak, each edge of their buildings ornamented with carvings of reeds bound into long cables that spiraled around the buildings. In the flat spaces between the carvings, Thux could make out patches of color where the buildings had been apparently decorated with additional ornamental depictions of what Thux could only assume were the lives of the titans. Some of these pictures actually looked sort of recognizable while others were simply strange angles and curves that did not mean anything.

It was another world from another time, and Thux had to remind himself to breathe.

The main avenue was just beyond the wild park, curving slightly as it rose up the gentle slope of the city's preserve. There were many side streets, all of which called to Thux, but he, being a devout scientist when it came to religion, determined that the most obvious course should be the first taken.

As he strolled slowly up the avenue, Thux was surprised how everything had remained so well preserved. The sheer cliff face that rose precipitously above the western boundary of the city had sheltered its inner trove from some of the harsher weather that habitually drove in over the mountains from the west. This had not stopped the rains, of course, but had sufficiently deflected them so that the center of the ancient city did not feel its full brunt. The avenue was mostly covered in silt from the erosion of the buildings themselves, but very often the drainage had been swift enough to expose the bare stones of the street beds. Sand banks had, however, built up in some corners where the drainage had not kept up with the silt. Here plants were also struggling to gain some purchase on the ground.

On either side of him, the dark doorways of the buildings called to Thux. It was all he could do to keep himself from diving into those intriguing holes of black promise and see what wonders each house held. However, there was something in the back of his mind that drove him up along the wide avenue toward the spires that towered just up the slope above even the impressive tops of the surrounding structures.

Thux continued walking, making his way into the heart of the city. He crossed the river, which ran through the city, at a wide stone bridge protected at each end by twin carvings of goblins with leathery wings. The wizard was astonished at the sight; they looked exactly like Lunki looked in his dream. Then, on the far side of the river, the avenue swung sharply to the right, climbing steeply along the side of the rocky hilltop where, he could now see, the tallest and most beautiful of the city's buildings stood.

Dried leaves skittered around his large feet, whose flapping steps echoed down the silent street as Thux followed the avenue onto the hilltop. The road ended abruptly at a paved ellipse that curved to both his left and right away from him. Directly in front he could see a choked tangle of growth that he guessed had once been the central garden of the city, but which now was quite impassable. He has seen this place in his dream—it had been a carefully tended lawn of short grasses and flowered paths. Ringing this morass, however, on the outer edge of the ellipse, were the grand buildings of the titans' central city just as he had seen them, each fronted by broad steps that climbed to their dark entrances.

Thux felt nervous. He had dreamed all these things—everything from the titan waiting for him outside Mimic's capital to the very buildings of this entirely forgotten city. Each had become real. He wondered if he dreamed them into existence but knew that was impossible.

But if the dream was of real things, then it was also something of a relief; for now he also knew where he was supposed to go.

Thux swallowed and began moving around the right edge of the ellipse. The sound of his own footsteps was making him anxious and he kept looking around behind him to see if anyone was following. He was lonely and missed Phylish terribly; indeed, if it had not been for her own safety he would never have come on this mad journey to a dead city. Yet come he had for her sake and, for her sake, he knew what he needed to do.

At the far end of the ellipse there rose an enormous structure. Its entrance was flanked by titans carved of marble, their outstretched hands reaching for a future that would never be theirs. The three domes behind them that capped the marble glistened in several places through the dark stains that crusted their metalwork.

Beautiful and alluring as the domes were, Thux stopped in front of a particularly familiar large, square building and considered it. The exterior face was supported by long, sweeping arches of stone. The top was a pyramid capped by a large prism that looked as though it was cracked.

This was the building in his dream, he knew. Inside was where he had to go and find what Mimic wanted if he had any hope of saving his Phylish and himself.

He stepped through the portal and into a wide corridor. He could see light, which puzzled him since it appeared to be in the middle of the building. He walked toward it, feeling not unlike the evening bugs that are drawn to their own destruction by a flame.

The light was shining toward him and he had to shield his eyes as he moved forward. At last he emerged from the end of the corridor onto a platform at the top of a set of wide stairs and out of the path of the light.

His eyes adjusted.

His jaw dropped.

There, on four separate concourses, as far as the eye could see, stretched shelf after shelf of books. They were the most coveted objects in all the goblin realms now that the Technomancers were in power, and to have a book intact could provide a goblin family with power and position, advancing them in the all-important social order of the goblins.

Thux had just discovered the only undisturbed library in the known world.

"I'm rich," he muttered to himself in awe. "Richer than . . . well, Mimic!"

In that next instant he realized something about wealth that he had not supposed before: that finding treasures and keeping them are entirely two different things. The ogres certainly wouldn't let him remove the books from the city, and when Mimic's titan army conquered the city, the goblin king would no doubt simply take it all for himself.

But for the moment, Thux was indisputably the wealthiest goblin in all goblin history. He had no idea how he could keep the wealth or use it to his advantage. Until he did, he decided, he had best keep his treasure as hidden as it had been for the last four centuries.

"Well, spy anything interesting today?" Istoe said each night when Thux returned.

"No, nothing yet," Thux would respond.

"You know," Istoe would observe, "the trick about spying is in knowing when to actually do something about it. Maybe I should help you."

"No, not yet," Thux would reply. "The Emperor doesn't want my 'faithful servant' to spy with me just yet. Maybe in a few days."

Each night they would then lapse into meaningless conversation as Thux avoided any talk about the Trove.

Thux reveled in his newfound—if as yet unrealized—wealth for three entire days. He would pass through the gates each morning, leave Istoe to his comforts and diversions, and come directly to the library to wander between its stacks of books admiring them. "Don't touch anything," he would happily say to himself, knowing that one day soon he *would* touch them and realize the dreams of every goblin who ever breathed: to be truly better than everyone else. He was sure it was only a matter of time before he figured out how he could make it all last forever.

It was a glorious time that, like so many glorious times, came to a sudden and terrible end.

He was wandering the lower levels. The light from the prisms set into the walls provided reasonable if somewhat undependable illumination. Its problems were due to the crack in the great prism that channeled the light into the building and the nuisance of clouds that often obscured the sun. Thux had learned this by following back the beams of light from where they shone on the walls and were somehow bent by reflective surfaces inside the odd-shaped glass. He still was not sure just how the light was bent by these clear devices but, after all, it seemed to follow Thux's Invariable Law.

"Stuff we do makes other stuff happen," he hummed to himself as he walked, "and when other stuff happens, someone did something to *make* it happen!"

He was ambling near the back of the rows of books. He had been counting them, trying to get some sense of their number, but in his reveries had forgotten how high he had gotten. It actually did not much matter since he had realized that the highest number known to all goblin-kind was one hundred and fourteen and he already knew that his find far exceeded that number.* It was there that he found the clear space among the stacks of books, a small area surrounded by benches. There were books taken down from the shelves and, uncharacteristically, left sitting about the floor. Though the light in this particular spot was a little dim—Thux mused that there must be a cracked crystal somewhere in the line of succession that was causing it—there was still sufficient light for him to see the pages that, for four hundred years, had waited to be looked upon again.

The goblin wizard leaned over the open book and gazed idly at the facing pages. There was a simple rendering of a common chirpy bird on the left page and two chirpy birds on the right. There were also a small number of those strange markings at the bottom of the page that were common to all titan books. In all, however, it was perhaps the simplest page ever created by the titans that Thux had ever seen. Not terribly interesting, he thought, and straightened quickly to pass it by.

His quick motion stirred the air, lifting one corner of the right-hand page, and turning it over. Thux was momentarily startled and

---

*One for each toe on the right foot (6), six toes representing sets of toes on the right foot (36), and two additional tips of ears representing six sets of toes on the right foot (72). Goblins never included fingers in their system of mathematics, as they were always in use keeping track of the numbers of toes and ear tips.

then amused. "Don't touch anything," he giggled, the sound of his laughter echoing down the long stacks of books. "I wonder, if I move and it stirs the wind and the wind touches the book, by Thux's Invariable Law, have I actually caused the page to be turned?"

Thux bent down once more and examined the new pages of the simple book. The pictures were different this time; there on the left page was a small titan—perhaps one of their child-titans—who was standing facing out of the page toward Thux. On the other page was a picture of this same creature joined by a second creature of similar creation, and, of course, the obligatory strange markings underneath both images.

It was all a matter of sequence, he thought; one thing leading to another. I move, the wind stirs, and the page is turned. The rain falls and the ground gets wet. One thing always seemed to follow another and you can track the path of its change through the little differences between where it was before and where it . . .

Thux blinked and bent down closer to the page. The symbols at the bottom of the two pages were mostly the same, he realized. Only the first symbol was different from one page to the other. Otherwise they were identical markings. "How odd," he thought with a frown.

Thux caught his breath as he stared at the two different symbols on the facing pages. "I've seen those before!" he breathed. Forgetting entirely the edict of the Two Laws, he reached down and gingerly took the edge of the left-hand page and turned it back. The two birds on the right were still facing the one bird on the left, but it was to the markings at the bottom of the page that his eyes moved.

"There it is!" Thux murmured into the vast, empty building. "The first marking on the left page is the same as the first marking on the next left page. I knew I'd seen it before. And the first marking on the right-hand page is the first marking on the next right page. But these second marks are identical across the pages. What's the same? What's different?"

It's all about connections, Thux thought. One thing follows another. Thux's Invariable Law.

One bird; two birds. One child; two . . .

Thux's eyes went suddenly wide.

The markings in the titans' books! The Technomancers claimed that they were designs of power left by the titans but otherwise meaningless. Thux knew, in a flash of insight that threatened to explode his head, that the markings were *symbols* for other things; the markings had a meaning all their own.

One bird; two birds. One child; two children.

Thux seized the book off the floor, sat down in the middle of the clear space, scattering centuries of dust in the process, and began turning pages. After an hour of careful examination, tears welled up in the wizard's eyes. "It's all in the sequence," he sniffed happily. He began giving himself a lecture, trying to organize his thoughts in some way that made sense to himself. "The symbols mean something on the page when you examine them in sequence. But that's not all! Look! Here this child tosses a round stone at this other child on this page. The other child catches it on this other page. The stuff that happens on one page leads to stuff that happens on the next page, which gives the pages all together a greater meaning as long as you take them all in sequence; of course, if the sequence were all messed up, then one page couldn't lead to the next and you would lose all the meaning."

Thux looked up happily from where he sat in the dust. "I wonder if the books themselves lead to other books? Maybe if you took all of the books in sequence . . ."

Thux dropped the book and stood up, shaking. He staggered over to one of the shelves. There were many different kinds of books but he found one group of them that looked to be bound identically. He stared at the bindings for a moment, then let out a shriek.

The markings were the same on the bindings of the identical books except for one symbol that changed.

One Book. Two books.

Thux whirled around. All these books meant something, he realized in sudden fear, but *only* when they were in order . . . only when they were in their proper sequence.

Don't touch anything . . .

The resurrected titans of Mimic's army would come. They would beat down the walls of the city and find this place. They would cart off the books without ever understanding that their organization had meaning and any hope of exploring this incredible find would be lost.

Thux sat down carefully, the open book lying a few feet away, and began to weep. Lithbet would be coming with her army soon, intent on destroying the city. They would cart off all the books and scatter them, making their original order meaningless and lost. What was worse, the ogres actually wanted the battle—seeing it as the culmination of their destiny and the fulfillment of ancient prophecy.

Thux looked up dejectedly, a tear rolling down his green cheek. There, from one of the ornamental posts supporting the ceiling, the carved figure of a toothy winged goblin gazed down at him but did not give him any answers. As Thux looked up, the grinning winged goblin figure seemed to wink at him, but when he blinked and looked again, it was just a marble statue.

All Thux knew was that he had to stop an army that had never known defeat from destroying a civilization that was spoiling for a fight. He had no idea how he could do it.

Another tear rolling down his cheek and his nose growing runny, Thux sniffed hard to clear the mucus, only to suddenly discover a foul smell in the library. But when he took a second sniff, the stench had dissipated.

When he returned to his suite that night, Istoe was gone.

Switchbacks

D oes that look familiar to you?" Eryn asked, pointing at the rock formation high up on the cliff wall to their right.

Jorgan glanced at it momentarily as he continued his climb up the winding canyon floor. He spoke in short spurts, his lungs working harder against the altitude of the steep climb. "Yes, it is the western face of what used to be called the Switchback Gap. Once we get up on top we should have a clear view of the Hrurdan Pass."

"No, that's not what I meant." Eryn shook her head. She was feeling the altitude as well. "It looks like the face of someone or something. See, that outcropping is shaped like a hooked nose and on the left there it has a long pointy ear. I'm sure I've seen it somewhere—maybe in the dream."

Jorgan shook his head. "You Soulless and your dreams!"

"Well, can't you see it?" Eryn demanded. "It's grinning at us."

"I suppose," Jorgan replied with a dark laugh, "that you'll tell me it's an omen or a sign of something which will cost me and benefit you—isn't that how it works?"

"Well," Eryn huffed, "at least I finally got you to laugh."

"Oh, I laugh all the time," Jorgan snorted in soft derision. "I find it improves my social life."

Eryn considered this for a moment. Jorgan was obviously in good physical condition; the man had always managed to keep ahead of the rest of their group as they were traveling regardless of the terrain. After crossing the fifty-mile length of the Aramun Plain, he had led them up into the Switchbacks—a winding slot canyon with an over-grown path that moved back and forth in a relatively steep climb—and never once complained of the exertion. Indeed, now that she considered him on the trail, he was a rather attractive man despite his bald shaven head.

Jorgan stopped ahead of her. The sparse trail had swung around another bend, this time cresting a large outcropping of rock that jut-ted from the steep face. Jorgan stepped out to its edge, a slight breeze pushing back his cloak as he looked back, surveying the canyon below.

"So how is your social life?" Eryn prodded as she joined him on the outcropping.

"Eh?" he answered absently, his fists set against his hips as he gazed down between the winding crags of the Switchback. "Oh, about as well as you might imagine it can be for a bastard priest. Of course, now that I've discovered that my father is the most reviled and notorious enemy of the church who ever lived, I'm sure my prospects will be ever so much improved. Can you see them down there at all?"

"Who?"

"Caelith and his hapless followers."

Eryn edged her way forward. The height, she had to admit, was making her feel a little dizzy. "No, I don't—oh, there they are; about halfway down, just past that ridge. It looks like that girl is having trouble prodding the torusk up the slope."

"I think the torusk is smarter than the rest of them combined," Jorgan scoffed. "Still, we'll be near the snow line soon. The pass itself is never clear and the first of our tests will begin. We need to make the caves before sundown or the going will be a lot worse for them."

"How do you know these things?" Eryn asked. "Have you been here before?"

"Do you doubt my ability?" Jorgan asked quickly, his cold, questioning gaze fixing suddenly on the woman.

"No—of course not!" Eryn said, taken aback by the intensity of Jorgan's response. "It's just that, well, you seem to have an intimate knowledge of every inch of the way—as though you had walked this same road a thousand times before."

"I've walked many roads, madam, but never this one," Jorgan said coolly. "Yet in many ways, each step on the path of my life was laid before me—the will of Vasska laying the course. This path is only a part of my journey; I walk it with the confidence of my faith. If my footing is sure, it is because only those who fight against their destiny stumble and fall."

"How can you be so certain?"

Jorgan stopped for a moment, looking at Eryn. "I once asked High Priest Tragget that same question. He was very much a father to me, growing up as I did in the temple, though few had any audience with him then or since. He asked me to come with him down below the foundations of the iconoclast and into the very caverns of Vasska's holy lair. I descended with him, down past the roots of the world, it seemed, until I was ushered into the most sacred of places—the cavern-throne where the high priest reads the dreamsmoke of Vasska and sees the fates of the Pir. I'll never forget his words to me that day, though I think I was only twelve at the time. He had me walk toward him past the throne and held my shoulders. 'The fates carry their own punishments for those who would rail against them,' he said. 'Penance is harder than obedience, Jorgan; always remember that.' Then he turned me to face the throne and said, 'Wouldn't you agree, mother?' "

"Mother?" Eryn repeated, aghast.

"Yes." Jorgan drew in a deep breath. "Edana, High Priestess of the Pir—or what remained of her—sat upon the throne. Her remaining hair was feathery wisps drifting in the cavern breeze, patchy atop her scarred and mottled head. Her flesh was almost nonexistent in places—I remember thinking her robes could easily slip from her skeletal frame. Her lips were pulled back from her darkly stained teeth in a most hideous grin, but it was her unblinking eyes that held my attention. They remained watery and perfect; fixed to stare out across the gulf in the cavern and forever look upon the dragonsmoke rising from Vasska. I felt as though I could see the person behind those eyes and experience the torture of their existence."

"How is it possible?"

"You should well know; Tragget was skilled in your arts. It is his penance that he uses them to keep his mother alive, continually weaving its spell to sustain her from moment to moment. But that was not what changed me—it was as I looked into Edana's horrible deformities brought on by her denial of the fates that I saw my own mother's face. She was beautiful still to look at, but she was just as scarred in ways that could not be seen; and this is what crystallized in me. My father had scarred her thus by rebelling against the natural order of faith. It was then and there that I determined my own penitence in dedicating my life to the will of Vasska."

"And that includes bringing your sworn enemies to the land of their faith?" Eryn wondered.

"It is Vasska's will. But what interests me is why *you* with all your faith in these so-called powers of yours could not see this path to your precious Calsandria without me. You Soulless—all your talk of dreams and visions and mystical energies and none of it has brought you a hairbreadth closer to your beloved Calsandria or done anything for you except make you outcasts and wanderers."

"If we're outcasts," Eryn said, feeling the warmth of her blood rushing into her face, "it's because the Pir cast us out. If we're wanderers, it's because we prefer life without a home to death with a permanent place of burial."

Jorgan's look suddenly softened, taking Eryn completely by surprise. She saw a flash of the pain behind his eyes just before he turned away. "I—I am sorry. Please forgive me. You—I don't know if you can understand how difficult this is for me. I've heard about corrupting influences of the Soulless all my life. Every sermon, lecture, and discussion as far back as I can remember blamed every ill known to civilization on the Soulless. Now here I am alone in the company of the very people I've been taught all my life to hate."

"I think I understand your anger." Eryn sighed.

Jorgan smiled shyly, still unable to look her in the eye. "No. Anger is my enemy—my knowledge of Vasska and his purposes is my strength and my shield. Doubt is the rust that threatens my armor. After everything I am and everything I've been taught—I'm afraid because now that I am here I *don't* hate you. I'm afraid because I enjoy your company—just your being here and talking with me. I guess I'm not making much sense. I mean, I accept that once I lead you to your Calsandria, you'll use your misguided powers to turn me into a rock or some squat ugly creature—but it's hard for me standing here to believe you would actually do it."

Eryn replied with a smile. "It doesn't work that way—in fact, we're not all that certain how it works."

"So far as my personal experience, it doesn't work at all. I have no understanding of this so-called dream that you're always talking about. As for the Election," Jorgan said, looking up at the top of his staff, "the Eye has no effect on me—I've never had the need to hide myself from its gaze."

Eryn was feeling a little dizzy once more from the height. "But—you're Galen's son! One of the few things we know is that the talent of the Elect is hereditary."

"Apparently not," Jorgan said, "but then, we may both have been mistaken about a number of things. I may even trust that you won't turn me into something unnatural when this is all over."

Jorgan's gaze dropped once more down the canyon to the advancing torusk and its struggling companions.

"On the other hand," Jorgan continued, "who's to say that someone else *might*. Be careful, Eryn; there may be others among us that are less deserving of trust than I am."

By the time the torusk crested the top of the Switchbacks, the sun was low on the western horizon, its rays glinting under a bank of dark clouds that moved in from the northeast. The temperature was dropping rapidly in the fading light, but Jorgan insisted that the entire company continue on to a set of large caves that he promised were sunk into an overhanging cliff face another two miles into the pass. A light snow was falling among the pine trees that blanketed the draw. Soon even the pines stopped abruptly at the timberline and the snows began falling in earnest. The company struggled into the caves just as the light of day gave out.

The snow fell as a deepening blue wall across the cavern openings. Several of the chambers were linked by openings of various size, allowing the members of the Mists of Arvad to move freely between them, each warrior free to seek his own place of comfort for the night.

Caelith moved wearily but methodically through his whole company. He spoke briefly with each, making sure of their condition thus far on the journey and to hear their thoughts. It was not, he knew, that he needed their report so much as they needed to connect with him, to hear his voice and know that they were each on his mind. The incident at the Gates of Aramun had, he knew, shaken their confidence in his leadership and he wanted to reassure them.

Or was it that it had shaken his own confidence and he needed reassuring? It was a dark consideration and one that he could not entertain long. He was the commander of his company—the Mists of Arvad. He would lead them and no other.

At last, each man accounted for and the watches set, he released Kenth for the night and trudged on aching legs into the last of the caverns. His lungs could not seem to catch enough air and all he wanted was sleep.

"Not exactly the sort of accommodations that one would expect in the larger cities," Margrave said, rubbing his chilly hands together in the cavern, "but certainly better than have been offered on the trip thus far. Of course, things could turn rather nasty for us all should the snow-serpents get the same idea as we and decide to crash our lodgings."

"Oh, please do give it a rest, old boy," Lucian grumbled from behind a stack of cordwood he was carrying from the stores on the torusk. "Bad enough that we had to listen to you all the way up here talk about the history of these blasted forests, but could you at least have helped us gather the firewood?"

"Truly I am sorry; I personally would have been delighted to assist but Anji put up such a fuss about the torusk and all." Margrave smiled as he shrugged. "What could I do?"

"That," Caelith said ruefully as he sat back against the gently curving cavern wall, "is the very question that I've been asking myself for several days—what *can* you do?"

"Well, perhaps I might regale you with a story from the majestic Hrurdan. Bloodcurdling tales from this very pass in which we are to spend the night!"

"By the gods!" Lucian sounded as though he were about to weep. "Can someone please make him stop!"

"When you figure out how, let us know," Caelith groaned, closing his eyes. "Say, where is that girl that's always with him?"

"Anji is tending to the torusk in a separate cave just south of us," Eryn said through a long yawn.

"Alone?" Caelith questioned.

"Couldn't talk her out of it, old boy," Lucian said as he set down his cordwood and fed several logs to the fire at the cavern's mouth. "And after all of us had a good whiff of wet torusk it was unanimously determined that it should reside in its own and most separate lodgings."

"Quite right," Margrave piped in cheerfully. "But it is not the smell of the torusk that is our gravest danger; for the snows of the Hrurdan Pass cover the frozen bones of many a brave lad whose tale ended in—"

"Margrave, we're wet, cold, and hungry," Caelith said, hearing a weary tone creeping into his own voice. "We really don't want to hear this right now."

"But it is a vital tale which—"

"Not now," Caelith said, his voice rising in sharp command.

Cephas, leaning against the wall of the cavern near the entrance, chuckled to himself. "Maybe as well you ask the river hold up as er Margrave to stop er talk!"

"I am only trying to help," Margrave sniffed.

"If Margrave stop er talk," Cephas roared at his own joke, "em words back up! Margrave explode er is!"

Jorgan entered the cavern, his cloak covered in thick patches of snow. "We have fog and snow tonight," the Inquisitas said, "so the fire should be all right. Still, we'll post a watch."

"I've already set a watch," Caelith said irritably.

Jorgan ignored him. "I will take the first; Caelith the second, and Lucian the third."

"Er now!" the dwarf piped up, lifting his cloth-wrapped eyes toward Jorgan's voice. "When Cephas watch er is?"

"I believe that for tonight we will skip the opportunity of putting a blind dwarf on watch," Jorgan drolly intoned.

"Bah!" the dwarf huffed. "Cephas hear danger before humans see er is!"

"Look, I said I've already taken care of it," Caelith said, his voice a bit louder than he expected.

"Caelith, give it a rest," Eryn said wearily.

"Give what a rest?" Caelith shouted. He was tired from the climb but mostly he felt tired of the whole situation. Somewhere in the back of his mind, he knew he was about to make the best speech he would ever regret. "I've been leading men into battle for years and this—this *priest,* who probably hasn't spent more than ten minutes outside the confines of his temple, is supposed to tell me how to set a watch?"

Jorgan smiled thinly, then turned and stalked out of the cave.

"Don't you walk away from me!" Caelith yelled. "Come back here and face me!"

Jorgan's dark form vanished into the snow and fog beyond.

Caelith drew in a long, shuddering breath. He sat there alone despite the people around him; each of them studiously looking anywhere but in his direction. He stared for a long time at the blank darkness of the snowfall beyond the cavern entrance.

And for a moment, he thought he saw the shadow of a young stick of a girl staring back at him from the veil of snow.

Whispers
and Echoes

The snow had stopped in the night, its clouds driven off by a stiff wind from the northeast, bringing a frigid, stark dawn to the Hrurdan Pass. None of this deterred Jorgan from his determination, for Caelith found him awake and busying himself for travel as the snows beyond the cavern entrance brightened with the dawning light.

Caelith quickly ensured that none of them would be left wanting before his dogged brother. He and Kenth quickly roused the company, supervising their refit into heavier, lined cloaks and fur leggings, hats, and mitts from the stores on the torusk. They were nearly finished with the chore when Caelith noticed the young girl staring at him with huge, questioning eyes.

He returned her gaze for a moment, then, finding her stare uncomfortable, turned his attention to her outfit. She had found a fur-lined cloak which almost fit her, though its ends dragged in the snow. Her own rough tunic, however, had frayed ends that were, in contrast, too short for her. He could see her hands curled in against the cold,

245

shaking as they held the long pole with which she guided the torusk by its tusks.

"I'm sorry I've put you through this," Caelith said to the waif. "You haven't done anything to deserve this."

The girl said nothing.

Caelith smiled ruefully, glancing down at his own gloves. They were soft brown leather, lined, with luxuriously deep cuffs. "Well— Anji, isn't it?—well, Anji, these may be a little large for you but I think they'll keep you warm."

He held out the gloves to her, but she took a hesitant step back.

"It's all right," he insisted with a smile. "They were always too small for me and I have others. Please?"

The girl hesitated for a moment, then reached out and took the gloves without a word. She quickly pulled them over her hands, the cuffs nearly reaching her elbows, then looked back up into Caelith's face with her large, watery eyes.

He could hear Kenth calling for him, his voice getting closer by the moment.

"You're most welcome," Caelith said to Anji with a sad smile before he turned. "Yes, Master Kenth."

"It's that Jorgan, sire," Kenth said, shaking his head. "He's given his morning pronouncement and started off to the south. Mistress Eryn took off trailing him, but we'll lose sight of her, too, before long."

Caelith cleared his throat. "We'll catch them both soon enough in this snow. Tell Beligrad to choose five companions and set out after our guide at once. Then have Phelig get whoever he needs to organize the gear and secure it to the torusk. You get the rest of the company moving and I'll—I'll try and get our dignitaries packed up as well."

"Aye, sire." Kenth nodded. "Is this how it's going to be from now on?"

"I certainly hope not!" Caelith bellowed as he moved quickly toward the next cave.

"Now where are we?" Eryn said, her words carrying into the chill afternoon air on white puffs of labored breath.

"Why ask me," Caelith returned, blowing across his achingly cold hands. "You're the one on speaking terms with our guide."

They stood knee-deep in the snow at the crest of a ridge outcropping. To their left rose a towering peak whose face curved around a deep draw far below. Along the face of the mountain, a single line cut through the pristine snow with a lone dark figure at its head.

Lucien pointed. "It looks like he's making for that deep cut to the south. I say, if I had my druthers I'd walk along this mountain, too, rather than go down to the bottom and have to climb all the way back up."

Longer but safer.

Caelith blinked. The words had been quiet yet distinct in his mind as though someone had spoken them within his head. It must be the altitude, he though ruefully. He had heard of the Mountain Madness, and there were others of his own company that seemed to be a little slower in their reactions than he remembered them being. He glanced back at the company behind him, awaiting his decision. "Well, to quote our guide, 'This way.' How about you, Cephas? Are you up to this?"

The dwarf was almost waist-deep in the whiteness, his hair caked with ice. "Dwarf on a mountain er is! Watch Cephas and see if he passes yon Pir priest eh?"

The dwarf pushed past Caelith, his squat body cutting a wide path across the steeply slanting snow. Caelith smiled and started along the path himself. It was a difficult position to be in; pushing down the new snows for those that followed, although, he thought ruefully, not nearly as difficult as that of Jorgan or Cephas ahead of them.

The noon sky slanted farther toward the west as they continued on their path. The going was slow and their lungs ached for air in their exertions. By mid-afternoon, they were nearly three quarters of the way to the deep cleft between the mountains, and the far side of the mountain bowl looked to be only about a half-mile before them. They had caught up with Jorgan and, their goal being obvious, the Inquisitas had agreed to allow the dwarf to go ahead of them and cut the trail.

Caelith looked back. Behind him, the rest of the company was spread out in single file along the long curve of the mountain face, the torusk and Anji in the rear pushing forward with the balance of their supplies. Directly behind him, Lucien, Eryn, and Margrave trod along, the bard unusually silent.

"I am astonished, Margrave," Caelith said haltingly, his breath labored in the thin air, "that you haven't had anything to—to say in the last—mile. For a man who seems to know a—story about every rock—and tree along the way you can't—you can't possibly find this area that boring."

Margrave looked up suddenly, recognizing that he was being spoken to. "Oh, sorry—I've been composing a terribly tragic lyric about the Hrudan Pass."

"Tragic?" Caelith scoffed but the voice within his head seemed to sound an alarm. He shook his head to be rid of it. "What is so tragic about snow? Perhaps frostbite is the subject of your—"

The sound of commotion down the line of march behind him suddenly drew Caelith's attention. The line had broken in the middle, with several of his raiders scattered both up and down the slope, their weapons drawn. Several of them had raised their hands, their fingers splayed out as they appeared to be tapping into the Deep Magic. Their shouts echoed back across the hills, making their words muddled.

Caelith began pushing his way back toward the disturbance. "Quiet!" he shouted as he slogged through the deep snow back toward his scattered men. "Quiet, I say!"

The shouting diminished slightly. Caelith felt as though he were moving with impossible slowness through the thick snow. "Kenth! What is it?"

"Don't know, sire," the lieutenant called back, his own weapon drawn.

"Something's moving!" Lovich squawked, his voice breaking with his anxiety. "Something under the snow!"

Caelith looked down the face. Rivulets of snow slid straight down the slope from where the men had scattered, but these were impossibly crossed by long curving lines that disturbed the snowpack from just under the surface. In the afternoon light, flat against the snow, however, they were difficult to see. Caelith suddenly caught sight of the end of one of the lines, moving with incredible speed parallel to their own line of march and toward the end of the column.

"By the gods!" Caelith cried out. "What is that?"

"Snow-serpents," Margrave answered sadly.

Jorgan, standing just beyond, suddenly paled. His eyes widened and his jaw set. "They never hunt before nightfall! They must be desperate." He pushed his way back toward Caelith. "We've got to get everyone off the face! Now!"

Caelith turned to face his older brother. "There's no cover here and it's almost a half-mile to that pass. We can't possibly outrun these things, whatever they are. You take the lead group and head for that cut. We'll hold them here and—"

Suddenly the ripping line just under the snow turned abruptly toward the torusk. The great beast bellowed loudly, its thick, scaled legs churning at the snow. Caelith could see Anji trying desperately to calm the enormous creature.

In that instant the snow around the torusk exploded. Three hideous beasts flew upward around the animal, attaching themselves to its neck, back, and flank by sinking long, razor-sharp talons from their short but muscular forearms deep into the torusk's flesh. The beasts' wide, powerful jaws gaped open, showing their long fangs. Thick white fur ran from just behind their flattened heads down the length of their long, tapered bodies. They had no hind legs, for they were not creatures of the land but of the snows and glacier lakes, their bodies flattening after their broad shoulders into a smooth, articulated tail.

The torusk howled again, churning its legs backward in the snows as it lost its footing.

"Kill them!" Caelith shouted, his voice raw in the frozen air. "Raiders! Attack!"

The company broke ranks on the trail. Several charged the serpents directly, drawing their weapons. A cloud of ice shards flew from the hands of Tarin, who was up the slope from the Torusk and had a clear line for his mystic formation. Their keen edges lanced through the first of the serpents near the torusk's throat, causing red stains to run down the monster's fur. It pulled back its grotesque head, howling in pain.

Caelith drew his own weapon but a strong hand pulled him around. Jorgan stood slightly above him on the slope, his hand grasping Caelith's shoulder. "We can't do this here! We've got to get off the face!"

"Damn you, Jorgan! Those are our supplies!" Caelith shouted. Beyond Jorgan, he could see Eryn, her bow already releasing one of her arrows past their heads. "How long will we last out here without them?"

"Longer than if we die here and now," Jorgan replied.

Caelith pulled his shoulder away from his brother's grip as Eryn's second arrow let fly. "I told you we've got to salvage those supplies— now let me do my job!"

Caelith turned back. Eryn's arrows had flown true; the second of the beasts had been pierced by them. It, too, howled, then leaped away from the torusk, curving backward through the air as it plunged back into the snow. The arrows protruded from the surface as the beast ran in a circle under the surface around the back side of the torusk. The first serpent, still bleeding, launched itself over the torusk's head, its talon claws reaching out for Phelig, who was still charging. Caught by surprise, the raider tried to raise his sword in defense but the creature was too swift for him. Both Phelig and the serpent vanished under the snow in a violent flurry. In moments the snow where they entered was marred by a growing red stain.

"Follow them!" Caelith ordered. "Kenth! Get the company into a defensive circle!

Jorgan's right. Caelith gritted his teeth, pushing through the snows, still too far from his own men. *Get off the face.* "Leave me alone!" he shouted at the voice in his head.

The rivulets in the snow began circling his warriors. The torusk beast was making its own trail, back up the slope and dragging the hapless Anji with it. The warriors seemed to have gotten the attention of the serpents, however, for they were ignoring the retreating beast for the time being.

Caelith was nearly there. Several of the men were already casting their mystical energies into the snow around them. The dull thud of their electric explosions illuminated the snow around them.

"Master Kenth, have the men aim ahead of—"

With a building roar, the snow began to move. What had once seemed so solid underfoot in moments became a river, liquid and deadly. Slowly but with ever increasing speed, the field of snow began to slide under the circled company, carrying them downward, tumbling them under a cascade of white death. The snow-serpents of the Hrurdan Pass had long hunted in these mountains; they knew well how to draw their prey into their snare.

"No!" Caelith's scream was swallowed by the echoing roar of the avalanche rushing away before him. He caught a fleeting glimpse of his company—the Mists of Arvad—as they cried out, screaming in rage against an enemy that had taken them so unexpectedly. The snows under Caelith's feet shifted slightly and he fell forward on the surface. He watched helplessly as the shattering inundation tore down the mountain face, carrying with it all his strength and purpose.

The light was failing as Caelith entered the steep canyon. The sheer walls would provide shelter that he would not feel through a night that he thought would never end.

With him came his lieutenant, Master Marash Kenth, whom Caelith had pulled from a snowy grave, and four others of his company: Lovich, Beligrad, Warthin, and Tarin, who had been uphill from the avalanche when it began. Lastly came the wounded torusk, still burdened with supplies for a company that no longer existed and a girl wearing brown gloves that were too large for her.

The Mists of Arvad were no more—and Caelith knew it was he who had failed them.

Ruins

The night wind whistled through the seams of Caelith's carefully and tautly pitched tent. Next to him sat his pack, placed just so on a stone protruding from the cleared, frozen ground. The ties on the pack were all neatly done up even to the extent that the ends of each leather cord lay at equal length from the knot that bound them together. Beneath him, he had arranged the layers of his ground cloth so that their corners precisely pointed to matching corners of his enclosure. The toes of his boots pointed toward the carefully secured door flap as he sat, holding his knees close to his chest. He had tucked his thick cloak around him fastidiously, his hood perfectly centered atop his head. The soft woven cloth he normally used as a pillow was now rolled and bound so tightly as to make it nearly as hard as the rocks of the crag in which they were encamped. That roll, too, he had meticulously placed in its customary position behind him, yet he was not putting it to any use. He simply sat, curled in on himself as tightly as his bedroll and holding as still as possible.

Throughout the evening—it must have been evening, he thought somewhere in the back of his mind, though he was having trouble recalling the passage of time—diverse members of what remained of their expedition had come to his tent. He seemed to recall Lucien at one point and possibly Eryn, though he could not be sure. Kenth had come; Caelith recalled his lieutenant wanted permission to search for more survivors and care for those recovered. Caelith had given his consent in a single word, but that was more than he gave to anyone else who came to him; the rest were answered only with an unfocused stare and silence.

It wasn't, he reflected with that part of his mind that could manage, that his mind was no longer functioning. Quite the contrary; it was working all too painfully hard. Behind the mask of his blank stare, his mind howled, it screamed in its agony, rage, and fear; it was a whirlpool of regrets and recriminations. How had he missed the significance of their unsteady ground? Why didn't he get them off the face as Jorgan had insisted? Did his own pride kill all those people who trusted him to care for them? What else could he have done? What should he have done and why didn't he? The shattering, tumultuous noise of anger, torment, name-calling, self-loathing, contorted faces, blame, and doubt in his mind was so loud that he could not hear the soft words nor see the concerned looks that tried to contact him in his distant place. How could they reach him when he was so far away, falling down through a black and bottomless well of his own recriminations?

Someone else was undoing the ties on his tent flap. Another visitor, this one in the darkness. Well, let them come, he thought; let them give their obligatory, pitying looks and say their socially awkward words, clear their conscience of him and be done.

He could sense the person enter the darkened tent, heard him carefully retying the tabs on the tent flap and then sitting down near him. He did not see him—did not wish to see him.

There they sat in silence together for an eternity of moments. The wind swept time away. He concentrated on his breathing, part of him wondering why he bothered.

It was then that he heard the quiet, distressed sniffing and muffled sobbing next to him.

Anger, white-hot, welled up inside of him. Bad enough that I have to carry my own guilt, but must someone come into his tent and pile their guilt on him as well? He suddenly reached out, grabbing fiercely at the person in his tent. He heard a stifled yelp as the figure tried to pull away from him.

His hand closed on the soft leather of his own gloves and the small, thin hand within it.

Caelith, without thinking, reached up and summoned a lightglobe from the Surface Magic—quite literally—at hand.

It was Anji. The girl quivered in the sudden light, her wide eyes, partially hidden behind her unkempt bangs, brimming with tears. She was still dressed as she had been for traveling earlier in the day; still wearing the gloves Caelith had given her.

He released her hand, sorrow threatening to overwhelm him. "I—oh, Anji I am so sorry," he stammered. "I—I didn't mean to . . ." His voice trailed off. He could not make himself go on.

The girl continued to stand, watching him with her intense gaze. Then, slowly, she sat down once more under the light of the globe still glowing in the air next to Caelith's head.

"So, you've come, too, eh?" Caelith nodded. His head felt heavy and he longed for sleep but could not welcome it. "Come to comfort the poor fool who lost his way and all his men with it."

She simply sat quietly, bowing her head and averting her eyes at last.

"I'm beginning to see what Margrave sees in you." Caelith chuckled darkly, then rubbed his hands vigorously across the stubble on his face. "I've campaigned for many years, Anji; did you know that? I've been fighting battles nearly as long as I can remember. I've seen men and women and children die—good or bad, one can rarely tell—sometimes at the hands of my enemy and sometimes at my own hands. You would be well to stay away from me, Anji; death is an old companion of mine." He drew in a painful breath, trying to speak with control through his emotions. "But today I dealt death to my friends—to those who looked to me to guide them and keep them safe. It was my own—my own pride that got in the way of my better judgment. I knew better than that, Anji; they died because of me."

"Caelith Arvad . . ."

The warrior captain started at the sound. "What?"

The voice was tiny, barely perceptible over the howling wind outside the tent, but it was clear and sweet—and astonishing coming from Anji. "You are blameless, Caelith Arvad."

He was so amazed, he stammered. "No—no, I could have prevented it—I knew but did nothing . . ."

"Because you ignored the voice," Anji said and nodded quietly.

Caelith blinked, his mind focusing. "How did you know?"

"My mother told me we all have the voice inside us." Anji shrugged, looking shyly at the frozen floor of the tent. "It's just that with swords banging and people shouting all the time, no one tries to listen."

Caelith held his breath for a moment and then let it out slowly. Anji sat quietly watching him.

"This is different," he said at last. "People died."

Anji cocked her head to one side, her dirty hair falling over her face. She shook it out of the way before she spoke. "People die. I've seen 'em; they're a lot like ruins. Margrave has shown me lots of ruins. I think about who lived there and what it must have been like. It's as if the place is only alive when the people are there. When they leave, the place goes to ruin right away just like dead people. Only they just probably moved away to a different place. So you got ruins, but the folks in 'em have just gone somewhere else."

Caelith was not sure what the girl was saying. "Maybe we're looking for dead ruins, too, Anji. Everyone seems to be shouting about Calsandria as though it is the greatest prize ever to be won— maybe it's just a dead ruin, too."

Anji brightened a little. "I saw someone win a prize once! Margrave and I were at a fair in Pantaris and one man won a prize for being the strongest in all Enlund."

Caelith laughed gently. "That would be *very* strong, indeed."

"Yeah." Anji nodded, then paused. "I remember thinking, though, that the *prize* didn't make him strong—but *winning* it sure did. You feeling better?"

Caelith nodded slowly, still feeling the gut-wrenching sorrow of the day but somehow calmer.

Anji nodded in return, reached up with her oversized gloves and somehow managed to undo the flap once more. Pulling her hood over her head, she slipped back into the night.

By the seventh day of the expedition they left the southern end of the pass, entering into a large mountain bowl formed by a glacier lake. All along that difficult route, Caelith was unapproachable; his words to Kenth were short answers to direct questions and not even the dwarf could coax him into any further conversation. They made camp on the shores of that ice-chilled water high in the mountains, taking the opportunity to refill their water skins.

That night, Lucian had made a somewhat impassioned speech in favor of abandoning the ill-fated expedition altogether while Jorgan argued for their continuing. Caelith sat near the fire, seemingly distracted until he unexpectedly stood up and said simply, "We keep going!" then stalked off to his tent, ending the discussion.

So it was that on the fourth morning, Caelith silently folded his canvas tent, repacked his provisions, and mounted it all onto the torusk. The breath of the beast hung in great clouds in the chill, still air. In every direction he looked there were towering peaks capped in snow, mirrored in the still and undisturbed waters beneath an achingly brilliant blue sky overhead.

The glacier lake was tepid compared to the frost-caked relationships between the travelers themselves. Caelith knew with every step across the ice-crusted ground that it was his own fault, his own frozen soul being reflected in everyone around him. The loss of so many of his own men was a wound that could be torn open at the slightest provocation. Caelith knew it was easier for the rest of them not to talk to him than to risk saying something that would hurt everyone. Let them think they are protecting me, he thought. Let them leave me alone.

The exception to the general chill was, of course, Margrave. As everyone else had stopped listening to Margrave altogether, he busied himself with an endless conversation—one-sided—with Anji. The girl simply trudged along mutely, her eyes forever downcast as the bard would babble on about his previous adventures and the lore of such-and-such a place during the reign of somebody-or-other.

Anji never spoke a word and Margrave would occasionally agree or disagree with, complain about, or praise something that the girl did not say. Caelith decided it was the way Margrave preferred his conversations, with him speaking and everyone else listening.

Caelith considered the young girl as they walked through the seemingly endless snows past a procession of mountain peaks. She had not said a word to him since that night or, for that matter, to anyone else so far as he could tell. He wondered sometimes whether it had happened at all, yet her words still rolled through his thoughts like a quiet, distant thunder, never quite leaving him.

Lucian and Cephas had also both grown quiet along the trail, speaking only a little and then only about matters of the road. The lark that was the adventure had vanished for Lucian in the deadly cascade of snow and he mostly thought of bringing the whole sorry business to a close. Cephas's silence was more understandable; dwarves were never much for conversation in the best of times, and in the high mountains, the dwarf seemed to be wrapped in his own thoughts.

As for Eryn, she was constantly ahead of the group of travelers with Jorgan now, walking at his side far in front. *I should be there,* Caelith thought. *I should be leading us with Eryn next to me instead of . . .* Even as he thought it, he felt again the pain of the loss, his own guilt, and knew he was not worthy of their trust to lead again.

Jorgan stepped toward the rest of the assembled group as they milled around the beast, awaiting the inevitable.

"This way," Jorgan said, pointing to the west.

"I say, old man," Lucian spoke quickly, "could you tell us how much further we will be traveling before we reach this Calsandria?"

Jorgan stopped and turned to face them. "Three days to the falls, if we make good time."

"Three days then?" Lucian sighed.

"Three days, if you can hold out," Jorgan said, a slight mocking tone in his voice. "This way."

"By the gods," Eryn breathed with wonder. "Can we really be here?"

They all stood next to the rushing river at the top of the falls. The thunder of its plunge was far below them; where they stood at its crest they could hear only the hiss of the water cascading over the edge and falling a thousand feet down the sheer cliff face.

Before them to the south, a magnificent vista lay; a valley wider and longer than the Aramun Plain and rimmed with distant mountains. The river from the base of the falls wound across the valley to the south, emptying into a lake which shimmered in the evening sunlight. In the haze of distance, they could make out the sharp edges of buildings, the glint of the sunlight shining off one of its towers, and roads nestled around the shores of the lake—a city of the Rhamasian Empire.

"Margrave," Lucian asked anxiously, speaking to the bard directly for the first time in more than a week, "what do you think? Have we found the lost capital of the Rhamasians or not?"

"Calsandria the Beautiful," Margrave answered with a smile. "The legends put it in a mountain plain next to Behrun Lake. Ships plied its waters, bringing goods from the Dwarven Road to the port markets in Calsandria itself."

"Ships?" Eryn asked. "In the middle of the mountains?"

Cephas chuckled. "Aye, ships as er is. Calsandria maybe er is but er good hammer knock is dwarf sure."

"What is he talking about?" Lucian asked.

"It's an old dwarf saying," Caelith answered.

Only Jorgan failed to look at him with surprise. It was the first time Caelith had addressed any of them in days.

Caelith continued speaking to the wind. "It means you have to touch something to be sure it's real."

The ancient road was broken but could still be followed. It wound its way down next to the falls and then ran straight across the basin toward the towers in the distance. The air was warmer on the plain, and with each step Caelith could feel his spirits rise. They were out of the frigid mountains, and their objective was in sight.

More encouraging still were the lands they passed: great stands of fruit trees that may once have been tended orchards; fertile fields waiting to be turned once more by anxious hands; and tall grasses that were wild and moved like a green ocean in the wind. The hand of man had abandoned this place and nature had given it rest. Now it was ready to be tamed once more.

On the second day, however, the glory of the distant city began to fade as they approached it. The magnificent towers they had perceived from afar proved to be but broken remnants of their earlier form, the glinting light mere reflections from a cracked remnant of glass. Indeed, as they entered the outskirts of the city, they discovered that nature had nearly reclaimed it in its entirety. What had looked like a grand vision in the distance was an illusion; the city was nearly vanished.

The life has left them, Caelith thought.

"What is on your mind, Lucian?" Caelith said absently as he stirred the glowing embers at the base of their campfire.

Lucian sat on a large, flat stone hunching toward the fire as well. There was an uncharacteristically troubled look on his face. "Never much, old boy—though I'm glad you've decided to speak to us again."

"Come now, I know you better than that." Caelith leaned his back against another large stone on the opposite side of the fire. "We're here. What do you think of this lost empire after all?"

Lucian glanced around. Eryn was some distance away gathering wood for the evening. Margrave was yammering at Anji next to where the torusk had dropped exhausted for the night.

"There's a reason they call it a lost empire, old boy," Lucian said quickly, his voice low. "A valley this rich—fertile soil, rested fields, and fruit trees all ready for the harvest—and no one has plucked this gem in four centuries? The Dragonkings have been at war for over two decades now and no matter how many times their villages are burned or their cities laid waste, humanity puts their shoulder down and rebuilds. Yet here, in this choicest of lands, not a single human seems to have bothered to stake their claim in over four hundred years—in the very spot where civilization once flourished. It's just nonsense."

"The road to get here wasn't that accommodating," Caelith countered thoughtfully.

"But it wasn't that difficult either," Lucian said, shaking his head, then, seeing Caelith's pained and angry reaction, continued quickly. "I'm not belittling our tragedies, old boy, but consider: by my reckoning, we haven't traveled much farther than I did from Enlund just to attend your father's rather silly conference. For four hundred years this Calsandria has remained completely inaccessible to mankind—mystic or otherwise."

"Are you saying this is a trap?" Caelith said quietly.

"All I'm saying," Lucian replied, "is that if this is Calsandria, then I'm High Priest Tragget!"

"Nice to meet you," Eryn said as she walked up to the fire, her arms filled with sticks. "I've always wanted a word or two with the Dragon-Talker of the Pir."

Caelith smiled thinly. The warmer air had apparently thawed Eryn's spirits, too. "Lucian was just speculating on the existence of Calsandria—particularly whether we have found it or not."

Eryn nodded as she dropped her bundle noisily on the already large pile away from the ring of stones. She then turned around, folding her arms as she contemplated the flames. "I'm not sure that it matters."

"Ah." Lucian smiled. "In an argument with two points of view, trust our friend Eryn to come up with a third."

"What does it matter if this is the real Calsandria or not," Eryn continued, "so long as the clans believe it is."

"I don't follow you," Caelith said.

"Think of what this place has to offer," Eryn said, gesturing all around her. "Fertile land, ample fresh water, already established food sources—and a promise from the Dragonkings to be left alone. Calsandria or not, it's still a far sight better offer than the life the clans are leading now."

"I don't know," Caelith said, shaking his head.

"What's not to know?" Eryn replied.

Caelith considered for a moment. "Eryn, I came looking for Calsandria—not just as a place. Calsandria means more than farms; it was the home of the ancient gods. There was a—I don't know—a *life* to it."

"You're looking for living gods," Lucian asked skeptically, "here? I'd say by the look of things, these gods of yours haven't taken good enough care of their old worshippers."

"You may be right," Caelith replied, tossing another stick onto the fire. "And if I find them, I'll be sure to ask them about that."

"If these gods exist, then Lucian's right," Eryn said. "They haven't done us any good. The clans need land where they can put down roots and build homes. After all the Pir have put us through, the last thing they need is another religion."

"But there's got to be more to us than farms and struggle and war," Caelith said. "I can't explain it, but somehow I know this is true. It isn't something I've seen in the dream—but it's got to be true nevertheless. I'm not all that sure what it is I'm looking for—hoping for—but I only hope that I'll know it when I find it."

"If you *do* find your gods," Lucian replied, "then I certainly hope you will ask them for considerable assistance. Without divine intervention, I have serious doubts about anyone ever hearing about us or your gods ever again. We walked into this valley, but I doubt very much that we will walk out as easily."

Shaeonyn

"Look! Look at Aislynn! Look what she is doing now!"

The laughter rains down all around me, suffused into my tears, which only seems to make the crowd howl all the louder with ridicule. I am not dancing the dance that the crowd expected of me as I move to a music that is all my own. My feet bleed from the shoes that I wear and I cry out in horrible pain but the crowd beyond the bright globes of light blazing in my eyes finds my positions comical and my dance an awkward travesty. No matter how hard I try, my fluttering is agonizingly inept and my steps on the stage faltering and wrong. Each more careful move only pushes me into another of the dancers that encircle me, wrenching my feet in the terrible shoes and sending a lightning bolt of pain up my legs.

The dancers around me are faeries clad in dark colors, their wings a smoky gray, their faces all hidden behind ornate masks of steel. They are eyeless, dancing blindly behind the masks, their hands linking them in a circle moving around me. Their movements are different from my own and no matter how carefully I move, I keep colliding with them. Each time I do, they scream at me in outrage, and their voices pierce me to the bone.

Yet I cannot stop the dance, for to do so will, I know, anger the crowd. They would destroy me in their hatred and not me *alone; for I do not dance for myself but for the others who are also on the stage anxiously watching me and knowing somehow that everything depends upon me.*

Then, as I struggle onward, dancing through my own sobs and tears, the circle around me breaks, dancing away from me across the stage and forming once more around a dancer whose movements are like their own.

"Please," I call out into the darkness beyond the lights. "Please let me stop!"

But the crowd laughs all the more at me — and my shoes keep forcing me to dance painfully on . . .

FAERY TALES
BRONZE CANTICLES, TOME VIII, FOLIO 3, LEAF 23

"Aislynn," a voice came from the darkness. "It is time for you to wake up."

"Why—what is it?" Aislynn asked, still groggy from sleep.

"You must get dressed," Shaeonyn said simply.

"Why? What is the matter?" the Princess asked as she sat up in her bed in the captain's cabin. She blinked, trying to see. A thin line of morning light could be seen outside the windows to the rear of the cabin but it was not yet sufficient to illuminate the pools of night in the corners of the compartment. It took her eyes a moment to focus in the darkness.

"Where is everyone else?" Aislynn yawned. The other bunks were empty.

"They are all waiting on us, Princess," Shaeonyn said flatly.

"Oh." Aislynn wondered how it was she had not heard them rise. She stood up, pulling her nightgown over her head. She quickly tugged on her breeches and reached for her gown, yanking it on over her head. She reached around for the back panel between her wings and started lacing it up on the right side as she spoke. "Has something unforeseen happened?"

"No," Shaeonyn replied. "Nothing unforeseen."

Aislynn nodded, lacing up the other side of the panel. There was something changed in their surroundings but she was having trouble grasping it fully. It suddenly came to her. "We've stopped! Have we arrived?"

"Yes." Shaeonyn smiled. "We most certainly have."

"Wonderful!" The Princess beamed, pressing her feet into her traveling boots. "That's so much sooner than expected!"

Shaeonyn only smiled. "There is only a little time left to us, Aislynn . . ."

The Princess did not hear her. She reached up out of habit to brush her fingers across the pearls at her neck . . .

The pearls!

Aislynn's eyes went suddenly wide. She turned at once, her hands flying through the bedclothes on the bunk, pulling the blanket free. She ran her hands once across the boards. She turned around twice, her eyes darting all around the deck. "They're gone!" she cried. "Where are they? They must be here! Where could they have gone?"

"They have gone here," Shaeonyn said, pulling back the high collar on her tunic.

The black pearls lay around her neck.

"Give them to me," Aislynn demanded, her hand reaching out at once for them.

Shaeonyn, however, was ready for her. Her right hand flicked upward, the air suddenly igniting in front of the senior Sharajin. Aislynn fell backward against the bunk rail, knocked nearly off her feet from the blast of heated air.

"Take the counsel of one who is far better trained in the arts of the vision," Shaeonyn said calmly, her beautiful eyes bright as she spoke. "You and the other Fae representatives of this ill-conceived quest are jeopardizing my mission here. The others are merely inconvenient, but you are worse; you are untrained, soft, and spoiled— a danger to yourself and others. This, truly, was foreseen, and now the political necessity of your attendance has ended."

"This was never part of Dwynwyn's plan nor—" Aislynn stopped abruptly. "But you aren't in the service of Dwynwyn, are you? This is not Dwynwyn's mission that you are fulfilling, is it?"

Shaeonyn spoke. "Take only what you think absolutely necessary. It's a long way."

"Who are you working for?" Aislynn was furious.

Shaeonyn held her silence.

"Who do you serve?" Aislynn screamed. Without conscious thought, she pushed both her hands out in front of her. Darts of ice formed in the air, ripping instantly toward the treacherous Seeker. Shaeonyn crossed her hands in front of her face, light pooling suddenly in front of her and its heat nearly vaporizing the shards as they flew to their mark. One of the darts slipped through, however, cutting deeply into her perfect cheek. A bright line of blood suddenly marred her flawless complexion. Shaeonyn cried out from the pain, falling to her knees as her hand reached up to press against the wound.

The door to the cabin flew open. Bachas leaped toward Aislynn but the faery was too quick for him. She pressed upward with her wings against the ceiling just as the Mantacorian reached for her. Bachas slammed against the bunk, smashing the side rails, and tumbled to the floor.

Aislynn saw Djukan and several more Mantacorians struggling to come through the door. She turned at once, flicking her hand. The heavy door to the cabin swung back, slamming against Djukan's fingers holding the door frame. He cried out but his hand kept the door from latching shut.

Aislynn spun in the air to face Shaeonyn once more but a large hand suddenly closed around her neck. She struggled for a moment but its grip was like steel and as cold as a mountain stream before the thaw. It pulled her down from the ceiling with brute force. Aislynn looked up with dismay into a familiar face.

"Deython," she rasped.

"Your Highness," answered the Commander of the Dead, his powerful grip still firm on her delicate throat. "Please do not struggle."

"But you can't do this," she said, tears streaming down her face. "You're mine."

"No longer, Your Highness," Deython intoned sadly. "No longer."

★ ★ ★

"This is an outrage!" Gosrivar bellowed as Aislynn was dragged up onto the quarterdeck, gripped painfully from behind by Captain Bachas. "I demand to know the meaning of this!"

The Kyree guards were all on deck, each with a drawn sword facing the faeries, and there was a line of Mantacorian archers with their bows waiting just behind them as well. Everyone was facing the faeries with grim determination as Bachas shoved Aislynn unceremoniously from behind out across the quarterdeck toward Obadon, Valthesh, and Gosrivar, who were all standing against the aft railing. Obadon was tense, his fists alternately clenching tightly and unclenching in his rage and frustration. Valthesh was quiet and contemplative, her wild hair blowing in the slight breeze. Gosrivar was nearly purple with indignation.

"Djukan!" Aislynn said quickly. "You've got to stop this!"

"I'm sorry, Princess," the Kyree leader replied as he climbed to the quarterdeck and stood next to Bachas. His voice was heavy and thoughtful. "I have little choice left in the matter. At least one of them has been harboring a terrible secret that jeopardizes this mission—indeed, we suspect several of you of conspiring to commit murder."

"Impossible!" Obadon said flatly, his anger simmering in his eyes.

"The Fae are incapable of lying," Gosrivar snapped. "That's entirely a Famadorian failing."

"Yet not incapable of scheming against one of your own," Djukan said quickly, "for events have proven otherwise. One or more of the four of you most certainly assassinated Ularis; a fact we have known since leaving port. The body was found and the matter was brought to me directly as soon as we returned from town."

"Then why include me in your accusation?" Aislynn asked. "I was with you that night in Kel Cliff and, as you no doubt recall, certainly in no condition after that to have committed such an unspeakable act!"

"Certainly not afterward—but quite possibly before. Ularis's flesh had long grown cold," Djukan returned. "You could well have killed him before we left that night. Indeed, we have evidence that Ularis specifically set out to find you after you left camp that night. In any event, where we are going we cannot afford to bring a murdering faery along nor have we the ability to return to the faery lands and sort out this entire mess. One of the four of you did the deed—if not more than one—and that makes whoever did this doubly dangerous."

"So what do you propose to do about it?" Valthesh asked calmly, her arms crossed defiantly in front of her.

"Leave you here to sort it out among yourselves," Bachas said with a sharp-toothed grin. "We all discussed it and it seemed like the most polite thing to do."

"Leave us? Leave us *where?*" Aislynn asked, gesturing at the sea.

"Why, where else?" Bachas smiled and pointed off the port-side beam. Aislynn looked to her left. Against the horizon she could see low, dark green mounds rising out of the sea.

"The Wingless Isles," Djukan said. "The Kyree used this place to exile its most violent offenders from all over the empire. They are actually a group of islands in a long chain, but not one of their shores is close enough to any other land for even the strongest of the Kyree to fly the distance all at once—let alone the delicate Fae."

"The wind is freshening," Bachas advised Djukan as his eyes searched the rigging overhead. "We had best hurry this along, if you please."

"My men and, for that matter, Bachas's crew are prepared to kill you if you attempt to return to this ship or try resisting us in any way," Djukan said in warning. "Your only hope—like many others before you—is to Walk the Sky."

"Walk the—what?" Aislynn asked incredulously.

"It's an ancient tradition of the Kyree actually," Sargo said as he examined his map most carefully. "Kyree agitators, mutineers, traitors, and criminals have been marooned by this same rite for centuries."

"This is not to be borne!" Gosrivar stammered.

"Fly straight north—keep the rising sun on your right," Sargo said, "and you should be able to see a tiny spot of land jutting upward from the middle of some nasty reefs about twelve miles away."

"Twelve miles!" Gosrivar gasped.

"That's Merlock Atoll," Sargo continued as he once more consulted his map, "and you would be well advised to rest there. There is no food, no water, and no shade on the atoll, but it is fully another ten miles to the north before you'll encounter Chytree Island. That's the main island in the group and where most of the penal settlements were located."

"And just how will the criminals of the Kyree welcome four faery ambassadors?" Valthesh asked in tones that dripped sarcasm.

"They won't," Sargo chuckled. "We anchored among these islands when we fled the fall of the empire. Whatever happened to the Kyree mainland happened here as well. There will be no welcome—warm or otherwise—for there is no one left there to greet you."

"We're wasting time," Djukan spat. "We will return for you as soon as it is feasible to do so, but—as Shaeonyn has aptly pointed out—for now this mission is too important to endanger it with unnecessary and dangerous unknowns."

Aislynn glanced around her. She had to do something! She searched within herself and found the magic there, burning as it gathered within her. She concentrated, her mind shifting through different thoughts and dreams, images and connections for just the right combination that would somehow take shape and make everything right.

"Oraclyn-loi!" Shaeonyn had come up from the cabin at last. "Do not show your foolishness in an act that will get you and others killed. You are untrained and have only a minor talent for the vision. You are no match for me and certainly no match for the Guardians of the Dead whom I now command. You know this is true."

Aislynn turned to the young Kyree lord. "Djukan, you're making a terrible mistake."

Djukan shook his head sadly. "No, Princess. You were among those who did not answer my questions."

Aislynn eyed the Sharajin with bitter hatred, her black pearls draped around Shaeonyn's neck. "But it was you who told me to hold my silence!"

"No, Lord Djukan," Shaeonyn said evenly. "I did no such thing. She lies."

Aislynn gazed on the Sharajin in shocked disbelief.

"But," Sargo stammered. "I though you said that the Fae *cannot* lie."

"That is true." Shaeonyn took a step toward her Oraclyn-loi, eyeing her critically. "But if this one has somehow acquired the ability then she would be doubly dangerous to us and our quest."

Aislynn looked at Djukan. The Kyree lord's face was set, his mind made up. The weapons of all the ship's crew and the Kyree were against them, but none of this was as terrifying to her as the fact that her Sharajin-loi had lied. She alone knew it in that moment—and feared that the knowledge would die with her.

"Go now," Shaeonyn commanded, as cool as the morning breeze. "This is no place for a princess to die."

Aislynn considered this for a moment—then smiled.

"You are quite right, Shaeonyn," she said. "This is no place for either of us to die."

With that Aislynn flapped her wings and rose from the deck—heading across the waters with the rising sun off her right hand.

The Wingless Isles

Aislynn heard the laughter and jeers of the crew falling behind her as she rose higher into the air, her eyes stinging with her tears. She heard Obadon curse and the flapping of other Fae wings behind her as well; Gosrivar and Valthesh were rising with the Argentei warrior to follow Aislynn into the sky above an unforgiving expanse of sea.

For a few minutes Aislynn concentrated on the simple beating of her wings, their rhythm and motion through the air. There were a great many questions tumbling through her mind. Ularis murdered—it seemed inconceivable. Death was a common enough occurrence among the faeries in a world where Famadorians often hunted them for sport if they strayed from their protected borders, and warfare among some of the different houses of the Fae was almost an art form in itself. Murder, too, was known among the more impassioned of the Fae, and the problems of assassination conspiracy were common among the royal houses of the Fae. That Djukan had used the word "assassination" probably meant that Ularis had, indeed, died from such a plot.

But what if a faery could lie? Shaeonyn *had* lied. That prospect frightened Aislynn more than the murder itself.

Everything had gone wrong, she thought, but at once she banished such thoughts and questions from her mind; better to survive now, she reasoned, and deal with betrayal and other questions afterward.

Only then did she turn and look behind her. The *Brethain* was already weighing anchor, her sails tumbling down from her yardarms. As she watched, the ship was already picking up headway in a quartering wind, moving off toward the southeast.

"They didn't waste any time," Valthesh tossed off.

"No, indeed, they did not," Gosrivar replied heavily. "Nor should you. You must be off at once, if you have any hope of making the safety of the island."

"So must we all." Aislynn nodded toward her companions hovering in the air about her, but her eyes remained fixed on the older faery sage.

Gosrivar shook his head. "No, Aislynn. You and the others are strong. I am the weakest among us and cannot survive this journey."

"You will survive," Aislynn answered. "We will help you."

Gosrivar laughed darkly. "And if you did, you would only make your own fate uncertain—you would die because of me and this must not be. I accept my weakness and know the truth of it. We Fae claim to be immortal . . ."

"But no one has ever lived long enough to know," Aislynn finished the old joke for him. "No. I do not accept that nor will any of us. Are the warriors of House Argentei strong, Lord Obadon?"

"There are none stronger," the warrior replied in absolute truth.

"And are you not a talented disciple of the Sharajin, Lady Valthesh?" Aislynn said, turning quickly to the female faery hovering on her right.

She smiled at some private joke. "It was a truth with which I was content to hold my silence. I have not attended the Lyceum so the depths of my talent have not yet been tested, Aislynn of Qestardis— but talented I truly am."

"Then does anyone here know how to swim?" Aislynn snapped.

Each of them looked at the undulating surface of the water below them and responded in most earnest negatives.

"Then we fly for the Wingless Isles together," Aislynn said flatly, "and will do so—together—without further argument."

With that she put the climbing sun on her right hand and scooped the air with her wings to fly.

The shores to the north seemed tantalizingly close but Aislynn kept telling herself that it was all an illusion; they were slightly less than twenty miles distant—a long distance for most faery to travel under normal conditions. Of course, the faery kingdoms themselves were scattered over far greater distances—Vargonis was just over eight hundred miles from the courts of Qestardis—and such distances could be covered in relatively short times by the use of nightrunner airships or the various fleets which the different houses maintained either to sail the western shores of the Qe'tekok, Incadis, or Dunadin Seas when the need arose. A faery on its own, however, was limited in the distance it could traverse by its physical endurance, the weather, and its ability to stop and rest along the way. There was something of a slight breeze from the south, which was encouraging, but only something of a minor help, for to traverse eight miles, let alone twenty—and to do so with only a single resting point—was madness.

Madness, Aislynn thought. *Is that what this is all about? Had Shaeonyn gone mad? And why did Deython and the pearls now answer only to the Sharajin?*

"Not too fast," Obadon called out. "A steady pace will get us further."

Aislynn felt a surge of pride as first Valthesh and then Obadon and Gosrivar both came into view next to her, their wings beating with her own, undulating through the air in an easy and natural synchronization. She smiled to herself and slowed down to match her companions, looking across the tops of the waves as they passed under all of them. Each stroke of their wings brought them closer to rest, water, and life.

For Aislynn, it had become more than just a question of life. She felt a resolve that she had not known in years. She remembered the dream she had the night before and knew now that it had tried to warn her of what was coming, but she had not understood it. Now she felt the grim determination to follow that dream wherever it took her—and find this new truth that had thus far eluded her.

The air warmed perceptibly as the sun climbed higher into the sky. The purple-tinged green of the island had grown and lengthened, but its shores still remained far beyond them.

Aislynn was finding it difficult to catch her breath. Her lungs ached and the muscles in her back threatened to seize up altogether. Still she pressed on. She continued to scoop the air because she had to; because to stop was to give up, and more than anything, to give up was to allow Shaeonyn to be victorious over her.

"Please!" Gosrivar croaked. He had fallen behind them, struggling to keep up. "I can't—I can't go on."

"Come on," Aislynn rasped. "We're almost there. Then you can rest all you want."

Valthesh looked sideways at her. She, too, was breathing heavily with the exertion. "Almost where?"

"Almost to the atoll," Aislynn said. "Look—off to the—to the left."

A spark of light flashed above the water ahead of them and just left of their line of flight. It flashed again moments later; a rhythmic pulsing light amid the waves. The longer Aislynn watched it, the clearer she could make out the white water of breaking ocean waves.

"That's it!" Aislynn altered her course toward the outlying reef surrounding a large, circular shoal. Just north of its center, the flashing light obscured a tiny piece of land.

"I can't," Gosrivar sighed. "It's too far."

"You can," Aislynn said, gulping air. "You know, it's surprising what you can do. Did you know that I used to be a princess? Look at me now, Gosrivar! I've dropped all the way to Seeker of the Shara-jin. How low do you think a person with talent and ambition might possibly sink in faery society, eh, Gosrivar?"

"In your case," Obadon said with a smile, "I might say one's potential is unlimited."

Valthesh laughed.

Aislynn smiled grimly. "What do you think, Gosrivar?"

"I find it—appalling that the youth of—of your generation have so little respect for the—for the traditions of your elders!" Gosrivar said, his voice breaking with the effort. "To think that I should live to—to see the day when a princess of the—of the First Estate should say such things!"

"Indeed," Aislynn said, swallowing hard, her mouth dry. They had carefully angled toward the atoll. The flashing light was getting closer. "I don't understand. Tell us what you mean."

"You don't want to hear what I have to say," Gosrivar croaked.

Keep talking! Don't think about the pain and just keep flying! Aislynn thought as she said, "I do—I think all of us could benefit from your wisdom. Of course, if you don't think you have anything to teach us . . ."

"Not have anything—why, you young whelp!" Gosrivar roared. "I've forgotten more truth that you'll ever learn!"

They were crossing the outer barrier reef of the atoll. Aislynn was struggling to stay airborne; the gentle waves of the shoals seemed to reach up to pull her down into their cool and eternal rest. The waters were so clear that she could see the bottom and wondered how far she would sink before she reached it.

She snapped her head up, concentrating on the white-sand shore ahead of her. The flashing light was coming from the top of some sort of bone-white structure—apparently the only shade on the entire spit of sand jutting up from the surface of the water.

"Forgotten?" Aislynn said, gritting her teeth against the cramps in her wing muscles and back. "What have I forgotten, old man?"

"You've forgotten your manners, for one! I've never—ACK!" Gosrivar's wings suddenly seized. He slowed dangerously only a few hundred feet above the water.

"Obadon!" Aislynn called. "Quick! Help him!"

The large warrior wheeled quickly. With a great cry, he folded his wings, plunging downward toward Gosrivar as he pinwheeled to the water below. He pressed open his wings just as he got hold of the old faery, pressing hard to stop his descent.

"I can't hold him," he called, his wings fluttering hard but unable to keep them from descending.

Aislynn wheeled back and dove toward them, calling after her. "Valthesh! Come on!"

Valthesh's eyes locked with Aislynn's for a moment—a look of decision on her face—and then the wild-haired Seeker turned away, her wings beating furiously toward the shore.

Aislynn shook her head in disgust and plunged down toward Obadon, who still was straining upward with all his might to lift the groaning Gosrivar still in his arms. Aislynn quickly circled them once, getting below them. She wheeled over on her back, carefully wrapping her own arms around the old faery's quivering wings until she had a good grip around his waist. Then, with all the strength left in her, she began beating her own wings furiously.

Their descent slowed further still, but it was not enough. Straining as they might, they were making no progress against the water waiting below them.

"Let me go," Gosrivar sighed.

"No," Aislynn yelled. "We all go together!"

Suddenly, the water below depressed into a huge bowl nearly fifty feet deep. An enormous gust of wind erupted around them, a waterspout that reached into the sky. The mists kicked upward around the three faeries, the gale catching their wings and carrying them upward higher and higher into the air. Aislynn screamed; Obadon shouted in exhilaration. The waterspout dissipated beneath them as quickly as it had appeared.

Obadon and Aislynn glided through the air, the astonished Gosrivar still held between them. They were more than a thousand feet above the atoll now.

"Do you think you can just extend your wings?" Aislynn asked the sage.

"Yes, of course," Gosrivar said, still filled with astonishment. "I can make it now—thank you."

The three of them glided wearily down toward the white structure below set in the center of the white sands of the atoll. In moments, their feet lightly touched the warm sands and they collapsed onto the beach.

Aislynn pushed herself up on her hands. A few yards from her lay

Valthesh, seemingly unconscious. Aislynn pulled herself across the sands to where the Vargonis Seeker lay. "Valthesh?"

The Seeker's eyes fluttered open. She lolled her head in the direction of the sand-covered princess. "Sorry to leave you like that—I just couldn't figure out how to make it work without my feet on the ground. I take it I sent you high enough?"

"Yes—yes, you did."

"Then we all made it?"

"Yes." Aislynn smiled, reaching out and gripping Valthesh by the shoulder. "We all made it together."

Deep Trouble

The faery with the scarred wing dances with Shaeonyn on the stage, both of them eclipsing the light and casting me in shadow. They both are laughing at my feeble and fumbling steps on the stage. Tears fall from my eyes, pooling on the stage around me, but I dance on. I am shrinking, growing smaller and smaller on the stage as my own tears grow into an ocean around me. I now see my companions—Obadon, Valthesh, and Gosrivar—all lying exhausted on the white sands of a tiny island. I stand trapped among them, for far off I see the Wingless Isles, where a light flashes on the shore, a guiding beacon that calls us to that lush island with the promise of shelter, water, and food. I know that we shall die if we stay here—and that we shall die if we leave, for I cannot bear to leave Gosrivar and he cannot hope to fly such a distance once more. I see bones at my feet—our bones perhaps or the bones of a thousand others who have died on this minuscule shore—bleached and adding their brightness to the sands.

The white building is here, too. As I look more closely, it, too, is made of bones and skulls, all chattering at me strangely and in voices that are confusing. Then the pillars of the building rise up out of the sands, moving as though they were legs. The building walks across the sands and into the ocean, chattering brightly all the while. I call to it to come back, but it does not heed me and disappears beneath the waves.

The sun is suddenly blocked behind me and I turn but am astonished to see an enormous cloud in the shape of a wingless man. I have seen him before in my dream, though he has come to me in many guises — sometimes smoke and sometimes fire. Now I see him as a creature of cloud. His voice is like thunder, his laughter rolling across the waves monstrously loud. I shrink from his approach but there is no longer anyplace on the atoll where I might hide.

The cloud-man stops above me, his enormous size covering nearly half the sky. He seems to be waiting for something from me. I know better than to speak to him, for my voice has always shattered his image in the past. So I turn and point to the Wingless Isles. Can he bear us there?

His great hand reaches down, its brightness above becoming dark and laced with lightning. I expect it to reach for me, but it passes over my head and reaches down into the water at the shore. It pulls a gargantuan handful of water out of the ocean, but, to my astonishment, the sea does not rush to replace it; instead, it leaves a great hollowed void in its place where the seabed is suddenly dry.

I look back up at the cloud-giant, who smiles back at me. Hesitantly, I turn to the hollowed patch of sea and step into it. As I walk farther on, the enormous hand moves with my every step, the hollow of the ocean moving with me in any direction I step.

I smile. Gosrivar will not have to fly the distance after all! I gaze up in thanks to the vast man of cloud, my hands clapping together in appreciation. All around our little island, the bones of the dead rise up out of the sands as well, chattering and applauding with the clattering bones of their hands.

The cloud-giant looks at me with confusion, his hands open. He looks from side to side, uncertain as to the direction he should take next.

I realize in that moment that I am, indeed, Sharajin — a Seeker of the Dead. I whisper to the bones around me. They explode into dust, rising up into the air, and are carried over the water on a *gust of wind. Their dust forms into the shape of dancing figures leading the cloud-giant southward.*

FAERY TALES
BRONZE CANTICLES, TOME VIII, FOLIO 3, LEAVES 24–25

Aislynn shook herself awake. The sun was already lowering toward the western horizon. Her muscles ached terribly and it was all she could do to push herself up from the sands under the shade of a pavilion.

She stood uncertainly, examining the structure. The eight pillars supporting its roof appeared to be fashioned out of some type of bright coral that had been shaped into spiraling columns. There were deep markings in it with numerous depictions of fish and what looked to Aislynn like other sea creatures as well. All eight columns rose up in long curves to join at a single peak. The roof itself was a latticework that would provide shade but not shelter from a storm. Through the coral web ceiling, Aislynn could see thin, curved vanes arranged around a central spindle that turned in the breeze at the peak of the roof. The top of the spindle rotated an oval piece of flat mirrored glass that flashed periodically the rays of the setting sun across the sea.

"An ingenious contraption," Obadon said as he walked toward the princess.

"Yes," Aislynn agreed. "The Kyree can be clever when it suits their purposes."

Obadon looked around at the tiny, barren spit of land on which they stood. "We, apparently, do not suit their purposes."

"And with us," Aislynn returned, "they have not been clever." She turned to face the green island to the north, still temptingly large on the horizon and still seemingly just as far away. A flash of light caught her eye. "Do you see it?"

"Yes," Obadon replied, following her gaze across the water. "It is another beacon. I believe we are standing on what the lieutenant Kyree called Merlock Atoll. That beacon must be meant to lead us to Chytree Island. No doubt it was meant to aid those who were marooned here as we have been—though it will do us no good as a group."

Aislynn folded her arms, considering. "I believe there may be more truth to be had yet in this matter."

Obadon shook his head. "No, Princess . . ."

"Aislynn—you must call me Aislynn. I believe that out here—in such circumstances—we are of our own caste."

"A caste of outcasts?" chuckled a quiet voice nearby.

"Valthesh, you are one Sharajin to be respected," Aislynn said. "How are you feeling?"

"If this ache between my wings is the price for such respect," Valthesh groaned, "I believe I could do without it." She pulled herself up slowly to sit with her back against one of the pavilion's pillars. Her wings were still quivering slightly from the exertion.

"We will need to rest here for a day—perhaps two, but no more." Obadon sighed. "Even I could not possibly fly the distance before then but we dare wait no longer; there is no water to drink here."

"Actually," Aislynn said casually, "I was thinking we might leave as soon as Gosrivar gets up from his nap."

The two other faeries stared back at her.

"Too much sun," Obadon finally said.

"Or too little thought," Valthesh added with skepticism. "Oraclyn, not even Obadon's wings will bear him another ten miles tonight!"

"I agree," Aislynn replied. "None of our wings will bear us anywhere tonight."

"Well, then how . . ."

"How far do you think Gosrivar could *walk?*" Aislynn asked, turning once more to eye the distant beacon on the far shore and summon up a vision of the wingless man.

"This is most unnatural, Princess!" Gosrivar's teeth were chattering so badly that it was difficult to understand him.

The shifting rays of sunlight filtered blue through the clear waters overhead. The gentle surface waves rolled thirty feet overhead, sparkling slightly under the bright sky of a lengthening day. Fish—

singularly at first and progressively more in larger schools—drifted by, their cold eyes casting curious gazes at the four closely huddled faeries walking past them on the ocean floor.

"Is he that terrified or just cold?" Valthesh asked nervously.

"Both!" Gosrivar shot back, his voice a full octave higher than usual. "We shouldn't be here!"

"None of us should be here," Aislynn said quickly. "We should all be on a ship sailing toward some Kyree port city called Jugan Mee or Jugan Moi—or something like that. We should be on a ship with that traitorous Shaeonyn and her traitorous friend Djukan enjoying an evening meal with their traitorous Famadorian crew! But we're not; we're stuck out here on the ocean—"

"Under the ocean," Obadon corrected nervously.

"Fine, *under* the ocean," Aislynn continued testily, "and the only food and water available is this way. I honestly don't know what you're complaining about; there's a nice breeze in here and we're completely dry."

"I was curious about that," Obadon said. "Why is there a breeze under the water?"

"There isn't," Aislynn said. "I mean, well, there obviously *is* a breeze right here under the water, but that's only because there's a breeze where this water has been sent."

"Huh?" Obadon shook his head.

"I mean," Aislynn said, stepping carefully over a sharp rock protruding from the sandy seabed, "that the water that normally would be where we are is up above us, somewhere in the air—while the air that normally is where that water is—"

"Is down here?" Obadon completed, still unsure.

"Ah—an exchange." Valthesh smiled. "The water up there switches places for the air down here. So long as there's a breeze up there, we have fresh air here—at least as long as the magic holds out."

"What?" Gosrivar squeaked.

The sandy ocean floor suddenly dropped off, descending gently into darker regions before them.

"Now what?" Valthesh asked.

Aislynn peered into the shadowy blue before them. "Well, it

doesn't look too much different from where we are now—just deeper. We still have the sun on our left and we should have only a few more miles to go before we climb onto the shores of Chytree Island. Let's not stop when we're so close." She glanced at the old, quivering sage. "Somebody hang on to Gosrivar and let's press on."

"Wait," Obadon said. "What happens if it starts raining where the water is now?"

"We get wet?" Aislynn asked in response.

They started down the slope. Within minutes the contour of the ocean floor changed. There were more large boulders for them to make their way around, slowing their progress. Their course was also more obscure, for the light had dimmed considerably, making it difficult to plan their path.

They had walked about an hour when Obadon suddenly froze, his voice a strained whisper. "Wait!"

They all stopped at once, their eyes straining to pierce the murky waters around them.

"What is it?" Aislynn asked.

"I thought—I'm sorry, I was sure I saw something out there," Obadon said quietly.

"What did you think you saw?" Valthesh asked carefully.

"Nothing—I'm sure of it," Obadon answered. "I think it's just the quiet down here. Let's keep moving; the sooner we get out of here—"

A long dark shape, nearly ten feet wide and longer than any of them could say, slid quickly past the faeries just beyond the extent of their vision.

"Oh, now I definitely saw that!" Valthesh said, her open hands rising in front of her.

"No! Wait!" Aislynn said. "Don't! We don't know what it will do to this bubble!"

The shape loomed out of the darkness once more, this time on the other side of them. Aislynn caught a glimpse of a long, snakelike body plated in huge scales.

"We've got to do something!"

"Gosrivar! We're right here!" Valthesh snapped. "There's no point in yelling!"

"There!" Aislynn pointed. "Into those rocks!"

They began to run, the bubble around them moving with them. The sand under their feet kicked up behind them as they neared the rock outcropping.

Suddenly, the hideous face of the creature emerged from the darkness, charging directly at them. It had the long snout and deep mouth of a reptile, its jaws lined with long, daggerlike teeth. Horns fully fifteen feet long swept back from its heavy brow, ridges that were set over dull, lifeless black eyes. The monster rushed toward them through the water, its mouth gaping open as it surged out of the darkness.

The snout slammed against the rigid bubble with such incredible force that it was dislodged from the seabed. The faeries were thrown with it, losing their footing from the sand with the upward rush of the bubble's inner surface. They tumbled on top of each other within the tumbling bubble, rolling backward through the water until the bubble lost its momentum and drifted gently back to the seabed. The sands below them, by the quirky whim of the mystical forces Aislynn had called into existence, rose up once more through the bubble to support the dazed and shaken faeries.

"Name of our Fathers!" Obadon staggered to his feet, astonished. "The bubble held!"

Aislynn struggled to get back on her feet. "Come on!" she cried out. "We've got to get to shelter!"

"Where is it?" Obadon called excitedly.

Aislynn could see it now, silhouetted against the dim light from above. It was a colossal serpent but with fins on the forward part of its body like a fish and a long barb at its tail. It may have been hundreds of feet long; it was difficult for Aislynn to tell. The creature was writhing in the water, shaking its mammoth head back and forth in anger and confusion.

"Come on! This way!" She ran once more, her companions at her heels. They rushed breathlessly toward the outcropping. Aislynn stumbled over a rock obstructing her path, got her footing again, and continued.

"It's coming back!" she heard Valthesh yell.

"Don't stop!" Aislynn called back. She could see a path into the rocks ahead. She rushed forward between the pillars of stone.

Only to slide to a stop at the top of a precipice. The water below her fell away into blackness.

"Wait!" she cried out. "Stop!"

Too late. Obadon crashed into her, pushing her out over the edge of the sea cliff. Gosrivar and Valthesh hovered momentarily on the edge but the bubble followed Aislynn and pulled them over as well. The bubble, free again, fell gently down the sea wall, farther and farther into the darkness. Lying helpless against the lower wall of the sphere, Aislynn locked her eyes on Obadon's as the darkness enveloped them.

Then there was a jarring impact from beneath. Aislynn felt pressure against her back as they seemed to rush upward, back toward the light. But quite suddenly she wished for the darkness to shield her eyes, for the long fangs of the serpent were locked around the bubble, occasionally clicking against its stubborn, impenetrable surface.

The serpent was plunging through the water with its prize clenched firmly in its jaws. The ocean floor was rushing past them at a tremendous pace, but then vanished altogether. One thing only penetrated Aislynn's thoughts: the sunlight filtering down through the surface was behind them and to her right now.

The serpent was headed to the southeast, directly out to sea.

Smoke and Mirrors

Caelith stared into the roaring fire. He had been absently tossing pieces of wood onto it for some time and he barely noticed that the heat from the resulting blaze was becoming uncomfortable even in the chill of the deepening night. The stars overhead were a brilliant dome over the clear sky, but he took little notice before the fire obliterated them from his vision. Bright, hot light played and danced across the scattered stones of the ruins about him.

"You've grown quiet lately," Eryn said, choosing a spot near the fire which, Caelith noted, was carefully gauged so that they might speak without being too close. "That's a new approach for you—usually you try to talk your companions into the ground."

Caelith smiled absently, his mind elsewhere. "You're right."

"Well, that's a change!" Eryn laughed ruefully.

"Isn't it." Caelith nodded, tossing another long stick onto the fire. It knocked embers into the air, then cracked, igniting at once. "There was a time when I thought everyone was waiting to hear the next word falling from my lips. Caelith, son of Galen the Great! Then I realized I was just talking to myself—and I didn't find me that interesting."

They both lapsed into silence, watching the flames dance feverishly in the gaps between and through the logs. It was true, he realized. Back when they had first known each other, he thought he not only had all the answers but believed he *was* all the answers. How could he explain to Eryn what happened to him when he barely understood it himself. The pep talks in preparation for raids, the speeches about the nobility of their wandering, the need of sacrifice—it had all crumbled to tasteless dust in his mouth. He wondered if there really was something more to life—some purpose—in all this suffering. There had to be something beyond the service and study of a magic that most of the known world decried as a vile and blasphemous evil.

Anji's words came back to him once more. *The prize does not make us strong—but the winning does.*

Caelith looked away from the fire to the crumbling, overgrown foundations around them. He spoke as much to himself as to Eryn. "Just think about it; we supposedly sit in the ruins of the greatest human empire history ever knew. This was a street once. Merchants must have walked down it; maybe children played here without a care in the shadow of walls that they thought would last for eternity. What happened to them, Eryn? Where were the miracles of the Rhamasian gods when they needed them? Where was their divine power when humanity cried out to them and these stones fell for the last time?"

Caelith drew in a long breath as he turned back to the fire. The long tongues of flame danced above, the smoke from the damp wood rolling upward into the clear night.

"I don't know," Eryn replied quietly, her gaze also fixed contemplatively on the flames. "But I do know that our clans need a rest. They all hope for Calsandria, and we can give them that hope right here."

"What if it's a false hope," Caelith said, shaking his head.

"Then it will be a hope nevertheless," the woman replied. "It is more than they have now—more than any of us have."

"You may be right." Caelith sighed.

Eryn gave him an amused look. "Another first!"

"Maybe this place is an answer," Caelith said huskily, "but . . ."

"But?" Eryn coaxed.

"But the wind is still blowing in my dreams," Caelith said into the fire. "It still carries my soul with it, calling me to another place."

"Toward Calsandria or peace?"

"Both, I thought. There is a voice in it that calls to me. I hoped this would be it—the place where I could get the answers to my own questions—but we've come to the end of this road and I don't know which way to go."

The flames of the fire danced and shifted, suddenly twisting over the glowing embers. They drew together, curling inward, taking the form of a winged woman created out of the flames. She danced across the top of the logs.

Caelith and Eryn both stared, transfixed.

"What is it?" Eryn asked.

"It's me," Caelith replied in hushed tones. "It's the Deep Magic— I can feel it welling up from inside me—but I've never seen this before. Are you seeing this, too?"

"She's beautiful," Eryn whispered in awe.

The flames roared upward, reaching out with graceful arms, the long curves of its body spinning in a dance. Violet sheets of light flickered backward into translucent wings. The delicate woman of flame spun in her dance, her arms held out as if pleading.

"I know her," Caelith said with a smile. "I've seen her in the dream."

"She wants something," Eryn shook her head, puzzled. "What is it?"

"She wants—quickly! Where are the water skins?"

"There, behind you, but . . ."

Caelith spun on his heels, falling on the full skins. "Not enough! Where's the bucket?"

Eryn glanced back at the beautiful woman in flame. "Down the slope—I left it next to the river, but . . ."

Caelith was already charging down the embankment, a mad grin on his face. He stumbled over one of the foundation stones, rolling partway down the hill before regaining his feet. Giddily, he hurtled into the water, after snatching a bucket from the bank. He plunged it into the drifting waters under the starlit sky, dragging it back to shore and racing back up the slope.

"Help me," Caelith yelled to Eryn. "You use the water skins."

"Help you do what?" She was peering at him oddly. He realized he must look like a lunatic.

"What is all this about, old man?" Lucian said, struggling toward them, "and it had better be worth my waking up."

"Good, you're here. Help us put out the fire!" he shouted, setting the sloshing bucket quickly on the ground. He started tossing water skins at his astonished companions.

"No!" Eryn said pointing at the flame-woman still dancing above the embers. "You'll kill her!"

"I say," Lucian said, blinking at the flames, "are you developing a new form of amusement, Caelith?"

"Just do as I say," Caelith instructed, picking up the bucket. "When I signal, douse the fire. Ready? Now!"

The water arced through the air. The fiery woman reached upward in its approach as it engulfed her, and she collapsed with it into the embers. Thick smoke billowed upward from the flames, engulfing them all at once.

"That was pointless," Eryn said, coughing.

"Wait," Caelith rasped. "Look!"

The smoke churned around them, then twisted under the bright stars. It lay flat against the ground, its contours forming the perfect pattern of the cobblestone street that once paved the wide avenue here. Its translucent tendrils rose upward from the foundation stones, forming into the smoky images of storefronts, shops, and tall homes that once lined the streets. The ash from the fire fitted itself to the ghostly form of the city now long lost. The smoke continued to pour from the doused fire, flowing constantly down the facades and walkways, reincarnating farther and farther down the path the images of vanished ruins as they once stood in their prime.

Caelith carefully approached the gray, almost transparent storefront to their right. "Look," he said almost reverently as he pointed. "You can even make out the marking on the building."

"'Indro's Bakery,'" Lucian read from the etching in the barely undulating smoke. He raised his eyebrow. "Not terribly original of old Indro, was it?"

"Oh, no!" Eryn breathed. "Caelith?"

Caelith turned, following Eryn's wide-eyed gaze down the street. The smoke continued to flow, re-creating more buildings as it went. He could even see the faint form of incredible towers toward the center of the city—but something else immediately drew his attention back to the street.

"People," Eryn said and shuddered.

They were more like outlines in the smoke—clear spaces where the haze of the smoke was somehow absent. Here, the details were mercifully missing entirely. The street was teeming with them. A couple—the figure of a tall man and a shorter woman—walked past them down the walkway, the outline of their arms entwined, their heads cocked toward each other. Vacant forms of children scampered about one another in a game that remained unfinished for four centuries. The outline of a group of hollow men moved down the street in great animation, their voices unheard and the subject of their argument now moot.

"Is this what becomes of us," Caelith whispered, "when our time is done?"

"It's so—oh, please, Caelith, make it stop," Eryn choked out.

"Wait, Eryn," Caelith said in wonder. "Look."

The outline of a woman walked down the center of the street directly toward them. For a moment, Caelith was certain she would pass directly through him, but the figure stopped in front of him. She seemed to be staring directly at him and she raised her hand and gestured for him to follow her. She then turned and walked back down the ethereal street.

Caelith cleared his throat. "Let's go."

"In there?" Eryn croaked.

"The smoke is already starting to thin here," Caelith said, pointing to the walls of the street. They were already nearly transparent.

"This—phantom or whatever it is—wants to show us something and I, for one, want to see what it is. I only wish we had more than starlight."

"I wonder," Lucian said, raising his hand in the air. Almost at once, the pale light from a glowing sphere awoke in his upheld palm. It lit the gray smoke street more clearly, but did nothing to dissipate it. Still the outlines moved fluidly around them.

Caelith nodded, his voice not as sure as he would have liked when he spoke. "Thank you, Lucian—and in the famous words of our intrepid Jorgan: 'This way.'"

They quickly moved in pursuit of the spectral woman, following her outline down the broad avenue that drifted about them. Unsure of themselves, they stepped to the side whenever the outline of someone stood in their path, not wishing to disturb what seemed like an imprint of a soul. They passed down through towering edifices whose grandeur spoke of power and wealth—now gone from the memory of man.

"I say," Lucian spoke sotto voce, "where is the rest of our valiant party? We appear to be short several humans and a dwarf."

"You nervous?" Caelith asked anxiously.

"Not at all, old boy," Lucian lied smoothly. "I just thought that since we've all come this far together, it would be nice to die together as well."

"But then who would bury us?"

"Well, it hasn't seemed to bother these people." Lucian gestured around them at the hollow specters walking past.

"Will you both shut up!" came Eryn's tense voice.

Their shadowy guide brought them into an enormous circular garden in the center of the city. The trees, down to their leaves in each detail, were re-created in the smoke from Caelith's fire. The spectral woman led them to the center of the park, the blades of its grass re-created in gray, where she stopped to gaze up at a monument, now lost entirely to time.

Lucian brought his light closer to the markings on its surface, reading them aloud. "'I am Shushankh, Tribune of Segathlas City and all of Nharuthenia. Behold the power and the might of our works to the greater glory of Rhamas.'" He reached forward with his hand to touch the plaque but it passed through the smoke, dissolving the inscription into swirls of smoke, only to re-form once more when he withdrew his hand. Lucian looked around at the buildings that once were and now were no more. "Well, old Shushankh, your power and glory seem a bit faded, old boy."

"Caelith, can we move on?" Eryn said quietly. She was staring at the hollow form of a woman lifting the silent outline of an infant into the air nearby.

"Our guide—she's moving again," Caelith said, pointing across the square toward a building with towering smoke columns. They hurried to follow her through the main doorway, framed in ghostlike gray. Beyond was a hallway, perfectly rendered. They stepped cautiously into the dark space, close together under the radiance of Lucian's light.

"By the gods," Caelith muttered in admiration, stepping into the large space beyond.

The rotunda vaulted overhead, six courses of columns rising a full hundred feet over their heads. The dome at the top was incomplete, the smoke swirling in wisps with the bright stars shining down through it. Huge stones, once cornices on the concourses high above, lay strewn around the broken slabs of the floor, sticking up incongruously through the perfect smoke depiction of the building as it once existed. The spectral woman moved across this floor and stopped, her head bowed.

"What is she doing?" Eryn whispered.

"I think she's looking at something," Lucian offered.

"Come on," Caelith said. They stepped forward across the broken and shattered slabs of the floor, their feet disturbing the smoke rendering for only a moment before it re-formed around them. At last, they stood before the smoky apparition. Caelith looked down under the light of Lucian's mystic ball.

"It—it's a map," Eryn breathed. "The whole floor is a map!"

"Look! Over here!" Lucian moved off, taking his light with him. "Right here! This is Segathlas—this is where we are! It's all marked— this whole valley was known as Nharuthenia—and look over there!"

Lucian moved a few steps farther on, his light traveling with him. "Here is Mount Hrudan and the pass we came through! There's the Aramun Valley! Caelith, old boy! What a find! Caelith?"

Caelith continued to look down, his breathing heavy. "Quickly! The smoke won't last and we've got to mark everything! Get stones—anything—and mark everything!"

"What is it, old boy?"

"I've found it." He could barely speak. "I've found Calsandria."

Change of Plan

"I've found it . . . I've found Calsandria!"

We stand on the hilltop in the dream, the wind blowing at our backs as rain falls in torrents about us. The Masters from each of the six clans are present — as they have been each night for the last week. We have come here in our masks, strangers so far as others in the dream are concerned, to stand on this spot and call upon the dream around us for some sign. Our efforts have stirred the powers of the dream, for tonight the sky is an angry waterfall, weeping in unrelenting sorrow for the lost Calsandria, for its glory now gone and for its people now all but forgotten. The sheets of water are driven by the wind, but over its moan I still can hear the voice of my son in the rain. As I peer into the gray, his face forms in the large drops. I see the joy in his face for a moment as he gazes down.

"Is it him?" shouts Flaming Mask to me through the wind.

"It is," I call back, my eyes still trying to penetrate the shifting veil of the downpour. Caelith's face appears again for a moment. The images of a street lined with magnificent buildings drift behind him as shadows in the rain.

"Then the information given to us by the Pir is correct," the figure in the Starlight Mask says anxiously. "He has indeed found the City of the Gods?"

293

The rain shifts once more. His voice once more calls across the gale-swept hilltop.

"I've found it . . . I've found Calsandria!"

I see the look of joy on Caelith's face. What sights must he be looking on? What sights shall we soon see when we join him?

"Yes, he has found Calsandria," I reply, unbridled relief filling my voice for the first time in many days. "Spread the word among the clans. We have not a moment to lose."

"Wait! We must not be too hasty," Seafoam Mask calls out. "We should wait for him to return—to give his report to the Council."

"By the time he returns, thousands could die," snaps the Flaming Mask. "At best it would take him weeks to return—even if he were aware of the Edict's spread to all the Five Domains."

"But that was not our agreement," Seafoam Mask shouts back.

"Everything changed after he left." I speak over the wind. "They were too deep into the Forsaken Mountains when the Edict was issued for us to get word to them. Now that they have found Calsandria, they do not know there is a reason to hasten their return. Many days could be lost."

"Days we do not have," Flaming Mask adds.

"But to call our nation into the open," Seafoam Mask says, shaking its head, "on such thin evidence . . ."

"Why else have we come to this hill each night?" Starlight Mask asks, water running off its surface and curling away in the wind. "How much evidence must we wait for—how many innocent people must die while we await more proof?" Starlight Mask steps forward. I see the mask more clearly now; a jagged line of stars cutting across the dark face. It troubles me somehow. "We must remember one thing! We did not send these scouts to find Calsandria—the Pir had already done that; we sent these scouts to tell us if the Pir were lying to us—to tell us if their information was correct. Now we have seen Caelith—the very son of Galen—say that he has found Calsandria! We watched the course he took up until two days ago; we now know the way. The Pir spoke truth to us and we must act now."

"Shout to the people that Calsandria has been found by Galen's son," Flaming Mask agrees, *"and they shall rise up out of the night and gather. Shout to the people of Calsandria, and they will follow us to a place of safety that is beyond the reach of the Edict."*

"Yes," I agree, turning back to peer into the drenching rain. *"Let all the clans gather here in the Naraganth Wood. Call them from their hidden places and their fearful holes; call them from the far-thest parts of the Five Domains. Let them come by night and all quiet paths; let them drain silently from the lands of the Dragon-kings and come together as one clan out of the Six. Calsandria calls them home. It calls us all."*

As I watch, once more I see Caelith's face shimmering in the gray wall of the weeping sky.

BOOK OF GALEN
BRONZE CANTICLES, TOME IV, FOLIO VII, LEAVES 63–66

"Blasphemy!" Jorgan sputtered, his eyes blinking furiously. He stared from under the soft light of the glowing globes Lucian had conjured for them, the stars shining overhead. Under their frantic hands, shards of stone had been transformed into mountain ranges, broken tiles and slabs had become lakes, and deep ruts cut into the dirt signified rivers. The smoke had cleared but a hasty, crude rendition of the ghostly map remained. Master Kenth stood a respectful distance apart from the Inquisitas, with Lovich, Warthin, and Tarin hovering nearby.

"I might have despaired of finding you at all in this city of ruins had you not been so loud," Margrave called out cheerfully as he, with Anji and Cephas in tow, jogged up to join the rest of them among the ruins. "Ah, discovery in the night, eh? Now that's the spirit!" He began composing out loud as he walked up to them. "There they stood—the Heroes of the Lost City among the ruins of a once proud and noble civilization! The spheres of forbidden light cast an eerie pall across the—ah! A map!" Margrave said happily as he came upon the scene. "Now that would be helpful! Any idea where we are?"

"I thought you said we were in Calsandria," Lucian said wryly.

"No, not at all." Margrave beamed. "I only said that it *looked* like Calsandria. I assume that this fine—well, actually, now that I look at it, this rather *crudely* rendered map would either confirm that or not. So, where are we?"

"Segathlas," Eryn said, wiping her sleeve across her forehead, then pointing down near her feet. "Here."

"Ah, Segathlas!" Margrave spoke in suddenly hushed tones, his arms opening up into a dramatic arc, his face turning upward into the glow of the lights. "Segathlas of Woe; that place of tragedy where the glory of Rhamas came crashing down and its pride was made low in its heartrending demise." He suddenly clasped his hands to his breast, averting his face as its features contorted in agony. "Weep! Weep for the children who played within her streets, their hearts gay and with no thought of the doom that approached! Weep for its graceful towers that shone white in the bright sun, only to crumble—their stones raining swift and terrible upon her startled women! Weep, too, for the music silenced and the hope now crushed below the—"

"Margrave, old man, please be so good as to shut up," Lucian said with annoyance, placing his hand firmly on the bard's chest and shoving him backward. "You just kicked Mount Shandar completely out of place with your wailing. We're not looking for Segathlas—woeful or otherwise. Calsandria is the point, or have you not been paying attention."

"It is profane knowledge—wicked and sinful at its base!" Jorgan sputtered, more agitated than Caelith remembered seeing him. "It is false and depraved! The reading of the smoke is one of the most sacred rights of the Pir!"

"I believe that is *dragon*smoke, old boy," Lucian observed. "I don't recall anything overly sacred about campfire smoke."

"You profane disparager! How dare you mock my faith?" Jorgan was nearly shaking in his outrage. "You are unworthy thieves who cannot even comprehend the worth of what you have stolen!"

"Stolen?" Caelith asked, confused. "What have we stolen?"

Jorgan turned his face away suddenly, holding his tongue.

"Oh, I can help you there," Margrave piped up, his smile brightening as he looked up from the crude map. "The Pir—especially the

Inquisitas—believe that the power of the Mystics is *their* power, intended for them by the dragon-gods, you see. Galen—your father,
Caelith; oh, and of course, your father too, Jorgan—supposedly stole
this power from Vasska during the final battle on the Election Fields
just as Vasska was presenting it to Tragget. It really is a rather new legend but I've been working on an exquisite epic poem about it. I
could perform part of it for you right now if you don't mind listening to a work in progress—"

"Not now," Caelith said in a quiet but forceful voice, his eyes
fixed on Jorgan. "You aren't looking for our home at all, are you?
You're looking for your *own* home."

Jorgan looked back at Caelith, his eyes steady, his voice smooth
and controlled. "I've come to claim what is ours by *right*. All we have
studied in the ancient texts tells us that Calsandria is the center of this
power. Somewhere in these ruins is the spring from which the
Dragonkings' might pours out over all the Five Domains, and when
I find it, you and all your kind will know who are the true heirs of
your so-called magic!"

"And wouldn't it be convenient if that spring were controlled by
only *one* of the Dragonkings?" Caelith nodded with sudden understanding. "Wouldn't it be more practical for the Pir to deal with only
one Dragonking?"

"Calsandria is the ancient home of the dragons," Jorgan asserted
with unwavering faith. "It is our home by right! And when the scattered clans of your misguided Soulless gather here they shall be
brought to an understanding of their own guilt!"

"And that would be here, in Calsandria—see?" Caelith said
calmly, indicating a spot amid their makeshift map on the broken
floor of the ruins. Jorgan seemed upset that the ruins around them
were not Calsandria and did not seem to know how to deal with it.
He suddenly looked confused—and Caelith had to admit that he was
enjoying every moment of it.

"No, I do not see," Jorgan said with a deep frown. "All I see is a
jumble of rocks."

"It may not look like much to you, old boy," Lucian said, out of
breath either from excitement or his exertions. Lucian had darted

feverishly about the area, scraping what markings he could in the dirt or with soft stone on harder slabs. "But it rather makes sense to us—I suppose you just had to be there. I am rather disappointed in my markings; shoddy job, that."

"But *this* is Calsandria," Jorgan said stubbornly. "The research, the maps, all of it says that this is where Calsandria once stood. You said yourself"—he thrust his hand out in Margrave's direction—"that this place had all the signs of being Calsandria."

"Well, you must understand," Margrave said with a shrug, "both cities were built by a lake in a mountain valley. Both of them had river commerce; so you see it would be quite possible on casual observation to mistake one for—"

"This is an outrage!" Jorgan shouted, his voice echoing among the ruin stones around them. "I've shown the good faith of the Pir and lead you to your precious city of dead and false dreams. Now you don't believe you are here? I tell you, this *is* Calsandria!"

"Nay, lad; Calsandria nay er is," Cephas said casually.

"What?" Jorgan's voice broke, his word finishing as a squeal more than a word. He wheeled around, his face contorted in rage and disbelief as he stared at the dwarf.

"Calm, Master Inquisitas; calm be as er is," Cephas rumbled ominously. "These the stones of Segathlas be. Know I the feel of these stones well, for their quarries be er my home far to the west. Where find ye Calsandria, lad?"

Caelith had known the dwarf for most of his life. Without thinking, he walked around the map until the markings he had personally set were between him and the dwarf. "This direction—about four feet in front of you."

"Aye, good lad." Cephas nodded. "Now, where be Segathlas on yon map?"

Caelith moved once more. "This direction—six feet."

"Aye, thank ye—and one more; know ye Mount Hrurdan er is?"

Caelith was about to move but Lucian, understanding the process, stepped to one side. "This way, old man; eight feet."

"Aye." The dwarf nodded again. Caelith wondered and not for the first time at the dwarf's ability to understand spatial relationships so exactly without being able to see. "Aye, far Calsandria er is. Home or Calsandria—distance be the same."

"We've got to go back," Jorgan stated.

The wind blew through the dream. It carried a whisper, beckoning him southward, far beyond the mountains. In that other place he shook his head, trying to refuse, but the wind whispered to him still.

"No," Caelith said sadly. "We've got to go on."

Everyone but the dwarf turned to Caelith, astonished.

"Go on?" Jorgan almost laughed. "Go on to *what?*"

"We set out to find Calsandria," Caelith said, a pained smile playing on his lips. "We were told to find it."

"Fine." Lucian shrugged. "So you've found it—congratulations. Now we should return so that the Council of Six can appropriately reward us all—hopefully by not sending us out on such an errand ever again."

"But that's not why Eryn came, is it?" Caelith said, turning to face the young woman. "It isn't enough for your clan mistress to just *know* where Calsandria might be located; you have to have seen it for yourself."

Eryn looked away. "Yes—that's right."

"And it is not enough for me; we have to go to Calsandria," Caelith added, sighing.

"This is insane," Jorgan sputtered. "But what should I expect when nearly everyone I'm traveling with *is* insane! I'm not convinced that this ruin *isn't* Calsandria. Even if is isn't, just look at your own map, Caelith! That's got to be another three hundred miles from here."

"Three hundred and twelve," Cephas announced.

"Fine! Three hundred *and twelve,*" Jorgan growled. "And that's through uncharted mountains. You'd break yourself and the rest of us with your trying to push through those peaks. Even if you could somehow find a passage to this phantom Calsandria, what hopes have any of us of surviving to return and tell anyone about it—including those sinners who lead your clan."

"Excuse me," Margrave said, "but I know the way."

"He's right, Caelith." Eryn sighed. "It's too far."

"We can do this," Caelith said. "We have plenty of supplies on the torusk."

"Only because so many have died getting us *this* far," Jorgan said flatly.

Caelith drew in a long breath and looked away.

"Look at us, Caelith; could we survive another three hundred miles? Even if we could, by the time we get there, it will probably be too late to help the clans—there may not even be clans left for us to lead anywhere," Eryn replied, her face suddenly filled with compassion. "I don't understand why you are so insistent on finding this mythic place of gods that, if they ever existed, don't seem to exist now or at the very least care about us at all. But I *do* understand that it is important to *you* and how important it will be to the clans. You've just got to face facts, Caelith. If you have found Calsandria, then the best thing for us to do is to return to the Council, report what we have found, and then, if the Council wills it, mount a proper expedition to cross this wilderness."

Caelith stared at her. She was right, absolutely right, and he knew it. He looked up at the stars. They seemed so far away as they shone down on him. The Pir taught that those were the souls of their ancestors in Surn'gara—the Vault of the Sky—looking down on their children. He had, of course, never been raised in the traditions of the Pir but had always been drawn to the stars when he looked for answers. Were the ancient gods—the gods of Calsandria—in Surn'gara? Were they looking down on him?

A breeze kicked up and drifted across the ruins, blowing sand into Caelith's eyes. He quickly turned away from the wind, blinking. Then the breeze subsided just as suddenly as it had come, and Caelith found himself staring at Margrave and Anji.

The young girl knelt down next to the map, her matted hair hanging down around her face as she leaned over the stones that represented the mountains to the southeast. Margrave stood smiling over her, his hands folded defiantly across his chest. "Excuse me," he repeated. "But I know the way."

"Here," Margrave said, pointing down past the young girl. "This is the way that I would lead you to Calsandria."

Caelith carefully stepped across the map toward the Loremaster, motioning Lucian to join them. Margrave continued to point down among the stones. "What is that? I can't make it out."

"It's writing," Lucian said, leaning forward. "Must have been something I copied in a hurry."

"What does it say?"

"Khagun-mas," Lucian replied, then shrugged. "It says 'Khagun-Mas.'"

The low rumbling chuckle of the dwarf rolled across the map. Caelith looked up.

"Look ye for the way to Calsandria?" the dwarf laughed aloud. "Yon Margrave find ye the way fast as er is!"

"Why? What is it?"

"Khagun-Mas!" the dwarf roared. "That be the lost Dwarven Road!"

Khagun-Mas

I walk but the plain beneath my feet does not move. The vast arena all around me is filled shoulder to shoulder and still more audience is shoving from the back in the hopes of getting a view. I find this bizarre since all I am doing is interminably walking. The stones beneath my feet are moving as I walk, but I remain in the same place, the wind at my back. I search the faces of the audience for some recognizable sign, but there are too many masks staring back at me—all of them unfamiliar and anxious.

I am running toward the painted scene at the back of the stage. A road is painted beneath me that continues up onto the backdrop of flat mountain peaks to a glittering light flashing between the mountains—the treasure that I seek. It draws no closer, however, no matter how quickly I run.

The snakes enter. They have been waiting quietly in the wings, impatient for their part. Now, as the lights on the stage dim for their cue, they slither onto the stage, their serpent motions a tandem dance as they circle around me.

The crowd boos as the snakes' hooded heads widen, rising up in preparation to strike me with their long, bared fangs.

Then the winged woman rolls onto the stage encased in a ball, a mesh lattice of spun water that moves of its own accord. She *tumbles uncontrollably within this globe, the snakes rearing back, distracted and confused. I think for a moment that the winged woman has come to destroy the snakes with the watery globe, but it careens wildly across the wide stage and veers suddenly toward me.*

"No!" I gasp. "Watch where you're —"

Too late! The woven liquid tumbles over me, engulfing me in its mesh, and suddenly I am tumbling within the globe. The dark-haired winged woman snatches desperately at me, gripping me tightly and binding me up in her embrace. Her face is filled with panic and desperation, her grip like iron. We both revolve inside the sphere, spinning madly about the stage. The snakes do not appreciate the deviation from the scripted scene and move quickly to strike at us both.

I glance frantically about the stage. Fish jump into the air from a hole in the floor of the stage. I throw my arms around the winged woman, tossing my entire weight in the direction of the opening. The water-latticed globe veers in its course, skittering. I shift my weight again and the globe swerves once more.

The hole in the stage is much larger now, a gaping orifice waiting to swallow us both. A gust of wind blows across the stage, causing the torches on either side to flicker. The globe swerves sharply in the wind, rolling along the rim of the widening hole in a moment of hesitation — then it falls, taking us both with it.

The crowd jumps to its feet, roaring their applause as we tumble into a darkness blacker than any night — the disapproving hiss of the frustrated snakes receding above us farther and farther by the moment.

Book of Caelith
Bronze Canticles, Tome IX, Folio I, Leaf 63

"Let us gather and begin anew the great quest!" Margrave called out through the morning stillness, his voice echoing off the walls of the ruins south of their encampment. He sounded bright and alive. "The dawn is breaking, and there's ground to be taken underfoot! The

Heroes of the Lost City strike out this day for the Dwarven Road . . .
To seek their doom and their glory as they follow their humble Loremaster down mysterious paths!"

Lucian groaned, managing only with the most supreme effort to
push himself up from his bedroll and slump aching into a sitting position. His eyes still resolutely closed, he could manage only to croak
plaintively, "Caelith, please do shut him up."

"Gladly," Caelith said with a deep groan. The dawn seemed to
come earlier than he expected. "However, the last thing I recall is that
he is now our leader; the newest chosen one to take us to this Dwarven Road—whatever that may be—and to Calsandria beyond."

"Well, it's your own fault." Lucian rolled onto his side, stubbornly
keeping his eyes closed as he spoke. "Keeping us all up more than half
the night arguing about this Dwarven Road business and playing 'who's
going to be the leader' until the darkest hours of the morning."

"Look, it was really very simple—"

"*Should* have been simple, you mean." Lucien propped his head up
on his elbow, eyeing Caelith resentfully. "Jorgan no longer knows the actual way, thank you very much, but insists on leading anyway. Never
mind that no one else in the company cares to follow him; they would
just as soon send him packing, except that now he insists on staying with
us just to prove how wrong we all are. Everyone else wanted to follow
you . . . But, no; you *won't* lead us and don't bother with any reasons.
Not that everyone here doesn't already know the reasons—"

"Shut up, Lucien. Let it go."

"I'm not the one holding on." Lucien closed his eyes, laying his
head back down on his bedroll.

"Hey, we came to a compromise." Caelith shrugged.

"Oh, yes." Lucien nodded, his face toward the lightening sky. "We
picked the one man everyone was equally loath to follow: Margrave,
master of the quest."

Caelith sat up and looked about him. A morning fog had filled
the valley earlier but was now quickly burning off. Through it, a figure approached him, his shadowy outline giving Caelith a start as it
reminded him of the holes in the smoke from the previous night.
This figure, however, soon resolved itself into someone familiar.

"Begging your pardon, sire," Kenth called as he approached. "That Margrave seems to have roused the camp."

"Well, he's in charge—"

"I took the liberty of setting a watch last night," Kenth continued quickly, his voice low but clear. "There's something you need to see, sire."

"Master Kenth, I—"

"I'll just be waiting over here for you, sire," the old warrior replied quickly, stepping away but not so far as to fall out of Caelith's thoughts.

Caelith craned his neck painfully around, then turned to look at his old friend. Lucian had curled back up under his thick blanket.

"Time to face the light," Caelith grumbled as he snatched up Lucian's blanket, tossing it at the Enlund mystic's head. Its impact startled Lucian, his eyes flashing open. "What was that old nursery song that your mother use to sing to us in the morning?"

"Oh no, Caelith!" Lucian groaned. "Please don't—"

"Oh, I remember now," Caelith said as he stretched. 'Good morning, mother mystic, the dreaming stars away! Awake and do your goodly work beneath the sunny day!'"

Lucian groaned and then rolled his eyes. "My good fellow, you should understand that your singing is not contagious but is sickening."

"A minor difference," Caelith agreed, standing.

"To some of us it is a vital difference," Lucian growled, falling back sideways once more onto his bedroll, his eyes tightly shut. "Honestly, Caelith, you find the City of the Gods and suddenly you're showing distinct signs of being motivated. It just isn't becoming; the whole thing has the smell of something entirely too close to ambition."

"Then ambition it is," Caelith said, drawing in a deep breath of the chill morning air, "or at the very least resolution. Come on! Get up!"

Caelith kicked at his friend's feet. Lucian snarled with annoyance, but when Caelith refused to stop, the tall young mystic scrambled to his feet.

"I'm up! I'm up—as well you can see. Now will you please go off with your soldier friends and annoy someone else?" Lucian sputtered. "Honestly, old boy, Calsandria isn't going anywhere. It's waited for you this long, I suspect it can manage to wait until after a decent breakfast!"

"Destiny waits for no man," Margrave replied, bouncing up to them. "I've found a bridge over the Torin about a half-mile down the road—"

"The what?" Lucian asked.

"The Torin—you know, the river," Margrave said easily. "It was all on the map, these names of fable and lore. This is the River Torin that runs next to the road. We'll have to cross another to the east before we can get around Lake Evathun and head south toward the Dwarven Road. In all it looks to be about forty miles and the end of it is all uphill."

"Uh, sire?" Kenth asked, insistence in his voice.

"If you will excuse us, Master Margrave," Caelith said quickly. Caelith stepped after Kenth with a nod for Lucian to follow. In moments they had left the bard behind them in the swirling mists, bereft of an audience. "Now what can possibly been seen in this fog, Master Kenth?"

The craggy-faced warrior quickly fell into step beside his commander. "Sire, I took the last watch last night—not that I could sleep anyway after hearing about those ghosts in the smoke—oh, up this way, sire."

Caelith turned, picking his way through the broken stones up the side of a gentle slope. "Go on."

"Well, sire, I stationed myself up here, hoping for a better view round about, if you know what I mean," Kenth continued. "The ground fog was just welling up but I managed to stay above it. It's thick but not very deep—if you catch my meaning, sire."

"What an odd thing." Caelith was puzzled. As he came to the top of the knoll, he emerged from the bank of fog. He seemed to be standing atop a sea of clouds that covered the ground around him in all directions for as far as he could see, broken only by the remaining stones of the city's ruined towers. The morning sun had not yet crested the mountain range to the east, though its rays were already illuminating its brother peaks on the western boundary of the great valley. The sky was an achingly brilliant blue. He could even make out the distant peaks of the Hrurdan Mountains, their snowy caps shining in the morning sun.

Caelith blinked. "Did I see something moving up there?"

"Aye, sire," Kenth replied. "I did too, so I thought I might prevail on the dream for a little assistance." The old warrior began to hum to himself an odd tune that seemed to carry two or three notes at once. He closed his eyes, and raising his hand, moved it in a circular motion in front of him. In moments, a clear oval formed following the arc of his fingers, the air compressing. In moments, the mountains in the distance appeared larger and much closer.

Lucian gasped in delight. "Really, old boy, you must teach me that one!"

Kenth smiled. "I've been trying to teach Master Caelith for some time, but he's yet to get the knack of it."

Caelith gave no reaction, but his eyes darted here and there at the magnified image before them. "I don't see—by the gods! No!"

Before the gently wavering image of Hrurdan Peak appeared distinctly a form with massive leathery wings, a serrated spine, and a long spiked tail. Its neck was craned downward, its great head lolling from side to side as it searched the ground below it.

"A dragon on the wing," Caelith said darkly. "And on the hunt. Could you make out which one?"

Kenth nodded. "Yes, but keep watching, sire."

Emerging from between two intervening peaks, two more of the enormous monsters hove into view, the downbeat of their wings causing the snow beneath them to flurry up behind them.

"Three?" Lucian breathed. "How can that be?"

"Three, aye, Master Lucian." Kenth nodded. "And they are all of them on the hunt and unmistakably together. I'm not sure of the third, sire, but those other two are Satinka and Ormakh. I can't tell if they have their Dragon-Talkers with them."

"But they are at war," Lucian said, perplexed.

"Aye, but apparently not today." Kenth collapsed the mystical viewer with a small pop back into the air from which he formed it. "Today they are hunting."

"Hunting what?" Lucian asked.

"Us." Caelith said, his arms crossed over his chest. "We've got to get to some cover before this fog burns off. Out here on this plain, it will be only a matter of time before they find us."

"Maybe they're looking for someone else?" Lucian asked.

"Have you *seen* anyone else?" Caelith countered. "I didn't think so. Margrave says he'd like us to get moving. I suspect that is a pretty good idea. Master Kenth, gather the—"

Caelith stopped. There no longer was a company.

"Sire?" Kenth asked into the sudden silence.

Caelith shuddered. "Gather everyone together. If those dragons are looking for us, they'll naturally come toward these ruins. We've got to move as far from here as possible while this fog holds."

They turned and quietly slipped back down the hill and into the mists once more, only to meet Eryn coming up toward them from below. "What is it? Margrave says that we're to leave right away."

"Well, he's in charge," Caelith responded, his eyes cast down to the ground as he moved past her toward the shadowy form of the torusk down the road. He could barely discern the thin form of Anji coaxing the beast to kneel in the deep grass to the side of the road.

Lucian's voice was accusing. "You really are enjoying this, aren't you, leaving us in the hands of that idiot?"

"You heard him last night," Caelith said, clearing his throat. "Margrave knows the way; we follow him."

"Caelith, be reasonable," Eryn said.

"My dear Eryn," Lucian sniffed. "Reasonable was never one of his strong points. Say, are you quite all right?"

The shadows of the night still seemed to haunt the long, drawn lines in Eryn's somber face. "He's right. Let's just pack up and get out of here. The sooner, the farther, the better."

The fog held in the chill dawn. It blanketed them as they crossed the first river, the Torin, at a wide stone bridge just inside the ruins, then moved eastward down the remains of an old road that skirted the limits of Segathlas along its northern side. The road straightened to the east, passing into large tracts of abandoned and overgrown fields. The morning sun then broke in their faces as they made their way, swiftly burning away the protective shroud and exposing them to the harsh, clear sky. It was not entirely clear, however, for it was marred to the north by dark flecks whose scales occasionally flashed in the light of day. The dragons were now soaring over the Nharuthenia plains, many miles away yet still much closer than Caelith would have thought possible in so short a time. By noon, Margrave found the River Naraganth, its wide, slow waters cutting across the overgrown fields. The bridge here had fallen, and though the humans might have crossed on the massive stones that protruded from the deep waters, the torusk certainly could not. A fording further upstream was found and, though delayed by an hour, they had passed the last major obstacle and were moving quickly southward around the shores of Lake Evathun.

Eryn ran ahead with Caelith—who had been given long and overly involved instructions by Margrave—but she kept a profound and ashen-faced silence as they moved ahead. Margrave, now in the role of heroic leader, rode on the long-suffering torusk, spending his breath on a cascade of words, which by now Kenth and the remaining raiders had learned to ignore in all their particulars. Anji, if it were possible, was more silent than ever, trudging along at the front of the torusk, her eyes fixed in a stare at the road. It seemed as though she cared nothing for their path farther than a few steps ahead of her.

Lucian, walking beside the torusk, observed it all with a jaded eye. Every step was taking him farther from home, and he wondered just what the point of it would be after all was said and done. Searching for the City of the Gods was a fine romantic notion, to be sure, and one that was politically charged; it had become the mythology of the clans over the last few years and no other idea had so struck the fancy of the mystics as a whole. It was all nonsense, he knew, but very powerful nonsense in terms of the politics of the Circle of Six.

So he walked beside the torusk, nodding occasionally and saying a meaningless "Yes, I see" toward Margrave so that he would not have to engage the bard in any real conversation. Lucian had a lot to think about.

Eryn was right, he decided; it didn't really matter so much if they found Calsandria so long as everyone *believed* they had found it. Dreams are powerful and Lucien knew how to turn power to his advantage. Caelith should have understood that, too, but now he seemed bent on actually *finding* this place. That was all well and good for the son of Galen, but where there is change there is profit; all one had to do was figure out how to leverage it.

Lucian glanced around behind him. Past the torusk, well behind them, he could make out Jorgan walking along beside the dwarf. What a Pir Inquisitas has in common with a dwarf, he could not fathom. He suspected it was actually the kindness of the dwarf that brought the two of them to walk together. Jorgan was probably back there licking his wounds now that Margrave—of all people—was running things. The dwarf probably just felt sorry for the bastard.

Lucian chuckled to himself. Bastard? He wondered which of Galen's two sons was the real bastard. Jorgan, if he understood it correctly, was conceived in wedlock sanctioned by the Pir, yet their marriage was dissolved when it was discovered Galen was of the Elect. The Pir maintained that such marriages were dissolved, so that would make Jorgan the bastard. But the subsequent union between Galen and Dhalia—which resulted in Caelith's birth—was not recognized by any kingdom or clergy known in the Five Kingdoms. So, if their marriage was illegal, didn't that make Caelith the bastard?

Lucian considered that for a moment. The way each of them had acted over the last few weeks made up his mind for him; they were both a couple of bastards. So, where did that leave him regarding this quest that was taking him farther from his clan?

Lucian shook his head in frustration. There just had to be a way to make finding the gods pay off.

Jorgan held his pace in check—a difficult thing for him. Discipline had always been a trial for the young Inquisitas, though his calling had required discipline above all. He had come to accept this frustration as part of the price of his existence and his penance before the dragon-gods. He knew his family's guilt and shame—the blasphemy of a father who dared defy the dragon-gods with arcane powers stolen from the church's rightful and righteous inheritance from the ancient Rhamasian Empire. He knew that only he fully understood and felt the culpability of his father and the shame with which it stained his own soul. So he carried the blame on his own shoulders, wrapping his life in its pain and humiliation and wearing the shame openly. It was a wound he kept picking at and reopening himself— forever bleeding. In his mind it was just, for how else could he atone for his own father's sins and free himself forever of his past? Indeed, he had come on this distasteful quest with just such hopes of freedom in mind.

His unquestioned and unquestioning faith would see him triumph.

Jorgan looked up at the mountains towering over them to the south. He could see where the deserted road on which they walked crisscrossed the face of the mountain, each twist a little higher until it turned into the cleft of a deep canyon. It would leave them exposed to danger until they got to the top. That was his road, he realized, and his life. His path was never straight or easy but always carried him a little higher than before.

Yet now as he and the dwarf lagged purposefully farther behind the itching ears of the rest of the expedition, he was impatient for some answers.

"Master dwarf," he said at last, as they walked along the ancient and broken roadway, "where are we going?"

"To Calsandria er we go," chuckled the dwarf. "Jorgan er listening not to old Cephas."

"But that was not what you presented to the Inquis Requi," Jorgan said, looking away. "It was never the plan."

"The Inquisition, their problems er is; Cephas and Jorgan have problems of our own. The City of the Gods the home of the Dragonkings er is. Find that and your Vasska-god triumph over all else. Jorgan worries far too much—even for an Inquis Requi," the dwarf added quickly.

"You lied to us, dwarf," Jorgan said, fixing his gaze on the wild-haired creature whose feet shook the ground slightly as he quickly walked. "*Your* Calsandria turned out to be the wrong city."

"Forgive Cephas; I knew all along," the dwarf admitted. "But that necessary to save the mystics if a deal not forged between us."

"You are still looking after your friends," Jorgan said, shaking his head.

"As Inquisitas Jorgan does also, I think." Cephas nodded. "You not wanting just to *be* right; you want everyone *else* to know you right, too. Soon your proof all shall see er is. Galen's clans gather like rain into a river. Slowly they flow south into the Naraganth Basin. You need not fear; the Dragonkings will have their due."

"So you have actually been to this City of the Gods?"

"Knelt at its altar as er is," the dwarf said proudly. "Show your brother, Caelith, truth as er is."

"He is no brother of mine," Jorgan snapped.

The dwarf chuckled once more. "More than blood binds brothers—and binds us all. Say you Calsandria was the fountain of the ancient gods. It was the only power the Dragonkings feared in the days of Rhamas. It is the power that your own father used to nearly topple Pir rule after four hundred years of order."

Jorgan looked up. The torusk had already traversed several of the courses and was high above them as they approached the first turn in what had suddenly become a very crooked road climbing up the mountainside.

"The power of the gods," the dwarf whispered for Jorgan's ears alone. "And in whose hands would it be better put to use than your own?"

Caelith was confused, frustrated, and awestruck at the same time. It was an odd combination of feelings that, coupled perhaps with their increasing altitude, left him feeling slightly disoriented.

"What is it, Caelith," Eryn asked, her own breath labored with the climb. "What's bothering you?"

"Nothing," he said a little too quickly. "Really—it's nothing."

"I've known you too long for that." Eryn shook her head. "Tell me."

Caelith shook his head. "I never could keep a secret from you."

"Which, as I recall, was one of the reasons you left," she replied. "So since you're going to tell me eventually, can't we get right to the point?"

Caelith stopped, looking back down the canyon. She was right, of course. The fact that she could easily peer into the secrets he held was both a comfort and a dread. It had hastened his departure from her. But this was no place to begin an explanation that needed time and courage. He wondered if there would ever be such a place. The shadows were already lengthening across the long plains of the Nharuthenia. The surface of Lake Evathun shimmered in the late afternoon light far below, and the ruins of Segathlas were visible against the far shore. The dragons soared above the ruins in the distance. Occasionally, jets of flame would rain down from their throats, the sound of their impact rolling up the canyon many heartbeats after the flash of their flame. They were looking for them, hoping to dislodge them from the maze of blasted and fallen stonework. Caelith shook to think what it would be like under their terrible and constant barrage, and fortunately they had left the city. But soon enough one of them would find their tracks and there would be little time for them to find cover. They had to get up higher and off the road. Which reminded him . . .

"It's this damn road," Caelith said, pushing forward. "I just don't get it."

"What's to get?" Eryn shrugged. "Who understands dwarves or why they do anything anyway?"

"Yes, but they always make sense in the end," Caelith said, gesturing at the way before them. "I mean, look at it."

"It's a mess," Eryn replied. "Why shouldn't it be after four hundred years?"

Caelith shook his head. "It's damaged, sure, but really look at it; it's thirty feet wide. All the way from the bottom and up to here it's thirty feet wide even when it would have made sense to narrow it by just a foot or so."

"Maybe the dwarves like thirty feet." Eryn sighed. "Or maybe they only brought the thirty-foot measuring stick that day. Keep moving!"

"Then there's the low wall on either side," he said. "Whole sections of it are missing now, but it obviously ran the entire length of the road even when there was no obvious need for a wall. Then there are these pits on both sides of the road . . ."

"I don't see what's confusing," Eryn said, taking a deep breath. "The path between them is wide enough for two torusks—let alone you and me."

"Exactly, but look at this one." Caelith picked up his pace and dashed a few yards up the road.

Eryn shook her head in disbelief and followed him up the hill to one of the "barrel pits," as Caelith called them—long rounded trenches cut into the surface of the road in matched pairs.

"Look," Caelith said, gesturing along the length of road beneath them. "These are situated horizontally across the road every five feet on either side of the path. Most of the pits are just open gouges in the road but this one"—he pointed with his open hand—"has these rusted metallic fittings holding the ends of an old, weathered log. It's a turning drum."

He looked back down the canyon. "Try to imagine the entire length of road fitted with these massive drums. Not only that, but the mechanism on the end appeared to permit the roller to turn only one way, as though allowing something to roll higher up the road but preventing it from falling back. What was so important that they had to roll it up this road—and only one way?"

"I don't know," Eryn said uncomfortably. "Are you sure this is the right road?"

"That's what Margrave says and you and I both saw it on the map. But one other thing," Caelith said quickly as he turned to face up the canyon and pointed to a sheer cliff face rising up above a ridge. "That waterfall up there."

"Another mystery?"

"It's an absolute torrent," Caelith said, shaking his head. "An entire river thundering down that cliff every second."

"So?"

"So do you see a river in this canyon?" Caelith asked in puzzlement. "That old riverbed below us is as dry as dust. Where is the water?"

"Caelith," Eryn replied wearily, "I don't know, but you're going to find out soon enough. Those falls have got to end around the other side of the ridge. Let's just get there and decide what to do next, because, and I want to be very honest with you, so far this Dwarven Road has not been any improvement over any other road we've taken. I can't see how it can possibly help us cover the almost three hundred miles to Calsandria any faster than we're moving now. So let's just get up there, find where the water is, and hopefully discover someplace to hide before the dragons find us."

Caelith noticed that the rumbling from the distant city had stopped. He looked back across the plains far below.

The specks in the distance that were the dragons wheeled through the sky and then seemed to stop in midair, bobbing only slightly from time to time. Caelith knew what that meant, for he had seen it before: the dragons were flying directly toward them. They would be searching the ground as they did, but it was obvious they had found their trail.

He glanced back down the mountain. Jorgan and Cephas had finally managed to catch up with the rest of the group, Anji silently guiding the torusk in the rear. They were still about a half-hour below them on the road at their pace but, Caelith shook his head, it was not as though they could choose another way nor could he get them to move any faster.

"They're coming, Eryn," Caelith said urgently. "Come on; we've got to find somewhere we can all hide."

The towering peaks around them were like stone daggers thrust up out of the ground, but the road stubbornly maintained its uniform structure. Caelith and Eryn followed its path, quickly rounding a turn around the jutting ridgeline and—

Caelith froze on the road. Eryn look up and stopped, slack-jawed next to him.

The road descended into a wide mountain bowl, filled with the roaring of not just one but three waterfalls dropping precipitously down from separate peaks rimming the bowl. These gathered into three wide rivers that emptied into a single, tempestuous, stone-lined lake. The road, too, ran straight down the gentle slope and directly into the churning surface. On either side of the lake were the ruins of buildings, large and glorious.

Magnificent as the ruins were, however, it was the beautifully crafted cliff face that arrested their attention. Towering columns carved into the stone reached fully fifty feet overhead, capped by an intricately engraved arch. The people and dwarves represented in the frieze between the columns remained clear as if it had been carved that same day, lustrous in the evening light with the faces of long-dead men, women, and dwarves, whose names were now lost but whose likeness lived on in the aching clarity of stone. All of these surrounded an arched gullet plunging into the heart of the mountain that was twenty feet tall and fifty feet across. The combined waters in the frothing pool surged into this gaping maw, slipping with ever increasing speed into the deep darkness beyond.

Next to the road, on the shores of the lake, Caelith saw three barges. Two were hopelessly ruined but a third appeared to be intact—its splintered platform lashed across twin hulls whose resin still glinted under the dust of centuries. It was a large, beautiful craft and, Caelith realized, just under thirty feet wide.

Caelith threw back his head and howled with laughter into the growing twilight.

"Caelith?" Eryn asked.

"A fast road indeed!" Caelith hooted. "Eryn, don't you see? The Dwarven Road is a *river!*"

Dwarven Road

H urry!" Caelith called out. "Keep moving!"

The torusk bellowed, its trumpeting sound nearly swallowed up in the roar of the rushing waters nearby. The beast was confused and unnerved by the urgent, frantic activity all around it. Anji did her best to keep the creature calm, raking its tusks with her guide-stick and rubbing its jowls soothingly.

Little, however, could dissipate the near panic that surrounded the creature. The humans swarmed around its flanks and sides, unloading the packets and canvas sacks mounted across its wide back as quickly as the ropes could be loosened. The provisions were then whisked to the side and set or hastily tossed onto the flat surface of the ancient barge, where Lucian and Eryn did their best to keep up and at least attempt to secure their cargo to the warped and weathered deck.

"Lovich!" Caelith shouted. "Where are they?"

"They've crossed the lake," Lovich called back, his voice breaking slightly. The young raider had obeyed Kenth's instructions and climbed up the low ridge at the head of the road ascending the mountainside. It was a good position from which to observe the plain below and the ruins of Segathlas in the distance. "I can see—all three of them are coming directly toward me. It's hard to see, the sun is in my eyes."

"This is insanity," Jorgan groused over the rumble of the rushing waters nearby.

"I thought all mystics were insane by definition," Caelith replied, grabbing another sack from the back of the kneeling torusk and swinging it onto the deck of the barge. The sky overhead was deepening into a salmon color, the sun now completely hidden by the western peaks. "What's the point of being crazy if you can't do something lunatic now and then? We need to hurry and get everything loaded before we lose the light."

"Lose the light?" Jorgan's voice broke. "You want to drag us down a river that flows *under* a mountain and you're worried about the sun setting? If you're afraid of the dark, then you're taking the wrong path!"

"I can't get these knots loose," Warthin growled from behind clenched teeth.

"Just cut them," Caelith replied, pulling another canvas wrap free of the beast. "Never mind the harness!"

Lucian stood on the deck of the barge, adjusting the load, but even as he worked there was an element of tension in his voice. "Caelith, old boy, maybe Jorgan is right. We should find cover in these ruins. There may even be another path out of here. A good night's rest might make our course, well, a little brighter in the morning? Maybe some nearby caves we can hide in?"

"No!" Caelith said with a vehemence that surprised even him. He took in a deep and considered breath before he continued. "Now listen, all of you. We have to leave tonight—right now. I can't explain it, it was something in the dream, but this is the way we must go; there is no other cover and we cannot wait out the night and survive."

"The snakes?" Eryn asked loudly.

"You were there—in the dream?" Caelith asked quickly, tossing a bundle of cake rations onto the deck.

"In the wings, watching." Eryn nodded, and then spoke quickly to everyone else. "This—I think this is the way. In the dream it was snakes, but it must have been a metaphor for the dragons and Caelith escaped by falling down some sort of well. By the gods, Caelith, where are you taking us?"

"Nonsense as er is!" the dwarf huffed. "Safe as er is the Dwarven Road!"

"Nonsense or not, we're about to see the handiwork of your ancestors firsthand," Caelith said, tossing the last of the packets onto the barge. "Cephas: you, Tarin, and Warthin help Lucian with that far runner. Margrave: you'll help Kenth, Beligrad, and me push this near runner with Jorgan. Eryn?"

"Yes?"

"You get Anji up on the barge while I untie these ropes. We'll push it down this ramp and climb on as it hits the water. You take the rudder in case something happens."

"Like what?" Eryn snapped.

"I don't know . . . anything," he shouted angrily.

"Great," Eryn groused as she climbed onto the barge. "Fine time to learn how to sail."

"Excuse me," Margrave said as he stepped uncomfortably close to Caelith, "but what about the torusk?"

Caelith looked over at the huge, long-tusked beast. Stripped of its burden, the mammoth creature had stood and wandered several yards away, taking interest in a tall clump of highland grass.

"Not now, Margrave," Caelith snapped.

"Well, how does *he* ride with us?" Margrave asked.

"*He* doesn't," Caelith grunted, having no success undoing the ancient knot wrapped around the rusting cleat. He drew his sword and neatly cut through the dry, splintering rope. "We're going on without the torusk."

"But, my lord!" Margrave said with shock.

Caelith straightened, crossing the ramp leading down to the rippling surface of the water before the cliff. "He's a foraging animal, Margrave; he'll be just fine."

"But what of us?" Margrave whined. "We may need the beast again at the other end of the majestic and mysterious Khagun-Mas—and consider Anji; she is absolutely beside herself with concern!"

Caelith glanced over at the waif. Her expression reflected the same blank, silent resignation as always.

"Yes," Caelith said dryly, "poor kid. I can see she's overcome with grief. Look, you're the one who led us up here—who said this road would lead us to Calsandria. Does it or doesn't it?"

"Well, of course it does." Margrave's laugh was colored by a tint of uncertainty. "I mean . . . eventually . . . no, it does."

"And you *can* lead us down this road, can't you?"

"Certainly!" Margrave asserted.

"Then we cannot stay here any longer." Caelith raised his sword once more, swinging it down quickly. The blade sliced through the wide braids of the rope, severing it at once. The cable, released from its tension, sprang back slightly as it fell to the ground, a thick coating of dust exploding on impact.

"Lovich!" Caelith yelled toward the ridge. "Get back here now!"

"I've lost them!" Lovich called back, his right hand trying to shield his eyes against the low, burning light of the sunset. "I can't see them!"

The hull of the barge groaned.

"It doesn't matter!" Caelith shouted.

The young raider turned to face Caelith.

The ridge exploded into white dust and hurtling rock, engulfing Lovich at once. An instant later, the gigantic form of a dragon, its leathery wings clawing at the air, emerged as a terrible shadow against the reddening sky. The pale scales soared over their heads, clutching in the talons of its hind claws the screaming and struggling Lovich. The dragon's wings pushed downward, its powerful force churning the waters of the small bay, its body climbing upward. It released Lovich just feet away from the cliff face, his body slamming against the carvings with a sickening, wet thud. A dark stain followed the limp and now silent body and it tumbled down the face and into the churning waters below.

"We're leaving! Put your back into it, Margrave," Caelith shouted as he grabbed the edge of the barge's platform just above his head. "Everyone, *now!*"

With a shout, they all pushed against the barge. The river ship protested but Caelith could feel it shift. He called out again; once more they pushed and the hull moved a foot further. Emboldened, Caelith shouted out a third time; they all pressed against the hull and the barge began to slide down the slanting quay. The men and the dwarf continued to yell, pushing harder as the barge picked up speed across the slick stones. In moments, the bows of the twin hulls slid into the water, lifting the keel free of the ramp.

Caelith glanced up. The dragon was wheeling overhead, seeming to float for a moment in the air as it poised for another attack. In that moment, Caelith caught a glimpse of the empty harness on the dragon's back—the Dragon-Talker's position that had been empty since before he was born. It was Satinka, the Silent Dragonqueen.

"Now!" Caelith shouted. "Get on now!"

Lucian, Tarin, and Warthin clambered up one side of the hull. The dwarf was struggling, however, so Lucian reached down quickly and grabbed the puffing dwarf by his wide belt and hauled him unceremoniously onto the decking. Margrave and Kenth both managed the feat without assistance. Beligrad, however, slipped on the wet stones underfoot, faltered and fell in front of Caelith. Caelith stumbled over him, falling forward even as his hands clung desperately to the edge of the barge. The boat continued to move forward, dragging Caelith through the icy water, shocking the breath from his lungs. He thrashed about with his legs but they found no purchase. He tried to pull himself upward, but the water dragged him back as the ship rode forward. The churning water lapped into Caelith's face, his nose, and down his throat. Still he hung on, gagging, feeling the panic well up within him.

Someone took his arms and pulled him up from the water's grip. At last, wet and sputtering, Caelith flopped onto the creaking, ancient deck.

"Thank you," Caelith sputtered.

"Don't thank me yet," Jorgan returned.

Caelith looked up in shock at his brother standing over him.

"Master!" Beligrad called out, as he staggered back out of the water to the ramp they had just left.

"We've got to go back!" Kenth demanded. "We can't leave him here!"

A terrible trumpeting shattered the air. The Dragonking Ormakh, its ancient leathery wings beating dust of the ground, alighted on the ridge, its hind talons nearly crushing the rock beneath him with its grip. It craned its huge, terrible head downward, then leaned forward and, folding its wings, began deliberately to claw its way down toward where Beligrad stood.

"Caelith!" Eryn yelled.

The young mystic stood up, water falling off him to soak the aged boards underfoot. "What is it?"

"I—I can't go back; I don't know how this works!"

Caelith scurried to the back of the barge. He could see that the current had already taken them, drawing them with ever increasing speed toward the wide maw of the Dwarven Road.

Margrave moved to the front of the barge and struck a noble and tragic pose as he spoke. "So it was that the intrepid Heroes of the Lost City, after braving the terrors of the road, and battling the spectral ghosts of tragic Segathlas, came at last to the darkest part of their journey: the unknowable terrors of the forgotten—and cursed—Dwarven Road."

"Cursed?" Lucian clucked. "I say, nobody said anything about a curse!"

Caelith stared helplessly back at Beligrad, who thrashed about in the water, unwittingly with his back to the approaching dragon. Ormakh's clawed foot plunged down where Beligrad struggled, drowning the warrior in his own crimson stain.

"So the heroes bold and true sailed past the silent quays, devoid of well-wishers to send them on their great and tragic quest. No goods filled the docks; no songs rang from the streets. For the Dwarven Road of Khagun-Mas was a tomb, the stagnant vein of a dead empire."

Caelith heard Satinka overhead, screaming with rage as she plunged, too late, toward them. The fallen towers and broken domes, their white marble stones stained by time, wind, and weather, were behind them now. Only the enormous face of the cliff filled their vision, the delicately carved figures staring back at them with stains streaking from their eyes and the black, enormous shaft of emptiness that drew them inward with increasing insistence and speed.

"Down the hole," Lucian called out more to himself than anyone.

"Tell me you're right about this, Margrave," Eryn said, her face pale. "Tell me we'll come out on the other side."

"Have no fear, good lady," Margrave replied, "fortune favors us through the darkest peril!"

"Just hold on," Caelith said with more confidence than he felt. "And we'll get through."

The arch passed high over them. The water, constricted by the tunnel, suddenly pushed them forward with a speed that seemed more appropriate for arrows in flight.

"Fearlessly they raced into the depths of stone!" Margrave shouted, the wind blowing back his thick, long curls. "Companions in search of their past that they might find for themselves and those who follow after, a future as bright as the blackness they faced!"

The barge rushed onward, the red light of sunset quickly falling behind them. In moments the subterranean river turned and an impenetrable black engulfed them.

The last sound that escaped the darkness was swallowed up entirely by the rage of Satinka, who snarled once again at being denied her prey. Could it have been heard in the light of that falling day, it would have been Lucian's plaintive and pained cry:

"By the gods, Margrave, could you *please* just give it a rest!"

Talons

"P erhaps you just need rest," suggested Emperor Oguk.

Thux paced frantically at the edge of the ravine, stopping occasionally to peer into its depths. "He's gone! That little back-stabbing, self-centered creep of a stench has bagged me and run off!"

"You say there was a Titan-Blakat here?" the giant ogre asked calmly.

"Yes! It was ten—maybe fifteen times your size with a hollow head," Thux said, peering once more into the shadowy bottom of the crag.

Thux had bolted from his suite as soon as he discovered Istoe missing. He frantically searched the market although in his heart he knew that the imp must have followed him into the Trove. The dreadful smell he noticed in the library haunted him. *"You spy on the ogres,"* Istoe had said, *"and I spy on you."*

In desperation, he had gone directly to Emperor Oguk to plead with him for help. The Emperor, not being particularly busy at the moment, volunteered himself to assist the little spy even if he did not quite understand the nature of the frantic goblin's concern.

So Thux left the main gate of the city on the shoulders of the Emperor and they both made their way quickly to the south. If the

324

titan was still where they left it, then Istoe would certainly not be far away. When they reached the ravine, Thux climbed carefully down from the Og's shoulders and was at once disappointed. He plunged down the slope but there was no denying it: the titan was gone.

"Perhaps you left it in another place?" Oguk suggested, sincerely trying to be helpful.

"No—I'm certain this is the place," Thux said, pointing to the opposite side. "Look—there are the footfalls of the titan coming down the slope from when we came here. He must have followed the course of the stream to the west before he headed north."

"Then he has got back among the Titan-Blakat," Oguk intoned, balling his massive right fist and slamming it into the palm of his left hand. "It is as the prophecy foretold. Blessed is this day that we should be tested and rise to battle against the Titan-Blakat!"

"You don't understand," Thux said, shaking his head sadly. "They will destroy you, your people, your city, and everything you have tried to protect. You cannot stop them."

"Foolish little goblin spy," Oguk said, shaking his head as he bent over and patted Thux as gently on the head as he could. "You do not understand these things. It is unimportant whether we win or lose the battle—so long as we fight with bravery and all our strength. Then our souls shall be acceptable to the Titan-Whitat, and we shall sleep in justified peace among the stars of . . . wait! Where are you going, Master Spy?"

The goblin was trudging back up the slope of the ravine, his head hanging down and his long ears drooping. "I'm going back to the Trove," he said dejectedly.

"You work too hard, Master Spy," Oguk said in solemn appreciation. "It is late in the day; have you more spying to do?"

"No." Thux sighed. "I've done all the spying I care to do."

"Then why go to the Trove?"

"To say good-bye," Thux wailed, his big feet carrying him slowly back toward the gates of the ancient city.

Thux stepped into the overgrown plaza with both the tips of his ears drooping.

It was truly beautiful, he thought sadly, gazing down from the wide steps of what he had come to call Thux's House of Books. The wild tangle of overgrown vegetation was barely confined by the elongated circle of road running around the central park he had dubbed the Ellipse, its wide roots extending outward and breaking up the flagstones in various places. He had never been one to care for vegetation—there was nothing mechanical about it to call his fascination—but over the last weeks he had come to appreciate it for its natural power and grace.

Phylish would have loved it, he thought—and tears welled up in his large eyes. He missed her terribly. He missed the grinding of her teeth in the middle of the night that let him know he was not alone in the darkness. He missed her big feet kicking him out the door each morning. He missed the way she tended to hiccough when she laughed; the slate-screeching sound of her voice whenever she was frustrated with him. Most of all, he mourned terribly that he had made one of the greatest discoveries in the entire history of goblins—perhaps even rivaling the roots of Technomancy itself—and had no way of sharing it with his beloved.

It had occurred to him that if he could get the Og to surrender to him, then he could barter with Mimic to exchange the Trove for his wife. The ogre lords had been sympathetic to his feeling for his wife and had offered what comfort they could in the form of large meals for their "dear master spy," as they had come to call him. Still, despite his efforts, Thux had been unable to convince them to surrender to him. As Oguk made plain, they were determined and anxious for the war to come. For them it was a prophecy fulfilled and they were not about to mess that up.

"We will defend this place until they return," is all they would say, "and not touch anything!"

So the Technomantic army of reanimated titans would soon come, unstoppable and inevitable, and his incredible discovery in the House of Books and all its carefully ordered books would be irretrievably mixed up, its sequence and meaning forever lost, and his hopes for being reunited with his beloved Phylish crushed under the iron heels of Lithbet's gigantic ambitions.

She might as well step on him while she was at it.

Thux wiped his runny nose on his sleeve—now deeply stained with many previous attacks of longing—and looked around. His House of Books sat on one side of the Ellipse and he had searched the structure for weeks for answers to his questions. He now knew a number of the ancient symbols and their meanings—dog, cat, boy, girl, ball—but there were so many more that he did not understand. He noticed that all the buildings surrounding the Ellipse had symbols on them as well, but none of them related to dogs, cats, boys, girls, or balls.

Only the great building at the farthest end of the Ellipse displayed any characters that he understood. One of the books he had been studying the most lately had pictures in it of titans kneeling before one larger titan. It was a difficult book to study because it lay only partially open on the floor and, without touching it, he was unable to view much. Still, one of the symbols was coupled with another from his first basic book—which he now had dubbed Thux's Book of Boy and Girl—and gave him a partial understanding of the inscription over the main entrance to the far building with the three bright domes.

"Throne of—something," Thux pondered aloud. "Throne of—what?"

His large feet padded down the steps, carrying him along the broken cobblestones of the Ellipse. He was heartsick, without hope, and needed some diversion. He spoke to himself idly as he walked, his footfalls echoing against the walls of the empty Trove.

"Throne of—Iron? Throne of—Doom? Throne of—what? Throne of Instant Death to Curious Goblins? Throne of All the Answers to My Problems?"

Thux stopped at the foot of the steps leading to the great building. A gust of wind blew up behind him, tossing dried leaves up the stairs until they spun against the wide doors.

"What is it, then: instant death or answers?" he asked himself, and then shrugged dejectedly. "Well, either way, *my* problem would be solved. So, I suppose it's time at last to break a rule or two."

He followed the wind up the steps and grasped the handles on the door. He pushed but nothing happened. He pushed harder but the doors would not budge. Finally, he took several steps backward, ran at the door with all his might and slammed his shoulder into it. He bounced off it, yelping in pain.

And the door swung out toward him and then rebounded shut again.

Thux glanced around in embarrassment to make sure no one had seen, and realized how ridiculous he was being. He grasped hold of the handle and easily pulled the door open.

The hallway beyond extended thirty feet above to a ceiling crafted in an arched stone lattice fitted with slabs of milky, polished quartz that allowed daylight to fill the expanse. The floor still shone under its light through a thin layer of dust. Between tall, slender columns on either side of the hall stood titans—three on each side—unlike any known in Thux's experience. They were shorter than other titans by more than half for one thing, and built more like the ogres—strong, broad, and compact. For another, they appeared to be completely intact—yet another unheard-of find. Each of them stood as they had stood for centuries, unmoving, with each holding a ten-foot-long sword in one hand and a metallic hook in the other.

Thux stepped between them with reverence, hoping not to wake them from their four-hundred-year slumber. His gentle footfalls left light impressions in the dust down the length of the hall. The sight of the titans should have thrilled him as an engineer but the wind seemed to be pushing him further down the hall. He had left the door open when he entered and now the evening breeze continued to blow gently against his back, urging him onward.

The end of the great hall opened onto an enormous rotunda surrounding a large object in the center.

Thux smiled for the first time that day.

"So there you are!" he murmured.

He had seen it before; though the details of the device were different, the shape was unmistakable. The statue of the upper part of a titan, its metal corroded and pitted, rose out of the floor in a graceful curve, its strongly muscled arms extending over the center of the rotunda, its hands holding a large globe. It was difficult to look directly at the globe itself, for the light that shone from within was a deep purple color that was difficult to fix one's eye on. The globe seemed to have a depth that transcended its size. On the back of the titan sat a metallic and corroded goblin, which held a smaller globe that was smoky gray in color with surface markings that seemed to shift as Thux moved. Two statues stood to the left and right of the globe-wielding titan; both were tall and too thin, Thux thought. They appeared to be the images of females—their stomachs sickeningly flat and their breasts unhealthily small and too firm. Perhaps they had been tortured, Thux thought, to be so deformed. Each of these held globes over their heads, gazing up at them with expressions that Thux could only interpret as pain.

Magnificent as all this was, it was the small object resting on a pedestal in the center of the floor that commanded his attention. It was a bronze globe of intricate latticework exactly as he had seen hanging over the stage in his dream. A turned shaft with a tapered knob protruded from one side and held something in its center, a dimly throbbing light that he could not quite see.

There was no doubt in his mind; this was the device he had seen in the dream. At last, he had found what Mimic was looking for.

Wandering around the pedestal, Thux found an ornate stone chair.

"Ah, the throne of—the Throne of Thux!" exclaimed the Wizard of Jilik, his high voice echoing in the vacant dome above. He quickly clambered over the scattered benches, stepped around the polished bronze ball, and sat down.

The throne was, to be truthful, too tall for his legs and too deep for him to sit back properly. Still it was grand, he thought, for a lowly goblin to be sitting here on a throne of the titans and be the master of the Trove. All their glory and all their power and who had it come down to at last . . . to Thux, Lord of the Trove!

Thux amused himself for a while, striking several royal poses on the throne, stern and compassionate in turn, but he soon got bored. Being Lord of the Trove just was not terribly interesting when there was no one to lord over. So he leaned forward to examine the bronze globe that sat within his reach on the pedestal before the throne.

"I wonder what it does," Thux asked idly, forgetting the weightier matters in his life in the excitement of his discovery. He reached forward, grasping the handle and moving it upward. The intricate bronze globe sat before him, still filled with its strange, pulsing light.

It was a curious ball; within the bronze filigree swirled an intricate pattern of lights. Its ornate surface was crisscrossed with long curving lines and deep symbols etched into the bronze latticework.

Symbols? Thux leaned forward on the throne.

A shaft of light pierced the darkness from a broken tile in the dome high overhead, leaving the globe before him in silhouette but with enough light for him to examine the device. He could not be certain but he thought that perhaps this symbol here was glowing.

He touched it.

Suddenly, the symbol burst with a brilliant orange color as if it caught fire. The incandescent light ran quickly down several of the lines etched in the bronze sphere, igniting other symbols which now glowed as well.

A loud, metallic groaning shook Thux. The deformed statues were shifting around the floor. Even the great titan above him was moving now, its arms drawing in slightly, shifting its own, drawing in the large purple globe toward it. "I hope I'm awake," Thux thought, more than a little afraid that he was not.

Thux looked up. One of the short titans stood in the archway of the rotunda, staring at him.

Thux gazed back at the titan with huge eyes. He could not decide whether to be shaken to his core with fear or to scream for joy. Then he decided to try a third approach.

"Nice titan," Thux croaked out, his voice small in the vastness around him. He slowly reached forward toward the globe once more to press the first symbol a second time. "Go back to sleep—that's a good titan."

He pressed the symbol once more. The lines of fire retracted to the first symbol only to run down different lines to other symbols.

The twenty-foot-tall metallic titan suddenly raised its sword with a speed that belied its size. It took a quick step into the rotunda.

"Just a minute. Just a minute, now," Thux said, trying a different lit symbol. This time more glowing lines ignited a completely different set of symbols.

The titan charged toward him, its cold metallic eyes fixed on Thux, both its sword and its hook raised alternately as it thundered toward him, kicking aside benches as though they were kindling.

"Just a minute!" Thux exclaimed, his hand desperately pressing more and more symbols. The proliferation of fiery lines was quickly becoming a confusing web of light on the surface of the globe. In a moment, the globe itself began to rotate, presenting new symbols toward him that glowed. "I just need another minute!"

Suddenly the charging titan stopped, spun completely around twice, and charged toward the left side of the rotunda. It slammed into a support column, cracking the stone. The impact shook the room around Thux, cascading dust from the ceiling far above. The titan continued, however, now raising its fists and pounding against the column with tremendous blows. Chips of stone began flying across the room. A low groan filled the hall, the shifting of the structure as the support column crumbled.

The titan turned, smashing into a second column, and once more commenced pounding.

"No! No! No!" Thux exclaimed, pressing more and more of the glowing symbols, trying desperately to remember the order in which he had pushed them.

The lines in the globe flickered and then changed suddenly to a completely different pattern as the globe shifted under Thux's large hands.

The titan stopped pounding the column and straightened itself to stand upright.

Thux realized that he was breathing rapidly. "Well . . . touch nothing indeed!"

He examined the symbols more thoughtfully this time and found one that he had seen many times in the halls of the ogres. "Ah," he said to himself. "Defend! A bit late for that, after all, eh? Well, if we are all going to die, we might as well do it with some style."

For a moment, Thux thought he saw ghosts or shadows moving around him. He hesitated for a moment, glancing quickly over his shoulders. "Is there someone there?" he said, his voice echoing into the hall. When after a moment nothing moved, he shrugged and pressed the symbol.

A low rumble rose under his feet, almost inaudible at first but getting louder until it began shaking the dust from the floor. The titan that had entered the Throne of Thux moved quickly to the hall from which it had come and was soon joined by his fellow titans in ranks facing the door.

The noise had become overpowering. Thux held on to the arms of his shaking throne. His shout was unheard, even by himself over the din.

"Now what do I do?"

Thux placed both hands on the bronze globe before him. He suddenly felt himself become lighter and lighter. The walls around him became transparent and smaller. It was as though he were becoming the entire Trove, his legs its foundations, and his arms its towers. It was an odd sensation, to be sure, since he now felt that he had eight legs and an equal number of arms at his disposal. He felt himself in two worlds—the waking and the dreaming—and then suddenly a clawed hand seemed to reach for him and drag him away from reality.

One moment I am in the waking world and the next I am in the dream.

Future students of my theories would no doubt like to know the thought processes underlying my conclusions and selected observations as I stand here. That's too bad because I don't have any—science, what I have learned, is largely a matter of speculation and discovering which parts of research pay really well.

However, I know that I had been purposely pulled into the dream. It occurs to me suddenly that this may be a good thing, for here in the dream I might contact Mimic and offer my own report before Istoe reaches him. The imp no doubt followed me into the building of books—I realize that now—but he knows nothing of the discovery I made there and the critical importance of keeping the books in their original order. Istoe will counsel plunder of the city, but Mimic, surely, will understand—if I can find him here in the dream.

I stand in a strange place. I am on some sort of platform situated in front of a number of long benches arranged in rows on a floor that slopes upward and away from me. These stone benches are empty and presumably wait to be occupied. From the back of these seats rises a curving hemisphere of a ceiling which arches overhead.

As I stand looking about, I hear a tremendous groaning from above. I look up to see a giant globe of ornate wrought bronze — exactly like the globe in the Throne of Thux room — with three long poles sticking out of it. From each of these poles hang odd symbols carved from sheet metal; one that looks like a mountain, another that looks like waves on water, and a third that is the image of a titan. The groaning becomes louder and more pronounced; a horrendous squeal takes up until the entire assembly breaks loose from the ceiling! I leap out of the way with a startled cry, scurrying as the bronzework crashes to the stone floor of the platform, narrowly missing me.

I stand up slowly, the dust still settling about me as I examine more closely the wreck on the floor. The bronze globe has broken into three equal pieces along its ragged seams, laying bare the interior. Each of the three arms protruding from the exterior of the sphere apparently also penetrates to the middle. Two of these rods end in a smaller sphere of dim light, although the third now lies in a bent and mangled mess.

"Sad, isn't it? Broken on the ground and so sad!"

I turn toward the voice. "Lunki?"

The winged goblin grins at me from the side of the platform, his eyes more narrow than I remember them. "So you _have_ learned a secret, eh, Thux? Beginnings and endings; endings and beginnings. Sometimes the same, aren't they, Thux? Sometimes an end is a beginning."

"I found something — something in the Trove — and it brought me here," I tell him. "It's what I have been looking for but now I don't see why. It's just a broken device like all the others."

"No, it is very important. You have done well, Thux," Lunki replied, his dark eyes shining. "For your part you have done quite well."

"I've got to find someone here," I say quickly. "Can you help me find them?"

"Poor Thux." Lunki speaks sadly. "So little time and so much to do."

"I've got to find King Mimic," I say, becoming more frustrated with the creature by the moment. "I saw him in this place once, not too long ago. Do you know how I can find him?"

"Oh, I think I know right where you need to go!" Lunki says quickly. "I'll take you there, good Thux."

Lunki flaps his shredded wings and draws me back toward the edges of the platform where long, black drapes hang falling from somewhere in the dark void above. The two of us pass through a portal and down a long stone hall. The hall branches into two halls and then branches again. Doors on either side are shut, barred against us, but we walk on, turning one way and then another. The ceiling appears more in disrepair the farther we walk until it is completely gone, with only the twisting walls remaining and the blood-red sunset sky showing above. Black clouds streak overhead, blown by a steady, fierce wind in our faces.

"Where are we going?" I ask.

"Each of us has a part to play," Lunki says, his bony hand gripping my upper arm. "You've done your work, and quite well for an amateur. Quite well indeed! But now it is time that you left this stage. There are others now who will take your place."

Lunki pulls me through an ancient, squealing door and into a large circular arena surrounded by broken pillars and arches. All around me lie the rusting remains of my own inventions; the Thux Variable Grabber, the Thux Variable Rod Lifter, the Thux Variable Rock Tosser, and a dozen more mechanical experiments. Each is a ruin, half buried like an ancient Titan in the sands of the arena floor.

"You're hurting me," I say, wincing from the pain. "Let me go."

"You are, indeed, being 'let go,'" Lunki replies fiercely. "You are being released in the most permanent of ways. Thank you for your grand performance—but your usefulness is at an end."

He pushes me away with such force that I stumble and fall flat against the ground. I push myself up with my hands to kneel, turning to face him. "What of my wife? What of Phylish?"

"Why, sadly, she, too, has finished her run and has but her own final bow before she joins you here," Lunki purrs, then gestures grandly about him. "And what fitter place for you to end your

performance than among the failures of your life, eh? A dead goblin resting in his dead hopes? How I love poetic justice!"

I struggle to stand as Lunki is transforming. His feet have become black, razor-sharp talons, his hands have grown rapier claws,
and sharp teeth are joined by long fangs. He spreads his wings,
screeching horribly, and he dives toward me.

I stagger backward away from the unexpected onslaught, my
arms rising in panic. My heels smash against a half-buried Thux
Variable Hammer and I reel backward, losing my balance. Lunki's
deadly talons miss their mark but still rake my chest, tearing long,
ragged cuts deep in my flesh.

My scream from the searing pain is silenced as I fall flat against
the sands, the air pressed from my lungs. I desperately roll over,
scrabbling at the dirt and clawing my way to my feet.

The Lunki creature wheels against the red sky, its cry of delight
echoing among the broken stones. His eyes are locked on mine, his
talons forward in his flight as he folds his wings once more, diving
toward me.

I spy the Thux Variable Rod Lifter and dash toward it. From
parts of my soul unknown to me, I feel an amazing surge: my goblin blood is running hot in my ears, my anger kindled and aflame.
I pull the rod from the ground in a single motion, not losing a step
as I dash toward a broken pillar at the side of the arena.

Lunki changes course in the air. I can hear his predator's cries
behind me as he approaches. I do not turn to look but I know the
talons are opening up behind me, the claws flying at me faster and
faster as the monster sails across the arena floor.

Suddenly, I fall back, jamming the base of the iron rod into the
sands of the floor, holding its pointed end up in the path of the
oncoming Lunki. The creature's scream shakes my bones as its left
breast is impaled on the makeshift spear. Its long-clawed hands
slash at the air frantically, raking my hands, which are still
wrapped around the rod.

I stagger backward, my hands on fire. The Lunki creature has
wrenched the rod from the ground, its screams still reverberating in

my bones. It staggers backward, but even as I watch, it is pulling the rod out of its chest.

I do not wait. I dash through the archway at the entrance, running back down the winding corridors, darting down junctions heedless of their direction.

The cry of the Lunki creature follows me, rolling between the roofless walls.

I remember the wind; the clouds overhead are still racing past; their direction is like a guide. I start running once more, following the direction of the wind, making my turns in the labyrinth so that they take me closer and closer toward the cloud's destination as well.

A tall creature suddenly appears before me in the maze. He wears a mask that is familiar to me — I have seen it in my dreams before. He gestures for me to follow him.

I run toward him but in the same moment the Lunki monster rises over the tops of the labyrinth walls. I run nevertheless, desperate for the help of the tall, masked figure before me. The figure reaches out for me —

The talons plunge into my back, lifting me from the ground. I wonder through the searing pain if it is possible to die here in the dream — and if that would mean I would never wake up. The pain pulses through me; an unending fire burning my very existence.

"I'll be here waiting for you," Lunki shrieks. "Every time, Thux — I'll be waiting to bury you here! You've played your part — now stay out or die!"

The walls of the labyrinth explode, as does all reality, tumbling downward into a blackness that has no bottom. Lunki releases me and I, too, fall into the nothingness below. My last thoughts are wondering if my memories will die with me.

CONVERSATIONS WITH THUX THE FIRST
THE RECONSTITUTED MEMORIES
BOOK I, PAGES 82–94

The imp Istoe stood in the darkened throne room. It was the deep of night, safe from the ears of courtiers. It was the time when real business was conducted.

"It is even better than you had hoped, Your Majesty," Istoe said in hushed tones that nevertheless echoed through the empty hall. "I gave Thux the freedom you suggested and, I've got to admit, that while I'm not much of a supporter of freedom, it certainly exceeded anyone's expectations in this case."

"What did he find, Istoe?"

"Not just a city of the titans, Your Majesty—but an entirely *intact* city at that! Wealth beyond anything known anywhere—an entire building filled with books alone—"

"Books!"

"Enough books, Your Majesty, to power our titans for a thousand years, and the whole thing is guarded by a group of idiot ogres who are not only ready to be killed by your titan army but who are looking forward to it!"

"Then it would be wrong to disappoint them; the Grand Subjugation Army shall depart at once," said the voice from the dark-shrouded throne. "Once more, you have served your kingdom well, Istoe. You shall accompany our force of titans and be on hand to claim your share of the looting."

"You are most generous, Your Majesty." Istoe bowed deeply.

The goblin on the throne stood to leave.

"May I be permitted one question?" Istoe asked.

The goblin stopped. "You may."

"Should I inform the king, Your Majesty?" Istoe asked easily.

The goblin turned and stepped toward the imp, coming as close as his stench would allow.

"I should think not," Gynik said with an easy smile. "And I believe an extra share of the loot would show my appreciation for your consideration in this matter. After all, why should we trouble my dear Mimic when he has so many other troubles of his own?"

Pillars of Agrothas

I think we're making progress!" Margrave said cheerfully.

Eryn conjured another light-globe with her left hand and anchored it to one of the four corner posts of the barge. Each of the mystics present had taken turns igniting the lights and staggered the times of their conjuration lest all of them failed at once and they be forced to endure the darkness. Satisfied that the globe would both remain aglow and at the upper end of the post, she responded quietly. "Yes, I believe we are, Master Margrave."

"In er day," Cephas said with pride, "the Dwarven Road bright as er was. Light filled the whole road so as men might comfort take in their sight. Alas, such days er no more."

Eryn peered over the edge of the barge to the waters around them. She and most of her companions had lost all concept of the passage of the hours, but the dwarf, fortunately, proved to be an admirable timekeeper. By his reckoning they had traveled through the night of the world above and were well into the morning of the second day since entering the Khagun-Mas.

To Eryn, it seemed like an eternity.

The channel had narrowed somewhat since they first entered the gaping maw that swallowed them two evenings before. It twisted in its course considerably through what Cephas had called the Slot Crags, a channel of rough white-tipped water. It banked up against the sharply curving walls that suddenly appeared out of the darkness before them by the dim light of their glowing magical illuminations. Eryn remained outwardly calm though she was terrified by the thought that they were being swallowed by some great beast. Soon enough, however, the passage widened again and the surface smoothed out considerably, although their speed did not diminish. The black waters around them moved as swiftly as the barge they carried, so it was often difficult for her to gauge their movement except for those occasions when the flow of the river brought them close enough to the rock face for their dim globes to illuminate it. At those times, Eryn could see that their speed was often frightening—faster than anything she had feared to experience.

Dangerous as it seemed, she slowly learned to trust the river. Initially, the roar of a waterfall cascading down the walls of the river had unnerved her, but as Cephas explained, their cascade was deliberate; a safety measure put in place by dwarves now centuries gone so that should the flow of the Dwarven Road be interrupted for any reason along its path, the lower portions would continue to flow to their destination. They were called Continuance Falls and Eryn soon became accustomed to the occasional cascade, finding comfort in its marking their progress. The waters, after their initial turbulent beginning, had unexpectedly slowed nearly to a standstill in one large cavern where the dim outlines of an underground town hovered at the edge of their vision. Its dark windows and portals seemed to look back at Eryn like the dry sockets of a long dead skull. Cephas called it Gateport and only shook his head sadly in response to her questions about its fate.

The current then picked up once more, driving them into a narrow slot between the walls, constricting the water and causing its speed to increase precipitously. Lucian feared for a time that the rush would capsize them at the first turn, but to their considerable amazement, no turn was forthcoming.

"The Medras Chute," Cephas intoned as the barge beneath them groaned ominously. The walls flew by. "Fast as an arrow and true as er is! One hundred and eight miles from Gateport to the Pillars of Agrothas er is. We make the time in just more than three hours and a half sure thanks to chutes like this!"

Eryn could only assume the dwarf had been right about the time. Now past the chute and with another two hours before they reached the Pillars of Agrothas, they were deep under the mountains and certainly well past exhaustion. The river widened again and slowed to a more docile rate. Three more of the Continuance Falls were passed without incident. Caelith had finally succumbed to fatigue and lay sleeping soundly, his head pillowed by his own bedroll. Lucian, too, lay curled up next to the pile of supplies on the center of the barge. Even Margrave had stopped his incessant chatter and lay snoring softly, with Anji curled up tightly on herself in the crook of his arm.

Caelith had assigned the first watch to Eryn, Cephas, and Jorgan. She knew his reasoning; between her and the dwarf, Jorgan could be watched. So she kept busy with the illumination globes and tried not to think of how very much stone there was hanging over her head.

Across the waters, their globes dimly illuminated the outlines of another dwarven city, carved out of the cavern wall on the farther shore. The angular lines of the dwarven architecture cast shifting, stark shadows from the lights on the barge. At the water's edge, Eryn could make out docks and the gaping maw of giant warehouses. The city buildings rose in concourses up from the shoreline, extending past the limits of their vision toward the unseen cavern wall high overhead. As they drifted past, Eryn could see that the huge city jutted out into the waters on a peninsula, its farthest tip crowned by a graceful tower of carved onyx. It looked like a great underground ship.

"Kunjung Het er is." Cephas nodded, then sniffed. "Here be the road from Westwall Basin joining with us. Confluence er is. Yon city be its port. Songs, food, and rest for weary travelers; alas er is no more."

"Should we stop there for the night?" Eryn asked, gazing at the columns and walls barely discernible from the blackness.

"Nay, lass," Cephas said, shaking his head sadly as he settled down, resting his head against a pot and adjusting his blindfold. "Tragedy were there as ever er was. Spirits find no rest in Kunjung Het. Best we travel on; leave the dead to their woes."

A city of the dead, Eryn thought. She believed she had seen such a place in her dreams. The dwarven ruin slid past them quickly as two rivers joined around the black polished tower, quickly carrying them once more into the dark tunnels.

For another half-hour she tried to keep her mind focused on their progress, but she knew she was tired and could feel herself falling into reverie. She pictured the abandoned Kunjung Het as though it were bathed in sunlight. There was an elliptical garden, now overgrown and wild in the center of the city surrounded by beautiful buildings. A curious little figure ran frantically along the bright curve of the streets, perhaps looking for the other dwellers and wondering where they had gone. Then the vision vanished and she knew again that the city was not alive and in the light; it was a tomb for its past rightly buried deep underground with its dead.

She shivered once more.

Silently, a cloak slipped about her shoulders; she turned quickly, startled.

Jorgan raised his hands as he stepped cautiously back. "You were cold—I thought the cloak might help."

She gazed into his eyes and saw only pain.

Jorgan looked away from her, his gaze seeming to search for anything other than Eryn to fix on. "It's—it's these caverns—the stones seem to pull the warmth right from the bones."

"Don't they," Eryn said, smiling, "although I don't think I'd care to say so in front of the dwarf."

"No," the Inquisitas replied rather self-consciously. "I suppose not. Well . . ."

Jorgan turned from her and stepped carefully toward the edge of the barge.

Eryn drew the cloak in closer around her. She considered Jorgan. What did they know of him, really? He was the first son of Galen— acknowledged by everyone including Jorgan—and had been reared among the Pir monks under the care of his mother. His manners were abrupt, even for the Pir, but so far as she knew he had never deliberately led them wrong. In all their long and rambling conversations on the road, he had never shown her anything of his heart, his life, or his soul beyond his unshakable and abiding faith in Vasska and the Pir. He was a mystery. But then so was his brother. She knew what little Caelith had revealed of himself to her beyond the armor of a warrior's life had cost him dearly, because it was a gentle place in his soul. It was something those who are most capable in battle can ill afford to reveal. She had guarded that gentle place with her own heart and it had been broken in return. Why had he left? Why didn't he at least offer her an explanation now? She grimaced and realized how neither brother liked to explain himself to anyone. Long ago she had learned to turn the key that held Caelith's secrets. Would knowing Jorgan's secrets help her? Would Jorgan trust her here in this strange place enough to reveal his inner workings? The siblings were alike and yet vastly different. One brother found strength in his faith, the other in his sword arm, and both were willing to reveal little else—*two sides of the same blessing coin.*

Eryn shook off her thoughts and took a step toward Jorgan. "I should have said thank you for the cloak."

He turned his head slightly in her direction. "It is not necessary."

"Perhaps." Eryn smiled gently. "But I thank you nevertheless."

Jorgan, his back still to Eryn, crossed his arms and continued to stare out into the darkness.

"What are you thinking?" she asked quietly, stepping up to stand beside him. She held still, wondering if he would answer.

His eyes remained fixed on the darkness. She waited patiently for his response.

At last, he drew in a deep breath. "We are blind, all of us, you know. We think we see where we are going and that we somehow determine our own fate—but it's not true. We are set adrift like this barge and float down our destiny. We struggle, we toil, we learn, but after it all we just ride out our fate to its end—a fate determined by the dragon-gods from before our births and played out to our final breath."

"Are you playing out your fate, Jorgan?" Eryn asked evenly.

Jorgan shifted his weight from one foot to the other, the river continuing to push them deeper under the mountain. "No more than anyone else. No more than you."

Eryn shook her head. "I don't believe that the gods would be so cruel as to give us our will in life and leave us without any hope of changing our fates. Why struggle at all?"

"Because the struggle is the point," Jorgan said firmly, his voice carefully controlled. "The struggle is ordained by the dragon-gods. My struggle—everyone's struggle—is ordained by the gods, who foresee our ends to their purposes; not ours."

"Then was it the will of your dragon-gods that your father became the first of the mystics?" Eryn asked quietly. "Was it the will of Vasska that left you without a father or a brother down all those years?"

Jorgan shook his head. "You do not understand—"

"Then help me to understand," Eryn responded quickly.

"My father," Jorgan began, his voice heavy with emotion, "abandoned my mother and me to pursue a blasphemous and sinful study that has brought nothing but pain and degradation to all those who have pursued it and blinded them to the truth of the Pir and the doctrines of Vasska. He destroyed my mother's heart and robbed me of a home I might have had . . ."

"But the magic chose him," Eryn said. "He didn't ask for it."

"That is my very point," Jorgan said calmly in return. "That was his fate, every bit ordained and foreknown by the dragon-gods. My sufferings—my pain—all have been passed to me through the fate of that terrible, cursed man and it is my destiny to balance that out; to endure its shame and to pursue my own destiny in the service of the dragon-gods that I might blot out the shame of my father and undo with my own destiny that which my father has wrought in his."

"Your gods, I think, ask that you carry too great a burden," Eryn said quietly. "I've listened to everything you've said along the way—about your mother, your father, Tragget, and your destiny. I know you see wrong in your past, but the wrong isn't your doing. You shoulder the weight of everyone else's sins as though you alone were responsible for them. What if you left it behind—forgave your father and looked for a new destiny of your own?"

"Are you a woman of faith?" Jorgan said sharply, turning to face her.

"I don't—well, I believe in the Deep Magic. I believe it is up to me to choose my life."

"Then from what you tell me, your faith is in your own ability, the strength to change the course of your destiny through the force of your will," Jorgan said, his gaze fixed intently on Eryn's eyes. "To presume to change our fates is to take onto ourselves the very power of the gods. What arrogance! Look!"

He grasped her shoulders and turned her to face outward once more. The barge had drifted toward the near wall with the current. Now, towering above them from below the level of the water stood rank after rank of carved colossi: mammoth figures of dwarves whose heads vanished into the darkness beyond the reach of their dim light. About each were deeply engraved figures which shifted as their light moved past them.

"Here are the dwarf kings of the Khagun-Mas!" Jorgan said, his powerful grip pressing into Eryn's shoulders. "Here is what is left of them and their gods! They believed themselves lords over their own fate and worshipped such gods as pleased them! Where are they now, the great builders of the Dwarven Road?"

Jorgan pulled her shoulders backward into him. She could feel his breath on her cheek as he pressed his face against her hair. "Would I change my fate? I am tired of living with the pain of my own existence! If I could, I would choose the life of a tender word, a quiet place, and a moment of rest. I would choose a passionate embrace and the hot blood of ecstasy—or for nothing more than a simple cottage in a land that had never known war."

His mouth slid closer to her ear. "But I cannot, for that is not my destiny."

He released her and moved slowly to the corner of the barge.

It was some time before Eryn thought to move from where she stood.

I sit cross-legged at the edge of the barge, the river carrying us flowing over the stage below. The lamps of the theater are dimmed and I can see nothing more of the stage than what is illuminated by the globe of light directly overhead.

The young girl Anji stands on the opposite side of the barge smiling at me. Everyone else in my party is also on the barge, but their voices are faint and distant, their bodies transparent. They take no notice of me or the girl. It is as though they were ghosts from another place and a different time.

The girl speaks. "You are still sad, Caelith Arvad?"

"That is a strange way to start a conversation, Anji," I say ruefully.

"Nevertheless, you are still sad," the girl replies.

"I don't know where all this is leading; what it all means," I answer her from across the barge. "We struggle — we die — and for what? Some legend that may not even be true. I'm not even sure I care anymore."

Anji looks up and around her at the darkness and says, "Sometimes, when I think the road is too hard or too long I have to remember that all roads lead <u>somewhere</u> — else why would someone have made them? I mean, there may be more roads beyond, but they go somewhere, too, don't they?"

I smile at the thought. "Yes, I suppose they do."

Anji lowers her head for a moment, biting at her lip as she considered. "People join us on our travels, Margrave and me. Sometimes they only walk for a day or so and sometimes they stay with us for months and months; but they always leave us sometime and the road keeps going on, and so do we. People come and go but the road goes on. Every hello had a good-bye to follow it, but we just don't know when and we don't get to choose. Is it that way with you?"

My eyes squeeze tight against the pain. "I've said a lot of good-byes lately, Anji — and it wasn't their choice to leave."

"No?" She frowns. "But they're just on another road, Caelith, traveling same as you and I. Trust me, I've seen enough of the road to know."

"Trust you?" I ask sadly, shaking my head. "How can I trust anyone?"

*"Well," Anji answers with a bright smile. "If not me, you can
trust yourself! There's always another road, Caelith Arvad; all we
have to do is find it."*

I smile. "How come you only talk to me?"

*"That's funny!" Anji giggles. "I talk to everyone when I have
something they want to hear."*

BOOK OF CAELITH
BRONZE CANTICLES, TOME IX, FOLIO 1, LEAF 74

"Caelith! Wake up!"

The young warrior sat up quickly and found himself suddenly
disoriented. "What? What has happened? Is it time for my watch?"

Lucian's face was grinning down at him, his face a strange pale
green color. "No, old man, it is not time for your watch, but you've
got to see this!"

"See what?" Caelith said, standing unsteadily on the deck of the
barge.

"See that you can see!" Lucian smiled enigmatically.

"Of course I can see! The globes are—"

It was then Caelith noticed that the illumination globes at the
corners of the barge were gone. He glanced up and smiled. "I've
never seen the like!"

The ceiling, more than thirty feet above the river, shone down on
them with a dim glow of its own. Long patches of moss radiated
greenish flecks of cold light. Its illumination was faint, but for the first
time, Caelith felt some sense of his surroundings and was comforted.

"It's like the night sky underground," Lucian said in awe.

"Aye," Cephas said. "'Tis star moss. 'Twere cultivated by the
Khagun. Means we be nearing the Agrothas."

"The what?" Lucian asked.

"The Agrothas!" Margrave intoned. "The Starless Sea of Khagun-
Mas! Deep below the roots of Mount Shandar, the gods took the
blessed waters of their most precious tears and hid them from the
sight of man. Held sacred by the dwarves of the Khagun, the waters
of the Agrothas flowed at the whim of the dwarven kings and

brought life to their cities. So important were its waters that each of
the different clans of the dwarves lay claim to it by divine right and
the Starless War was fought below the mountain for over a hundred
years. Then, in the early days of the emperors of Rhamas, Imperator
Mnarish the Second brought peace to the dwarven clans who had
been at war for nearly a century. In gratitude, the clans of the Khagun built the Dwarven Road. The northbound road and the southbound road both passed through the same place only twice; at
Calsandria and here, at Agrothas."

"Margrave?"

"Yes, Master Lucian?"

"I am astonished," the mystic said, beaming. "You have just said
something completely useful!"

"Indeed?" Margrave sniffed. "Then may I suggest that you observe wonders that words cannot convey? Behold, the wonder that is
the Agrothas!"

Docks appeared on either side of the cavern, carved buildings of
dwarven design reaching back into the living stone. It was another
port but this was somehow different. Some sort of mechanism was
mounted on the ceiling above, fitted with rusted chains and hooks
that ran down to capstans on the docks to either side. Caelith caught
a glimpse of several small bays set back away from the current of the
river sailing quickly past. Then, abruptly, the buildings ended, the cavern ended, but the barge and river sailed on.

Caelith crouched down, his eyes wide. Eryn cried out, quickly
grabbing one of the corner posts on the barge and holding on to it
for her life. Lucian and Jorgan also reached for one of the posts, their
mouths slack with awe.

They saw the surface of the Starless Sea glittering beneath the
soft glow of the star moss—two thousand feet below them. An immense stone aqueduct carried the river high above the sea below,
bridging the gap from the cavern wall to a tunnel carved through one
of several huge limestone columns that rose out of the sea to spread
against the roof of the colossal underground space. The cavern was at
least thirty miles in length, most of its entire expanse lit by the soft

glow of the star moss, though they could not see the farthest end, for it lay completely in shadow.

"By the gods!" Caelith murmured. "The river flies!"

The barge moved fast down the aqueduct, passing quickly through one of the columns, turning slightly and then emerging once more high above the sea. The river was accelerating, its noise against the sides of the barge and the stones of the aqueduct growing louder.

"These be the Pillars of Agrothas," Cephas called out. "Lugjen be the port the far side er is. Be there soon as er is!"

"Why is it getting darker?" Lucian shouted.

"Star moss dying er is," Cephas shouted. "Nay worry be."

The dim shape of a tunnel flew past them; then they emerged into darkness. Caelith could still see the glow of the cavern behind them but could not make out where they were heading. "Lucian, we need some light again."

"I'm still a bit tired, friend," Lucian called back. "What about Eryn?"

"No, I've got it," Caelith yelled. He held up his arm, then searched within himself for his connection to the magic.

"What is that sound?" Eryn cried out.

"What did you say?" Margrave shouted. "I can't hear you for the noise!"

"It's getting louder!" Eryn yelled. "Caelith?"

Caelith connected with the magic, concentrated—and the globe of light flared into existence.

"*No!*" he shouted.

He stared past the bow of the barge. The Dwarven Road had come to an abrupt end. A section of the aqueduct had fallen, the waters of the road cascading over the edge and down toward the distant sea now beyond the limits of his feeble light.

Eryn screamed.

Caelith turned toward her, trying to reach her, but it was too late.

The barge shot from the top of the broken aqueduct, tumbling downward with Caelith's light into the darkness below.

Merfolk

Aislynn was pressed against the back of the sphere, terrified. Her companions lay about her as well, their arms and legs extended, trying to find something to steady them. Behind them lay the dark, gaping gullet of the serpent, while above and below they could make out rows of razor-sharp teeth and no fewer than four sets of long fangs, their curves locked around the edges of the sphere that held the serpent's jaws at bay. Out the front of the sphere, between the forward set of matching fangs, Aislynn stared at what they all could see for themselves, the dim, distant surface of the ocean passing swiftly overhead. Small bits of ocean debris would occasionally flash past them with unthinkable speed as the serpent drove relentlessly onward. Now and again, the creature would shake the globe in its mouth, tumbling the occupants painfully about. It would release its jaws, trying to gnaw into the orb, but each time its long fangs failed to penetrate the sphere. Then it would once more rush onward through the ocean, frustrated with its efforts.

Inside, the wind of the air above, displaced into the sphere by Aislynn's magic, had become a gale with the speed of the serpent, over which they had to shout to be heard.

"So, now I suppose we just wait until your magic fails?" Gosrivar shouted, his voice even more nervous than Aislynn had remembered.

"We've got to do something," Obadon called back. "Valthesh! What about your magic?"

"Well, on the positive side, I think there's a very good chance I could get this creature to let us go," Valthesh responded quickly.

"And?"

"On the negative side, if this monster *did* release us, then our little protective bubble would sink to the ocean floor."

They all looked down into the dark blue abyss below.

Valthesh raised her eyebrow. "Anyone think we have much chance of walking out from the bottom of the ocean?"

"So what are our choices again?" Gosrivar asked through chattering teeth.

"We can wait until the monster eats us as we drown," Valthesh replied, "or . . ."

"Or?"

"We starve on the ocean floor."

Aislynn closed her eyes. She could not get the pavilion back on the Merlock Atoll out of her mind. There was something familiar about it; something she had seen before but that hovered on the edge of her memory.

Suddenly she remembered.

"Everyone, cover your ears! Now!" Aislynn shouted over the rushing wind around them. She reached forward with her hand against the wind, pressing it against the cold surface of the orb around them. She closed her eyes against what she knew was coming.

THON! The sphere suddenly rang like a deep bell, its surface blurring under her touch. The noise within was horrendous, reaching into their bones and filling their heads with the sound. The serpent reared, dragging the orb backward through the water and sending everyone tumbling forward.

"What are you doing?" Obadon demanded. "You're going to get us all killed!"

"Silence!" Aislynn responded at once, holding up her hand.

The silence of the depths engulfed them.

"Again!" Aislynn said, pressing her hand against the cold, curved wall.

"No!" Obadon reached out to stop her.

THON! The sphere once more resounded with an awesome thunder that rattled them down to their core. Obadon fell back, shouting against the sound as he brought his hands up to grab at the pain in his ears.

"Quiet, everyone!" Aislynn shouted, then fell silent. The serpent adjusted the grip of his jaws around his prize, the scraping sound of its teeth grating against the exterior of the sphere. Then the gentle rush of water running past them resumed, though slower than it had been. The serpent, it appeared, was warily making slow circles in the water.

"What is it you think—"

Then a distant sound penetrated their globe. Quiet and indistinct but nevertheless audible—a *thon*.

"Is that—an echo?" Gosrivar asked pensively.

"It's possible but I don't think so," Aislynn said with a hopeful smile. She reached out her hand one last time, ringing the surface of the dome at last.

The answering *thon* sound came more quickly and louder. Then it was followed in quick succession by two more answering sounds— from different directions. Within moments the sea around them was ringing with the same sound.

The serpent began circling closer now, its movements more swift.

"What was that all about?" Obadon demanded.

"I used to sneak down out of the tower at Qestardis when I knew my mother was going down to the sea," Aislynn explained. "At the base of the sanctuary, there was a special dock for receiving—"

Suddenly, a brilliant light exploded in the water ahead of the serpent, its thunderous sound shaking them all from their already unsteady stance. The monster reeled back, a terrible roar coming from deep within its throat.

Aislynn looked anxiously out the globe. There, emerging from the dim waters beyond, came what seemed at first to be a school of large fish. Within moments, however, their shadow forms resolved into heads, arms, and flanks that tapered to long, sleek tails ending in wide flukes. The long, greenish hair on their heads waved behind them as they swam with determined speed. They wore a dark, fitted armor around their torso, from which jutted incredibly muscular arms. Each of them held a long trident in their hands, the shaft of which ended in a glowing jewel.

"Famadorians!" Obadon shouted.

"By the Elders!" Gosrivar breathed.

The serpent suddenly twisted, writhing around and then rushing forward through the dark waters. Aislynn fell backward with her companions, pressed by the accelerating serpent once more against the back of their globe.

The Famadorian creatures, however, easily kept up with the monster, several of them drawing close enough to the bubble to shine their lights on the faeries. One pressed its face against the surface of the globe for a closer look.

Obadon gasped.

The creature's face was horrific to look upon, for though he appeared, in most respects, to have the upper body of a faery, his face had only a thick ridge where the nose might be, while large gill flaps extended upward from the back of his jaws to either side of his head. His features were blotchy but smooth, with his black eyes set far apart and a wide mouth that smiled at them from a jutting jaw and sharp, pointed teeth. Then, just as quickly as it had appeared, the face left them, undulating quickly into the dark waters around them.

"Oh, this just keeps getting better," Valthesh muttered wryly.

Another light flared in the water to their right. Aislynn felt the orb quiver around them, shivering with the convulsions of the serpent. The monster screamed, the shrill sound cutting painfully through Aislynn's magical globe. Two more bursts flashed, illuminating for a moment scores of the underwater warriors circling around the serpent. Then the behemoth shook again with the blow, thrashing his head. Aislynn and her companions slammed from one side of the globe to the other, painfully colliding with the curving walls and one another.

Suddenly the motion stopped.

"We're freed!" Gosrivar exclaimed.

Aislynn looked up. Their globe was slowly falling away from the serpent's gargantuan head. The long fangs snapped but not at them, for their rescuers continued to pass quickly through the water in great arcs around the beast, their tridents firing bolts of blue-white lightning into the creature's scaly hide. The serpent recoiled, snapping its huge jaws at its attackers. The sea warriors scattered, then schooled together as a second group charged in a sweeping arc around the serpent. Their lightning flashes seared the creature's underbelly and it reared back in pain.

The flashes, however, were getting dimmer and more distant.

"Aislynn," Valthesh said, "was this part of your plan?"

"We're descending again," Obadon said grimly. "I'm hoping there is a bottom to the sea."

As the light dimmed, Aislynn could make out darker forms moving about the globe. In a moment, large, pale hands reached out and pressed against the globe. The light from their tridents was dimmer now, but they still provided sufficient illumination for each of the faeries to make out the hideous faces once more.

"What are they?" Obadon asked.

"Merfolk," Gosrivar offered in a contemplative voice. "Famadorians of the sea. I have heard stories of them but did not believe them to be true."

Aislynn gazed out. The surface was a dim lighter blue that was rapidly darkening. She folded her arms as she spoke. "They are taking us deeper."

"And may I point out something more disturbing still?" Obadon said quietly.

"What is that?" Aislynn asked.

"They are Famadorians—but they are Famadorians who appear to have the power of magic."

"Then," Valthesh offered, "it would seem that our situation has not greatly improved."

The seabed rose up beneath them as the mermen glided swiftly over trident-illuminated sands. Aislynn had no idea how long they had been traveling. She knew she was hungry but had no way of equating it with the hour of the day.

"How did you come by that trick?" Obadon asked absently as he watched their gentle progress over the bottom of the sea.

"What trick?" Aislynn asked back.

"Making that noise—calling these merfolk—how did you come by that?"

Aislynn smiled. "I tried to tell you before. When I was young, I used to sneak out of the sanctuary. My mother, Tatyana, would go down to the private docks of the First Estate and had her guardians clear it of all eyes and ears. They eventually caught me and gave me a long scolding and swore me to silence. But this sound was how she called the merfolk to her and conversed with them. They always had valuable news of the comings and goings of the Argentei fleets."

"You should not have told us," Obadon complained with a frown. "It was a secret of your house."

"If you did not wish to know, then you should not have asked. Besides, I felt it necessary to tell you," Aislynn responded. "You may tell your house masters what you wish, provided we get home alive. But here—now—we are our own house and you are the only brothers and sister that I can count on. Much depends on what is about to happen. I cannot do this alone. Are you with me?"

Gosrivar smiled. "I should have died a number of times today—I think my time may be borrowed from you, Princess Aislynn. Yes, I am with you."

"Obadon?"

The Argentei warrior considered for a moment, then spoke. "I am a spy, Aislynn."

The Princess raised her eyebrow. "You perform your duties remarkably well, Obadon. I did not know."

"I, too, am a Seeker but trained in a hidden place in our land. I have powers as you have, though, I observe, not nearly as powerful or refined as Shaeonyn has shown. I have kept this from you as it was my duty."

"And why do you tell us now?" Aislynn asked.

"Because I see a greater truth," Obadon replied. "You must know this about me to use me effectively and you must use me to stop Shaeonyn. The Argentei Seekers also feel the wind drawing them into the Kyree lands and fear what they may find there. I am with you—for the greater good of House Argentei."

"Well enough," Aislynn said, then turned to the Seeker from Mnemnoris. "And you, Valthesh? Are you with me in this?"

Valthesh opened her mouth to speak and then caught the sound in her throat. She gazed on Aislynn for a time, slowly closing her mouth before she looked away.

Aislynn smiled sadly, her voice gentle. "Your silence is acceptable to me, Valthesh. Whether you are not yet ready to give your answer or you fear the answer you must give, I value you all the same."

Valthesh looked up at Aislynn but held her silence.

"Something is happening ahead of us," Obadon said, moving toward the front edge of their bubble.

"It's getting lighter," Gosrivar observed.

"We are nearly there," Aislynn nodded. "Just as I had hoped."

Leviathan

The air within the bubble was growing decidedly cooler. Night
had fallen over the surface of the waves far above them, bringing a chill to the displaced breeze that drifted among the
faeries. Aislynn folded her arms in front of her, rubbing her hands up
and down quickly in an attempt to draw some warmth into them.
She lowered her head, her eyes staring intently forward, and then
spoke. "Gosrivar, you said you heard stories of the merfolk? What do
you know about them?"

"Aislynn," the elder faery said with slight discomfort, "I don't
know anything beyond the tales gathered from the few of our Shi-
vashian seamen who have encountered them. They are mercurial at
best; fascinated to distraction with the world above the sea yet preferring to keep their world isolated from it. They will just as readily
save one faery seaman from death as let his companions drown next
to him. They respect strength, deplore any sign of weakness or uncertainty, and are, by one report, admirers of both physical and mental prowess to the point that their leadership is determined either
through combat or games."

"Games?" Valthesh glanced over in surprise. "A Seeker's tool?"

Aislynn's lips curled into a one-sided smile. "Don't ever play a game with the merfolk, Valthesh. I'd have better fortune wrestling a centaur than to beat one of the merfolk at a game. Anything else, Gosrivar?"

"Just that they are certainly liars★ and, therefore, clearly some type of Famadorian. In truth, Princess, you would have more experience in these matters than I would through my reports."

"Perhaps," Aislynn sighed, "but they are valued nevertheless."

The growing brightness before them began to take on definition. The frozen undulations of sand at the bed of the ocean ended at a hard, jagged line, falling away down a sea cliff to even greater depths below. As they were propelled over its edge, their eyes widened at the vista opening below them.

It was a city of the merfolk; a sight never before seen by the eyes of the Fae. Great platforms jutted out from the seawall, shaped underneath to appear as a variety of enormous shells, kelp, or, in several cases, heads of serpents. The central and greatest part of the underwater city rested on what looked to be the inverted shell of a gigantic turtle shaped entirely out of the sea cliff stone. Atop these dark platforms rested the city's fluid, graceful architecture of shaped coral, spun as though by a delicate craftsman's hand, which covered the face of the sea cliff with a dazzling array of patterned domes, delicate columns, and spiraling towers. Each building glowed from within, suffused with a soft, bright light that was tinted by the coral into an incredible display of patterned hues. The faeries were astonished by the brilliant new display. Not even the fair Qestardis rivaled the beauty before them.

"Well," Valthesh breathed in wonder, a smile playing on her lips. "I hope they are still fascinated by our world above—what could we offer them that could possibly compare to what they already have?"

Aislynn glanced at the Vargonis Seeker, considering her words. They were four faeries in a bubble at the bottom of the ocean; with what could they possibly bargain?

The merfolk in their company propelled the bubble between the

---

★Faeries, as has been noted elsewhere, have no closure in their thought processes and, therefore, no imagination. Seekers demonstrate limited abilities in these areas, but any creature whose communications are incomplete or even colorfully illustrative are considered "liars" by the strict faery standard.

outer towers of the greater city. There were no streets below them—the merfolk having no need for anything resembling a vehicle much in the same way that faeries have no need for stairs—but Aislynn could make out that they were heading for a large open space near the back of the city against the seawall. The area was covered by a beautiful lattice shaped into a pointed dome.

"What is that?" Obadon asked suspiciously.

"That is perhaps our best hope," Aislynn responded quickly, straightening her rumpled clothing as best she could. "Everyone look confident and pleasant!"

The merfolk slowed with Aislynn's sphere, allowing them all to drift downward toward a smooth floor. They could now see that a considerable crowd of merfolk had gathered in the clear space under the lace dome. There were large males and the slightly smaller females and, to Aislynn at least, a surprising number of children dashing excitedly about. Several of the young bolted directly toward their bubble, darting about it and staring curiously inside. Their globe settled slowly before a delicately formed arch. In it was a curious structure: a smoothly carved granite stone that resembled a large chair with several smaller chairs carved around its perimeter.

One creature sat languidly atop this strange throne—a male of the merfolk larger than any they had encountered. His barrel chest was massive, his arms gnarled with powerful muscles. A great mane of bluish green hair flowed back from his mottled head.

The merfolk that still held the globe halted and raised it several feet above the floor in such a way that the large male could more easily examine it.

"Bow," Aislynn commanded her companions quietly as she knelt. "This is their king."

Her companions dutifully stooped in careful obeisance.

The large male barked his laughter. His voice resonated through the globe when he spoke. "I not king! I K'ktukah—Skuelar of Umuurha, North Shallows of Huuluk Delving!" K'ktukah then casually turned his face away and made a series of sounds that were foreign to Aislynn's ears: clicks, whistles, and pops in quick succession.

The crowd answered back in a cacophonous cascade of sounds.

"What did he tell them?" Gosrivar asked through chattering teeth, his eyes still averted.

"I tell skuel you think me king—big joke!" K'ktukah replied, baring his rows of sharp teeth in what might have passed as a hideous smile. He slid easily from his throne, the slow undulations of his long, powerful tail driving him easily through the water as he circled the faeries in the globe with a critical eye. "Tell if true or lie; aermen keep fish in glass house for amusement?"

"Yes, sire," Aislynn answered truthfully as, being of the Fae, she had little other choice. "This the aerfolk have done."

K'ktukah reached out with his large fist and struck the bubble. It shook with a loud, low ring from the blow.

"Now K'ktukah keep aerfolk in glass house!" He threw his head back, barking once more with his strange laughter. He then apparently communicated his joke to all the assembled skuel, for they roared once more in response. "All skuel pleased! K'ktukah keep glass-house-aerfolk for all skuel can play. Tell names! Tell names!"

Aislynn rose to face the Skuelar. "I am Aislynn of Qestardis, daughter of Tatyana. These are my companions . . ."

"Avast!" K'ktukah said at once. "You tell name again."

Aislynn drew in a breath. "I am Aislynn of Qestardis, daughter of Tatyana."

"This name I know," K'ktukah responded, his black eyes narrowing. "Urumhuul Delving with T'tyan of K'taris much trade. Great Queen of aerfolk this T'tyan. Friend to D'nwyn, mage of souls— stealer of magic."

Aislynn looked up sharply. Valthesh and Obadon exchanged shocked glances as Gosrivar stared openmouthed.

"You—you *know* of Dwynwyn?" Valthesh asked.

K'ktukah grinned broadly once more. "Think merfolk foolish of aerfolk—foolish of magic? D'nwyn called dead aerfolk from sea. Powerful magic D'nwyn; dead steal merfolk magic to serve D'nwyn."

"Your magic—your magic is leaving you?" Gosrivar asked, stepping forward.

"Aye, true speak." K'ktukah nodded solemnly. "Strong current takes merfolk magic to D'nwyn at Dead Shoals."

"But before this—this D'nwyn," Gosrivar continued, "your magic was strong?"

"Aye," K'ktukah replied suspiciously. "What lies you asking?"

"No lies," Gosrivar said, glancing at his companions as he licked his lips. "Where does your magic go—when it leaves, I mean? Do you know where it is taken when it leaves you?"

"To old D'lar," K'ktukah replied. "Lands of K'ree long ago. Now Dead Shoals."

Gosrivar turned to Valthesh and smiled. "We may have something to bargain with after all."

Aislynn looked at them both. "What is it?"

"Great K'ktukah," Valthesh said, turning to the merman just beyond their globe. "We have come across the land and across the air and into your waters on a great mission. This—this aerfolk," he gestured at Aislynn, "is not only the daughter of Tatyana but a servant of Dwynwyn."

K'ktukah suddenly flashed backward in the water, putting a little more distance between them. "A dead-mage of the aerfolk!"

"What are you doing?" Aislynn asked urgently under her breath.

Valthesh turned to her, speaking quickly. "Their magic started to drain from them, and then sometime later they heard tales of the dead being taken from the sea. They think the two events are connected—and, in a way, perhaps they are—but K'ktukah says the magic is moving toward Dunlar; that's Kyree lands. The Kyree were destroyed at the same time the magic started leaving the merfolk."

"They are the same event?" Aislynn murmured.

Valthesh nodded. "And apparently whatever happened is still happening. Their magic is still draining."

"Their magic is going to Dunlar; Shaeonyn is going to Dunlar; and now *we're* going to Dunlar!" Aislynn said, then spoke to K'ktukah beyond the edge of their glass bubble. "Sire, I am Aislynn and a servant of Dwynwyn. She is unaware that your magic was taken. She would wish to restore it to you if she can. What she would do, we shall strive to do. Help us, and in Dwynwyn's name, we shall do all we can to restore your magic to your people."

*   *   *

The quiet hiss of the water around them had lulled Gosrivar to sleep. He lay curled up on one side of the globe, his arms folded tightly around him. Now the water's hiss was interrupted occasionally by the deep and grating racket of his occasional fits of snoring.

Aislynn looked up from where she stood near the front of the bubble. The surface of the water far overhead was churning and dark. There must be a terrible storm up there, she thought. Here, however, well beneath the waves, their little bubble of air was calm and quiet—Gosrivar notwithstanding.

Obadon and Valthesh had been speaking in hushed tones for some time before they approached Aislynn.

"What is it?" she asked quietly, not wishing to wake the Shivash scholar.

Valthesh glanced at Obadon.

The warrior whispered. "We've had nothing to eat or drink for three days."

"This I well know," Aislynn responded.

"I am not complaining," Obadon snapped, then relaxed. "We can go for perhaps another day without water before we will have serious problems."

"K'ktukah would have offered us both food and drink but none of us could figure a way to get it into this wonderful curse of a bubble," Aislynn said, banging her fist against the impervious surface in her frustration. "They can't fly and we can't swim. I think we'll be all right—K'ktukah said our friend would have us there by the fourth day."

Aislynn gestured toward the back of the bubble. There, still pushing them with its tremendous snout, a leviathan, an incredibly huge fish with a broad, flat snout, undulated its enormous body through the water, effortlessly pressing across the oceanic expanse through what K'ktukah called the Serpent Shallows. Merfolk had accompanied them for some time, but bringing the leviathan to a halt, their leader explained with broken Fae words that they had reached the Dead Shoals and that the merfolk could not go further. Then K'ktukah made a series of sounds to the leviathan, who answered him back in kind. The gigantic creature was apparently willing to do the behest of the merfolk lord, for it at once maneuvered to place Aislynn's magical bubble before it and began pushing it with speed through the water.

"Are you sure he knows where he's going?" Valthesh asked, nodding toward the beast.

"That's what K'ktukah said," Aislynn replied, "that the merfolk have an unerring sense of direction and that this beast is loyal to him."

"Look! Up there!"

Aislynn and Valthesh both turned to follow Obadon's pointing hand.

There, suspended above them and silently crashing through the waves, was the underside of a ship's hull.

Aislynn smiled. "It must be the *Brethain*."

Valthesh lay back against the inner curve of the globe, her hands comfortably cradled behind her head. "They appear to be having a more difficult crossing than we are at the moment."

"There appears to be some justice after all," Obadon said through a tight smile.

"Perhaps a little for now," Aislynn replied, her eyes fixed on the hull. It was making little headway in the storm, as they were quickly passing under it. "Storms blow over, and I'd never count Shaeonyn out. We may beat them by a day—perhaps—but then we'll be four of us against Shaeonyn, the Kyree, the entire Mantacorian crew, my own dead guardians, and for all I know there is some unknown horror that awaits us when we surface, and we *still* have to find something to eat!"

Her eyes followed the rocking hull above her until it fell behind them, vanishing in the black waters.

The Starless Sea

I plunge toward the black waters. The Dwarven Road had ended abruptly and catastrophically; our barge, racing at an unbelievable speed, tumbled from the broken end of the ancient, collapsed aqueduct. I no longer see anything—I hear the cries of my companions. I tumble. I fall. The dim light from the moss is a blur. I plunge from unthinkable heights toward the black and fatal waters below.

Yet somehow everything around me alters in the darkness. I am no longer falling toward the unforgiving reality of the underground sea, but have entered the dream and am falling with the winged woman into the darkness below the stage. My hold on her is not firm; the liquid makes her arm slick and she slides from my grip. The lattice of water that protected us from the snakes collapses. The delicate structure engulfs me; its black waters spin me around, as though in a whirlpool. It drags me under the surface toward a deeper blackness, one that I know will be cold and eternal. My lungs ache. I fight the urge to let go my breath and take in the deadly, chill blackness that surrounds me.

Then a shaft of light shines dimly down at me through the spinning waters. The figure of a woman is silhouetted by its rays, which stab downward through the water. I cannot see her clearly,

but she beckons me, urging me upward from the water. Her light
gives me strength I did not have, and I pull myself upward, out of
the hole through which I had fallen.

Soaked and sputtering, I glance about; the stage is dim and
deserted. Even as I watch, the stage, too, fades to blackness, its
boards crumbling into slick stones under my hands. I am suddenly
in the grip of numbing cold and a pitch-black darkness that no eye
could penetrate.

BOOK OF CAELITH
BRONZE CANTICLES, TOME IX, FOLIO 1, LEAF 77

Caelith cried out with all his might. It was a primal shout from
the depths of his soul, mindless and primitive. It echoed around him
through the darkness, amplifying his raw feelings, and he raged back
at the sound of his own fear again and again until his emotion was
spent and his mind slowly came to understand that he was still alive.

He could see nothing. There was a dim sense of faint light in one
direction, but it barely registered on his human eyes. He was soaking
wet; he must have somehow survived the unimaginable fall from the
broken "road," tumbling down through the black air to the water
below. He had very little recollection of it, nor did he desire to remember. Now he sat on smooth, frigid stones. A gentle lapping water
splashed around his frigid feet, its sound asserting itself as the echoes
of his own anguished cries diminished into nothing.

Though he knew that he must be on the vast shores of the Starless Sea, he felt the darkness press closely in around him. His mind
conjured notions of terrible beasts lurking just beyond arm's reach.
Shivering, he exerted a tremendous effort of will, calmed himself further, and struggled to reach that place of mind where he might call
on the Deep Magic.

It was not there. It had not been there during his fall and it still
failed him. Caelith shuddered, his hands gripping his upper arms
tightly as he sought to find even the simplest of conjurations from the
dream.

It answered him at last, and a single globe of light struggled to life in his hands. Though it gave off no heat, its presence warmed his soul. Blinking, Caelith held the glowing orb above him, his confidence improving slightly under its feeble illumination, an island of calm reaching no more than thirty feet in any direction.

He was, indeed, on the shores of the Starless Sea. Its chill water lapped against the stones of the shore, which were worn smooth by the gentle waves since before time was measured by men. The hardscrabble stones of the seawall gave way to earth and rocks higher up from the shore and, beyond that, the vague hint of a ridgeline of a subterranean bluff. He stood up, his breath loud in his own ears as he looked down the wide shore that swept in both directions from him.

"Hey!" he shouted. His voice bounded back from a great distance, diminishing with each repetition. "Lucian! Eryn! Answer me!"

. . . Answer me! . . . answer me . . . answer me . . . The echoes died off as he strained to hear a reply.

Only the soft, lapping waves answered him.

Caelith sat down slowly on a large, broken boulder at the water's edge. Setting the light carefully to attach at the peak of the massive stone, he drew his knees up to his chest, held them close with both arms, and pondered what to do next. He was alone, it seemed, miles beneath the Forsaken Mountains. His Deep Magic was feeble and unpredictable at best. He had lost his supplies. His training during the years of war and hardship seemed useless here.

"By the gods," he said to himself as he shook his head. "Just what am I to do now?"

A slight breath of air rustled past his ear; it was a moment before he actually caught the word that it carried.

"Walk."

Caelith stood quickly. "Who—what did you say?"

. . . did you say? . . . did you say?

The slightest of breezes continued around him. For a moment, the young mystic thought he might have imagined it, so he stood still on the boulder in the shelter of his dim light.

"Walk with me," the voice whispered on the wind.

Caelith remained still, unsure. He had heard this voice once before; on the mountainside just before the disastrous attack by the snow-serpents and the avalanche that had cost him nearly all his men. He had ignored the voice then—

The wind rose slightly around him, blowing past him along the shore. That, too, gave him pause, for the coastal winds that he knew of on the surface always blew across the shore rather than along its length.

"Trust me," the voice murmured. *"Trust yourself."*

Caelith drew in a deep breath, then reached down, gathering up his meager ball of light and raising it over his head. He knew he was going to die here, buried under a range of mountains so deep that no one would ever know his fate. He jumped down off the rocks.

"Follow the wind."

"Why not?" he said aloud to the wind as he started down the shoreline. "Okay, voice in my head! If you know a better place to die, then lead on. I hope you know where we're going, by the gods!"

. . . by the gods! . . . by the gods! . . . by the gods!

He had no idea how long he traveled before he saw them; his companions lay on the shore as he must have lain, scattered down the rugged beach. Caelith cried out, running toward them, his wet boots sliding awkwardly on the wet stones of the shore. Cephas was pulling the limp form of Jorgan from the water. Lucian lay still on his back, his arms spread wide but his chest moving. Caelith passed him, running at once into the water where Eryn was coughing as though she had swallowed most of the sea herself. He reached down, steadying her as she was racked by another coughing seizure, holding her up with his free hand as they both staggered up the shore.

Their barge—or what little remained of it—lay broken on the rocks and half submerged. A number of their supply bundles lay strewn along the shore, though a cursory glance proved that there were far fewer than they had possessed when they started down the Dwarven Road.

Caelith sat Eryn as gently as he could on the smoothed stones, then stood over her, watching her with concern. She was still coughing but was slowly improving. He looked up at the dwarf. "Cephas! How is the Inquisitas?"

"Right enough er long be," the dwarf intoned sadly.

"Good! Let me know when he's conscious." Caelith stepped over to where Lucian lay. He held his light up close to his friend's wet, pale face. Lucian's lips parted a few times and he voiced several indistinct sounds before he blinked open his eyes.

"We're still alive?" he groaned. "By the gods, Caelith, what does it take to die with you?"

"I don't know," Caelith said with a relieved smile. "Personally, I don't know why any of us are alive."

"Speak for yourself. I feel like I've been dead for years, but you just never listen to me, do you?" Lucian said, struggling to sit up. "Speaking of listening—do you hear something unpleasant?"

Caelith cocked his head to one side and shook his head. "I don't believe it."

They both turned. Down the shore floated a cheerful tenor voice singing.

> *"Caelith and all his merry band*
> *Fell from the sky to a sunless land,*
> *In the dwarven fast, known as Khagun-Mas*
> *They were doomed on the shores of a starless sea!*
> *To their deaths on the shores of a starless sea!"*

Lucian just shook his head again and moaned.

Approaching from farther down the shore were the dim outlines of three figures. Margrave was bounding toward them, happily reciting his newly forged epic while Kenth, Tarin, and Warthin followed from behind.

"Master Kenth!" Caelith called out with relief. "Good of you and and your companions to join us."

"Aye, sire," Kenth called back wearily. "Slightly worse for the wear but we're here."

"Are you all right, Margrave?" Caelith asked the approaching bard incredulously.

"Never better, good Caelith!" Margrave answered with a broad smile. "I must say that was a most incredible spell you conjured by those forbidden arts of yours! Absolutely top-rate! You must tell me all about it so I can fit it properly into the epic; was it something you had mastered long ago or was this some newfound power that sprang up from within you, eh? Say, where's Anji?"

Eryn held her arm across her eyes and drew in a breath. "I'm sorry, Margrave. She's gone."

Margrave blinked. "Gone? What do you mean, she's gone? She can't just be *gone.*"

"I was near her when we hit the water." Eryn sighed. "I came up—she never did. I hung on to the barge, calling out for her, but she never surfaced."

"She isn't gone! That's not possible!" Margrave pushed past Caelith, staring at Eryn in disbelief, panic rising in his face for the first time since Caelith knew him. He cried out and darted to and fro along the beach. "Anji! Anji, please! Where are you?"

Caelith grabbed the crazed Loremaster, holding on to the panicked man with great difficulty. "Margrave! Stop it, man!"

"You don't understand," Margrave yelled, his composure completely lost, "we've got to find her—right away! Oh, gods, she just has to be here!"

"Margrave, I'm sorry but—"

"You're *sorry?*" the Loremaster roared angrily, breaking free of Caelith. "You've no idea what's going on here! We've got to find the girl—got to find her now—or it's the end of all of us!"

Caelith held his hands out open in front of him, trying to speak calmly. "Easy, Margrave; we need your help. I'm sorry—we all are—but your knowledge led us down here and I think it can lead us out again."

"Idiot!" Margrave screamed, tears suddenly coursing down his cheeks.

. . . *Idiot!* . . . *Idiot!* Caelith stepped back.

"It was *her,*" Margrave sobbed suddenly, turning his face away. "I mean—I was a pretty good Loremaster in my day—well, apprentice Loremaster in any event. But Anji was something special—I mean *really* special; the kind of special you just don't meet every day. She knew everything—histories that had long been forgotten. By the gods, with her at my side, I could stump the scholars of Evanoth themselves. And nothing—*nothing*—ever touched us. I was always safe, no matter what dangers we faced, so long as she was with me. And now I'm going to die in the oversize cave without ever having written my history! I'll depart an unknown Loremaster, unsung and unheralded in death!" He broke down completely.

"What?" Caelith stepped forward, grabbing Margrave by his tunic and spinning him around. "You don't know *anything?*"

Margrave sadly shook his head. "Well, some—but most of it came from Anji—she'd whisper it into my head and I'd perform it."

"She whispered it into . . ." Caelith suddenly let go of the Loremaster.

"Trust me . . . trust yourself . . . Walk with me."

Caelith blinked. "Anji?"

"What is it, Caelith?" Eryn stepped forward.

Caelith quickly started to gather objects off the beach. "Everyone! Let's salvage what we can from the barge. We've got to press on."

"Begging your pardon, sire?" Kenth asked, perplexed.

"We've been pressing on—and nearly died for it!" Lucian argued emphatically.

"But we *didn't*—by some miracle we don't understand we didn't when by all reason we should have," Caelith answered. "That has to mean something."

"Mean something? What it means is we need to take a lesson from all this, be grateful we're alive and turn back," Lucian snapped. "Caelith, what's wrong with you?"

"We can't stop now!" Caelith argued. "We are so close—I just know it, Lucian. We've just got to press on!"

"How? With what?" Lucian gestured toward the shattered barge. "In case it missed your notice, we don't have supplies anymore, let alone a barge to carry them."

"We get back on the Dwarven Road."

"We fell *off* the Dwarven Road, Caelith!"

"Then we press on from here!"

"Difficult it be to press on from here, even if enough supplies er be," Cephas sniffed. The dwarf looked unusually troubled. "Thar Dwarven Road be river, aye? One set flows north by south. T'other set flows south by north. We fell from yon south road. All roads from here Starless Sea flow north. Only back home do these roads lead from shores of Starless Sea—north only to Nharuthenia. The road ye want be two thousand feet above these shores. That be the road we need reach."

"A road two thousand feet above us?" Kenth bowed his head, his eyes looking anywhere but at his master's face. "We may be able to repair the barge enough to float, but it seems the only road available to us is back toward where we came."

"So, you're giving up?" Caelith said darkly.

Lucian looked up. "We found Calsandria, Caelith! It isn't going anywhere. We can come back in the spring with a proper force and well supplied . . ."

"He may be right," Kenth added, looking away from Caelith as he spoke. "Some roads have ends, Caelith."

"Not this road!" Caelith said, the force of his voice echoing among the rocks. "I can't explain it, but we can't turn back now!"

"What is this obsession, Caelith?" Lucian shouted. "Who are you trying to impress here? Eryn? She's sick to death of this insane quest. Or maybe you've got something to prove to your father or your brother here? Are you that unsure of who you are that you've got to drag the rest of us into your grave with you trying to find out?"

Caelith suddenly lunged forward, gathering the breast of Lucian's tunic into both his fists. He pulled the man's face toward his own, his eyes burning. Then, just as quickly, they softened as a smile played on his lips.

"You know, up until this moment, I didn't know myself," Caelith said softly. "Thank you, old friend."

Caelith released Lucian and patted his tunic smooth with his open hand. "Take them home, old man," he said. "I'll come back when it's finished."

"You're—you're leaving?" Lucian was dumbfounded.

"Yes," Caelith replied. "I'm going to finish what I started. You take Eryn and the others back; report what we found to the Circle and come look for me when you're done."

"No," Jorgan said.

They all turned slowly toward the Inquisitas.

"What do you mean—no?" Caelith asked.

"I mean that we must continue," Jorgan replied easily, his hands folded across his chest. "We must press forward and not return. It is a spiritual imperative."

"A—a what?" Lucian gaped.

"If Calsandria is the City of the Gods, then is this not a quest to discover the gods themselves?" Jorgan said, stepping forward among them. "For over four hundred years the question of the gods of humanity being overthrown by the god-Dragonkings has been at the heart of war and death throughout the Five Domains. The question should have been settled when Rhamas fell. Yet down these centuries the question has still burned in the hearts of humanity and fueled wars. You want to find your gods—I want to put an end to their false rumor. Either way, should we enter this City of the Gods we will save many more lives than those that stand on this forsaken and sunless shore. For the sake of Pir and sinner alike—Caelith is right. I go with him."

"And I with both," Cephas affirmed. "I'll nay be sending human kith down the Dwarven Road without a dwarf er is."

Kenth sighed. "I am your man, Caelith—I'll stand by you wherever your road takes you."

Eryn stood up unsteadily, then reached down, gathering up one of the bundles on the shore.

Caelith looked at Lucian.

"Well," his old friend said slowly, "if I *must* die, I would at least like the satisfaction of dying in good company. I don't suppose you know where we are going, do you?"

"Trust me . . . trust yourself . . . Walk with me."

"Oddly enough," Caelith answered Lucian. "I believe I do."

"Look!" Eryn said, pointing in wonder. "Is it real?"

They had picked their way across the sloping floor of the immense cavern for, as the dwarf calculated it, nearly a day before they came against the sheer vertical wall of granite. Though Caelith had led them unerringly to the right location, it took them a few minutes before they spotted the rising cut in the cliff face.

"By my beard! The Lugjen Stair er is!" Cephas said excitedly as he ran his fingers along the cut steps and wall.

"Wait! I actually *know* this," Margrave said, most pleased with himself. "It was a remarkable passage cut carefully into the cliff face, and it runs from the shores of the Starless Sea all the way up to Lugjen Port on the southbound road. Grathas, King Under the Mountain, claimed it was a means of running supplies up to the port, but in truth, it was a strategic passage that he used during the fifth year of his reign to move his armies against the Rhamasian trade princess. The most remarkable thing about it now is that its entire length is occupied by a symbolic representation of the Trade War and the stories of its different dwarven commanders. What?"

The rest of the group was just staring at him.

Margrave sighed. "No one is interested in the details. Fine! I'll make it simple for you: it looks like Caelith found the big old stairway up. At the top of the stairs is the lower part of the road from which we just fell. Climb stair—get back on road."

With that, Margrave started walking up toward the top of the bluff and the steadily climbing light on the distant cavern wall. "Honestly, people just have no appreciation for craft."

Caelith looked at Lucian with questioning eyebrows.

Lucian moaned. "I'd *still* like to know how we survived that fall."

"Well, when we get to the City of the Gods," Caelith said, turning to follow Margrave, "perhaps you can ask them."

"And how did *you* find this stair?" Lucian asked.

"I just followed the wind." Caelith smiled.

City of the Gods

The climb up the Lugjen Stair took a full and exhausting day, all the more exhausting to Caelith, who was sorrowful thinking of Anji left behind somewhere in that darkness below. He could see he was not alone in his contemplation; everyone was quiet during the long ascent. He was grateful in an odd way that the cavern was so terribly dark and his own light so very feeble; it meant he did not have to acknowledge the chasm that fell to terrible depths just off the edge of the stone stairs. But it left him to reflect on the chasm of his own doubt, as he advanced step by step into the unending darkness. That he had led them to the stairs was no less amazing to the others in their group than to himself. He heard, or perhaps he felt, a voice calling him, but it was unlike any voice in the dream; a whisper through his soul.

It was such a new and wondrous experience, but he was not sure how he could explain it to the others—especially Eryn. There was a time when he could go to her whenever new mysteries presented themselves. She would listen intently as he described the knot of thoughts that troubled him and then, somehow, always unravel it into clarity and order. It was one of the things he missed most about her;

and he longed for her to help him make sense of this voice that led them through the darkness.

He thought again of her as they continued the laborious climb. There was so much he wanted to say to her, so much he had left unsaid; and just when he thought he found the words, the world would flip on its head and another crisis would threaten them all. Perhaps after they got back on the Dwarven Road, when things quieted down again, he could find the words once more, explain that he knew how badly he had treated her and ask her forgiveness. Then she could help him understand this quiet prompting that urged them on, when there was a little peace.

As their silent climb finally came to its end, the stairs led them to the dwarven port of Lugjen. The abandoned harbor lay just inside the lip of an immense tunnel that bored out of the cliff wall. The wide stonework of the aqueduct protruded from the tunnel out into the dark space over the Starless Sea. The level of the water was considerably lower in the channel than it had been before their fall, but there *was* water in it—water that was rippling.

"Well, we've made it up here," Lucian observed dryly. "Now where do we go?"

"Listen!" Caelith said quietly. "Do you hear it?"

"Hear what?" Jorgan snapped.

Caelith nodded his head with a grim smile. "The Continuance Falls—down the tunnel. Come on!"

"Wait a moment," Lucian countered. "You mean you want to get back *on* this underground water trap?"

"Look, Cephas said that the dwarves built the Continuance Falls to take care of just this sort of problem, right?" Caelith prodded the dwarf.

"Aye"—Cephas pushed his chest out proudly—"said that I did."

"We passed several ports like this one," Caelith continued. "Each of them had several barges down the side quays. Most of them were ruins, but there were still a few that were afloat. That rumble down the channel is another Continuance Falls. All we need to do is find another workable barge past the falls and we're back on the road."

"Back on that river?" Lucian scoffed. "You've got a death wish, lad!

It's not enough that we should nearly fall to our deaths once, you want this Dwarven Road to have another chance at our blood? Not me!"

"Where did you think we were going?"

"Up! Out! Light and sunshine!"

Caelith turned to the dwarf. "And how far is it to the nearest exit from here, Cephas?"

"The Starless Sea be direct under Mount Shandar," the old dwarf grumbled. "Nearest exit south er is. One hundred nineteen miles yon exit be."

"So," Caelith said as he looked around, "anyone here want to walk the distance?"

"Caelith, please," Eryn said, gazing uncertainly at the building on either side of the Dwarven Road. "Isn't there some other way out?"

"Nay, lass." Cephas shook his head, reaching up and taking the woman's smooth hand in his own rough, hardened palm, patting it gently with his other. "No be another way. Don't look to close er yon doors ye pass. Don't stop in doorways and safe be ye as er is."

Caelith moved down the quay bordering the channel, his own light leading them on. It swung from side to side as he walked, causing the shadows it cast to shift and dance with his steps. The shadows of the buildings lining the sides of the great canal danced about the ancient columns, steps, windows, and doorways. Within, Caelith thought he could see things moving, awakened by their passing, but he could not be sure if they were real or just a figment of his light.

Lithbet, the general of the Grand Subjugation Army, felt a thrill course up her spine as she stood atop her titan and gazed about at her command. A rather excitable young goblin, she was prone to throwing fits when she thought it would get her way—and it almost always did—but there were few things that brought her genuine joy. Crushing a village under the feet of her titan; marching victoriously over the bodies of her foes; beating a stubborn enemy into groveling submission—ah, she thought, those were the moments that made everything worthwhile.

But to command a fierce army into battle; there was nothing better in Lithbet's eyes. The titans were drawn up in a line that stretched across the ogre home plain to either side of her in a long, shallow arc nearly two miles in length. She commanded no fewer than seventeen of the great machines, if you counted the one without legs as she invariably did. While none of the titans were entirely whole—each great machine missing some major component like an arm or head—they were nevertheless things of powerful beauty that stood at her command.

Directly behind the titans were the grumps of the GSA—the foot soldiers. Arrayed in whatever clothing they brought, they were marked with a single strip of red cloth around their heads to distinguish them from any enemy. They were largely a volunteer army, which, in Mimic's reign, meant that they were on their own for food and arms and often only showed up when they thought there was something in it for them. They were without much training and came to the battle primarily to help pillage whatever the titans "liberated" in their conquest. Just counting an army of this size presented a challenge to the goblins. It took one hundred and fourteen goblins called hunneds, each representing one hundred and fourteen grumps, just to tally the number of troops at her command. Each hunned was commanded by a hunned leader and six sergeants whose jobs were to keep everyone in reasonable line and make sure that none of the grumps carried off anything more valuable than their pay, which was generally calculated at one tenth of whatever they showed their hunned leader. Despite being volunteers, they were a remarkably effective fighting force; especially if the prize was obviously a rich one. This campaign was so full of promise that nearly every volunteer in Mimic's kingdom who could walk had come and everyone was anxious to kill anything between them and the glorious treasure of the ogre city of Cyderdel.

Finally came the Technomancers at the rear of the formation, all flying their banners and keeping their precious books in special carts just in case one of the titans faltered during battle and needed more of the magic by which they were animated. The long list of recent conquests had, however, left them woefully short of books, the mysterious power in them waning with repeated use. It was part of what made this particular engagement so exciting for Lithbet—the slight edge of desperation. They were short on the very thing that kept their army supreme, and she knew now that the ogre city Cyderdel held the promise of practically unlimited power.

If the little imp was right.

"Tell me again about this building filled with books, Istoe," Lithbet said as she surveyed her warriors far below. "Tell me of my triumph to come."

"Your Majesty." Istoe stood grinning next to the goblin warrior princess. "The building is filled with them, intact and undisturbed by time. You shall break through the city gates, crush the ogres beneath the feet of your mighty titans, and make your way to the center of the city."

"There I will find Thux," Lithbet said, her eyes staring to the southwest as though she were trying to see into the future.

"Yes, Your Majesty," Istoe replied. "No doubt waiting for you in the House of Books."

"Glorious victory, unprecedented wealth, and a consort that will ensure my reign—ah, what a fine day!" Lithbet murmured. Then she leaned down, screaming through the empty head of the titan to the pilot below. "Get this thing moving, Funj! It's time to kill us some ogre!"

The sphere around Aislynn and her companions began to brighten as the leviathan pushed them into the more shallow waters.

"Wake up," Aislynn said hoarsely, her throat dry. "We are nearly there."

Obadon roused himself more slowly than on previous days. Valthesh lay where she was, though her eyes were open. Gosrivar only moaned.

"We'll have to walk soon," Aislynn said roughly. "The leviathan can push us only so close."

"I don't think I can," Gosrivar muttered.

"Of course you can," Aislynn spoke with a certainty she did not feel.

"It—it's so dark above," Obadon said, looking up through the orb.

A drop of water fell lightly on the back of Aislynn's hand. She looked down on the wet spot in some confusion.

"Aislynn?" Obadon said with rising urgency.

Several more drops fell through the top of the globe, landing on the faeries.

Gosrivar's eyes widened in fear. "Aislynn! Water! Water's coming in! The globe is failing!"

"Wait, I don't think—"

Suddenly, torrents of water began pouring down through the globe.

"We're going to drown!" Gosrivar cried, standing quickly up and pushing himself higher against the side of the globe.

"We are not going to drown!" Aislynn asserted, pointing downward. "Look; the water is falling out the bottom just as quickly as it's coming in from the top. Besides," she said, tasting water that she collected in her upturned hand, "it's not seawater . . . see, no salt! It's—"

"Rainwater!" Valthesh smiled, cupping her hands in front of her. "Don't put it to waste! Drink while you can!"

The parched faeries gathered the rainwater, satisfying their thirst even as they became soaked. They were so busy in their relief that they did not notice the leviathan give them one last gentle push over the sea ledge before it turned with haste back toward the open sea. The bubble settled slowly and in moments Aislynn was surprised to find her feet settling into the sand.

"We're here," Aislynn stated with hesitancy.

They stood for a moment on the seabed, water pouring down on them and pooling in the sand at their feet. A chill wind whipped through their globe.

"I never thought I'd be rained on *under* the ocean," Valthesh observed, her soaked hair matting down around her face.

"It's the Sharaj," Aislynn observed, looking overhead. "The bubble displaced the air from an identical sphere above us. It's obviously raining there—so it's raining in here as well. Everyone ready?"

"Wet, but ready." Obadon nodded.

"I'd do about anything to get out of this bubble!" Gosrivar exclaimed. "No offense intended to you good friends, but there have been some aspects of our close quarters that I have not enjoyed."

"Then let's see this wretched city of Tjugun Mai and find out what terrible thing happened here," she said, walking up the inclining sand. Her companions followed, the bubble moving with them. The waves overhead tumbled in the storm, opaquing any view of the world above. They passed the shattered hulls of ships lolling restlessly against the bottom of what must have been the harbor. They skirted the pilings of the docks, climbing a sharp incline to a shallow shelf. The rain continued to pour down on them through the bubble, a torrential storm whipping around them though they were beneath the waves.

"It's not much drier in here than out there," Valthesh shouted.

"We're nearly there," Aislynn said over the wind howling through their bubble. Waves were already breaking just over the crest of the globe. "Be ready!"

"For what?" Gosrivar asked.

"For—I don't know what for; just be ready!" Aislynn turned and led them up out of the water. As their mystical bubble cleared the last of the waves, it burst, dissolving into nothing as it freed them.

The faeries stood there, their feet in the sand with the storm-surged waves crashing around their legs. The curve of the harbor lay to their left, a twisted apparition whose wooden piers were curled and deformed. The row of buildings facing the waterfront was ruined as well, most of the roofs having collapsed or having been torn off as though by some giant hand. The torrential rain obscured their view, graying out the buildings farther down the wharf. Aislynn stepped across the short beach toward the deformed wood of the boardwalk.

A heavy pylon rose from the sands at the edge of the beach. The upper part of the column resembled the closed eye and forehead of one of the Kyree. Yellow straw resembling hair whipped through the wind from the top of the pylon while a single carved wing stuck out of one side. Aislynn thought it more hideous with every step she took toward it.

She shook her head, reaching out toward the monstrosity as she approached. "Why would anyone carve such a deformed—"

The eye of the carving blinked open, its expression filled with horror and pain. The carved wing began to flap frantically.

Aislynn screamed once, stepping suddenly back against her companions.

In that instant, lightning flashed over the city, illuminating in silhouette tall domed towers in the distance. The wind howled about her, pressing against her back, urging her forward toward the distant towers.

"That's where we will find our answers." She shivered, her tears mixing unnoticed with the rain pouring down her face. "There, in that nightmare!"

The Shandar Peaks lived. The lives of mountains are measured only by the dwarves, who have the patience and inclination for such things. They pace their breaths in eons and they shift in their slumber over millennia. But shift they do. Their formations tumble and shift the course of rivers—even those rivers engineered by dwarves.

Caelith stared blinking into the light of day. The Dwarven Road emerged from under the Shandar Range, by Cephas's calculation, some thirty miles short of their expected destination, the Paulis Plateau. An earthquake, perhaps, or some other event had broken open the Dwarven Road and now its path wound into a long mountain valley.

"By the gods," Lucian murmured. "Look!"

Caelith, his eyes still adjusting to the light, blinked in the direction his friend pointed. "Can it be?"

"The tower, the impossible buttresses extending upward from the bounding wall, the climbing circles to the center," Margrave said as he, too, peered to the southwest. "Yes, Caelith, I believe you have found the City of the Gods."

"Er good hammer knock is dwarf sure," Cephas intoned.

"The dwarf is right," Jorgan said huskily. "We have to be sure."

"Wait! There in the valley beyond!" Eryn reached out, her hand pointing into the distance.

Beyond the towers of the temple, beside a huge lake, shone the towers of a city.

"Calsandria," Caelith whispered. "It's our past and our destiny all at once. It's a dream made real."

"Now we shall see, brother," Jorgan said confidently, "to which of us the dream truly belongs."

The
Citadels

Dead Testaments

Aislynn trudged slowly up the fitted slate cobblestones of the street, her once beautiful traveling outfit now hopelessly stained and heavy with rainwater. Though it had been only four days since their unceremonious dismissal from Bachas's ship, it seemed like an eternity. She was weak from hunger, tired and cold, yet she still placed one foot before the other as they moved deeper into the tortured city of the Kyree. Obadon, Valthesh, and Gosrivar all followed behind her. She knew that if she stopped she would fail them; and she would rather die than fail them now. So she lifted her weary eyes and searched for their way into the heart of madness.

The ferocity of the storm over the city continued unabated and, she began to suspect, had done so since before the city's fall more than twenty years before. It was an eternal tempest, nature railing with fitful sobs against an offending abomination in its midst. The tempest hid behind its misty veil the more terrible aspects of the tortured city, but the horror would not be suppressed, only obscured. So through the sheets of the chill, gray downpour Aislynn and her companions saw glimpses of the towering architecture of the Kyree city.

At first they made their way along the waterfront of the harbor, a long bowl of seething whitecaps nearly two miles in length. There, the towering buildings of the Kyree leaned not so much toward the angry water as away from the center of the city. Each long wharf that they passed was buckled, the wood planks used to fashion it warped and curled. Next to the wharfs, the masts of the ships sunk at their moorings jabbed awkwardly at the sheets of rain from odd angles, their tattered sails and buckled rigging moaning in the storm—but not the gale alone; for the tattered sails prove to be composed of large, stained feathers embedded in the tarpaulin, and the masts were pocked with the shapes of open mouths that screamed in chorus with the howling wind. The fevered waves of the harbor crashed against the rigging, forming watery, panic-driven hands that struggle to grasp the slippery ropes momentarily before descending once more to join the frothing surface. Even Obadon—a fierce warrior of House Argentei—recoiled at the sights and sounds of the harbor.

They quickly crossed two bridges along the waterfront that seemed to lead them toward the towers that appeared occasionally set against the flash of lightning and called to by the crash of thunder. On the other side of the second bridge they were stopped short by the sight of a Kyree woman fused with the street underfoot. She appeared to be emerging from the cobblestones; indeed, she looked as though she were made entirely of the same material as these stones, yet moving with grinding agony. One of her hands held a loose rock with which she had been chipping at the stones in front of her, as though clawing herself free to the harbor just beyond her reach.

The figure stopped and, screeching with the effort, turned to face them with stone, featureless eyes. It reached for them—

Aislynn paled, stepping back suddenly. She turned and focused on the thoroughfare snaking up into the heart of the city and she ran for a distance between the slanting, empty buildings. She stopped when she lost her breath.

In some ways, Aislynn reflected as her teeth chattered, the Kyree architecture was not so different from that of the Fae. The Kyree were winged creatures and, as such, had little use for such Famadorian foolishness as stairs. Roads and streets, apparently, were as much a necessity for the Kyree as for the Fae; both finding their civilizations dependent upon distant commerce and, thus, the necessity of moving bulk goods along the ground. While building entrances were found in open archways high above the street where one might fly up and honor their host—as appeared to be the case with the Kyree structures that towered over her on either side—the roads in and between the cities were the deep veins of a city's lifeblood.

It was an unfortunate comparison in the current circumstances; the water running in thin sheets down the street beneath her feet was tinged with crimson. Decades of rain, she thought, and the city still bleeds.

She continued to force her feet to step one before the other. All along the street, they saw the partial bodies of the Kyree; some fused into the walls, their faces obscured by door frames, pillars, or windowsills, their arms and legs still twitching, grasping, and clawing for a surcease from an agony that seemed never to end. Other partial faces gazed at them from where they were suffused, their mouths working with terrible sound but without mind or thought to form words.

"We've answered one question," Obadon observed grimly. "We wanted to know where the Kyree had all gone."

Aislynn agreed wearily. "I wish with all my heart that they had gone; but the terrible truth is that they are all still here."

She drew in a long, shuddering breath, then looked up. Beyond the tops of the tormented buildings—their walls made into prisons for the very hands that had crafted them—she could see they were drawing closer to the forbidding central towers of the city.

Even from several miles away, the City of the Gods was an impressive and imposing sight. The center of the city was built around a small rock peak situated at the edge of a plateau that dropped precipitously down into a wide valley beyond. Surrounding the entire rock peak were rings of wall rising up from the base in successive tiers. At the top of the peak, in its center, great flying buttresses rose in tall, impossible arches over a great dome to support the central, graceful tower. Though several of the buttresses had fallen and shattered and the top of the tower seemed to have broken off, the walls still shone in the sunlight. Framing it on either side were the towering snow-capped peaks of the Paulis Range shining brightly in the afternoon sun.

"The City of the Gods," Margrave spoke in the most reverential of practiced tones. "Here the emperors took counsel that they might know the will of Hrea in their judgments and appeal to Ekteia for good fortune and profit."

"So, you're saying it *is* the City of the Gods?" Lucian asked skeptically.

"Well," Margrave sniffed. "It certainly *looks* like a city of the gods. I mean, if I were a god, that's what I'd like *my* city to look like."

"You also said that the last ruin we found was the City of the Gods," Lucian grumbled. "It's getting so that every pile of stones we see stacked on each other is the City of the Gods."

Caelith stood at the leading edge of the barge, considering the glorious ruin as it drew closer. "What do you think, Jorgan?" he asked flatly. "Have we found the City of the Gods at last? Is this where both of our questions will be answered?"

"We shall know soon enough," was all Jorgan would say, his arms folded tightly across his chest.

"It is glory day!" Oguk shouted with religious fervor from atop the outer wall of the city. "Today our promise is full!"

Below him, the ogre warriors stood outside the city walls and shouted back in response. Their deep, booming voices obliterated all other sound and their stomping feet shook the foundations of the battlement. Each was arrayed for battle, strict formation lines in blocks of combatants sixty-four square on a side. They all wore face and body decorations unique to their family and ancestry, carefully and proudly painted onto their skin by their ogre women and directed by the elders of their families. Each carried the ancestral weapons that had been lovingly cared for down the generations— hooked blades with serrated edges or long pikes with strange blades affixed to both ends. The blades and shafts gleamed with their preserving oils. In the rear of each formation were several phalanxes of ogres carrying slings and sacks of glass balls filled with white powder. These ogres wore thick hide vests, but the vast majority of them wore nothing more than a wide wrap of cloth around their waist.

To Thux, standing next to Oguk on the wall, they looked frightening, formidable—and completely doomed. "Emperor Oguk, your army is, well, pretty impressive, but don't you think they would be better off *inside* the walls? I mean, you're supposed to *defend* the city—not run out and attack."

"My dear Master Spy," Oguk said, shaking his head with a patient parent's smile on his wide face, "you do not understand the way of such things. The prophecies are clear; we are what the Titan-Whitat called kenon-foder, those who charge in defense of the city. Then, in the hour of our most desperate need, the Titan-Whitat will return and bring glory and honor to the fallen. The Titan-Whitat will defend us."

Defend!

Thux felt a cold rock form in the bottom of his stomach. He could see the symbol in his mind, feel the chill of the bronze globe, and hear the voice of Lunki laughing at him—waiting to kill him in the dream-place. He tried to consider what would happen if he did not do what he feared he must.

"They will all die," Thux answered himself aloud.

Oguk nodded. "It may be so; then we take glorious rest with the Whitat."

But Thux was already running down the stairs. His large feet carried him through the cheering throngs of ogre women and children and their proud cries for battle. They carried him past the vendors and merchants who were closing their shops. They carried him farther into the city until they brought him through the now unguarded gates of the Trove itself. And before he quite realized what they were doing, his feet brought him to the closed doors of the Throne of Thux. Tears welled up in his eyes; the House of Books was to his right around the ruined plaza. It was not the thought of his own life or even his dear Phylish that moved him. Even the destruction of the ogres, terrible as that might be, did not move him—but the mere thought of Lithbet tearing apart the ordered ranks of books drove him past reason.

He pulled open the doors, his feet slapping quickly against the cold, polished stones of the entry hall. In moments he stood panting, gazing down at the throne and the bronze globe that he had come to loathe as a gateway to his own death. He made his way over to the throne, standing between it and the globe. A voice seemed to whisper to him, words in his head, and he knew what he needed to do. He reached forward and twisted the handle, rotating the globe until the handle was upright. The symbol he was looking for was turned toward him.

"Defend it is, then," Thux said to himself as he reached forward, closed his eyes, and pressed his finger to the globe.

"By the gods!" Caelith exclaimed. "What is that?"

"Something is happening in the central tower," Jorgan said anxiously as much to himself as in response to Caelith, his brow clear with delighted astonishment. "A light—a beacon sign to the dragon-gods!"

"A beacon?" Lucien was incredulous. "In the middle of the day?"

Jorgan turned calmly toward the Enlund mage. "Have you no faith? You sorcerers are always conjuring tricks, selling your souls for false lights and fakery; then when true miracles shine before you, you scoff! You cannot even believe your own eyes. The City of the Gods—your own supposed legend made real in front of you—and you can't believe it. I don't know who is blinder, you or the dwarf!"

"Well, *someone* is making very clear to us where they want us to go," Caelith observed thoughtfully, "but the question is whether it is an invitation to guidance or a lure to a trap."

"So now you fear the truth." Jorgan laughed. "You fear knowing that Vasska reigns supreme over the earth and sky!"

"The Rhamasian gods reigned long before your Vasska began to soak the earth with blood," Caelith answered back. "If anyone has cause to fear, it is you."

Jorgan suddenly lunged at Caelith, his hands closing around his brother's neck in a fury. Caelith reached up, trying to block the Pir Inquisitas, but the priest was strong and his rage white hot. "The Dragonkings are the only lords of this world; the only true hope for mankind! You'll destroy us all—just as your precious Rhamasians nearly destroyed us four centuries ago!"

Caelith reached across suddenly, thrusting his hand over one arm of his attacker and under the other. In a quick motion, he pried Jorgan's hands free of his neck, grabbed his far hand and twisted it, driving his opponent quickly downward. "You want to save your people?" Caelith shouted. "Well, I want to save mine! You've been killing us for centuries—your own ancestors—and for what?"

"For the peace." Jorgan grimaced. "For the hope that humanity would have outgrown you!" The priest pushed forward, dragging Caelith off balance down to the deck of the barge with him. In a moment, the two were locked in a fierce struggle.

"Stop it! Both of you!" Eryn shouted. She leaped forward, struggling to pull the two combatants apart. "Lucian! Margrave! Help me!"

The two men joined her, wading into the fray. In a few moments, Caelith and Jorgan stood facing each other, panting and red-faced on the deck.

Nearby, the old dwarf sat, chuckling to himself.

"And what do you find so amusing in all this?" Eryn asked angrily.

"City of the Gods er is." Cephas laughed loudly. "Knock on the door we be—see who answers er is; then we know who be god er no!"

"Aislynn!" Gosrivar called out. "What is that?"

"I don't know," the Princess called back down the lane. "I think we had best hurry—something is changing!"

They had made their way up the hill and now stood between two gigantic statues of Kyree that faced each other from opposite sides of the road. The buildings here were of a grander nature; taller and statelier than those they had encountered thus far.

Waves of deep blue light had begun pulsing out from the dome covering one of the buildings. It washed as a wall across the buildings and down the streets. With each passage, the Kyree horrors screeched with pain and woe, an ear-splitting sound that shook bone and soul. The rain was driven back with each pulse, its power undeniable.

"I believe we are getting closer." Valthesh spoke in even tones but Aislynn could see uncertainty in her eyes.

"What manner of truth is this?" Obadon muttered nervously.

"Stay with me," Aislynn shouted over the keening of the Kyree around them. She wished she could fly, but the rain had left their sodden wings useless and their clothing hopelessly heavy. She gathered her strength and ran between the colossi and into the center of Tjugan Mai.

The road before her was buckled and deformed. She could see that it ran up into a great plaza surrounded by massive buildings, yet it was a smaller, unimpressive domed building lying down a side street to her left that immediately drew her attention. Every other building in the area leaned away from the domed structure. Without hesitation, Aislynn turned and made her way past the twisted faces and leaning columns of several stately buildings. She was astonished, in fact, that she could make out the words on the faces of the buildings as she hurried past them, for the inscriptions once more bore an unsettling similarity with Fae shortscript. "Hall of Glory," she read aloud as she ran, "Hall of Heroes . . . Hall of Destiny . . ."

She stopped before the glowing, domed building. Although large, it was smaller and seemingly of no importance compared to those surrounding it.

But it was the undeniable epicenter of the waves of light.

"Hall of Conquest," Aislynn read aloud.

"The Kyree were a race who prized conquest above all other things," Gosrivar spoke up, his voice shaking. "They would keep their most important treasures in such a place."

"Then perhaps they plundered one treasure they had best not have kept," Valthesh observed. "What do you recommend now, Aislynn?"

"The dead drove us here," she replied. "The Kyree seemed to believe we were responsible for both the dead in our own land and the dead of theirs."

"So we face death?" Obadon asked, flexing his hands.

"We face the truth," Aislynn replied. "And if we can, make right what was made wrong."

"Then we had better hurry," Valthesh said, pointing behind them.

Aislynn turned to follow the other woman's gaze. Between the buildings, the waves of light had drawn aside the curtain of perpetual rain.

There, in the harbor, the *Brethain* was dropping anchor.

Caelith scarcely could breathe as he led his companions into the ancient precincts of the City of the Gods. The outer buildings were in utter ruin, the vague outline of their streets barely visible through the grasses that struggled to hide the scars of four centuries before. Caelith paid them little attention, for the grandeur of the walled center of the city itself drew him.

He beckoned his companions through the outer gate and into a different world. Within it looked as though the city were still inhabitable. They followed the road to a circular plaza where a fountain of clear water splashed as though to welcome them. Curving streets ran to the right and left following the contour of the second and much higher inner wall. Shops and homes here all lay quiet and still, their doors closed as though their owners had just stepped out for the afternoon and would be returning soon. In his exuberance, Caelith led them straight forward toward a towering pair of gates but found them barred.

"The gods don't seem to be at home," Lucian observed wryly. "Didn't you let them know we were coming?"

"I believe I did," Caelith said in reply, "but I think I mentioned you would be with us. You don't suppose that offended them, do you?"

"Blasphemous unbelievers!" Jorgan scoffed. "You cannot even take your own false gods seriously!"

"Look, is this Calsandria or not!" Eryn demanded. "We'll need some proof for the Circle of Six and so far I haven't seen anything that's convincing."

"Patience, lass!" Cephas said in a kindly rumble. "Proof enough er is given time. Find proof Caelith will!"

"As my father told me: 'If you can't go through, go around,'" Caelith said, stepping back from the massive gate. He walked back down the street and started down the road circling the inner wall. "Let's try this way!"

Lucian shook his head with doubt, then shrugged and followed with Eryn as Jorgan walked slowly beside the dwarf.

The street curved past numerous houses, each apparently built with a common wall, as there was no space between them. The buildings ended, however, where the curve of the inner wall bent outward into a second, shallower curve. Three colossal statues sat on thrones against the high inner wall, looking out over the lower outer wall.

"What are they, Margrave?" Eryn asked in astonishment.

"I don't know," the Loremaster said, shaking his head as he smiled in wonder.

"Awfully glad we have you with us," Lucian said to Margrave through a pleasant smile, "now that we really need you."

"Lucian! Can you make this out?" Caelith stood at the base of the tower that rose at the apex of the curved inner walls. An inscription in Rhamasian was cut ornately into the tall, peaked archway that entered the tower base.

Lucian gazed at it for a moment before he spoke. "Pilgrim's Way."

"Pilgrims, eh? Is that what we are?" Caelith asked as he entered through the arch.

"What is he looking for?" Eryn asked.

"Knows he Caelith does," Cephas intoned with a broad smile. "Follow him and answers er is!"

The stone circular steps showed the wear of use now centuries past. Caelith trod them with an increasing sense of reverence for those forgotten souls that had walked this path before. An archway at the top of the stairs opened onto a large courtyard surrounded by high, curved walls. The light of the afternoon sun was lost in the shadows of that deep place. Lucian and the rest of his expedition joined Caelith as he approached a towering stela set atop a diamond-shaped platform.

It was the second set of stairs, however, that captured his attention. Rising higher still between where the two curved walls narrowed, the broad steps led directly to the tower at the apex of the city: the Pillar of the Sky.

They climbed the stairs in awe of the vision before them: a column of light stabbing straight into the evening sky through the shattered peak of the tower. Cresting the steps, Caelith found the tower itself surrounded by a wide garden. Nine flying buttresses rose from the soaring wall that circled the garden to support the central structure. Two of the buttresses had fallen, their stones scattered across the now dead garden, and the top of the tower lay as a ruined pile to one side. Yet despite the damage, the place was magnificent.

"The Pillar of the Sky," Caelith said in quiet wonder. "This is it. We've found it."

Colossal seated statues faced outward at intervals all around the base of the tower. Each held their arms up, seeming to support the tower itself on their bent backs and wide shoulders. A set of wide, curved stairs led up between two of the colossi. High above it all, the brilliant column of light shone upward from the tower.

Caelith dashed across the overgrown garden, taking the steps into the tower two at a time.

"Wait!" Lucian shouted as his old friend dashed across the garden and up the stairs. "Oh, by the gods! Come on!" he muttered to Eryn and then ran to follow.

Caelith slowed at the top of the stairs, suddenly uncertain about treading on holy ground. He stepped through the arched portal and gazed into the temple of the Mad Emperors.

The center of the tower reminded Caelith of the smoke-outlined rotunda they had seen in Segathlas but far grander. It was a forum of tiered concentric platforms surrounding a central dais and pedestal. There, atop the pedestal, was a strange object that felt familiar to Caelith: a bronze globe of intricate workmanship pierced by a single spindle. It was from this globe that the column of light shone upward and out through the missing ceiling of the tower high above them; its light illuminated the interior of the rotunda.

Jorgan came into the hall, Kenth, Tarin, and Warthin following just behind. The Inquisitas was rapturously gazing at the interior of the enormous tower. "The City of the Gods," he murmured, his eyes bright with joy and contentment. "Vasska be praised!"

Caelith gawked at everything in awe. Three tremendous statues, thirty feet in height, stood evenly spaced against the walls. One was of a beautiful woman holding three globes together in her joined hands. Another was of an exquisite winged man pondering three globes in his left hand. The third figure was of a monstrously peculiar, big-eared creature with a playful smile that was balancing two globes while keeping a third floating in the air. Each was separated by a fresco adorning the gallery twenty feet up the wall.

"Do you see it?" Jorgan asked with quiet satisfaction.

"What?" Caelith had not even been aware that his brother had joined them.

"The fresco; do you see it?"

"Yes, it's magnificent. I don't think I've ever—"

"No," Jorgan said. "Look at it! Over there. What does it show?"

Caelith looked. "That's . . . that's a dragon! It looks like Satinka. It's bowing down before that figure on the right."

"Yes," Jorgan said calmly, "and what is that figure holding?"

"Well, he's holding—" Caelith blinked. "That *can't* be right!"

"He's holding a dragonstaff." Jorgan nodded. "A staff identical to every one carried by my brother Pir monks throughout the Five Domains."

Lucian shook his head in disbelief. "The same staves they've been using to oppress and control us for four centuries. We never knew where they came from; we all assumed that they were created by the Pir in some ritual power that came from the dragons. But look around us, Caelith; look in the alcoves between the statues."

"No!" Caelith whispered.

Set carefully in each of the alcoves stood row after row of dragonstaffs, their gemlike eyes gleaming back at him with the light of the pillar.

"Caelith . . . Caelith!"

Eryn's voice intruded on his tumbling thoughts. He turned toward her. She stood in the center of the circular arena next to the pedestal on the dais. She was looking down at something behind the pedestal, obscured from his sight by the glare of the light.

"Come here," she said, a deep sadness in her voice.

Caelith and Lucian exchanged a quick glance before they moved toward the dais. Jorgan walked confidently with them as they circled around to get the glare out of their eyes and see what she was look-ing at.

It was small, looking like a bundle of old clothing carelessly tossed behind the dais. He drew closer, squinting in the bright light next to him. He could see tangled hair and realized suddenly that it was a body. He had seen enough of war to deal dispassionately with the dead, but then a shock ran through him.

The hammer in its hand was unmistakable.

"Cephas!" Caelith stammered. "This is . . . Cephas?"

"Yes," Eryn said quickly. "And by the looks of him, he's been dead for a long while. Perhaps a year."

The Jesters

Thirteen months, more like er is," said the dwarf from the edge of the rotunda, smiling wickedly through his unkempt beard. "Dead as stone er is!"

Caelith slowly stood up, facing the dwarf. Jorgan's head swung around, his eyes fixed on the dwarf. Lucian took a careful step, his hand reaching behind him to push Eryn back. In the light streaming from the bronze globe, they all watched the dwarf where he stood in front of the enormous statue of Ekteia, a satisfied smile playing across his tight lips.

The dwarf reached up and slowly unwound the bandages covering his eyes. He tossed the cloth aside, revealing startling red eyes.

"Who are you?" Caelith asked slowly, barely daring to breathe.

The dwarf shrugged, grinning through his widely spaced teeth. When he spoke, the voice was still low and gruff but all trace of the dwarf's strange speech was gone. "A traveler—a wanderer—a collector of this and that. Mostly, I like to watch the great play; to see the struggles of man on the mortal stage. You do struggle so!"

Jorgan glanced at Caelith, his face turned to a frown. "What is the meaning of this?"

Caelith took in a careful breath. "It would seem that we have been following a dwarf that has been dead for over a year. This"—he gestured down at the remains next to the altar—"is all that is left of Cephas Hadras, our father's closest friend. The question is: if Cephas is dead, who is this dwarf that has come all this way with us?"

Jorgan turned back toward the mysterious dwarf and took a menacing step forward. "You brought us here! You were the one who came to us! What do you mean by this?"

"Jorgan Arvad, Inquis Requi of the Pir Drakonis, I have come to make you more famous and more powerful than you could ever imagine," the dwarf replied smoothly. "It was I that presented this plan to the Pentach of your orders. It was so perfect a solution for us both. Of course, they, too, were deceived; they thought I was just the foolish old dwarf of Galen's long acquaintance, bartering for the help of the Pir on behalf of my friend, but it is of no consequence. Once they discover that we have succeeded, these little details will be forgotten and forgiven."

Caelith glanced at Jorgan. "You *knew* about this? You were in league with this creature?"

"No . . . I mean," Jorgan stammered. "Yes! I knew . . . He came to the Pentach, claiming to know how we might end the war. He said he had found Calsandria—knew the way—and could lead this sinful pestilence out of our lands. He said he had proof that the Pir were the heirs to the Deep Magic and came to us instead of Galen so that we could help the Soulless learn the truth. The Pentach believed that the mystics could be saved if they were brought to an understanding of the truth of Vasska; that they would renounce their stolen powers back to the proper province of the Pir—"

The dwarf's mocking laughter shook the hall. "Is *that* what they told you?"

The titans crested the riverbank, shining brightly in the late evening light as they strode toward the walls of the city. They were gruesome apparitions—skeletal remains of a glorious past—yet their power was seductive, their supremacy unquestioned by those who drove them across the landscape. Their strides shook the ground beneath them, reverberating against the walls of the city, shaking a cloud of dust loose from their centuries old hold.

The ogres answered with their own shouts. This was the culminating moment for every ogre of Og; a time of prophecy and destiny fulfilled. As they had practiced once every twenty-four days* since before living memory, each ogre took his place. Men, women, and children all moved to their appointed locations. Some stood on the walls next to the boulders piled there for this very occasion. Some took up their positions behind the city gate, anxiously gripping huge clubs. Still others took positions near the towers set at intervals along the outer wall. For many, the reason behind their location was a mystery, but they believed it would be made known to them when the time came. From each of them, however, came a common hymn: a low and rumbling song of unabashed joy that the gods should call on them in their time to fulfill the destiny of the ogres. Old ogres wept for joy to see this day. Young ogres strained within their ranks outside the walls, anxious to find their destiny in a righteous war that would secure an honored place for them among their ancestors. The aftermath of the battle was of no thought: the ogres had lived for this moment, existed for this moment, and now were enraptured by its power.

Death would be welcome and glorious.

Oguk moved among them quickly, his hooked blade gleaming in the sun. His heart was nearly bursting with pride in his warriors and his people. They had trained for generations for this day, and now that it had come, he knew he had done all he could to ready them. He faced his destiny with a clear conscience.

Oguk moved out onto the plain where all the ranks of his warriors could see him. He turned, standing alone as he faced the city and its legions. A tear formed in his eye at the sight of the banners flying from the city walls, his nation standing with one resolve before him. The Titan-Blakats were fast approaching, he knew, but this was the way of the Og. He swung his hooked blade over his head six times and then brought its massive pommel down against the ground.

---

*The ogres have six fingers on each hand and six toes on each foot; thus the twenty-four-day calculation.

The army cheered, its sound echoing off the distant mountains. Then he laid down his weapon and began beating the ground before him with a slow, rhythmic pounding of his massive fist. Before him, the massive host of his nation's warriors each set aside their own weapons and began a synchronous pounding of the ground with him. Soon the sound rolled like waves of thunder across the plain, the warriors shouting with their battle rage and building to a frenzy.

It was in that moment that Oguk looked up and saw a wondrous sight. Beyond his armies, beyond the towering outer wall of the city and its banners, beyond the ring of the city, Oguk saw the Trove itself begin to rise, its towers climbing high over the surrounding structures.

"The titans are returning," he stammered in wide-eyed wonder. "It is—*a sign!*"

He snatched up the blade from the ground at once, turned, and with a terrible yell charged across the plain toward his destiny.

As one, all of his warriors charged after him.

The power of the Titan-Whitat has been awakened, Oguk knew, and nothing could stop them now.

Aislynn held the handles with both hands, pulling with all her might, but the door remained steadfastly shut.

"Now what do we do?" Valthesh asked.

"Something's holding the doors shut," Aislynn said in frustration. "There's no latch—nothing barring it; there is no apparent reason why it should not just open."

"The Sharaj," Valthesh said. "The magic bars our way."

"Then perhaps the Sharaj can provide us a way in," Aislynn said.

"However we do it, we may be too late," Gosrivar said anxiously. "The boats have reached the docks. They'll be here soon."

"You're too late," the dwarf said easily.

Caelith slowly backed until he bumped into the altar.

"But don't think I'm not grateful to you. You see, you, Caelith, are the instrument by which all your people have been doomed. What a part you have played, one that will be held in horror and disdain through the ages! You are the means by which your future and the future of your people come to a fitting and rightful end. You mystics are so predictable. A little nudge, toss some lies about the greatness of their glorious past with a little hope of some false future, and they'll abandon their homes, their lives—maybe even their families—just to lay their responsibility, guilt, and blame at the feet of some convenient idea of a god. Puppets on my stage, Caelith! That's all you've ever been."

Caelith looked at Eryn. She turned her face away from him, her head bowed. Caelith knew that she had never believed in the gods but until that moment he had not realized she had still hoped they were, somehow, there anyway.

"Margrave," the dwarf called out.

The Loremaster peeked from behind the statue of Hrea.

"You didn't tell them about how the tragic citizens of Segathlas died?" the dwarf continued.

Margrave stepped carefully down into the forum. "Well, there didn't seem to be time, and right now may not be the appropriate moment to perform the—"

"How careless of him," the dwarf interrupted. "You see, in the last days of the Empire of Rhamas, Segathlas was attacked by all five of the Dragonkings at once. The valley provided no easy means of escape; Lucian was right about that—a lovely place for a trap. Those that escaped the city itself were easily hunted down and, well, let's just say that not a single child was burdened with the memory of their pain for very long. One of my better productions; one that certainly demands an encore."

Caelith was horrified. "You wanted me to lead them—"

"Ah," the dwarf sighed. "But you already have. As we stand here—indeed, as we have for many days been winding our way under the mountains on your 'noble quest,' all the clans have been gathering—journeying willingly, draining the lands of the Dragonkings like a gathering cyst."

"I never gave the order!" Caelith snapped at the high priest.

"Whether you did or not is irrelevant," the dwarf sneered. "They *think* that you did."

"But they don't know the way."

"Did you think your father would be so trusting, even of Berkita?" the dwarf scoffed. "He searched for you in the dream and I helped him find you—at least as far as Segathlas."

The dwarf leaned his shoulder forward.

Caelith saw at once the long white scar.

"The dream!" Caelith seethed. "You convinced them I had found Calsandria."

"But you *have* found it." The dwarf grinned. "Just not in the place they think you found it."

Caelith's eyes flashed over to Jorgan. "It's murder, Jorgan. Worse, it's genocide. I know what you think of me—what you think of all of us—but you must stop this!"

"Why should he stop it?" the dwarf observed gleefully. "He is about to become the greatest hero the Pir have ever known; Jorgan, the humble Inquisitas who on his own ended the War of Scales and brought the power of the mystics home to the Pir. More than that, he shall be the prophet who brought the ancient gods back to humanity."

Jorgan stood quietly gazing at the dwarf.

"The blood of thousands," Caelith rasped through clenched teeth, "just for your ambition?"

"No," Jorgan answered carefully. "To redeem my mother's soul! It is the word of Vasska to me!"

"You are quite remarkable, Caelith." The dwarf leaned back against the statue of the monstrous Ekteia, folding his arms across his barrel chest. "Not only do you put all the clans in our power, but actually manage to find the City of the Gods. How fitting and ironic that you should give this knowledge to the Pir. I am sure they shall guard it well."

"You mean bury it . . ."

The dwarf shrugged under his smile.

"So what now?" Caelith asked with finality.

"Oh, you want to know how it turns out? One never gives away the end of a performance. One final irony for my amusement. I have an old debt to repay," the dwarf said easily. "She'll be here soon enough. Even Margrave would agree that it is a fitting end to a sad tale. Satinka, Dragonqueen of Ost Batar, flies over the peaks of the

Paulis even as we speak. It was she, after all, that your father offended on the Election Fields. She wishes her vengeance personally."

"By the gods!" Caelith yelled at the smiling dwarf. "Who are you?"

They heard the call.

They brought their children out of cellars and caves, blinking into the light of day. Wives gathered up all they could, shedding tears as they closed the doors on their homes for the last time. Husbands managed whatever conveyance they could find for their meager treasures and their food supplies, using their own backs when nothing else was available. Fathers spoke of hope and mothers spoke of faith. Their faces were dark and light, wide and narrow, long and round, but they heard the call across the Five Domains. The word was whispered like lightning—Calsandria! The City of the Gods!—and in ones and twos, threes and fours, they stepped away from the tormented life of their past for the hope of a better future.

Some were too exuberant in their anticipation, revealing themselves and calling down the wrath of their neighbors and the local Pir monks despite the assurances of the Pentach. This was especially the case in Palathia, where Clan Nikau's more militant mystics were quite forceful in their expression. Instances of looting of local shops and markets were numerous in Maranth where the Black Guard of Jekard was called out to restore order and rout the Nikau mystics from their city. Open warfare erupted in the central market as the local mystics stole food for their journey, justified, they believed, because of their long oppression. The dead were mounting on both sides of the conflict, potentially bringing the direct and terrible intervention of the Dragonking Jekard himself, until Uruh Nikau intervened and convinced the mystics to abandon the city more quietly. Similar clashes to a smaller degree took place in Urmakand, Ost Batar, and Pantaris as the leaders of the Circle drew their clans to them and began what they soon came to call the Trail of Hymns. For as they walked on their journey, they sang songs of long ago that suddenly seemed more alive and real than ever before.

The mystics had for ages been individual tears scattered across the land, hidden in the shadows of brighter lives. Now they gathered; one tear became two, two joined with four, and soon small caravans, rivulets of the hopeful, were winding their way across plains and hills, across mountains and grasslands, through forests and across deserts. Their rivulets joined others; streams became rivers; and rivers became a torrent of people, making their way down the Election Roads that for centuries had carried their kindred souls to their doom.

Behind them lay the Dragonkings and their Five Domains. Their cities were oddly quieter and less crowded. The fear of the mystics lifted from the faithful Pir like an annoying note that had played so long that it was no longer heard until it was gone. Thus the Pir rejoiced, for their Dragonkings promised them peace at last now that the land was rid of this pestilence.

So, far from their homes, the mystics gathered; Clans Mistal, Myyrdin, and Caedon out of the north and western lands to the Naraganth Basin and Clans Harn and Nikau out of the east to the Vestron Marches. Then, when all were gathered, they moved once more, their footsteps shaking the stones of the ancient Imperial Road beneath their feet as they moved with one voice and one hope toward the Aramun Vale.

Oguk's call was answered.

Ogres thundered across the plain, charging directly toward the approaching titans. Oguk could feel the pounding of the earth behind him, hear their roar. He did not know if Titan-Blakat could bleed but he would soon find out. The ancient lore had been ingrained in the ogres from before time; each ogre child knew the weapons of the Og and the manner of their use against the Titan-Blakat. To demonstrate these skills was a right of passage for the Og; the moment a child became an adult. Never before, however, had they ever been tested in combat, for the Og were, otherwise, a peaceful and quiet nation.

We shall see, Oguk thought, *how well the elders taught us.*

The Titan-Blakat before him seemed to hesitate. Where they had been steadily advancing on the city before, several of them had stopped and were moving about in confusion. One large Titan-Blakat, however, moved among them, hitting the reluctant titans with its massive metal hand and pushing each one forward.

They are afraid, Oguk thought as a smile creased his face, his huge feet pounding the ground.

He could see these Blakat more clearly now. They were men of metal, standing three to five times his own height. They were hideous apparitions, deformed and unnatural. Their metal flesh was stripped in places from their arms or legs. The sky beyond could be seen through gaping holes in many of their chests. But in that moment, Oguk also knew clarity, for the ancient teachings that had seemed so strange suddenly made sense to him. He knew how to attack these monsters and bring them down.

Oguk reached the advancing line of his towering, creaking enemy. The first titan was missing its head, but this did not impair it from seeing the ogre leader and quickly shifting its foot to step on him. Oguk suddenly threw himself sideways, rolling over his left shoulder and back on his feet just as the huge metal foot slammed against the ground. He leaped at once, throwing his massive bulk with deceptive ease up onto the back of the Titan-Blakat's right heel, catching his hooked blade in the hoses and cables that dangled from the back of the creature's legs.

The titan raised its foot again as it stepped, carrying Oguk skyward. The air rushed about him, filling him with the thrill of battle. He grasped the back of a Blakat leg plate with his free hand and scrambled to find some purchase for his footing. The titan continued its advance, nearly jarring the ogre loose as it smashed against the ground, but Oguk held fast. The leg drew back and then moved forward just as the forward line of ogres rushed into it. Oguk watched as no fewer than fifteen of his warriors were kicked into the air, flying backward over the ranks, flailing through the air. The titan's foot came down into the charging ogre line, crushing five more under its tread.

Oguk pulled his blade free and began sawing on the cables at the back of the titan's heel. He was aware of ogres around him that were trying to avoid the titans' deadly feet while attacking them at the same time. Two other ogres had managed to cling to the creature's left foot and were assaulting that heel as well. Oguk barely heard the screams and shouts of his army about him, his attention focused on severing the cables and bringing the beast to the ground.

The titan reeled sideways, nearly throwing Oguk from his precarious hold. The fire-warriors had reached the line. Fist-sized globes of glass arched over the ogres, flung by the fire-warriors from behind the line. They crashed against the titan's skin, shattering. The white phosphorus mixture within touched the air and burst at once into searing white flame that clung to the titan where it hit. Thick smoke billowed out of Oguk's titan, the firebombs having ignited something else within the creature.

Oguk feverishly sawed on the cables. The ground beneath the monster was crimson and slick with the blood of his warriors. The cables were fraying, their strands splintering under the edge of Oguk's sword. He could see more of his ogres suddenly tossed into the sky, the smell of burning and blood filling his nostrils but he kept cutting.

Suddenly, the cable snapped. The release of the tension drew the jagged edge of the frayed steel with tremendous force across Oguk's wide chest, slashing a deep cut into his muscular flesh. Oguk grimaced through the pain, but the leg kicked suddenly backward and he lost his grip. For a moment he felt the sensation of floating as he spun, but then the ground came up to greet him most painfully.

Oguk pushed himself up, his hands feeling the ground as warm mud. His army ran about him but towering above their heads was the titan. It staggered, dancing a strange step as smoke poured from the neck of its missing head. Then it fell backward. The ogre's cries were renewed and victorious as they swarmed over the fallen enemy.

Oguk struggled to his feet. The battle raged, but the Emperor of Og could see that the remaining titans were advancing on the city.

For the first time, Oguk wondered what might happen *after* the battle was lost.

"They're coming," Obadon called over the shrieks of the damned Kyree. He stood at the top of the steps leading to the Hall of Conquest, looking down between the buildings. "It's Shaeonyn, and the Black Guard is with her. It looks like Bachas and his crew are waiting on the docks."

"You cannot kill the Black Guard," Aislynn said flatly. "They are already dead."

"What about Djukan?" Aislynn asked. "Where are the Kyree?"

"I don't see any of them," Obadon said, shaking his head.

"Shaeonyn may have betrayed them, too," Gosrivar said, shaking his head slowly. "They were undoubtedly needed to find this harbor. They may still be prisoners on board the ship—or dead depending upon Shaeonyn's whim."

Valthesh turned at once to face Aislynn, determination and resolve in her eyes. "Is this the center of the nightmare? Are you sure we've found it?"

"Yes," Aislynn replied. "This is it—but we've circled this building twice. We can't get in and Shaeonyn will be here with the guardians in minutes!"

"By the gods," Caelith yelled. "Who are you?"

"Do you really want to know?" the dwarf said, his red eyes bright as he started to advance across the floor. "I'm everything you really came to find, Caelith; everything you feared. But only the dead truly understand, you know. Here, let me help you."

"Stand back!" Caelith shouted.

"Or you'll what?" the dwarf replied easily. "Hit me with your sword? Oh, I see it's missing now, isn't it? How unprepared of you."

Caelith reached for his sword but found the scabbard mysteriously empty.

The dwarf grinned. "It has been so long since I have had the chance to kill with my own hands, to experience the pain and the gloriously terrifying surprise so intimately. It's a rather dull ending, I'll admit—but one that is deeply satisfying!"

Caelith needed a weapon; there was only one at hand. He reached over, turned the bronze globe on its pedestal and shone the brilliant light of the Pillar of the Sky directly into the dwarf's unbound eyes.

Aislynn blinked, the Deep Magic washing over her. The domed building became transparent to her eyes in a moment and she saw beyond its walls the wingless man stumbling, holding something heavy in his arms. The vision passed in a moment.

A terrible thunderclap rang out across the nightmarish city, its deafening noise painful to the ears of the Fae. In that instant, the great waves of blue light ceased radiating from the Hall of Conquest and the terrible cries of the city faded beneath the quiet howling of the wind.

Behind them, the doors to the Hall of Conquest slowly swung out toward them.

"Come on!" Aislynn called out over the wind. She turned at once, her worn slippers sliding slightly on the wet stones of the threshold as she plunged headlong into the darkness within the Hall of Conquest.

Thux could feel himself falling but, he told himself, everything else seemed to be falling, too. It might have led to an interesting observation about how things moving relative to each other may not actually be moving at all, except a jarring crash knocked Thux completely out of the throne and sent him rolling across the floor.

Everything was quiet once again. Aside from the considerable dust hanging in the air, one might think that nothing had happened at all.

Thux picked himself up and reminded himself that it was all part of the hard life of a wizard. You try stuff, if it works you get rich; if it doesn't, then it might kill you or it might not, in which case you get to try again. If he was going to save the city, keep his job, his wife, and his life, he had to figure out how to help the city defend itself.

He staggered over, still a bit disoriented from the fall, and seated himself on the throne. More than anything, he felt the need to sleep. "I wish I had some chains to hold me down," he thought but then laughed at the extravagance that would have represented. "Now, let's see—where was I?"

Thux examined the bronze globe and found the symbol he had used before.

He pressed it.

No lights.

No sound.

Nothing.

"I broke it?" Thux asked himself sadly just before he lost consciousness.

Revelations

I shout "Run!" to Eryn and Margrave as the brilliant light falls on the faces of the startled Jorgan and the dwarf. I bolt across the floor, the strange device still in my hands. I hope that I may find some cover, passage, or shelter against the deadly attack that surely is coming. As I draw the blinding ornament away from the pedestal in the center of the room, the column of light flashes out of existence, and plunges the entire room into a strange, unnatural darkness. It confuses me for a moment, as I find myself running headlong into sudden and complete blackness. Confused, panicked, I slow my frantic pace, fearful that I might run blindly into one of the stone walls.

I hear applause.

The darkness parts like a curtain before me. I am standing on the stage of the dream. The rows of benches are filling with thousands of masked creatures, mystics flooding into the hall rising to a standing ovation. Their wild cheers resound through the hall.

The globe is no longer in my hands.

"Father!" I shout from the stage. "Father!"

"Ah, the noise of the crowd," says the dwarf with the ragged scar running from his shoulder down his back. "So hard to hear when the world is cheering so loudly. That applause is for you,

Caelith! You've found the land of promise! You showed them the way to their dreams."

I turn toward the dwarf in horror. "No! It was you!"

"Me? How modest of you." The dwarf smiled. "I never make anyone do anything, I thought you knew me better than that by now! They are coming because they _want_ to come! They come because they _want_ to believe. Now they are coming to the land of dreams and there is nothing that anyone can do to stop it. And they _will_ get there, of course, to the land of eternal dreams where they need never wake again!"

"Father!" I shout into the crowd.

"He cannot hear you!"

I search desperately around the stage. There, emerging from the shadows, is the winged woman I have seen so often in my dreams, her face drawn and haggard. She is desperately searching for something among the many masked players that are on the stage, all taking their bows before the enthusiastically cheering audience. I try to move toward her, but the other players on the stage remain in my way. I shift about them, desperate to reach her, but I make no progress.

One of the masked figures, clad entirely in crimson red, turns toward me. In his hand he holds a dragon by its neck. It writhes slowly under his grip.

"He has followed you here," the dwarf hisses through a tight smile. "Everything is as it should be—so well wrapped up to please the crowd, eh? Your doom and your brother's doom; it is the same doom, and isn't it fitting that you should meet it here?"

BOOK OF CAELITH
BRONZE CANTICLES, TOME IX, FOLIO 1, LEAF 82

Aislynn gazed in horror at the hall, unwilling to look further, unable to look away.

The treasures of a thousand conquests lay scattered in a careless jumble across the polished floor of the long hall between pillars of stone supporting the arched ceiling high over their heads. The columns, however, were twisted and warped as though some heat from an unimaginable forge had melted them where they stood, bending them away from the center of the room. The room was as silent as death itself, yet in every gleaming surface, every polished tile, every glistening jewel she saw the desperate faces of the dead staring back at her in envy and despair as though they were trapped within the objects themselves. The images of their hands clawed at her from polished casings, struggling to get out. The reflection of their screaming mouths gaped silently at her from the floor beneath her feet. Mirrors lining the hall were filled with the desperate dead.

Aislynn trembled.

"What—what is this abomination?" Obadon breathed through clenched teeth.

"The Kyree never left their homeland," Aislynn said with a shudder. "They are all still here."

"Aislynn!" Valthesh said urgently. "There is not much time!"

Aislynn drew in her breath, taking courage from it. "It's here—somewhere—we just have to find it."

"Find what?" Gosrivar asked.

"I don't know," she said, frustration in her voice. "I—wait, I see something—something in the Sharaj. Creatures in masks and—"

"What is she talking about?" Obadon asked.

"Quiet!" Valthesh commanded.

"I see it," she replied, her eyes narrowing as though trying to see something at a distance. "It's—quickly, come with me!"

She dashed across the floor, her companions following, her wings still too wet to accommodate her with flight, her footfalls wet against the pleading faces trapped in the marble below her. She tried not to think of them, of what anguish they might be enduring, as she ran between them, their eyes and faces following her every move. She passed several of the pillars, then turned to her left, drawn by a vision of the dream that seemed to impose itself on her waking eyes.

She found it on the far side of a broken pillar.

"This is it," she said as the others approached.

"But it's so small," Obadon said uncertainly. "It looks like a dagger."

A bronze sphere, of intricate workmanship, lay in two halves atop a pedestal, one with a long spindle extending through it, its sharp end pointing into the bowl while a crystal bead stuck out the rounded side. A strange darkness surrounded it, making it difficult to look at in the dim hall.

"How curious," Aislynn said as she reached toward it.

"No."

Aislynn stopped, glancing back at her companions. "Why? What is wrong?"

They were not looking at her, however. Gosrivar and Obadon stared up at the pillar behind them, Valthesh taking several careful steps back from it.

The creature's legs were missing, as were its lower arms and hands; both submerged in a giant rock. Only its torso and the left side of its head protruded from the stone, bent backward in a tortuous position. Near the crest of the broken pillar was the unmistakable carved outline of featherless wings pressed back against the curve of the stone, a great white crack running down through one stone wing.

"A faery of the Sharaj!" Aislynn gasped. "The Kyree stories were true!"

The stone head pulled free of the rock with a terrible cracking noise. There were no features on its right side; only broken, ragged shards from the rock pillar. The creature gazed down at them with its single eye.

"You have come for me?" the stone faery asked with hope and agony. "You have come to free me?"

"What have you done?" Gosrivar asked quietly.

The stone faery turned its gaze to the scholar. "Too much—not enough. I was a child given the power of death for a plaything. How could I have known? *How could I have known?*" The stone faery pulled back its head, screaming in its unending anguish.

"You've found it, right enough," Valthesh said to Aislynn, her voice shaking slightly. "Whatever you have to do, be quick about it!"

"What must we do?" Aislynn asked the stone faery.

"I—I do not know."

"What?" Valthesh gaped. "You do not know? You *caused* all this!"

The grotesque stone head lolled in her direction. "I was captured, brought before the Emperor of the Kyree. I had a gift—a new truth of a place where visions could be made real."

"The Sharaj!" Aislynn nodded.

"The Kyree have always been conquerors," the stone faery said with a sigh. "Down the long centuries, their plunder of a hundred nations was brought in tribute here for the glory of the Emperor. Each proved the military supremacy of the Kyree Imperium save one; a mystery that troubled the Emperor's mind. Some years before my capture, the Kyree discovered a nation that had vanished, leaving all its wealth behind as though they had simply walked into the night. In the center of their greatest city, the Kyree scouting party found a single, secured vault. With great difficulty—and no small loss of life among them—they managed to open it—and found that object."

The torn-stone head nodded toward the spindle and bronze-tooled hemispheres on the pillar.

"It was in pieces when they brought it back here as spoils of conquest, and so it remained here," the stone faery said, "until I came."

"You tried to put it back together," Gosrivar finished.

"He convinced me to—told me that it would lead me to greater power in my new truth," the stone faery wailed.

"Who? The Emperor?" Obadon asked.

"My companion in the vision—the faery whose symbol of a scarred wing I now bear—my mark that I am his and my shame." The stone faery breathed out with difficulty. "And in my act my soul was anchored to this place, my torment unending along with the spirits of the Kyree I have condemned with me!" The stone faery's face contorted in agony once more, its screams resounding through the hall.

Aislynn turned away from the terrible sound, facing the device once more. The bronze globe shifted in her vision. She saw it smashed on the ground, with a pointy-eared monster shifting the pieces around. He sat on the wide platform she had seen so often in her dreams of late. He held the device up toward her, smiling with hideous sharp teeth.

"Wait," she said slowly. "This is wrong."

"Of course it's wrong," Valthesh said, nodding, urgency rising in her voice. "*All* of this is wrong!"

"No," Aislynn said. "I mean this artifact. I've seen it in the Sharaj, but it did not look like this. The pieces aren't in the right places."

"You mean," Obadon said, incredulously, "all of this happened because this faery put it together *wrong?*"

"Yes," Aislynn said, looking up. "That's exactly what I think!"

"But the question is," Valthesh pressed, "do you know how it is *supposed* to go together? We've seen what the wrong assembly can do—what other horror will you unleash if you put it together in some *other* wrong way."

"We need help," Aislynn said, her words hurried. "We need time."

"We don't have time!" Gosrivar shouted. "Shaeonyn is already on her way!"

"Then we've got to find a way to slow them up," Valthesh said, "to give you time to put an end to all this madness. Obadon! Are you with me?"

"Yes," he replied. "But against the undead of the Black Guard—what weapon is of any use?"

The dwarf with the white scar draws near me. "Time for your final bow, Caelith! Whether you die in your world or in mine will be of no consequence. You have served your purpose. It is time for you to leave the stage."

He motions to the crimson masked man, who approaches and removes his mask. It is Jorgan, the dragon in his hand stiffening, its eye getting larger and larger as he draws near.

In that moment, a crash is heard on the far side of the stage. A small, ugly demon has tumbled onto the stage, his long, pointed ears quivering as he sits up. His large eyes look dazed as though he did not expect to be here.

The dwarf turns, his voice rising to an ear-piercing screech. He speaks with the sound of steel on slate, his long hair and beard vanishing as his skin darkens to a reddish brown and dragonlike leathery wings sprout from his back. He springs into the air with a terrible sound, long talons thrust from the ends of his fingers as he swerves toward the hapless little monster.

I see it then; the demon holds a device identical to my own — a sphere of bronze surrounding an ornate shaft.

Jorgan turns, distracted by the ferocious spectacle. I reach out, stripping him of the dragon in his hand. Its head writhes horribly in my grip, struggling to be free of me, but I hold it fast. I charge forward, pointing the sharp tail of the dragon, now a hardened spear in my hand, and thrust it suddenly into the back of the winged demon.

The stage crumbles around me, the stones flashing into dust, the audience swept away as dust before a sudden gale. The darkness engulfs us just before . . .

BOOK OF CAELITH

BRONZE CANTICLES, TOME IX, FOLIO 1, LEAVES 83–85

Jorgan's dragonstaff quivered in Caelith's hands. It had passed completely through the dwarf, impaling him. The faux-Cephas stood with a look of surprise on his face. Caelith, too, was shocked, releasing the staff and stepping quickly back.

Caelith choked out, "Jorgan, look!"

The dwarf began to laugh.

Jorgan blinked, stepping forward.

"No blood," Caelith rasped.

The dwarf turned, his now booming laughter ringing through the hall. He reached down with his thick hands, drawing the dragonstaff directly out of his body and casting it carelessly onto the stone floor. Not a single drop of blood flowed from the closing wound; the staff remained unstained. "You surprised me, Caelith! That's rare indeed! You shall have a great place in my kingdom!" The dwarf vanished, his visage shifting once more but growing. Larger and taller, stronger and more powerful, the figure enlarged until its head nearly touched the dome of the rotunda overhead. Its hair shone with brilliant light, its eyes blue fire. Lightning burst from its fingertips, its voice shaking the stones around them.

"Your quest is over, mortals!" the voice intoned, booming through the hall. "Now you shall avenge me and my faithful of ages past! I shall lead you and all my people in taking back with blood that which was stolen from us; for I am the god of Rhamas, the god of retribution for all humanity!"

"No, you are not," spoke the quiet voice from before the colossal statue of the woman.

Light and Dark

aelith turned, incredulous at the sight that greeted his eyes. Directly before the colossal statue of Hrea stood the frail, diminutive form of a young girl.

"Anji?" Eryn cried out.

The waif had fixed her gaze on the gigantic figure towering over them all. "You are all lies, Ekteia, and have been from the beginning."

Ekteia beat his breast, the thunderous sound reverberating throughout the dome. "I am the god of power and war! I am come to justify my people and release them from the chains of oppression!"

"You are a temperamental, spoiled child who is blind to the greater truths of the spheres," Anji replied with a small, stern voice. "You meddle with the gifts of mortality without any understanding of their consequences."

"I know the founding decrees as well as you, Hrea," the huge being replied, his voice seeming to shake the ground.

"But no part of you knows the mind of truth or the power of faith these mortals wield. Their free will is the greatest gift given to mortals; you have squandered it long enough."

"That was not my fault! It was that dreadful device that held me here among them," Ekteia grumbled.

"It was you who inclined others to break it," she countered. "That they did so was to their shame, but it was your fault nevertheless. Your prison was of your own making."

Anji gestured with the slightest of movements in her right hand.

A thunderclap resounded through the rotunda, so loud that Caelith ducked. When he looked up, the colossus of Ekteia had vanished. In its place stood what appeared to be a surly little boy, the twin of the young form of Hrea. The young goddess folded her arms with impatience. "Come, brother, you have caused enough trouble."

"We could have been great together," Ekteia said, turning to Jorgan, his voice now young and full of mischief. "But it doesn't matter now, does it? The worlds are all set in motion and there is nothing to be done but watch them spin down to their mutual doom." His visage began to thin, dissolving in the air as it receded into the great statue behind him. "Soon enough will your souls be weighed before us and *that* to my great amusement!"

With that, all that remained was the cold, silent statue smiling above them.

The young waif they had known as Anji turned with a satisfied sigh and stepped toward the statue that bore her true name.

"Wait!" Caelith called out, hurt and anger in his voice. "Are these—are *these* the gods of Rhamas—small children behaving badly? Is this the hope that my people have sought in their hearts?"

Anji stopped and turned toward Caelith. "Mortal Caelith, the ways of the gods are both simple and complex; their eyes see further and their minds contemplate truths for which you are not yet prepared. Some mortals turn their sight toward the false comfort of darkness; they see less and less until they are blind, like Ekteia, to anything that is real. Others—like you, I believe—turn their eyes toward the light and see more and farther with each new dawn. Each takes comfort in where they are relative to the light. We appear as we do before you here because *this* is as much as you are ready to understand. Ekteia had no power over you that you did not willingly give him; I have no more power over you than you willingly give me. Yours is the power of choice and choose you must; for you both stand on the precipice of your destiny, the fates of worlds hanging in the balance. Ekteia has tried to topple that balance, to manipulate and confuse your course, but there is still time for both of you and for your worlds."

"Both of us?" Jorgan said, his voice shaking.

"Think on this, young Jorgan," Hrea said, turning her large eyes on the Inquisitas. "Your salvation is not found among the false gods of the Dragonkings, for they have not the power to grant the forgiveness you seek—nor is it found in making your pride a slave to vengeance and hate. The end of the mystics you hate is your own undoing; for the appetite of the dragons has turned to the flesh of men, irrespective of the Pir or the mystics. Your answer is Caelith's answer; you must find it and soon, young mortal. Satinka approaches, and should you fall, both your nations shall fall with you!"

"Then stay with us," Caelith said urgently. "Help us!"

"It is not given to me to intervene in the fates chosen of men, Caelith. You have been given all you need in this place, mortal," Hrea said softly, her visage fading into nothingness until only her voice remained. "It is here that men decide the fate of the worlds."

"Anji?" Margrave asked quietly.

"Yes, Margrave," came the quiet, now disembodied voice drifting through the hall.

"Thank you," the Loremaster said, "for putting up with me."

A strange silence descended on the great circular room. Caelith looked at Jorgan; the Inquisitas was breathing hard, his hands shaking uncontrollably. Even Margrave was silent, looking back at Caelith with a questioning look on his face—unsure as to what they were to do next.

Caelith looked up past the faces of the three enormous statues that graced the hall. Ancient Rhamas was there arrayed before him in the fresco overhead, the Emperor holding a dragonstaff, commanding the dragons around him to bow before him. He looked more closely at the fresco; the Emperor held the dragonstaff in his right hand but his left was reaching back behind him, his palm hovering over . . .

Caelith gasped.

There, in the fresco, pictured under the extended arm of the Emperor, was the bronze globe from the pedestal. Caelith quickly looked around the wide floor, panicking until his eyes caught sight of the bronze globe between the statues of Hrea and Ekteia. He stepped over, reached down and picked it up. The exterior globe was formed like a cage of intricately forged and carved bronze, two halves held together with intricate fasteners. A single shaft pierced the surface with a long spindle on the outside and a crystal globe—pulsing with an odd light—held in its center. Caelith looked up once more at the fresco. There was no doubt now; the device was the same.

More than that, on either side of the Emperor stood two other figures—winged Hrea and demonic Ekteia—each holding a globe identical to the Emperor's and facing him. Rays from all three of the globes combined over the Emperor's head, forming with their shared radiance the single column of light that was the Pillar of the Sky.

A winged woman . . .

Caelith's eyes went wide as he looked to the bronze spherical device in his hands. He looked up quickly at his brother. "Jorgan!"

The Inquisitas shook his head nervously—he was staring at the statue of Ekteia above him.

"Jorgan! Please, I need—"

"No!" Jorgan snarled between clenched teeth.

"Jorgan! I can't do this without—"

"No!" Jorgan's entire upper body was shaking.

A distant screeching penetrated the hall.

Caelith's blood suddenly ran chill. It was a sound, once heard, that was forever burned into the mind; the cry of Satinka—Dragonqueen of Ost Batar—cut through the walls and into their souls.

"Eryn! We need Jorgan! We've got to convince him—"

"No!" Jorgan screamed, sweat pouring off his shaved pate, his eyes bright and filled with tears. His body shook with rage. "Soulless! Blasphemers! It's a trick! You've conjured all this up! You did this! You killed the dwarf, and you'd kill me, too, but that's not enough to kill my body! You want to kill my soul as well!" Jorgan collapsed onto the floor of the temple, his hands barely holding his head above the fitted stones of the floor. His voice fell to a whimper. "Everything I've wanted . . . everything I was promised . . . forgive me . . . forgive me . . ."

Caelith took a step closer to his brother. The sphere cradled in one hand, he reached out with the other.

Jorgan's head snapped up, hatred burning in his eyes. "No! I do *not* believe it!" He lunged for his staff lying but ten feet away from him across the floor.

Caelith leaped backward, trying to find cover behind the short pillar—knowing it would not be enough.

Caelith glanced quickly at Lucian. His friend stood transfixed halfway between the wall and the center of the vast room, his hands held still but with a building tension in their muscles. Lucian was reading for the Deep Magic.

Lucian moved, his hands suddenly rising. Great arcs of lightning ran from his fingers across the ground, tearing at the stones as it flashed toward Jorgan. A pungent smell filled the air after the electric blue snapped across the distance.

Jorgan saw it and spun his dragonstaff suddenly, connecting its head with the ground. The crackling bolts ran up the staff but stopped partway, gathering themselves into a flashing ball, each bolt snapping at the heels of another. Jorgan deftly spun the staff once more in his hands, reversing it around its crackling center.

Caelith, astonished, crossed his arms, weaving them into a pattern before him, searching within for the magic as well. He could almost see the stage from the dream superimposed around them; the winged woman stood beating on glass doors, unable to reach Caelith, while a little demon played with the bronze globe next to him. The winged woman looked terrified and the demon was not paying any attention to him, yet he had to draw on them somehow.

Lucian raised his hands reflexively, reaching once more for the magic to defend him. Caelith had nearly finished, the Deep Magic welling up within him.

Too late; the bolt flew from the end of Jorgan's staff just as the air before Lucian began to frost over and solidify. The frozen air shattered as the bolt passed through it, breaking against Lucian's chest. Caelith's friend flew backward with a cry, falling hard against the stones of the forum floor.

Caelith released the power within him. The shattered stones that lay scattered across the forum floor leaped up, tumbling through the air toward Jorgan.

Jorgan quickly tossed his staff into his left hand, then raised his right. In that instant, Caelith realized that Jorgan, too, was on the stage in the dream, not just as a symbol or metaphor but a participant.

The hurtling stones exploded at Jorgan's touch, shards flying away from him. Eryn ducked behind the pedestal while Margrave yelped, diving behind the statue of the woman. Caelith threw himself flat against the ground, the shards tearing burning pain as they sliced across his back.

"Deep Magic!" Caelith shouted angrily at Jorgan. "You *are* a mystic!"

Jorgan slowly lowered his outstretched hand, his eyes fixed on Caelith. "Yes—the only legacy I received from my father, though it was left to High Priest Tragget to train me in the art! How ironic that you should die by the very power that—"

A tremendous crash filled the room as a section of the dome collapsed inward, its massive stones raining down on the floor below. Jorgan snatched his staff and rolled quickly out of the way, barely missing being crushed by a falling slab. Eryn tried to run from the cascade but was caught on the back by a large chunk of stone and slammed to the ground. Caelith could no longer see Margrave, Kenth, or anyone else through the choking dust that had erupted in the hall. Blinking, he looked up.

The dragon had arrived, its huge head craning through the opening. She trumpeted, her voice deafening in the confined space, as she began clawing at the shattered opening in the dome, scrambling to reach her prey.

I am in a strange place for a faery indeed. I stand as though in two places at once. In one place, I stand with my companions in the Hall of Conquest, fearful of our impending doom. In the other place, however, I stand once more on a stage. I see the ranks of the dead before me, watching me, screaming at me from their benches in the hall. Many strange creatures surround me here but two are familiar to me; the wingless man and the little long-eared Famadorian creature holding something in his hands.*

The little Famadorian is being attacked by another of his kind; a winged, vicious creature whose long talons rake the poor little fellow mercilessly. I step forward to try and stop the assault, but the wingless man runs forward, a long blade in his hand. He thrusts it through the body of the evil creature. It shrivels and dies from the blow, falling to dust and scattering before me.

I hear myself speaking, though whether to my companions or to these strange visions, I cannot tell. "We need help," I say urgently. "We need time."

The wingless man covers his ears at the sound of my voice; it is painful to him and the small creature as well.

"We don't have time!" It is Gosrivar speaking from the hall.

"Then we've got to find a way to slow them up." Valthesh is speaking to me, though her words seem to come from a faraway place. "To give you time to put an end to all this madness. Obadon, are you with me?"

I glance about the world of the stage. The small green creature holds a device—a globe of bronze, its halves brought together. The wingless man holds another that is of an identical fashion.

"Yes," I hear Obadon from the waking world. "But against the undead of the Black Guard—what weapon is of any use?"

I look into the hall in the waking world and cast about for something that may be of use when my eye settles on it: a long sword of gleaming metal. I see the faces of the dead writhing within. I bolster myself, reach down, and pull it into my vision of the stage.

Lightning flashes from the bronze globes of the wingless man and the little Famadorian, arcing down the length of the sword. Its hilt becomes curved and gnarled, the straight edge of its blade bends into a wave pattern like the path of a snake. As I watch the

---

*As mentioned before, faeries classify all creatures other than themselves as Famadorians.

souls within the blade fly free, rising up from the blade, spreading their spectral wings and soaring into the rafters above the stage.
"This weapon!" I cry out.

FAERY TALES
BRONZE CANTICLES, TOME VIII, FOLIO 3, LEAVES 67-71

Aislynn's voice rang through the hall as she raised her arm, brandishing a sword she had pulled from the treasures scattered about them.

Obadon looked dubiously at the three-foot-long wavy blade. He reached forward, taking its handle and visibly quaking at its touch. "It speaks to me," he declared. "It is repulsive."

"Perhaps, but it is a frightful blade for frightful work," Aislynn replied, her eyes strangely unfocused. "I think I know how to make this right, but you've got to give me time."

"And if we fail?" Obadon asked.

"Then the dead will have no rest and the living shall pay the price for their suffering."

A Matter of Time

Valthesh stepped warily back out through the main doors of the Kyree treasure house, her dark eyes searching the long curve of the street before her. The strange waves of blue light that had previously cleared the rain were no more and the sky was again pouring down an inundation.

"Where do we go?" she said to Obadon. "Where will they come from?"

The Argentei warrior glanced down the deep shadows of the street in either direction. "We are behind a ridge above the waterfront. They entered the city near the same place we did, so they will have to make their way up the ridge from that side." Obadon pointed back down the way they had come.

"There are a lot of roads, friend, which lead up here from that side," Valthesh said. "We cannot cover them all."

"We do not have to," Obadon replied briskly. "We are not an army; we cannot form anything like a defensive line. If depleting their forces or their will were at issue, I would consider stalking them individually—but that would take more time than we have."

"A few inconvenient deaths certainly would not stop Shaeonyn,"

Valthesh observed. "Ours did not. So now that you've exhausted what we *shouldn't* do . . ."

Obadon smiled sadly. "We do not try to stop them where they are—we make them come to us. The objective in this private little war is to buy Aislynn time to repair the damage the magic has done. We have to lead them off, keep them busy with us, and do what we can to draw them away from this place for as long as we can. We buy as much time as possible."

"And what is the price?" Valthesh asked, her eyebrows arched over her sleepy eyes.

"Our lives," Obadon answered directly. "Did you expect it to be otherwise?"

"No." Valthesh smiled wryly. "I just don't usually shop at such expensive markets."

With that, she plunged down the street into the pouring rain, with Obadon running at her heels.

"There is a ring at the base of the glass sphere," the stone faery said in a voice laced with agony.

"I see it," Aislynn said, wiping the sweat from her brow as she turned the device over in her hands yet again. "It's stuck. What am I supposed to do with this?"

"I don't know," the stone faery keened. "But the shaft won't move while it remains."

"But you put it there!"

"I don't remember!" the stone faery wailed.

"This is hopeless," Gosrivar grumbled.

"It should just come apart," Aislynn said, frustration seeping into her voice. "I can't see anything holding it in place."

"I'm a scholar. I don't know anything about such things!" the sage shouted. "Magical devices; honestly! I have never understood this whole business about the Sharaj! It's like you people are never all here at once."

"Gosrivar, if you can't be—wait a moment." Aislynn blinked, a new truth entering her mind. "What did you just say?"

"Just that I have never understood—"

"No, after that."

"What? About your people never being all here at once?" Gosrivar replied, a quizzical look on his face. "I don't mean to be insulting, Aislynn, I just—"

"That's it!" Aislynn said. She reached over, taking the head of the sage in both her hands, drawing it toward her and kissing him on the top of his balding pate. "You are a genius!"

"I am?" Gosrivar responded, still puzzled.

"The device, it is magical," Aislynn said. "That means it is probably like me; with one foot in two places at the same time. Parts of this device are here—the pieces we see—but I see them being connected to other parts in the Sharaj. The answer isn't here, Gosrivar—it's *there*."

Obadon drew in a slow breath. He knew what he had to do, but it went against all his instinct and training.

Through the curtain of rain, he could see the group striding up the street toward the intersection where he and Valthesh lay in wait. Shaeonyn was drenched, her light hair painted dark and flat with water, her wings soaked and keeping her feet to the slick ground. She appeared completely unconcerned with the arms of the dead that reached up toward her from the pavement beneath her feet; her eyes fixed as they were on the path before her, her face a mask betraying no emotion. The Black Guard followed behind her, their weapons sheathed. They, of course, were dead, unsurprised and unconcerned with the horrors that surrounded them. It was Shaeonyn's unemotional acceptance of her surroundings that chilled Obadon's blood.

But not more so than the weapon he held in his hand.

Obadon considered it for a moment, turning the dark, hideous object. The long blade was waved and, through some trick of the eye, seemed to writhe like a serpent in the dim light. The guard on the hilt seemed to move as well, strange images surfacing from the detailed carvings where no such images had been before. The handle itself burned cold into his hand. Aislynn had thought this weapon would be effective against the dead of the Black Guard. He only hoped she was right; it was time to find out.

He turned to Valthesh beside him, speaking sotto voce. "You stay back; use your magic at a distance in my support as long as you can. I'll try to draw them off. When I do, you have to fall back. From then on, it will be up to you."

"What are you going to do?" Valthesh asked in return.

"Whatever I must."

Obadon drew in another steadying breath—then stepped out into the intersection of the streets.

Shaeonyn stopped; a look of astonishment on her face that all the dead of the Kyree city had not elicited. "Obadon?"

"Shaeonyn," he acknowledged in return, the rain cascading around him.

"It is not possible that you are here," she said flatly.

"And yet I am," he rejoined.

"Not for long, I should think."

Out of the corner of his eye, Obadon saw Valthesh step backward, remaining out of sight in the side street, her hands working as she searched for the Sharaj and its power.

Keep her talking, Obadon thought. *The longer she talks, the longer we live.*

"Where are the others?" Shaeonyn said menacingly. "If you are here they cannot be far."

"They will reveal themselves in their own time," Obadon replied. "What do you intend, Shaeonyn? What is there here that would cause the servant of Dwynwyn to consign her fellow Fae to the sea?"

"I do not answer the questions of the lower-born."

"Yet you banished the higher-born Aislynn. If you will not answer to me, will you answer to her?"

"Aislynn! That fool!" Shaeonyn snarled, then turned at once to the Black Guard. "Destroy him now! We've no more time to waste!"

The dead faery guardians strode purposefully up the street toward him. Obadon shifted his grip on his sword to both hands, readying the weapon as he began backing away from them down the street opposite Valthesh. The Black Guard was quickly closing on him, their powerful green legs pushing their huge, rain-glistening bodies over the cries and groping hands of the pavement below. Shaeonyn followed, her own quick steps suddenly anxious. Obadon backed further down the street, trying to maintain his stance on the slick cobblestones. He caught a glimpse of Valthesh lurking in the street beyond the charging wall of undead Fae.

The first reached him several steps ahead of the rest, its massive arms reaching for his throat, probably confident that Obadon's weapon was of no consequence, for all blades passed through their seawater bodies with little effect. Obadon quickly reversed, stepped forward with the blade and thrust it upward under the creature's chin.

The blade burned suddenly with a fierce blue flame as it exited the top of the guardian's head. The Black Guard opened its mouth in a terrible scream that shattered the remaining glass in the windows on the street around them. The undead faery convulsed, seemingly suspended by the blade that Obadon steadfastly held with both hands. Then, with a sigh, the figure collapsed, its saltwater crashing to the ground, washing across the stones and mixing with the rainwater as it ran down toward the sea.

The Black Guard slid to a halt, now uncertain.

Their leader, Deython, stepped cautiously forward, drawing his own weapon, a wide, keen-edged sword, as he did. When he spoke, his voice was dark and demanding. "What is that weapon?"

Obadon drew the wet sword back once more, his stance more firm, his countenance more determined. "It says its name is 'Soulreaver,'" Obadon said, rain cascading over his grinning teeth. "And it is anxious to make your acquaintance."

Deython raised his own blade with a great shout. His fellow guardians drew their weapons as well.

"Only thirty-five more to go," Obadon said grimly.

Valthesh watched the undead guardians turn the corner in pursuit of Obadon. She felt sorry for him, actually, and wished that there were something she could do for him. She knew that he counted on her help. She hoped he would understand when she did not.

The Black Guard was not her target; she had only ever had one from the beginning—one clear objective whose attainment had to be achieved at any cost or sacrifice.

It was then that Shaeonyn, following the Black Guard, stepped into sight.

Valthesh released the power caged within her, a combination of the Sharaj and all the hatred of her soul.

Shaeonyn wheeled around, sensing the tendrils of magic rushing toward her, but too late. A tornado of flame exploded around her, lifting the Sharajin off the ground, spinning her in its blazing vortex. Raindrops sputtered, flashing into steam against the whirling column of fire. Shaeonyn screamed in rage and agony; Valthesh smiled grimly, her eyes bright and wide as she watched. Valthesh gestured with her hand and the column pitched sideways, slamming Shaeonyn against the side of the building with a sickening thud. Valthesh laughed aloud. She repeated the motion again and again, giggling hysterically each time.

Suddenly, her laughter stopped.

The flaming figure of Shaeonyn emerged from the burning column, floating out over the street toward her. Her hair was ablaze as were her wings, her arms upraised, poised to strike.

Valthesh cursed, then turned and ran.

The street behind her exploded, sharp shards of stone ripping the air and cutting into her back and legs. She fell, tumbling across the wet stones. She could feel the ragged holes torn in her wings; they would be useless now even if they were dry. There was a pain in her left leg also, making it difficult for her to move, but she knew Shaeonyn was behind her and far from finished. Valthesh rolled over quickly to her back. Shaeonyn was closer still, the flames on her body sputtering out in the rain, her charred features smiling at her from a head now devoid of hair.

Valthesh thrust her hand up, a piece of lightning flashing in Shaeonyn's eyes. Valthesh knew it was a weak move, but it might work as a distraction. She rolled to her hands and knees, pushing upward with her good leg, trying to run.

But the hands from the pavement grabbed at her.

Valthesh struggled against them, crying out. The hands were pulling away the cobblestones as well, digging a hole beneath her.

Digging her grave.

She pulled herself forcefully away from them, their gray finger-nails tearing her flesh. Bleeding, she stumbled down the street back toward the treasure house.

The laughter of Shaeonyn followed her all the way.

Deython ran down the water-soaked street, his heavy footfalls splashing occasionally in the pooled water among the broken cobblestones.

Ahead of him ran his prey: the Argentei faery that stood in the way of the quest. The blank eyes of the Kyree damned followed him everywhere; their faces straining to follow him from the walls, posts, and roofs of which they had become a part. Their hands strained toward him from the stones below, desperate to touch him. He was alive and free and they longed for his touch. Deython heard their voices crying out for him and their sound made stalking him that much easier.

Deython matched him step for step. Already he could see that Obadon was tiring. Deython would have dispatched him without thought but the blade Obadon held was no ordinary edge of steel. It had already obliterated one of the Black Guard—something Deython had not thought possible. This meant that his prey was dangerous and required more than brute strength to bring down.

Deython smiled; the danger felt almost like being alive.

Obadon dashed across a circular plaza with the Lord of the Dead and his Black Guard still in pursuit. Deython pointed in rapid succession to four of the guardians behind him, indicating where they should attack. Each of them leaped into the roiling sky, the seafoam-color bodies rolling in the air and landing feetfirst against the plaza stones.

Obadon uttered a warrior cry, charging at once toward the surprised undead faery blocking his way. The guardian raised his own sword, but Obadon attached him with a fury unlike anything the guardians had seen among the living. The staccato of crashing steel rang across the plaza.

"Now," Deython commanded.

The guardians of the dead charged as one, but not soon enough. Obadon feigned an overhead blow, reversed and buried the blue-lightning blade into his opponent. A horrendous scream shook the buildings. Obadon leaped backward, deflecting the blows of two other guardians that had closed in on him. Grasping one of them by the arm, he pulled the undead warrior forward and off balance. It blocked the second guardian's swing and allowed Obadon the opportunity to thrust the tip of his blade through the eye of his opponent.

The third scream ripped the air.

The guardian remaining in Obadon's grasp, however, reared up, pushing his back into the Argentei faery's chest, tossing him backward off his feet. Obadon rolled as the guardian's blade slashed backward in a wide arc, its tip tearing through his calf muscle.

Obadon cried out fiercely but still got to his feet, throwing himself backward, his blade held with both hands at his side, tip toward the rear. The blade slid into the body of his attacker.

"Back!" Deython commanded.

The remaining guardians stopped and took several steps. Obadon stood panting as they carefully surrounded him in the plaza. Blood flowed freely from his wound as he leaned heavily on his good leg.

"You fight well, Obadon of Argentei." Deython's voice was hollow and deep as he spoke from the edge of the circle. "You have a unique weapon."

"It was a gift," Obadon replied with a grimace. "From someone you were sworn to protect. It would seem there is not only no truth among the dead, there is no honor either."

Deython slowly raised his sword. "I serve a higher calling. Shaeonyn has brought us to the knowledge of a higher purpose: to serve our fellow dead and bring them comfort in their torment."

"Liar," Obadon sneered.

Deython frowned menacingly.

"There is no comfort for the dead of Sharajentei!" Obadon shouted, taking several painful steps toward the towering sea-green faery. "Shaeonyn lied to you. Cling to this world, Deython of Sharajentei. I seek the enlightenment that you will *never* know!"

Obadon raised his sword and lunged toward the Lord of the Dead. Deython parried and at once their metallic blows pealed

throughout the plaza. Deython could see the fire of life in his opponent's eyes and felt himself pressed back by the intense flurry of
blows. Deython spun his blade, cutting deeply into the mad faery's
left arm but still his opponent pressed his attack as he screamed in his
warrior rage. Deython's blank eyes were wide as he desperately tried
to fend off the blows of a blade that he felt sure would erase his
existence.

Obadon stepped onto his injured leg but it would not hold him
and he reeled backward. Deython saw his chance, whirled his massive
blade in his hand and thrust through his opponent's chest.

Obadon stared back with a look of surprise. Blood trickled from
the corner of his lips as his mouth moved. "I—I found . . ."

Obadon collapsed, sliding off Deython's blade as he dropped his
sword onto the wet cobblestones.

Deython stood gazing down at Obadon's body, though he could
not tell for how long he was buried in his own thoughts. It was the
sound of Shaeonyn's laughter that awakened him from his reveries.

"Come," he said to his remaining guardians. "Our new mistress
calls."

*The stage is deserted. I feel uncomfortable here, for this place
seems abandoned and hollow. The light is dim and difficult to see.
I wander for a time, wondering where everyone has gone. Then I
see him.*

*My little monster friend with the long ears; he sits in the center
of the stage and I cannot account for why I did not see him at
first. His legs are crossed as he contemplates his own device whose
parts look so much like my own.*

*I step over to him, the piece of my own device in my hands. I
see that he has placed his device in a frame that seems to have
room for two more. He is frowning as he contemplates his little
globe and occasionally reaches out and touches it. Nothing happens and he sighs.*

*I kneel down next to him, holding the pieces of my device awk-
wardly in my hands. This interests the little fellow and he looks at*

my pieces as well. I fear to speak, for I know he will not under-
stand me and do not wish to frighten him.

I try to put my pieces together but this only amuses the little
green fellow. He points to the framework and one of the bowl-like
pieces in my hands. I see here where it connects with the frame
and easily set it in place.

As I do, the spindle slides free of the hemisphere in bronze. He
smiles and then points to another piece in my hands . . .

Faery Tales
Bronze Canticles, Tome VIII, Folio 3, Leaves 72–73

"You've nearly got it." Gosrivar was in awe.

"Just a few more pieces," Aislynn answered, her eyes intent on her work.

"Then what will happen?" her companion asked earnestly.

Aislynn shook her head. "I don't know, Gosrivar—I wish I did."

In the distance, the doors of the treasure house banged open. Aislynn and Gosrivar both looked up with a start.

"She is coming! She is coming!" It was Valthesh, her hoarse voice ringing through the hall. She was limping badly, her blood streaking the floor behind her from a wound in her leg. Her face was battered and one eye was swollen shut. "I'm sorry, Aislynn. I'm so sorry."

Gosrivar hurried over to her side, catching her just as she was about to fall. He laid her down quickly beneath the stone faery. "Aislynn, please—finish it!"

Aislynn turned back to the device. That part of her mind that was in the Sharaj could see the monster showing her how to put the device back together, but her time was running out.

"We will by all means finish it," came a new voice into the hall. "But not the way you think. Put it all back, Aislynn—put it all back exactly as it was before."

Aislynn looked up. It was Shaeonyn. Behind her stood Deython and several more of what had once been her own dead guardians.

"Don't listen to her," Valthesh croaked. "I—I'm sorry, Aislynn; I should not have kept silence. My father knew who she was—and she murdered him for it! I thought I could avenge him . . ."

Shaeonyn looked down at the broken woman lying on the ground. "Valthesh? You were Pelithei's daughter?" The Sharajin smiled. "Of course, I remember now—though after so many killings they all seem to blur in the mind."

"You killed her father?" Aislynn was aghast. "Why?"

Shaeonyn smiled. "It only seemed just—considering that he had killed me the year before."

"What?"

"Yes, little Oraclyn." Shaeonyn grinned through clenched teeth. "I've been dead for some time now. I find it extremely convenient to keep things just the way they are—which is why you will put that device back the way you found it. Or would you rather become like me?"

Confluence

Satinka thrust her head into the enormous rotunda, her mouth gaping open as she trumpeted her rage and bloodlust. The sound was deafening; Caelith felt the sharp stabbing pain of it deep in his ears. The sound also chilled him. Satinka was by far the cruelest of the dragons in the Five Domains, and no human in all those lands was more hated by her than his father.

No, he realized, not *his* father; *their* father. The story of Galen's battle on the Election Fields was legendary; how he used the Deep Magic to disrupt the war. That battle was supposed to determine which of the other dragons were to mate with Satinka; but Galen had spoiled it and Satinka had not gotten her brood. If Ekteia had made it known to the Dragonqueen that *both* of Galen's sons were here, nothing could have stood between Satinka and her most delectable revenge.

Jorgan stumbled backward, tripping over the debris and falling painfully, his back against the floor. Satinka snapped toward the clamor, her enormous head rearing back, drawing in air to fuel the flames of her terrible breath.

Caelith adjusted his stance, finding his footing. Conjuring up whatever was at hand within the dream, he lashed out, lightning and hail exploding from his fingertips, slamming against the jaw of the dragon. It deflected the dragon's head just as she released her spew. She bellowed at the insult, her gargantuan talons pulling fitfully at the stones of the dome, desperate to reach fully into the ancient hall and tear at her prey. The flaming discharge continued as her head reeled, its inferno circling the chamber overhead, its blistering heat radiating down on the instantly illuminated room.

Caelith saw clearly the frescoes, illuminated in the light of the dragon's flame.

"Jorgan!" Caelith shouted. "We have to do this together! Help me!"

Caelith looked around only to realize he was in the open, exposed.

He dropped the bronze globe from his hands, diving for cover behind a huge fallen ceiling stone.

Aislynn felt exposed. The device was nearly assembled. All she needed to do was slide the spindle properly back into place.

"I am sorry, Aislynn," Valthesh choked from where Gosrivar held her and tried to comfort the badly wounded Seeker. They were at the foot of the broken pillar, the stone faery moaning over them both. "I should have told you. Should have trusted you."

"Yes, but trust was never one of the stronger qualities in your family, was it, Valthesh?" Shaeonyn interjected. As she stepped forward, Aislynn could see that part of her cheek had been torn away, exposing a rotting jaw and gray teeth underneath.

"But we always keep our word," Valthesh gurgled, red-flecked foam gathering at the corner of her mouth. "I found you, after all."

"How very tragic you won't be able to keep all your promises." Valthesh sighed. "Your father thought he could stop me—it was his hand that killed me to begin with—but imagine my surprise when a little upstart Seeker from such a tiresome house as Qestardis called my soul out of torment and gave me form once more? To be among the living again and to find that I had powers like her own; it was a great gift this Sharaj has given me. Oh, and to be rid of the burden of truth! It allowed me to pay your father back for taking my life, Valthesh, and now it seems I get to take yours as well. How sad for you." She smiled, baring the charred, rotting region of her cheek.

"You killed her father?" Gosrivar asked quietly.

"Well—yes, I did," Shaeonyn sighed, "although it is difficult to remember after so many. One tends to lose track."

"Why?" Gosrivar asked in horror.

"It was my duty," Shaeonyn replied sharply, deep, painful sarcasm seeping into her voice. "My great duty to my great house! I spied; I seduced; I killed; all in the name of Lady Milindral and to the greater glory of House Mnemnoris. And when I was of no more use to them, I was betrayed to her father of House Vargonis so that he could destroy me and save them the embarrassment. But I knew my own past, old man! I knew I would have to face Aelar the Enlightened One for an accounting of my life. I clung to this existence with a will of steel rather than face his judgment of my soul."

"Ularis was from House Mnemnoris," Aislynn spoke, taking a step back. The device rested nearby but there were several pieces left to be set in place. She could never complete it before Shaeonyn stopped her.

"Ularis was foolish," Shaeonyn said dismissively. "Of all the people Lady Milindral could have sent after me, he was no challenge at all."

"Another death?"

Shaeonyn shrugged. "What's one more—especially with so much at stake? Give me the device."

"You missed a spot," Aislynn said.

Shaeonyn stopped, reached up with her hand to the blistered hole in the side of her face, and smiled with minor discomfiture. "How embarrassing of me," she demurred, gesturing over the regions with her fingers. In moments she was whole again, the perfect, chill beauty Aislynn had known.

Aislynn cast a quick glance behind Shaeonyn. There were but fifteen of the Black Guard remaining. Obadon had done well against so many. Yet it was Deython, the Commander of the Dead, standing behind Shaeonyn, that she looked at most carefully. He held in his hand the sword she had given to Obadon not so long ago. His blank eyes were focused on Aislynn as she spoke, listening carefully to everything she was saying.

"So, are you saying that there is a life beyond this one," Aislynn responded carefully, taking another step back, "and judgment that you are most anxious to avoid?"

Shaeonyn took a purposeful step toward the Oraclyn. "Why should the dead submit to anyone's verdict? Here we shall remain for all time, living out eternity without fear of retribution."

"And what of those who do not fear such judgment?" Aislynn asked. "This device was broken; it may have freed you from responsibility for your past, but it condemns all the other souls of the Fae from reaching their enlightenment."

"We must all die sometime, Aislynn," Shaeonyn said quietly, taking another step toward the Princess, her hand rising slowly over her head. A black globe was forming about her hand, a whirling mass of insectlike winged creatures growing in size and number. "What do I care for enlightenment? We shall rule all the face of the world, for there is nothing more inevitable than death! It is time for you to join us, Aislynn—you and your friends. Then I shall undo here what you have done; we will have cheated the gods!"

"But what of the spirits of those who seek the enlightenment?" Aislynn pleaded, taking a final step, her back pressed against the moaning stone faery of the pillar. "We are all flawed; what about them?"

"It's just a black unknown," Shaeonyn breathed. "Better they should live forever in shadows. Better they should never know enlightenment."

Deython let out a terrible cry. Shaeonyn turned. The Commander of the Dead was lunging toward her with all his strength. She loosed her magic on him, encasing him in a deadly globe, its winged members biting him as it tried to tear chunks of flesh from his body. But Deython was of the Black Guard pearls and his body was formed of the sea made solid. He reached quickly around behind Shaeonyn's neck, grasping it firmly in his left hand. His right hand thrust forward with the sword.

Shaeonyn cried out in horror.

Aislynn leaped out of the way, falling hard on her side, her hands still clutching the pieces of the device.

Deython's momentum carried them both against the broken pillar. The blade of the Soulreaver sliced through Shaeonyn's body and deep into the pillar itself.

"Free!" cried the stone faery from the stones above them. The stone began to bleed brilliant red from where the Soulreaver had penetrated the stone. "Blessed Aelar! We are free!" With that the stone faery crumbled, its lime cascading down around Deython.

The Commander of the Dead stepped back. Shaeonyn's body, maintained by the Deep Magic for many years, lay pinned by the sword to the pillar. Her hair had fallen to wisps of white, thin and pale, and her skin became mottled gray, pulled back from her lips in a hideous grin. Her eyes were vacant sockets of fading light. Yet, even as Aislynn watched in horror, the head lifted up, its bony hands reaching for her.

"No," Aislynn said firmly, a shudder running through her.

She turned back to the device and slid the last pieces quickly into place.

Satinka's head recoils, but I know it is more from the shock of my blow than from any real damage. She pulls backward in her panic, dragging down the entire northern wall of the rotunda. Dust fills the vast hall, and I cannot keep myself from coughing. I am having trouble seeing, yet there are figures that seem to be moving nearby. The winged woman and the demon! Each of them are here—or some form of them, for once again I seem to be both in the world and in the dream at once. Each of them holds a bronze globe like the one near my feet. I see the pedestal through the dust in the air.

Both of them seem to be placing their own globe-shaped devices on their own pedestals.

I reach down and set mine on my own.

BOOK OF CAELITH
BRONZE CANTICLES, TOME IX, FOLIO 1, LEAF 86

Thux woke up. He could hear the sounds of battle outside, the shouts and songs of the ogres and the dull thud of the titans beating down the outer walls of the city.

"How extraordinary," he thought. "I wonder if it is possible to actually fix something that doesn't exist?"

He drew himself up to sit on the throne in the dim hall. He examined the ball critically for a moment, found the appropriate symbol, and pressed it.

Instantly, the hall was ablaze in light. Thux smiled and encouraged himself. "Well, that's promising!"

When he placed both hands on the bronze globe before him, Thux suddenly felt himself become lighter and lighter. The walls around him became transparent and smaller. It was as though he were becoming the entire Trove, his legs its foundations and his arms their towers. It was an odd sensation to be sure, since he now felt that he had eight legs and an equal number of arms at his disposal. As he thought about it, he found that he was rising higher and higher into the air on his enormous legs, the massive titans before him looking more like toys than imposing machines of war.

I wonder if I might just kick them over? he thought.

Lithbet decided the battle was going well. The outer wall of the city was breaking apart nicely and, other than a number of unsightly dents in her fine titan, the local ogres—while no doubt capable of squashing any of her goblin Technomancers like bugs if they were outside of their titans—were no match for them *inside* their titans. Just a few more hours of smashing walls and the whole thing would pretty much be over.

Sad, really, she thought; there just was not much challenge left in combat any longer. You take your big old titan out on the field and smash whatever you need to smash in order to take whatever you want to take. Not a great deal of strategy was involved. Still, she would add the victories to her credit—after all, no one cares how you won so long as you win.

"General!" her driver squawked. "Come quickly!"

"Oh, what now," Lithbet whined.

"Probably wants to know when the victory dinner is scheduled," Istoe sniffed. "Say, when *is* the victory dinner scheduled?"

"Tonight after dusk," Lithbet replied, climbing out of the mouth of the titan—her command headquarters—and up the ladder to the right eyeball. "Well, what is it, Smesh? Are the ogres making faces at—"

Lithbet stopped, her jaw dropping.

Behind the inner wall of the city, the buildings seemed to be lifting up, rising higher and higher. Long arms rose out of the towers around the perimeter of the inner city, their clawed hands nearly a hundred feet across. Rising farther, the city stood on eight mechanical legs like some titanic beast. Dirt, bricks, and stone cascaded from the edges of the city as it continued to rise even higher into the evening sky. Soon the base of the buildings cleared the wall, revealing a stained metal dish on which the entire center of the city was apparently built.

"The city," Istoe gulped next to Lithbet. "The city is a titan!"

"What shall we do, General," Smesh asked nervously.

Lithbet gulped. "Does anyone here know how to surrender?"

Caelith stumbled through the debris, panicking for a moment, unsure where he had dropped the bronze device. He caught a glimpse of it, however, and quickly snatched it from the ground.

"Jorgan!" Caelith shouted. He could hear no reply; he only hoped the Inquisitas was still out there somewhere. In a few steps, Caelith reached the pedestal. He could hear Satinka pushing her way through the fallen wall. In moments she would be near enough to smell him.

Caelith placed the globe firmly down on the pedestal.

The light from the Pillar of the Sky unfolded, radiating outward from the globe, a wave of power that suddenly swept the dust from the hall with painful clarity. He could see the dragonstaffs lining the walls, the eye of each glowing brightly in the light of the bronze globe.

At once, Satinka saw him standing in the center of the room. She pushed herself further into the hall, her rows of razor-edged teeth separating in anticipation.

"Jorgan!" Caelith called out, stepping backward from the pedestal, not daring to turn away from the slathering maw that approached him. He raised his arms, trying to find one last breath of the Deep Magic within.

Then Satinka shuddered and stopped moving toward him. The great dragon convulsed and shook—unwilling to go back and unable to move forward.

Caelith stood breathing heavily, his arms aching.

Satinka's head drew back, her eyes filled with pain and rage. With jerking motions, she retreated, pulling herself back through the gaping hole in the collapsed wall to the surrounding courtyard. Then, with a mournful cry, she opened her wings, dragging herself upward to the rim of the courtyard wall and perched on the great platform at its crest, her head bowed down.

Jorgan stepped up beside Caelith.

"I may have been mistaken," he said shakily, the dragonstaff glowing in his hand.

Covenants

B achas had had his fill.

His fellow Mantacorians were a superstitious lot even before they had dropped anchor in this harbor of damned souls. The sights on the waterfront alone had been enough to unnerve his crew; not one of them could be persuaded to go very far into the city no matter how glowing the promise of riches just around the next corner. To be sure, there were plenty of objects worthy of looting in the shops facing the docks. But these were purchased at a dear price, for some of them were fused with the trapped bodies of these near dead creatures who were, understandably, reluctant to give up the possession to which they had become so literally attached. When Shaeonyn moved inland, up the street of clawing hands, Bachas made no move to follow her and his crew was just as glad to wait on the docks for her return.

The captain of the *Brethain* was beginning to wonder just how long Shaeonyn's task was going to take. Rings of bluish flame had swept over the city earlier, and for a time, Bachas thought that Shaeonyn was thus signaling the completion of whatever urgent task had brought them across the oceans to a land of the dead, or the perpetually near death. Yet the blue fire had stopped after a time, and no other signal was coming forth.

Then, quite suddenly, the angry clouds parted and a single ray of light broke through the rainy gloom. It shone down on the city some distance inland, illuminating one particular building with its brilliant ray.

"Faeries!" Bachas planted a fist on each hip with a satisfied snort. Surely this was Shaeonyn's doing; she would be back directly with her freakish dead guardians and they could get their ship out of these cursed waters. "That's about it, friends! Load up what we have and make ready to shove off."

Yet though the light continued to shine, there was no sign of Shaeonyn or her guards.

The sun drew lower on the horizon, its rays breaking red under the overcast, bathing the entire dead city in a salmon light. Bachas licked his sharp teeth nervously; his crew had been restless for some time and was now becoming vocal about the bad luck in being in a haunted city with the advent of darkness. Though Bachas would never admit it, his feelings mirrored those of his crew.

"All right, friends," he shouted at last. "Let's feel the wood of our own deck under our feet! Clear the moorings; we're done here!"

"Aye!" shouted his crew in a rush of relief, the jolly boats pushing away almost before Bachas's voice stopped echoing off the warped walls of the waterfront. The boatmen quickly set the oars, pulling with a fervor that Bachas could not recall seeing in any crew. The bow of Bachas's boat cut a white spray through the choppy water, the reddening sunset glinting off the crests of the waves. Two other boats followed Bachas's own, their crews anxious not to be left behind.

"I never should have listened to that Shaeonyn faery," Bachas muttered to himself, a habit that he indulged in only when he was upset. He should have known it was a mistake when she insisted they cast those first four faeries adrift—that should have been clue enough—but killing the Kyree? At least he had been able to stop that, insisting that they be imprisoned, rather than murdered outright, arguing that they needed Djukan and, more particularly, Sargo's cooperation in order to navigate the unknown waters to Tjugun Mai. Subduing the powerful and warrior-trained Kyree had been far more tricky than dealing with the faeries but they had managed it. Now, of course, Bachas had run out of reasons why Shaeonyn should allow the Kyree to live—but he would deal with that problem when it came up.

They were nearing the *Brethain* now, the furled sails and rigging silhouetted against the lowering sun. He should be able to see the watch on the weather deck, he thought, his eyes relieved to see several figures against the rail. "Ahoy!"

No answering call came back across the waters.

Bachas was puzzled. The storm had abated and the waters in the harbor were relatively calm. "Ahoy the ship!"

Silence was his only response.

"Make ready your weapons, lads," Bachas whispered. "Something's not right aboard."

"Ahoy the boat!" came the cry from the quarterdeck, a woman's voice.

"Who answers for the *Brethain*?" Bachas demanded.

"Her master," came the answer.

"I should have known it," Bachas muttered under his breath, then shouted again. "Shaeonyn, we had a deal! I've stuck to my end of the bargain—"

"Shaeonyn regrets that she is no longer among the living," the voice responded. "Indeed, circumstances have changed considerably. Are you in a position to listen to—how do you say it—a new deal?"

Bachas thought for a moment before responding. "That would depend on the deal—and who I am dealing with."

"I am Aislynn, Princess of Qestardis and Oraclyn to Sharajentei. You tried to kill us several days ago and imprisoned your Kyree guests; you also obviously failed on both accounts, as we are, as you can hear, alive and have managed to free the Kyree who now hold your vessel. Master Djukan is of the opinion that we should sail the ship back across the Tjugun Sea on our own, leaving you and your fine crew here to deal with the restless dead on their terms. But the burden would be lighter should your experienced crew sail here instead."

"What's in it for us?" Bachas shouted.

"Your ship back once you deliver us safely to our own lands."

"And what if we just take our own ship back?" Bachas snarled.

"Difficult and uncertain proposition," responded Ailsynn, "as we have not only released but have also armed the Kyree aboard, who are most anxious to exact their vengeance on you and your fine crew. That—or you simply return to the docks and find yourselves a home in this city."

Bachas looked back at his crew. Their faces made his decision for him.

"Both I and my crew would be delighted to sail under your flag, Aislynn of Qestardis."

Djukan leaned against the aft rail on the quarterdeck, flexing his arms to rid them of their stiffness. "I apologize, Aislynn; I misjudged you—and was taken in by Shaeonyn."

"We were all deceived by her—including Dwynwyn," Aislynn replied. "But how much greater is our own guilt, Djukan, for the loss of your nation and people. If one of our own had not assembled the device improperly—"

"Or if the Kyree had not brought back the device from one of our wars of conquest—these arguments could circle around forever, Aislynn," Djukan countered, straightening himself. "There is blame enough for all to share and far more than we can bear. You have done as you said you would; you have discovered the fate of our nation, tragic as it is. For this, I am grateful."

Aislynn nodded, turning to the rail and looking out over the water of the harbor. "And I, too, am grateful; the dead now have a means of leaving the mortal realms and attaining their enlightenment. Sharajentei need no longer be a place of pain, a prison for the souls of those whose lives ended before their perfection. Now Sharajentei can be a place of instruction, a place of healing, and a place where the restless dead can find their passage to peace."

"This will change the politics between the faery kingdoms once again, will it not?" Djukan chuckled.

"Yes, but for the better, I should think." Aislynn smiled, seeing the stars that rose above Tjugun Mai for the first time in more than twenty years. "We have accomplished much—you and I—however, there is one thing we must yet do."

Djukan sighed, his face falling. "I cannot see how it is possible."

"We came to honor your father," Aislynn said.

"The Halls of Isthalos are many hundreds of miles to the east of here," Djukan said, shaking his head sadly. "From what you tell me about our land, there is little hope that we could survive the journey. My father's bones shall have to rest in exile."

"I think not," Aislynn said and turned to the main deck. "Deython?"

The hulking warrior of the undead Fae rose to the quarterdeck and faced the young Kyree prince. "Lord Djukan of the Kyree, I am a warrior and my faults are many. It was I who wrongly followed Shaeonyn and led my brothers to do likewise. I unjustly killed a brave warrior of House Argentei. I have much for which I must atone before my soul will be ready for the enlightenment."

The undead warrior knelt before Djukan, holding out his hands. "May I and my brothers take the bones of your father to your sacred place?"

Djukan blinked and a tear ran down his cheek. "You honor me— and my entire house. I accept."

Aislynn stepped forward and lay her hand on Deython's frigid head. "Do this and I release you, Deython."

"I have always protected you, Your Highness," Deython replied.

"Yes, you have." She smiled up at him. "But I think I can stand on my own now."

Lithbet and Istoe stood uncomfortably before the throne in the center of the Hall of Defense. On the specific instructions of the Wizard of Jilik and Hero of Og, the ogres had allowed these two and these two only to enter the Trove and come to stand before him for the surrender.

"Look," Lithbet said testily, "all I want to know is: what do I get out of this?"

"You get to keep your army," Thux said pleasantly. "All your remaining titans get to walk away from the battle and go beat up on someone else."

"Yes, yes, yes; I understand that," Lithbet said quickly. "But I've already got my wedding scheduled, and now that you've won the war, it's upset the entire plan. I mean, unless you're willing to—"

"No," Thux said flatly. "Having my wife delivered to me here very much alive and very much unharmed is part of the surrender terms and you're just going to have to live with it."

"I thought that if you might be willing to compromise a little—"

"That is not negotiable."

"Fine!" Lithbet shouted. "Then what about my wedding?"

"Well . . ." Thux thought. "How about Istoe here?"

"Istoe?" Lithbet sneered. "He's an imp!"

"Yes, and a very fine Technomancer in his own right," Thux said, more interested by the moment in the possibilities. "He's already a hero of the realm, the greatest living explorer in all goblin history, so he's a natural for the post of your husband. Between your wars and his wanderings you'll probably never see each other—a perfect solution for a political marriage!"

Istoe looked at Lithbet in surprise. "He's right, you know!"

"Meanwhile, I will remain here after your surrender and set up a research group. We'll call ourselves the House of Books Goblins, an autonomous protectorate of the kingdom of Mimic."

"House of Books Goblins?"

"Well, we'll shorten the first part—H.O.B. Goblins," Thux said. "Hob-goblins."

"Wait." Lithbet's eyes narrowed. "If we surrender to *you,* then how is it you become part of *our* kingdom?"

"I understand that's how it always works." Thux shrugged.

"I'll have to go and talk this over with my mother," Lithbet said grumpily.

"You do that," Thux said happily. "Just remember one thing on the way out."

"What's that?" Lithbet asked.

"Don't touch anything!"

★　　　★　　　★

Satinka quivered on her perch, an anger and resentment nearly as old as herself burning in her eyes.

"By the gods," Caelith said quietly, "this is what the dragons feared most."

"It is what we all fear," Jorgan replied, "and the so-called gods had nothing to do with it."

Caelith looked at his brother with a puzzled expression. "How can you say that? You were here! You *saw!*"

"I saw?" Jorgan sneered. "What I saw—what *you* saw, for that matter—was nothing more than an aberration of the dream." The Inquisitas sighed heavily as he looked away. "There are—there are no gods save those we make ourselves, crafted out of our own inner fears and desires. There are no purposes or destinies save those we carve out for ourselves."

Caelith shook his head. "You are wrong, brother."

Jorgan smiled thinly. "Well, one of us has always been wrong—*brother.*" He wheeled suddenly, his hands filled with the blazing light of the sun.

Caelith stood with one hand pressed against the bronze sphere. "Think, Jorgan! Attack me and I'll topple the device. The dragonstaffs will lose their authority—and what will Satinka do then?"

Jorgan glanced up at the huge head of the dragon hovering nearby. Her eyes were fixed on him.

The Inquisitas relaxed his pose, the fireballs burning in his cupped hands suddenly fading. "The Pir will not understand what has happened."

"Then you explain it to them any way you like," Caelith said. "You always have. You have the opportunity to reshape the Five Domains—right here and now, Jorgan. Controlling the dragons puts great power into your hands, and I suspect it is a power which man will not use with great wisdom. However, let's be clear: one place you will never use that power is against the mystics. Should you break that pact, then we would be obliged to take your controlling power away from you, and I suspect that the memory of dragons is long indeed."

"As you say, the memory of dragons is long," Jorgan observed. "To take away our control would result in your own destruction as well."

"It would," Caelith responded, "but let us hope that it never comes to that."

"It seems we each hold a dagger at the other's throat."

"Yes, but we seem to be talking all the more civilly for it."

Jorgan smiled and nodded. "Very well, brother. A kingdom for a kingdom, eh? It's a bargain I accept."

Jorgan turned, and began walking toward Satinka's perch.

"What are you going to do, Jorgan?" Caelith asked.

"I'll leave you here. Satinka's domain has been without a Dragon-Talker for some time. I suspect I shall take that vacant place on the Pentach Conclave and make my home in Ost Batar. And what of you?"

"We'll stay here," Eryn answered.

"Eryn!" Caelith said with relief. "I saw you fall—"

"I'm a bit bruised, but I'll survive," she replied. "There's much to be done. We have our own people coming to join us."

"Which reminds me," Caelith said to Jorgan. "There is one more part of our bargain I expect you to honor."

"Indeed?" Jorgan replied. "What is that?"

"You will allow the mystics to pass down the old Imperial Road east of Mount Saethalan and into the Westwall Basin. From there they'll take the Dwarven Road south and out of your lands. We'll manage getting them home from there."

"The dragons will be disappointed," Jorgan replied. "They were no doubt looking forward to another slaughter in Nharuthenia."

"Then they shall be disappointed," Caelith said firmly. "What choice do they have?"

"What choice do any of us have?" Jorgan said. He raised his staff and turned it, the motions natural. As he did so, Satinka lowered her head, allowing Jorgan to enter the ancient, worn pouch still around her neck. "Farewell—brother."

"Farewell," Caelith called back. "Brother."

Satinka opened her wings wide and lifted into the air. Caelith watched for a time as the enormous beast wheeled around the City of the Gods twice before turning to the north. It was some time before her form vanished over the peaks of the Forsaken Mountains.

"Master!"

Caelith turned toward the voice. "Kenth! I was beginning to wonder what happened to you. What of the others?"

"Scattered about and a bit worse for wear," the craggy old warrior answered as he knelt behind a pile of stones from the fallen wall. "Lucian here may have broken both his legs, but he appears to be breathing. Tarin's arm's hanging at an odd angle, but I'll see to that. Warthin's a bit confused from a rock bouncing off his head, but he'll straighten out, I'm thinking."

Caelith shook his head. "Amazing. I'm almost afraid to ask about—"

"Marvelous! Simply marvelous!" Margrave chimed as he emerged from behind the Statue of Suthal. "What a tale this shall make—oh, perhaps a little ragged in parts but not to worry, I'll fix up the details in the end!"

Caelith shook his head again, smiling. "I've no doubt, Margrave, that by the time you finish it, the story will be not only entertaining but completely devoid of true facts."

"Well, Caelith." Eryn stepped up on the dais to stand next to him and looked around. "What *do* we do now?"

Caelith turned to her. "Come with me."

They ran down the steps of the Pillar of the Gods. Caelith glanced around until he found what he was looking for: a set of stairs that led to the top of the wall surrounding the pillar. He took her hand and led her to the top.

"There," he said, "that is what we do now."

Eryn followed his gaze. From the top of the wall they could see the river and the top of the falls. A valley lay before them to the southwest in the evening light. Behrun Lake glistened in the distance, the lost city of Calsandria nestled against its shore. Green and verdant lands surrounded it, inviting them to a new and permanent home.

"I will contact my father in the dream," he replied.

"Unmasked?"

"I see no other choice," he replied. "Then we'll have to find a way to get everyone past the broken aqueduct in the Starless Sea, but in time, our people will start to flow into the valley and we'll build a place for ourselves and our children."

"*Our* children?" Eryn said, her brows raised.

"Well, I meant 'our children' in general," Caelith said casually. "But it isn't a bad idea."

Eryn glanced at him sardonically, then looked toward the valley. "What happened to them, Caelith? Where did they go wrong?"

"I don't know," Caelith said, "but the past is done. The future is where our destiny lies."

Eryn nodded. "You should tell that to Margrave."

"Why?"

"He'll write it down," Eryn said with a smile. "For the future."

"With a few improvements?"

"Of course!"

"Eryn."

"Yes?"

"There is so much I have to apologize for," Caelith said haltingly. "So much I want to explain."

"Slowly, Caelith." She gently squeezed his hand. She looked down on the lush valley below. "I don't want it rushed. I want to hear it all, every word, and I feel like you have a very, very long time to say it."

Thrice upon a time . . .
there was one device
that existed in three places
all at the same time.
A gift of gods whose names were lost,
its power could doom or save.
But to be broken in one
was to be broken in all.
And so it lay waiting beyond the memory of mortal-kind.

Thrice upon a time . . .
An heir to a kingdom was sought.
A war threatened all of history.
And the veil between worlds was breached.
But that is a different tale.

Song of the Worlds
Bronze Canticles, Tome I, Folio 1, Leaf 17

THE END OF BOOK II